"Gritty and compelling. Cara McKenna is a master at capturing realistic situations and characters."

—#1 *New York Times* bestselling author Maya Banks

"Quenched my thirst for wicked-hot romance. Cara McKenna knows how to write sexy-as-hell bad boys."

—*New York Times* bestselling author Jaci Burton

"McKenna ratchets up sexual chemistry and danger in equal measure. . . . Readers will eagerly turn pages to learn the outcome of both the mystery and the romance."

—*Publishers Weekly*

"An intriguing cast of characters, a raw, honest backdrop, and a healthy dose of smexy."

—Amanda K. Byrne

"A crazy ride ense."

-Fresh Fiction

"I can never are always so gritty and di em."

-Fiction Vixen

"An intense, at times dark, heated romance."

—*RT Book Reviews* (4½ stars)

"It's different and sexy."

—Smexy Books

"Beautifully written and brilliant."

—Dear Author

"Intense, funny, and perfectly dirty all at the same time."

—*USA Today* bestselling author Victoria Dahl

"Exceptionally evocative writing . . . fascinating."

—Smart Bitches Trashy Books

"Mind-blowing."

—Scandalicious Book Reviews

"High-octane suspense and sizzling sexual tension."

—Under the Covers

Also by Cara McKenna

THE DESERT DOGS SERIES

Lay It Down

Give It All

Drive It Deep

OTHER NOVELS

After Hours

Unbound

Hard Time

CROSSTOWN CRUSH

A Sins in the City Novel

CARA McKENNA

A SIGNET ECLIPSE BOOK

SIGNET ECLIPSE
Published by New American Library,
an imprint of Penguin Random House LLC
375 Hudson Street, New York, New York 10014

This book is an original publication of New American Library.

First Printing, September 2015

For more information about Penguin Random House, visit penguin.com.

LIBRARY OF CONGRESS CATALOGING-IN-PUBLICATION DATA:

McKenna, Cara, 1979–
Crosstown crush / Cara McKenna.
pages cm.—(A sins in the city novel; 1)
ISBN 978-0-451-47605-0 (softcover)
1. Married people—Fiction. 2. Triangles (Interpersonal relations)—Fiction. I. Title.
PS3613.C5547C76 2015
813'.6—dc23 2015009443

Printed in the United States of America
1 3 5 7 9 10 8 6 4 2

Set in ITC Berkeley Old Style

Penguin
Random
House

With thanks to Laura, who helped me sneak into the party.
And to Christina and Claire, who keep on refilling my glass.

CROSSTOWN CRUSH

CHAPTER ONE

With the tab settled, Samira hugged her best girlfriend good night outside the bar, exchanging promises to meet up again soon.

She checked her phone's clock. Just enough time. On legs the tiniest bit languorous from the cocktail, she crossed Walnut Street and headed for Sephora, making a beeline for the fragrance wall. She held sample bottles of the various men's colognes to her nose until she found one she liked—a fresh, citrusy smell. Samira misted the cologne into the air and walked through it. She replaced the tester, pleased not to have earned herself any odd looks, as she had from the makeup counter ladies at Macy's.

Back in the open air, she had only a quarter mile's walk home. It had rained that afternoon, and the cool early-April air felt electric, charged with life and possibility. She breathed in spring, along with the cologne, imagining what man might have left that scent clinging to her hair and clothes.

She'd tried a different drink that night, a greyhound—vodka and grapefruit juice. Who was this mystery man, she wondered, who'd ordered her that cocktail?

Her husband would want to know.

He was tall, she decided as she crossed the street. Tall and built, with clear blue eyes and lean muscles, a soft, deep voice, and slow hands.

He was hung.

That was a given. That was what Mike would want to hear above all else. Sam named her imaginary lover Nick, and decided he was a rower. He rowed every weekend morning on the Allegheny, so he had big, cut arms, and during the day he was . . . an EMT. *Nice.*

What a dreamboat her imaginary piece on the side was.

Their apartment made up one half of an old brick Victorian, and as she drew close, she auditioned the faces of her favorite actors until she hit one that fit the bill. Sam felt giddy as she mounted the stone steps and dug out her keys, as though she really had just met this handsome, athletic, altruistic Nick for a drink and a fuck. No matter that she'd spoken to no men at the Elbow Room aside from the one who'd mixed her cocktails. *Ooh, bartender.* Her next fake fling would be with a bartender, she decided, pushing in the door. Not that Mike cared about their occupations.

She smiled to find no mail waiting on the floor before the slot. That meant he'd gotten out of work on time and had hopefully been home for a while, winding himself up with his own fantasies about where she was, what she was doing, and to whom she was doing it. The notion had a smile tugging at her lips.

Such a contradiction was Mike Heyer. Outside these walls, he was a badass—a lead narcotics detective with the Pittsburgh police, maker of snap decisions, with a body to match his demeanor. Rough and ready. Beyond these walls he was always on, always acutely aware of his rank and others' perceptions. Confident and sure. He could be the same in bed, and often was. But once or twice a month, within the bounds of these games, he let the burden of authority drop from his shoulders and embraced what Sam suspected to be his deepest, most defining fears.

You're weak, this game told him. *You're outmanned, and you can't measure up. You're failing.* Sam smirked as she locked up behind her, smug to know she was the sole keeper of his secret desires, the only one who got to see him reduced to such a happy mess. The only one who got to do the reducing.

There had been a time when she'd wanted nothing to do with those secret desires.

When he'd first confessed them to her, Sam had reeled from the blow they dealt to her confidence in both herself and the relationship she'd once felt so sure about. She hadn't known what had been going on with her then-fiancé; she'd known only that she'd begun feeling like a criminal in his eyes and that the sharper edges of their sex, which she'd enjoyed so much, had become too sharp, too coarse. Where he'd once been possessive, he'd become, at times, mean and accusing.

She'd dumped other lovers for less than that, but Mike had been different, right from the start. From the night they'd met. She had never felt so free with a guy before—so free it was like meeting herself for the first time, discovering how goofy she could be when she was relaxed around a man and how much better the sex was when it felt like an adventure instead of like a performance. But it had become painfully clear that there was something else at work that he wasn't telling her. So she'd threatened to leave, and meant it—the most painful decision of her life—if he didn't tell her what was going on. And he had. Since then, their motto had been: *Truth only. Always.*

She'd been intimidated at first, and even repelled. But the truth had told her, *It's nothing you've done wrong. It's what he secretly* wishes *you'd done wrong.*

In time, Sam's feelings about it had morphed from shock, to

skepticism, to acceptance, and eventually all the way to curiosity. It had taken her close to a year to get to the point where she was on board with his needs, and over the course of those months, Mike had changed as well. She came to realize that confession had been a ten-ton weight hovering above him, and with that crushing pressure gone, all those old red flags ceased to wave. No more accusations, no more confusing signals, no more too-edgy sex. The Mike she'd fallen in love with had returned, just with a kink openly in tow. And once she trusted that it wasn't her enemy, she decided to make it her friend. Her partner in driving her husband insane in the ways he craved most.

When they'd first started exploring Mike's kink, Sam did as she had this evening—stayed out past dinnertime and came home smelling of alien maleness. Back then she'd simply worked late, then swung by the drugstore and rubbed samples from the men's style magazines on her wrists. But having seen in the past couple of years what their games did to her husband, she'd learned to revel in it herself. The same kink that had once belittled her now turned her into a powerful, wicked devil-goddess. A sexual supervillain.

And goddamn, it was fun having these powers.

Once or twice a month, Sam would meet friends for drinks, secretly scouting the bar for men to imagine she'd gone there to meet. She'd try new cocktails, pretending they'd been sent to her, and browse those cologne samples with relish—all part of the casting process. Now, nearly three years after the ultimatum, it was hard to remember the time when Mike's kink had repelled her; now she couldn't imagine their marriage without it. It would've been like having a favorite spice taken away, their meals still nourishing but missing that exotic kick.

"Hello?"

"Hey, baby," Mike called back from upstairs.

His office was up there, and he must have brought the day's paperwork with him. He preferred to finish that stuff up at the station and leave his job where it belonged, but Sam knew that doing this at home was all part of the game. Waiting up, imagining her out somewhere, getting nailed on some strange man's bed.

Her pulse quickened as she hung her jacket on the rack, spiked as she slid off her wedding band and stowed it in a pocket. She smelled the cologne on her, breathed in that citrus zing, tasted the lingering bite of grapefruit on her tongue, and conjured the imagined man she'd just fucked behind Mike's back. *This was great, Nick, but I have to get home or my husband will suspect . . .*

She went upstairs to their bathroom, slicking herself with a measure of lube from the bottle in the cabinet. One, two buttons to free on her blouse, low enough that someone standing close could see she was wearing a lacy mint green bra. She gave her hair a mussing and decided she looked as if she'd been thoroughly, recently, convincingly ravaged.

Down the hall, Mike's office door was open. He swiveled in his chair when she knocked on the frame, looking her up and down with a tight smile. *Game on.*

"How was your day?" she asked innocently.

"Busy, and still not over. Guess I'm not the only one, huh? You're awful late. I had to heat up leftovers."

"Sorry. I had this conference call that just would—not—end."

"You're dressed up." He took in her skirt, her heels, her cleavage.

"Some of the donors were visiting," she lied, averting her gaze.

Mike got to his feet. He had changed out of his work clothes and into jeans and a T-shirt, the latter snug, which let bad guys know his morning rituals involved weights, not doughnuts, and that there was no softness to be found in Mike Heyer's body or justice. But as much as his physical capability excited her, Sam wouldn't acknowledge it that night—not while they were playing. When they played, he was a weak man, incapable of keeping his cheating wife out of the arms of stronger, more handsome, more virile men. Sam hadn't so much as kissed another man on the lips since her first date with her husband five years before, but according to the parameters of this charade, she'd fucked half of Pittsburgh.

"You smell . . . different," he said, coming closer. "What is that?"

"Gosh, I'm not sure. I don't smell anything."

"Smells like . . ." He brought his face to her temple and breathed her in. "Like men's cologne."

She shivered from his deep, smooth voice—a contradiction to his rough native accent. Tamping the sensation down, she slid into her role, shrugging. "That's weird. Maybe it's that new detergent."

"And your breath smells like liquor."

"I used some mouthwash before I left the office."

His blue eyes narrowed, calculating. He clasped her wrist, holding up her bare hand. "Where's your ring?"

"Oh. I must have taken it off before I went to wash out my mug at work." She felt around in the little pocket of her skirt and produced the band. "See?"

He watched her slip it back on, frowning. "Who was it?"

She finger-combed his soft, sandy brown hair, not meeting his eyes. She wanted to run those same fingers down his throat, over his chest and abdomen, and cup her palm between his legs to see how hard he might be, but her role was that of an ambivalent, dissatisfied wife just now, and his cock was beneath her interest. She'd found a better one, his fantasy dictated. She couldn't say she was turned on by these dynamics, herself, but knowing what it did to him . . . Nothing had ever made her feel so fiercely desired.

"I don't know what you mean," she bluffed. "Who was who?"

"Don't play games with me, Sam."

Oh, but I will. She huffed an unconvincing little laugh. "I'm not. I honestly don't know what you're talking about."

"You were out with some guy again. Who was he?"

Sam sighed, pretending to feel weary—not guilty—over being busted. Bored. She crossed her arms and leaned against the door frame. "Does it really matter?"

"Yeah, it does. You're my wife." He took her by the arm, leading her out of the room and flipping off the lights behind them, just the city's glow from the window at the end of the hall showing the way to their bedroom. An old floorboard on the landing before the door creaked. So many times she'd been awakened by that creak—that wonderful noise that told her Mike had come home from a late night, from a bust or investigation or stakeout, safe and sound . . . So many nights it was her cue to relax, though at moments like this it spiked her pulse, setting heat humming low in her belly.

He coaxed her into their room with a bossy hand on her lower back—a lingering glimmer of his domineering side, soon to be shed alongside his shirt and jeans. It had no place in this room with them tonight.

Sam switched on one of the bedside lamps. "It's Friday, Mike. We're both exhausted. Let's deal with this tomorrow."

"No, we're going to deal with it now. You're going to tell me what happened."

She sat on the bed, pulling off her shoes. Her throat was dry, as though she were thirsty for him.

He stood before her, hands on his hips. "Who was he?"

"Just some guy named Nick."

"What'd you do, find him at a bar?"

She nodded. "We only had a drink. Nothing happened."

"If nothing happened, how come you smell like him?"

She ignored the question, getting up and unclasping her necklace. "I'm tired, honey. Let's not get into this tonight." The heavy beads rattled as she set them on the dresser, and her fingers moved to her buttons. She could feel Mike getting close before he even touched her, his fingertips easing the top from her shoulders.

His voice heated her neck and the sternness had left him. "Tell me about him."

"I just met him at the bar, when Lisa stood me up for a girl's date. He bought me a drink, that's all." *A greyhound.* She pictured her imaginary fling, his warm, wicked gaze as he slid her glass across the wood, his cruel smirk as his eyes darted to her wedding band. Her imaginary flings were always colossal dicks, whatever that said about her.

"That's all, huh?"

"Sure."

Considering the size of his hands, Mike had deft fingers. They slipped free the clasp of her skirt and lowered the tiny zipper, thumbs sliding under the band of her tights before the skirt even hit the floor.

"Tell me about him," Mike said again, and his voice had gone gruff. The time for play denials was over. His kink was loose, pacing the room, and it wanted feeding.

"He's tall," she said. "Tall and handsome and built. With this smile . . . I wanted to tell him no, but I just couldn't, not the way he smiled at me." A couple of years ago this performance would've made Sam feel silly and self-conscious, but practice made perfect. She could teach a class on improvisational dirty talk now. It was all about commitment—better to say something cheesy and over-the-top and to own it than to clam up or hold back, afraid of sounding dumb.

"What else?" he demanded.

"Strong hands." She felt Mike's fingers at her bra clasp. She imagined her mystery man having freed those little hooks an hour or two earlier, imagined his palms as Mike slipped the straps from her shoulders and cupped her breasts. Electricity crackled through her body, a sharp, hot bloom snaking from her belly out to her fingertips and feet.

"You fuck him?"

"No." She sighed and paused for a beat. "He fucked me."

She heard the click of Mike's belt and finished her own undressing, dropping her panties and stepping free of them and her tights. Their bodies met at the bed. His touch was needy now, and unsure. He pushed her onto her back and knelt between her legs, sliding two fingers along her sex, slick from the lube.

"Christ, you did fuck somebody."

She smiled. "Like I said, he fucked me." She kept a stash of condoms in their bathroom, too, and sometimes she'd rub one along her labia, then make Mike taste the latex—the so-called evidence of her infidelity. The realism deepened the fantasy for him, and his pleasure spurred hers in this kink she couldn't *quite* call her own.

He was already hard, ready to go. A generous lover with a more than adequate cock, he was the best she'd ever had, whether their sex was tender or rough or desperate or any other flavor she might crave on a given night. But she wasn't allowed to say so, now. In this game Mike was poorly endowed, borderline impotent, hopeless at pleasing her. He was a weak, pathetic husband who drove his wife into the beds of superior males—and for whatever reason, that thought turned him utterly feral.

Even after two years of this play and a virtual dissertation's worth of research on cuckolding kink, Sam still didn't entirely get it. And she'd come to accept that she didn't need to. She didn't know precisely what caused a thunderstorm, either, but that didn't make the lightning any less exciting.

If she had to guess, she suspected it was something to do with letting go. Something to do with Mike surrendering to the pressure he felt to be in control, to be fearless, commanding, the leader with all the answers. His greatest fear, professionally, was that he wouldn't be good enough, that he'd let his partner down, that he'd fail his team, lose their respect, maybe even cost someone his life. But his job was dangerous and left no room for self-doubt. So it was here, in their bed and in their games, that he got to relieve himself of all that stress—not only to admit that he wasn't perfect and strong and capable, but to *wallow* in the idea. Wallow in whatever sensation it gave him to feel like a lesser man—some great gulp of air when the pressure of his job felt thick enough to drown in.

Sam stroked his cock. "I need more than you can give me, Mike." She felt his flesh twitch and tighten at her words, but she kept her touch lazy, fingers flaccid to help them pretend he wasn't as hard or big as he was.

"Tell me what happened."

She coaxed him to lie next to her and their legs tangled. She traced his collarbone with her fingertips and spoke against his throat. "He took me back to his place. A beautiful loft, with a view that overlooks the river. He rows on the weekends. And he's an EMT during the week. If we'd had the time, I bet he could have fucked me all night."

Mike's hand slid between them to hold his erection. She was meant to ignore it, scorn it, reject it.

"What else?" he asked, that deep voice sounding strained in her ear.

"He was a great kisser. His kisses got me wetter than fucking you ever has."

"How old is he?"

"Thirty. I'd almost forgotten how much energy younger guys have." No matter that Mike had completed a triathlon the previous summer. This other man was younger, fitter, hotter, better in every way. "And Jesus, what a body."

"And his dick?"

"Big. Thick. Long. I worried that maybe I wouldn't be able to handle him at first. But it didn't matter," she said with a mean smile. "He handled me just fine."

Mike shifted, getting to his knees, between her thighs, taking her quick and smooth. He'd be pretending she was wet from some stranger—wet with arousal or the other man's come. But even without the lube, she was wet for Mike, for her hot, fascinating, wonderfully warped husband. Though she ought to get the stars out of her eyes and focus on Nick if this was going to be an A-plus performance.

"Where'd you fuck him?"

"On his couch," she riffed, hatching the fantasy in her head. "I could see the park. On my hands and knees, and he took me from behind, right there in the window. The entire North Shore was watching. It was so hot."

It was Mike who truly wanted to see, though.

He had never come out and asked her about it, but she knew he was up for taking the past couple of years' play to a new level. A level that involved her actually sleeping with another man, and telling him all about it, perhaps taping it or having him watch from a crack in the door or listening from the next room. Having it rubbed in his face.

And after several months' deliberation, the idea had gone from an impossibility to something quite different. Something quite intriguing. At first Sam had dismissed it without any consideration—they could play out these scenarios, but nothing more, of course. Monogamy had always been implied, and anything beyond that was cheating. And she could never cheat on anyone, least of all Mike.

Then she'd asked herself—what made an affair *cheating*? Answers came back to her in time.

Deception. Secrecy. Selfishness.

Cheating was a greedy decision made by one partner, resulting in pleasure that the other got no part in. If Samira and Mike invited another man in together, though, it would be none of those things. It would be the precise opposite. A mutual decision, and far from a greedy deception—it would be her gift to him, in fact. Maybe even a gift to *her*.

Before, the idea of being with another man had stirred nothing in Sam. Not at first. Though the past couple of months, when Sam would be out, scouting those bars for fantasy men . . . and then back at home, in bed with Mike, remembering them . . .

Maybe I could. For me, as much as for him. Touch a new man, for the first time in five years. Kiss one. More. If that didn't threaten their marriage, was she really so saintly that she couldn't admit the idea excited her?

She held Mike's strong, pumping body tight, stroked his hair.

She could nearly see it happening, now. She wanted it . . . if the circumstances were *exactly* right. She was a levelheaded woman, a planner, a risk minimizer. Her marriage was the most precious thing in her life, and it couldn't be treated as some petri dish and experimented in—not impulsively. Plus she'd invented so many perfect strangers in her head, how could she possibly find a real one who'd measure up?

Mike drew her from her thoughts. "What else?"

"He was rough. And so strong." She pictured imaginary Nick's strained face and taut muscles. "I begged him to take me face-to-face just so I could watch his body."

"Just his body?" Mike's own body was as powerful and commanding as the one she'd made up—and never more so than at moments like this, when he was riled up beyond belief—but he mustn't be allowed to know that.

"And his cock," she said. "I begged him to let me watch his cock while we fucked. God, he was thick. You can probably tell that, though." She ran a patronizing palm over his short hair. "You can probably feel what he did to me."

He cranked into an entirely new gear at those words. *Proving mode.* Every muscle had hardened, along with his expression and his thrusts. He'd set his insecurity aside, overcome by the burning competition he felt toward this made-up rival. Those were the three acts in this filthy play they put on together—suspicion, humiliation, reclaiming.

"You think I'm not enough for you?" he demanded, taking her roughly with a dozen deep pumps. "This dick's not big enough for you?"

"Let's just make this quick. I'm sore." She let her tone imply more. *Make it quick—like you'd know how to make it any other way.* She slid her fingertips to her clit.

Just make it quick. She smiled to herself, remembering the vacation they'd taken to San Francisco after they'd been dating for two years. That first evening, Mike had made love to her for no less than an hour, woken her up twice in the night for more, and left her smirking and a touch raw the next day, in no doubt of what he was capable of. He'd proposed to her that afternoon, one knee sunk into the sand beside the bay, blue eyes full of hope and fear in the sunshine.

That—a marathon of sex preceding the proposal—should have been her first tip that he was a little different sexually. Skewed in such a way that his worthiness was wired to his cock, with not *quite* the right voltage conversion. After they'd gotten engaged, he'd gone through that brief but potent period of irrational jealousy, one that had grated on her terribly, made her feel hurt and distrusted and nearly had her giving back the ring.

But in the wake of her ultimatum and his confession, she learned that the jealousy didn't make his blood boil—it made his dick hard. He hadn't wanted reassurance that she *wasn't* cheating. He'd craved the fearful rush that maybe, just maybe, she was.

She stroked his neck, so in love with this quirky man. Though now wasn't the time to tell him so, not when insecurity had him this hard and frantic between her thighs.

"You should have seen him," Sam said, urging his hips with her own. "God, I wish you could have. I should make you watch so maybe you'd get a clue how to fuck me."

He answered with a pained sound, as though she'd struck him with more than her words. It gave her a moment's pang, but she trusted their game. A bit more intensity with her fingers had the heat and tension gathering, a tangling knot of pleasure in her belly growing tighter, tighter.

"He was just so, fucking, big. So deep. And I wish I could have stayed there the whole night. He could've gone that long. Next time you're out on a case," she promised, "I'll have to find him again. Maybe bring him back here."

"Not in our bed."

"Yes, right here." She stroked the pillow under her head and the sheets at her side. "Then every time I let you fuck me I'll remember how much better it was with Nick."

"You used a condom, at least?" His voice was a needy whisper.

"Oh, he offered. But I said no. No, I wanted to feel him that way. Inside me—like proof I really had been with someone like him."

Mike groaned. *Proof* was one of his trigger words—a verbal spur that jabbed his heart, a tight hand that stroked his cock. He had others as well: *ruined, dirty, wrecked.* His reaction had her arousal sharpening in turn.

"I wish you could have seen it. I really do." She'd taken to repeating that notion, a veiled signal she hoped he might pick up on. *Maybe I'll just let you watch* was the hidden message. Though for all she knew, he'd loathe the idea of actually going there, and that was fine. And for all she knew, it'd blow his mind clear into the next county. She was starting to suspect she was capable of it, herself. So she kept planting the seed, waiting to see if Mike would water it.

"He make you come?" he panted.

She laughed, a derisive, pitying noise. "So many times. I don't think I've ever felt that good, coming on such a big cock. God, I just felt . . . *owned.*" Another trigger word, and Mike's thrusts grew rougher. "He just owned me with his body. I was begging for him: Nick, Nick, Nick," she whispered in his ear. "Fuck me, please. Fuck me like my husband can't. Show me what a real man feels like."

Sensing he was nearing the end of his rope, she touched herself with purpose. She kept talking, as though the thoughts were what was edging her toward release, and not the hard, needy motions of her husband's gorgeous body and the exquisite expression on his face, that ecstatic psychological torture.

"Oh, it's got me close, just remembering his cock." She watched Mike's cock surging, and her imaginary male faded to a faceless shadow, no match for her real-life lover. "So big," she murmured. The pleasure had her body hot and angry, aching for relief. She wanted to touch Mike, and feel his damp skin against her fingertips, taste the sweat gleaming there. But for the game's sake she kept herself aloof, a limp, grudging vessel.

In lieu of her hands, she let her gaze stroke his strong arms, tight stomach, pistoning hips, flashing shaft. "So big," she muttered again, and when the pleasure flared and burst in her clit, it was from thoughts of one man alone.

Mike surrendered a dozen harried thrusts later, back arching to bathe his chest and shoulders in warm lamp light, his hips grinding her thighs with the sweetest twinge of pain.

After a few steadying breaths, he collapsed beside her.

Now she was allowed to smile fondly, to stroke his face and kiss him and admit whose name had been at the tip of her tongue as she'd come.

"Baby," he muttered, then laughed softly.

She pressed her lips to his temple. "Good?"

"So good. Always."

"I love you."

He wrapped her in powerful arms and she locked a leg around his hip. "Not half as much as I love you," he said.

And she let him believe such a thing, because there were no words available to mankind that could ever express how much she adored him.

CHAPTER TWO

Mike woke late—nearly ten thirty, the alarm clock told him. The smell of coffee had wafted up from the kitchen, and he pictured Samira cross-legged on the couch in her pajamas, with a book or magazine propped on a pillow in her lap, her mug's steam lit all pearly by the morning light. She'd go jogging later, as she did most Saturdays, and her unwashed hair would be wild and wavy, her face bare. She never looked prettier than she did on weekend mornings, and Mike had taken the mental snapshot so many times he could shut his eyes and relish every detail.

He smelled sex in the sheets, a scent darker and more exotic than the coffee in the kitchen. *Fucking hell.*

He rolled onto his back, remembering last night's game with a flush of fond, sheepish arousal, and a grin curled his lips. He and the other guys in Narcotics liked to one-up one another with evidence of whose long-suffering girlfriends and wives were the best. The women who waited up until two a.m. keeping dinner warm, who always covered for forgotten family birthdays in the midst of messy, endless cases, who never failed to record a single game.

Mike couldn't exactly crow about his own wife's beyond-the-call-of-duty cred. *Well, boys,* he imagined saying, *every few weeks my wife stays out late and brags about fucking another man, then makes me come so hard it's a miracle I haven't had a stroke. How about those Steelers?*

Still smiling, he tossed the lust-smelling covers aside and swung his legs to the floor. He was heading a small bust, starting at midnight tonight, but he and Sam had the day, and after next Friday, he was on vacation. Staycation or whatever the fuck it'd been dubbed of late, but that was fine by Mike. He could finally diagnose the mysterious squeak in the car, sleep in, putter and nap and breathe easy with no one relying on him for an entire glorious week. No one but Sam, and the rare demands his easygoing, self-sufficient wife might make were his pleasure to address.

He pulled on some clean shorts and jeans, a tee and sweater to cut the morning chill. He headed downstairs and found Sam just where he knew he would, mug in hand, gaze on an open book.

She smiled up at him from the couch, brown eyes sweet and dark as she liked her coffee, and shining in the sunlight. He wanted to record each and every detail of her, her laugh lines and the way she squinted, how her ears stuck out a bit, the molasses brown of her glossy hair. She was thirty-six and she looked it, but he wouldn't have her any other way. She might rue every new line and gray hair she found, but Mike loved them, each a tiny hint about the woman she'd one day be.

"Morning, handsome. Coffee's ready."

He stooped to kiss her forehead. "Thanks. When'd you get up?"

"An hour ago, maybe. So weird to out-sleep you."

He headed for the kitchen to fill a mug, speaking to her over the breakfast bar. "You must have worn me out."

"Oh yes, blame your wife for your laziness," she teased.

He grabbed last Sunday's paper from the table and joined her on the couch. Leaning over, he planted an extra kiss on her temple. "It wasn't a complaint."

His cock gave a twitch at the memories of last night. He'd come home that evening wound up from work, every muscle strung tight enough to snap, a stress headache brewing behind his eyes. Then he'd texted to see when she'd be home, and her curt *Stuck at work late* was all he'd needed to know what was in store for him. Work drama forgotten, the tension had shifted, and he'd started growing hot and impatient as he waited. He'd already been playing their game in his head for an hour by the time she'd come home. When he'd collapsed beside her after the sex, every muscle and nerve had been slack, all the tautness erased from his body and brain.

Other men could keep their anti-anxiety meds. Sam was the only therapy he needed.

Tonight he'd spoil her rotten. Whatever she wanted—be it an entire hour of head or just a quick peck and a night's reprieve from all sexual demands—it was hers for the asking.

He scooted closer so his thigh touched her knee. He reached under her pillow, disrupting her reading to give her chilly foot a squeeze. "Thanks."

She met his gaze, oh so innocent. "For the coffee?"

"For last night."

She smiled deeply. "My pleasure."

Maybe, but probably only to the extent it was *his* pleasure. "Whatever you want tonight. Or this afternoon or right now. Whenever."

"All I know is that I want to get takeout for dinner."

"La Feria?"

"I was thinking Soba." She shut her eyes, smiling. "Pot stickers. Oh yes."

"That all it takes to spoil you? Where's the challenge in that?"

She looked him up and down, mischievous. "I'm sure I'll think of some other ideas as the day goes on." Her tone confirmed his hopes, warm with flirtation.

"Anything," he said, and let her foot go with a final squeeze.

For a long time they read without speaking, the calm enriched by the smell of the coffee, the rustle of pages, the sounds of traffic and activity outside. After a half hour or more, Sam broke their companionable silence.

"You know last night," she said lightly.

A familiar, irrational surge of anxiety jabbed Mike—fear that she was done with their games. Though she gave him no good reason to, he felt this worry now and then, aware of how strange his needs were and how thoroughly he'd already been spoiled. She was patient and more than indulgent. But would she grow weary of their games, in time?

He spoke casually to mask his fear. "I seem to recall last night, yes."

"All this stuff we do. All the stuff you like . . ."

Mike's field had conditioned him to always expect the worst, and his heart sank in selfish mourning. "Sure."

She met his eyes. "How far were you thinking you wanted to take it? Further than we have?"

The fist around his heart loosened. "Oh, honey." He turned and cupped her jaw, stroking her cheeks with his thumbs. "I love what we do. I'm not going to ask you for anything more. I'm not going to ask you for anything you're not comfortable with."

She'd been dropping hints for a couple of months now, clearly curious to know if he intended to leverage his kink beyond fantasy talk into something serious. He should have assuaged her fears the first time he'd sensed them. "Were you worried I was planning for us to take things further?"

She averted her eyes, her expression not evidencing the relief he'd hoped to offer. "No, I wasn't worried."

"I can read you like this book," Mike said, tapping her paperback. He pulled her into a hug, but her body stayed rigid. "Jesus, Sami. I'd never ask you to do that." He searched her face for signs of impending tears but found none, thankfully. "Is it not fun for you anymore?"

She didn't answer right away, gaze focused on some nowhere-space between them and the far wall. "It's still fun."

"But?"

She bit her lip and met his eyes. "Have you ever *thought* about taking things further?"

He wouldn't lie, as much as he feared freaking her out. "I've thought about it, sure. But that doesn't mean I'd ever—"

"Would you *like* to?"

"I . . . In theory, yeah, maybe. But what we're doing, it's great. It's enough. Hell, it's *plenty*. Don't worry. I'm not biding my time, waiting to ask you to do anything you're not into. I'm not grooming you for some skeezy three-way."

Finally, a tiny smile. "I've thought about it, too."

His fearful heart thumped hard, then froze. "Thought about . . . ?"

"About maybe taking things further someday."

His mouth was dry as sand. "Like . . ."

"Like us, and another guy. Maybe."

For a couple of breaths, he felt that sensation he dreaded so much—that suffocating feeling of inferiority, of worthlessness, of being not-enough, never-enough, not-even-close. Then, as always, it shifted, like gas dousing fire. His cock grew heavy between his thighs and a flush crept from his chest up his neck. "Like, you and a guy, and me watching?"

She nodded, a practical gesture, as though they were discussing whether to get the Focus's tires rotated. "Yeah. Something like that. Whatever gets you hot."

Fucking Christ, he was hot right now. But it wasn't simply a matter of turning up the volume on their role-playing. They were talking about a real live other man, the real live sanctity of their marriage, and a scenario that demanded they both trust his turn-on wasn't going to go sour and rot through the foundation they'd built together over the past few years. He'd nearly driven her away once before with his jealousy—the scare of a lifetime.

"I don't know," he said. "Do you think we're up to it?"

"I think we're up to talking about it. The idea, and the logistics. Whatever consequences could come of it." She smiled. "I am an actuary, after all—I get off on risk assessment."

It reminded Mike of the conversations they'd had as newlyweds about whether to have children. Weighing the urges against the risks and reality; their easy, low-stress home life versus the ticking clock that demanded a decision be made. They'd ultimately decided against, and why? To keep things simple, keep each other at the center of their lives.

To keep ourselves free and open to exploring this marriage to its fullest, Mike thought. Would it be a disservice to their decision to let *this* question mark go unexplored?

He took Sam's hand and linked her slender fingers with his big ones, and focused on the baby steps. "How would we even find somebody?"

"Probably online," she said. "Put an ad on a personals site. Like, a kinky personals site. The background check would be a piece of cake, at least."

Mike nodded. True, he could get the dirt on any guy with a few keystrokes. But that didn't cover STIs, character, intentions . . . He wasn't exactly a public figure, but he *was* a public servant. If some sexual tourist found out Mike's position, what was the worst that could happen? Three-ways weren't illegal, and they wouldn't be soliciting. He'd face a hell of a lot of judgment and scrutiny and humiliation, but his job wouldn't be at risk. Neither would Sam's, though she still had her privacy and reputation to consider.

"What about if the guy, like, talked about us online or something?"

She smirked. "I think you're underestimating how likely you look to break his neck, honey."

"Oh. Maybe."

"Or that invisible gun that's always hovering at your side, even after you've taken your holster off. But if that's not enough, we could make him sign some confidentiality agreement, I bet. So we could sue him if he told anyone. But really, people do this stuff all the time."

"I know. I'm just trained to expect the worst."

She leaned into him, a hug without arms. Her hair was a whisper against his neck. "I know you are. Do you think if we did find someone, theoretically . . . How do you think you'd actually feel, watching another man with me? Would it be as hot as what we talk about, or would it be upsetting, in reality?"

Tell her the truth and risk crossing some line, being too kinky for her to stay on board with . . . ? *Truth only. Always.* "I think it'd be the hottest thing I can imagine."

She sat up and smiled, a mysterious, beguiling little gesture. "You're such an interesting man."

He felt his face heating and cast his gaze down at their linked hands.

"And after the sex was over?" she asked. "Would the hotness be tainted once the deed was done? After you went back to being Mr. In Control?"

"Once the deed was done, I'd know that guy would realize I have the sexiest, most decadent wife in the world. And that I'm the one who gets to wake up with her every morning, while he was the one who had to go home alone."

She nodded, seeming to like his answer. Her attention shifted and she picked up her phone, checking the time. "I better get running soon. I've got a haircut at one."

"You driving there?"

She shook her head and stood. "Walking."

"Cool. I'll check out that whining noise in your car."

She smiled and leaned in to kiss his forehead. "You're lovely."

He got to his feet, tailing her down the hall. "You need the bathroom, or can I grab a shower?"

"I'm good. I'll see you when I'm back."

"Have a good run," he said.

"I will. Could be a long one. I've got a lot on my mind now." She shot him a grin over her shoulder. "I think maybe I've got a project to start planning."

CHAPTER THREE

Samira's plotting officially kicked off two evenings later, when Mike was out on a bust that might take three hours or thirty. After a couple of days' soul-searching, she'd decided to give the first stage of planning a shot as a treat for him, a bit of wicked news to keep him buoyed through his rough assignment.

Step one was creating a post on a kinky personals site.

BULL WANTED FOR CUCKOLD SCENE, GREATER PITTSBURGH

Even typing that one line had her heart pounding, pleasure and fear mingled in every beat. It felt as though somebody were behind her, reading over her shoulder. But she'd already given herself permission to bail—if she got replies and they creeped her out across the board, she'd hit the abort button. If she received replies and they didn't *all* creep her out, but her intuition wasn't happy, she'd still abort. Though maybe she'd print out the more intriguing replies, in case they gave Mike a thrill, and further deepen the unlikely groove they'd been steadily etching into his libido.

But the more she reread the subject line, the less it intimidated her. She took a fortifying sip of wine, and a half hour later she examined her composition.

Me: married female, mid-thirties, professional, pretty, curvy, Persian roots, great skin and smile.

My husband: late thirties, calm, submissive cuckold fetishist, indulged in role-playing only so far. That's where you come in.

You: can pass for early thirties/late twenties. Single, safe, handsome, tall, built, and hung. No race preference, brunet a plus. Open-minded and kind on the inside, gruff and cocky on the outside. No penetration during the first visit or two—we can build up to more explicit stuff if things feel right. Ultimately my husband wants to watch us together and should be made to feel belittled and outmanned, and generally have his nose rubbed in how much manlier you are than he is.

We're fun, sane, childless, and STI-free. Ideally we'd love to find a man we have chemistry with, for a longer-term, casual arrangement. Please, no leather/rubber/intense BDSM stuff. You will pretend to be my normal old piece on the side, who just happens to be gorgeous and bossy.

If interested, let's chat via e-mail. Please send a photo, including face. If it feels like a good fit, I'd love to meet for a drink. Then if the chemistry's right, we can flirt and kiss while my husband watches from afar, pretending I'm meeting up with the guy I'm cheating on him with. We won't take you home on the first date, but if it feels natural, the sky's the limit for the future. Be warned, we will require your real name before we invite you into our home, and we will run a background check as a formality.

—S

"Not bad," she decided aloud.

She fussed with the wording for another hour—and another glass of wine—and was shocked at the confidence with which she hit POST.

Her nerves tingled, but her curiosity far outweighed her fear. She wouldn't get her hopes up—the fact that she was genuinely rooting for the ad to result in some candidates was thrilling enough. There was no deadline, after all. It would happen if and when it was supposed to.

The next morning, Sam sat with her coffee mug hovering near her chin, blinking, shocked by the e-mail flood that greeted her. Shocked and terrified and flattered and excited.

She was at her desk in the corner of the living room, and Mike was puttering in their tiny kitchen, beyond the breakfast bar. He'd gotten in around four a.m. and had to leave again in just a few minutes, but maybe this would give him a boost. The coffee alone probably wasn't enough on three hours' sleep.

"Honey, come here a sec."

"What is it?" He rounded the counter with his own mug in hand, and peered over her shoulder at the subject lines. "Whoooaaa . . ."

"I know." She'd opened a new e-mail account specially for the task, and it looked like a big old in-box full of sin, staring at her with accusing messages titled *Bull found!* and *Can't wait to meet a hotwife* and the like.

"Forty-three messages," Mike said.

"In about twelve hours. And here I thought you were an outlier."

"Wish I could stick around and see what the hell they say." But instead he kissed her cheek with a mischievous little grin. "Another late one tonight."

"I figured."

"But maybe you'll have some developments to share with me when I get in."

"Here's hoping."

But the number dwindled as Sam filtered out men who lived halfway across the country, ones whose pictures turned her off, ones who claimed to be "a very youthful fifty," and some plain old creepers. It ruled out a *lot* of candidates.

"We're down to six viable options," she told Mike when he got in at eleven that evening. She slid his dinner into the oven. "Is it unreasonable of me to also get rid of the guys who didn't bother punctuating or capitalizing their messages?"

He came up behind her, wrapping his strong arms around her waist and planting a kiss on her neck. "We're shopping for a man we think deserves to sleep with you. Be as picky as you want. It's not the kind of decision you should rush or force yourself into."

She smiled at that, pleased to know that no matter how much he wanted this, there was no pressure. He valued their relationship and her feelings above his fantasies. Of course, she'd known that all along, but having spent her evening in front of that intimidating screen, the reminder was welcome—as reassuring as the hug.

He left her to shower, and as Sam headed back to the computer, she gave herself permission to dismiss the messages with bad spelling and lazy capitalization.

It left only two candidates, but she liked their photos and introductory messages. She replied to both conversationally, asking if they were local, how old they were, if they had any experience with cuckolding, and what about it appealed to them. She also included a photo of herself. It seemed only fair, though she chose a long shot, one with an erstwhile haircut. It gave a sense of her body and her face, but wasn't detailed enough that the men would be able to recognize her in the supermarket, should she chicken out and abandon the mission.

After Mike ate his late dinner and disappeared to sink into a much-deserved coma, she sat down again at her laptop, intending only to shut it off. But there it was, a message in her secret in-box.

The reply was a disappointment. The guy was way too eager, with only fifteen minutes having passed between the time she'd hit SEND and when he had. His reply consisted of a rather dirty and not at all arousing missive about the things he wanted to do to her, and he was too antsy about setting a date for Sam's taste. Enthusiasm was one thing, but her gut said this was quite another. Pass.

The second reply was worse, in that it didn't arrive—not that night, nor by the time she was heading out to work the next morning. Two dozen new responses had come in from the ad, none of them especially appealing, all of them totaling discouragement.

"It's fine," Mike said when she debriefed him that evening. "What were the chances we'd strike gold the first time out?"

He was right. And having him home at dinnertime was treat enough.

But the following day, something changed.

Sam had checked her personal e-mail while her hair dried and her coffee cooled. She'd decided she wouldn't check "the dirty account," as it might just overwhelm her, the task now feeling impossible. Not a cloud she needed following her to work for the third day in a row. But even as she got her shoes on and shouldered her purse, curiosity had her crossing the floor, sitting down, clicking the bookmark, and typing in her password.

Ten or so new messages, but she didn't have it in her to tackle them beyond reading the subject lines. Then she recognized the e-mail address of the second short-listed respondent.

"You took your time," she muttered, opening the message. Though had he, really? Taking a day or more wasn't criminal. In fact, it struck her as rather encouraging that he had other things to do in a given day besides pursue his chances at playing sexual tourist in other people's marriages. A hobbyist, not a fanatic.

She sipped the last of her cold coffee and read the e-mail.

> Thanks for the reply, S.

Bless him and his use of commas and capitals. She opened a new tab and found his first e-mail, wanting to confirm he was the one she was picturing. Yes. Oh, good photo. It was a shot of him in a park, crouching with his hand on a yellow lab's collar. He looked big and strong, with a fearless sort of smile and a lot of stubble, messy dark hair. Could be any ethnicity—Italian or Hispanic, or just a white guy with a summer tan. She liked the shape of his shoulders under his T-shirt, and wished this were like Zappos, so she could rotate him and examine his design from multiple angles and browse other women's reviews.

But he looked good. Not *too* wholesome, despite the park and the dog, but not sketchy. There was something in his smile, something lazy and easy, just a touch cocky. *Mischievous.* She began to wonder about his voice, then realized she ought to read the e-mail before she got her hopes up too high. She clicked back to the first tab.

> To answer your questions, yes, I'm in Pittsburgh. I turn thirty-six in a couple of weeks, but I think I could maybe pass for a few

years younger. Maybe. May need to bust out the Grecian Formula on my temples, but—

Dear God, prematurely graying temples? Mike might get hot over the prospect of competing with a younger man, but Sam's legs always went a bit wobbly over salt-and-pepper facial hair and the like. She liked a man with a few miles on him. A man who looked like he knew his way around a woman's body. Yes, please.

—maybe that's negotiable.

Actually, I've got no idea what's negotiable. I've never been part of a cuckolding scene before. In fact, I had to look it up to make sure I had the right idea. I found your ad because I've got an exhibitionist streak I've been thinking about exploring. The idea of some guy watching me with his wife in the comfort of their home has more appeal than getting arrested for public indecency, and the latter seems to be what most of the people looking to be watched or get caught are after. So there was that, plus you're cute. So here I am, sleazing up your in-box.

Sam grinned. Then she glanced at the computer's clock, and realized she was going to be late. *Fuck it.*

You asked what about it appeals to me. I can't speak to the cuckolding, but as for wanting to be watched . . . Okay, I can't really speak to that, either. The idea just turns me on. And I'm not in the market for a serious relationship, so I'm not in a position to ask anyone to trust me enough to tape anything or let an outsider watch. And I don't really want to be out there on the Internet, in video format. But when I thought about what you and your husband are looking for, it made sense, especially when you mentioned a background check. I figure you're as concerned about keeping things discreet as I am. I'm not married or the manager of a day-care center or running for mayor, I just don't want to be another casualty of the Internet's infinite memory.

Anyhow, that was long-winded. I promise I can be utterly filthy and lecherous, if that's what you guys want in bed. Just thought I'd make sure we're on the same page logistically.

Oh, logistics. Sam's heart gave a flutter. If he'd attached a spreadsheet, she just might have climaxed.

If you don't mind, could you explain a little more what your husband gets out of this? I don't quite see what's in it for him, if you and I ultimately slept together. I'm curious to know what about the idea gets him off. I know you said you've never done this before. Sorry if you're looking for a "bull" who's a bit more seasoned, to facilitate. If we end up hooking up sometime, I'll require a little breaking in, myself.

Anyway, hope to hear from you again,

Bern

"Bern?" Mike muttered when he read the e-mail over her shoulder, late that night.

"I'm sure it's short for something. Bernard, maybe? At least he's not a Bernie."

"Or a Nard . . ." Mike's gaze skimmed the message a second time. He was wearing his poker face, feigning perfect apathy. "He seems sane enough, and he wrote in full sentences. What do you think? Could you sleep with a Bern?"

"I'd like to at least meet him. I like that he mentioned wanting to be discreet. And I like his photo. He looks kinda sexy." Kinda *very* sexy. "He's the best candidate I've seen so far. By miles."

Still, it was like ordering a dress online. It looks so good, seems so perfect; then it arrives and the color's off or it fits all wrong, leaves you feeling dumpy, and you're out seven bucks on return shipping.

"What did you say when you wrote back?" Mike asked.

"I haven't yet. I wanted to hear that you were still interested before I went any further."

"I am." He kept his voice businesslike, but Sam could sense his excitement. "You want to maybe do what we talked about? Meet him at a bar?"

"With you there, spying on us?" For both titillation and safety.

Mike nodded.

"I think I might." A rush of fear and excitement rolled through her, the whole venture suddenly feeling very . . . possible. "Would you like to answer his questions about what gets you off about the whole thing?"

He shook his head. "No. If we're going to do this, I want him and me to be as close to strangers as possible. Since that's how the fantasy's worked, with me being oblivious to the other guy's existence. As long as you're comfortable being the liaison, I don't want to have any contact with him, outside of the role-playing."

"Okay."

"Going forward . . . even if this guy is as decent as he comes off in an e-mail, I want to imagine he's the cocky shithead my wife's fucking around on me with. So if it's cool, I'm happy to trust your judgment the rest of the way. Plus you're better at wording stuff. You'll explain my freaky streak better than I ever could. And it'll sound better coming from a woman."

"Okay, then. And you're feeling . . . okay with it?"

"Sure."

She sighed, smiling up at him wearily. "I know you're trying to sound like you couldn't care less, so I won't feel pressured—but tell me honestly if this is exciting you or not."

Mike said nothing, just took her wrist, drawing her hand from the mouse and back to cup his cock, rock-hard behind his fly.

"I see."

He let go of her hand, smiling. "If I had the luxury of staying home tonight, I'd drag you to the bedroom and listen to all your horny theories about this Bern guy. I'm just trying to be blasé so if you're not into it, you won't feel bad about pulling the plug."

She turned onto her hip and held the back of the chair. Mike smoothed her hair, tucking it behind her ears.

"Don't be blasé," she said. "I know it's my decision. And for now, I'm excited, in no small part because you're excited. So don't downplay anything." She gave his erection another quick squeeze. "At least part of you is always forthcoming."

He leaned down to kiss her temple. "You're the most amazing wife ever, I hope you realize that. Wish I could stay and ravage you."

"Me, too."

"But I'll be happy all through this damn case, knowing maybe you're right here, writing an e-mail to some guy."

"You may be the weirdest husband ever, I hope you realize that. But good. Happy to make you happy."

Another kiss, then Mike had to go out to relieve a colleague on a marathon of a drug bust. The glow of Sam's computer screen had become her most constant companion of late, but in a way, it fed the fantasy. *My husband's never home*, she imagined telling some handsome stranger. *He won't suspect.*

So after she locked the door behind Mike, she poured herself a glass of red and got comfy before the screen.

Bern,

Thanks for such a thoughtful reply. And thanks for the offer of lechery, though your pragmatism was actually much appreciated. I'm new to all this, too, and not looking to rush anything.

But my husband and I are both excited at the prospect of maybe meeting up sometime. I know it sounds sort of drawn out, but I'll tell you how I'd been hoping it might go down . . .

She paused, and a bold thought overtook her. An impulse born of both curiosity and practicality. Though mainly the former.

Actually, would you be willing to speak to me on the phone? I'm home tonight, and I'll be up until about eleven. I'd like to hear your voice and your thoughts on how I envision all of this going. If you're comfortable with that, please feel free to give me a call.

She typed her number with a pounding pulse, and the second she sent the message, she worried it was a dumb move.

She worried he'd call. She worried he wouldn't. She worried herself through the rest of her glass of wine, and to her horror, her cell phone chimed as she was pouring a refill.

"Please be Mike. Please be Mike." Please be anybody but Bern.

Oh fuck, private number. She gulped a breath, grabbed the device from the coffee table, and hit TALK. "Hello?"

"Is this S?" Oh, what a voice. A deep, easy rumble of a voice.

"Yes. Is this Bern?"

"It is." A soft chuckle came through the ether, relaxing her by a small measure. "Wow. Weird."

She laughed herself, though it was tight and high and nervous. "I know, very weird. Thanks for calling."

"Was I too eager? I just happened to be checking my e-mail when yours came through." *Fuck, that accent.* Sam couldn't say if he was from Texas or Tennessee or Georgia or any other place, but his voice was steeped in bourbon and honey. Even if it was put-on, she prayed he'd keep it up.

"No, this is fine." She grabbed her glass and sank into the couch cushions, hugged a pillow to her middle. "I was worried giving you my number was too eager . . ." Sam bit her lip. "Jeez, now that I have you on the phone, I have no idea what I'd planned to say to you." His voice was as appealing as his photo—and his punctuation—and suddenly she felt like a stammering junior high schooler.

"Well, for starters, I feel kinda silly calling you S. Is there something else we could use?"

"Sam is fine."

"Sam. I like that. You a Samantha?"

The truth would be a bold move, given that there was probably only a handful of Samiras in the whole of Pittsburgh, but her intuition sounded no alarms. "I'm a Samira, actually."

"Oh, right, your ad said you're, what? Persian?"

"Yeah. My parents both grew up in Iran. What about you? Is Bern short for Bernard?" she asked.

"It is. Kinda geriatric, right?"

"Only a little."

"It was my great-grandfather's name. I think I got off easy, though—it was between that and Leslie."

"Close call."

"So, you were going to explain how you thought the first meeting might go." Some motion hitched his voice, like he, too, had dropped onto a couch and gotten comfortable. Though for all Sam knew, Mr. Exhibitionist had just taken out his cock and stationed himself in front of a mirror or a wide-open window or a webcam, but she'd run with the first notion.

"We were thinking that for the first time, I'd meet the man at a bar. We have a lot of scenarios, actually, just from . . . you know. Dirty talk and that sort of thing."

"Sure."

"So the idea was that my husband and I would go to the same place, separately. He'd sit off to one side and I'd sit at the bar, pretending not to know he was there. Then you'd meet me, and we'd act like we were having an affair, or that you were picking me up as a stranger, something like that."

"Right."

"And my husband would watch us flirt. Though, if you and I didn't feel any kind of spark, we could just talk about how awkward we felt and *pretend* to flirt."

Another soft, seductive laugh. "Fair enough."

"Then I'd head out and my husband would probably still be happy, just to have seen me getting hit on by some strange guy."

An unmistakable smirk warmed his tone. "I'd like to think I'm not *so* strange."

"That remains to be seen," Sam returned, smiling to herself.

"And so what if there *was* a spark?"

"On the first night, probably just a lot of flirting, and casual touches. As much as two people can get away with in a bar. Making out, maybe." She blushed, feeling silly. With two years' practice, Sam could wax filthy with no hesitation for Mike's ears, but no other person on earth had ever met this side of her before. Until now.

"Speaking of getting away with stuff at a bar," Bern said, "I imagine you'd need to meet me someplace pretty far from where you live, where you won't know anybody."

"I would. Shouldn't be too tough, though. I'm not a native and I didn't go to college here or anything. I'm willing to chance a meeting or two."

"Gotcha. I'm not eager to run into a friend, either, so we'll just have to settle on a neighborhood neither of us usually goes to. Can I ask where you guys live?"

"Shadyside."

"Ah, nice."

"And I work right downtown, so that's out, too."

"Well, I'm way down in Carrick," Bern said, "so maybe meet in the middle? Someplace around the South Side?"

"That could work." She swirled the wine in her glass, feeling relieved and more than a bit wicked. "So. You think you might want to?"

"Meet up? At the risk of sounding too eager, I'm intrigued. Very intrigued."

"Me, too. And my husband is as well."

"If you'll forgive me saying so, I can't wait to meet this piece of work you married."

She grinned, trying to guess what sort of wimpy beta male Bern was picturing. "You might be surprised. Can I ask what you do, or is that too personal?"

"Let's save all that for the bar. Don't worry—no shocking surprises or anything, but let's maybe conserve the small-talk topics. We might need them."

"I guess we're going with the picked-up-by-a-stranger routine, then," Sam said, pleased to catch herself flirting for real without even thinking about it.

"I'm game if you guys are. What's the next step?" he asked. "Do you need my full name or my social or something, for that background check?"

"That'd be good. Hang on." She rose and went to the counter, to scribble on the grocery list pad.

"Bernard Davies," he said, and Sam copied down his address and social security digits.

"Thanks. Do you want mine?"

"No, that's okay. You're in my call log now. That's probably enough for the police to track you down with, after you and your husband bury me in a shallow grave."

"Not before we've had our way with you," she countered.

There was a pause, and then Bern spoke, his tone different from before, firmer. "Speaking of that—of you guys having your way with me."

"Uh-huh." She headed back to the couch, suspecting a serious conversation was to follow.

"I looked this whole cuckolding thing up, after I read your ad," Bern said. "I saw a bunch of references to something called 'forced bi.' Did you guys have anything like that in mind? Your husband . . . you know, doing anything with me? To the guy you wind up with, that is."

"We haven't discussed it, no. That aspect hasn't come up in the couple of years we've been playing around with the idea, in the dirty talk. He's never said anything that made me think he wanted to go down on a guy or anything. Nothing direct. He . . . Hmm." She sighed. "Can I be frank, and kind of gross?"

"Sure."

"He's sort of into the whole sloppy-seconds thing. We've pretended that a guy's . . ." Her face flushed and she was glad Bern wasn't there to see how red her cheeks had surely gone. "We've pretended another guy was with me, and you know . . . came. Inside me. He likes to feel like there's proof. So there may be a bit of that."

"But you don't think he wants to touch me?"

"I don't think so. He's never made any noises about anything like that."

"And the whole coming-inside-you thing," Bern said, sounding not at all red in the face, unlike Sam. "That begs the question about condoms."

"Definitely condoms. Only if it seemed like everyone wanted it to be a long-term arrangement, then we could all get tested, I guess. I was thinking of maybe using female condoms, if my husband wanted to be able to . . . you know." She couldn't bring herself to utter "sloppy seconds" again so she let Bern infer it.

"Gotcha."

"Well, I have to talk to my husband about everything, but do you think you're interested in giving the first meet-up a try?"

"I am. I'm free this weekend, if you guys are. I imagine a Saturday night's best?"

Oh my. *This* Saturday night? It felt awfully soon. Then again, she and Mike were on vacation after Friday, and what better way to kick off the week?

"Yeah, that could work. Let me talk to my husband, and I'll send you an e-mail and we can nail down the where and when." Where and when to meet the man she might one day cheat on her husband with. So fucking weird.

"Sounds good," he said.

"Cool. Well, thanks for calling."

"Thanks for picking up. Maybe you'll pick me up in some other context in a few days."

She smiled at that. "Maybe."

"Have a good night, Sam."

"You, too."

As she set the phone aside, she felt deeply exposed. She got up and closed the curtains to quell the sensation, and put on a sweater. It wasn't entirely unpleasant, this psychic nakedness. She felt stripped down past her skin, way down deep to her ethics. Right into the core of her bones, like the whole world could see her marrow, what her marriage was made of.

Fine. Let them.

What good was an intentionally selfish lifestyle if they didn't take every opportunity to explore their relationship? They'd chosen to nurture their own bond and needs in place of a child, and she wasn't going to neglect something as fundamental as Mike's sexuality.

She unbuttoned her sweater and tossed it aside, flung the curtains open, and shoved the windows up to let in the sounds of the city. She poured a third glass and lit a couple of pillar candles, stretched out on the couch, and got to daydreaming about where all this fascinating nonsense might take them.

CHAPTER FOUR

The background check took a matter of moments—Mike ran it between eating his bagel and doing his push-ups the next morning.

It came back perfectly clean, and Sam toyed with drafting a confidentiality agreement for the three of them to sign, then decided not to bother. It could only ever be a formality; if Bern Davies turned out to be a sociopath and wanted to hurt them, it wasn't as though a piece of paper was going to stop him. And, most important, her gut said it was unnecessary, and she trusted that even more than she did tables and projections.

Now the only thing that stood between them and Bern was Sam writing an e-mail and inviting him, officially. Inviting him along for step one in the amendment of their wedding vows.

Or rather, step one in Operation: Let's See How Hot Our Sex Life Can Get. Yes, that was the attitude. This proposition had her equally excited and anxious, but whenever the latter felt as if it was winning out, she pulled up that photo of Bern from her e-mail, and his smile eased her mind. And thrilled certain other parts.

Saturday at eight, Bern agreed via e-mail, and they chose a decent-looking neighborhood bar neither had ever been to, just south of the river, halfway between Bern's place and theirs.

Saturday. One day, a wait that sounded at once like ages and seconds. Hell of a way to kick off her and Mike's first joint vacation in more than a year.

See you tonight, she wrote to Bern the next afternoon. *When I get there I'll head for the bar, whichever side is most visible to the rest of the room. I'll be wearing jeans and a dark green, low-cut shirt, and a necklace with a silver disc on it. And a wedding band. :-)*

A charge crackled Sam's nerves as she fastened the necklace in question. She was scared, but the good kind of scared.

She remembered all the auditions she'd had, all the teams she'd tried out for, all the résumés she'd polished and interviews she'd dressed up for, all the first dates. It was a healthy fear, the fear of losing out on something potentially life-changing. A delicious anxiety built of yearning. She checked herself in the mirror on the closet door, liking what she saw. She hoped Bern would like it, too. She hoped Mike would like watching Bern liking it.

They'd debated who would need alcohol the most, to handle whatever might come, and who'd abstain in the name of driving. The answer was that the both of them would probably need a couple of drinks. But it was a special night and they could afford it, so they splashed out and called for a taxi.

While they waited, they got a plan in place, in case things became too intense for either of them. If Mike got uncomfortable, he'd simply sidle up to the bar and pretend to study the liquor bottles before heading for the men's room. That was Sam's cue to wrap up her conversation, tell Bern it wasn't working for her, and politely pay the tab. If Sam got spooked, all she had to do was excuse herself and go to Mike.

Only time would tell if either escape route was necessary.

At seven thirty they climbed into the cab, and the click of Sam's seat belt sounded absolute. *Strap yourself in, kiddo. Who knows where the fuck you'll end up.*

As the driver wound them through the dusky streets, Mike took Sam's hand across the backseat and squeezed it.

"Was that a nervous squeeze or an excited squeeze?" she asked.

"That was a thank-you squeeze."

She smiled at that, and they settled into their own thoughts for the rest of the journey. When they reached their destination, Sam lingered as planned, taking her time counting out bills for the fare. It gave Mike a chance to enter the bar first and find himself a seat, so they could both warm up to the game and their roles, their separateness in this charade.

She thanked the driver and headed for the entrance, straightening the hem of her top and smoothing her hair. All those first-date jitters came back to her, and she was twenty-five again, thrilled and scared and hopeful.

An energetic Saturday din welcomed her as she pushed in the door—chatter and laughter, music. The bar felt like a sort of upscale dive—no frills, but lively and friendly, not too meat-markety. The crowd was mostly thirty- and fortysomethings, and Sam's worries about feeling like an old lady among college students evaporated.

She caught the briefest glimpse of Mike, who'd found a seat at a small table near the door. It took all her willpower not to flash him a smile. Their game had begun, and the impulse was selfish—she was supposed to be getting "caught," oblivious to his presence. As if she'd be able to forget for a second that his eyes were on her every move.

She headed for the bustling bar, and oh fuck, there he was.

Bern.

He'd told her what he'd be wearing, but it was his face she recognized. Funny how accurate her mental picture had been, based on only that one snapshot. She slowed to a halt, her stomach plummeting to her feet, the room feeling like an elevator with a snapped cable.

Be cool, kid. You're a shameless slut tonight, and don't you forget it.

She blew out a tense breath and kept on walking.

Bern's picture had attracted her, but he was so much . . . *more*, in three dimensions. Even seated on a stool, she could tell he was big. Big and substantial, with long legs and a strong, handsome profile. His hair was as messy as in the photo, tucked behind his ears, black in the low light of the bar. That picture must have been taken at the height of summer, as his complexion was fairer than she'd expected. A modest beard covered his jaw, neither wild nor fussy. He looked rugged and capable, as though he'd just come from the woods, doing something obscenely manly. Or that was what Sam's libido decided.

She swallowed, throat feeling thick. He was as sexy as any guy she'd covertly checked out during the girls-only cocktail dates, casting her fake flings. Sexier. A pang of pleasurable guilt warmed her skin.

Sexy and punctual.

Move aside, Nick.

Bern turned as she approached, and she thrilled at the recognition that flashed across his face. His smile was the perfect mix of mischief and shyness, so exactly what she felt, herself.

There were no free stools, giving Bern a chance to bank some chivalry points and kick off his role as smooth-talking, seductive stranger. He stood as she reached the bar. Sam kept her attention on the taps as though she were deliberating.

"Here," he said, patting the stool.

"Are you sure?"

"Please." He grabbed his half-drunk glass of beer and stepped back so she could have a seat. She sat with her back to the bar, crossing her legs. Just as her single self might've done if a handsome, actual stranger approached her, she kept her purse in her lap to camouflage any unflattering business her snug jeans might be doing to her belly. *Huh.* Twenty-five again, indeed. She hadn't felt this self-conscious in years.

"Thanks."

"Sure." Oh, he was tall. Taller than her husband, perhaps six-two to Mike's five-eleven, meeting one point of his criteria. As promised, he wore a plain gray T-shirt, and beneath it she could make out the contours of his chest and shoulders, trim and powerful as his bare arms. She liked the soft-looking hair there, the shapes of the fingers wrapped around his glass.

I could totally bang this guy if I wanted. Crazy. And did she want that? For herself, as much as for Mike . . . ?

"Can I buy you a drink?" he asked.

"Sure. Cabernet, please."

He came close, leaning between her and the next seat to get the bartender's attention. She studied the silver streaked at his temples and peppering his facial hair and nearly swooned right off her perch. His eyes were blue, but not bright like Mike's. More a stormy sea than a summer sky. Breathing him in, she found no cologne, just the faint but distinct smell of a new man, a scent you couldn't buy at Sephora. He ordered her wine and told the bartender to add it to his tab, his voice twice as rich and deep and thrilling as it had been on the phone.

For a split second Sam felt busted, realizing Mike was watching her checking Bern out. But *busted* was the name of the game.

Bern passed her a dangerously large glass of red and stepped back, tucking a thumb in his front pocket and sipping his beer. His thigh was only a couple of inches from her crossed knees, and she wondered how warm he'd feel through their two pairs of jeans.

"On your own tonight?" he asked.

She nodded. "You, too?"

"Yeah. My name's Bern." He freed his hand to shake hers. And what a shake—firm and warm and solid. She wished Mike could have felt it, too. *Meet the man I might just want to fuck while you watch.*

"I'm Samira. Sam's fine." And she stalled.

Oh shit, what were they going to talk about? But wait, they had plenty to talk about. It wasn't as though Mike could read lips. They were free to drop the act and he'd still get to pretend they were just meeting.

She offered Bern a familiar smile. "Are you nervous?"

His posture changed, visibly relaxing, and he smiled back. The gesture made him an entirely different kind of sexy. The warm and easy kind of man that you wanted sitting across from you at a diner, versus the wicked one you wanted to take you home from a bar. "A little nervous," he admitted. "How about you?"

She nodded. "I was terrified, up until I saw you."

"Worried that photo was from the seventies and I was really some retiree with no teeth and overgrown fingernails?"

"Well, no, but you know . . . Anyway. You're a very pleasant surprise." A very, very, *very* pleasant surprise.

"So are you. You're even cuter when you're not blurry."

She laughed. "I hope you hadn't worried I was trying to hide anything. I just didn't want to use a photo that anyone could pick me out of a lineup from."

"Of course."

He stepped closer so they could talk without being overheard in the din, and his leg brushed hers, sending a bolt of energy up her thigh to settle in her belly.

"I'm guessing you're not from Pittsburgh any more than I am," she said.

He laughed softly, a warm, airy chuckle that raised the bar's temperature by five degrees. "Whatever gave me away? But you're right—I'm from Kentucky. Raised in a tiny little farm town about halfway between Louisville and Nashville."

"That must've been a culture shock, when you moved."

"At first, but I love it here. I've always been a city boy at heart."

"I bet I wouldn't last an hour out in the country . . . Thanks for coming out of your way," she added.

He waved the thought aside as he took a taste of his beer. "Drive took me ten minutes. And I'll say this—you're the most interesting date I've had in ages."

"I'll bet. Have you not met anyone for what you'd gone on that site for, originally?" she asked, meaning his exhibitionist streak.

"I quit looking, after you and I started talking. It was getting discouraging. There's so few women on there, looking for that kind of thing. And I didn't even really know how to roll it out without sounding like a perv. I think it's sort of a lost cause. I got a hundred and one replies from so-called women, wanting to watch me . . . you know. On a webcam. But I wasn't born yesterday."

She frowned her sympathy. "You'd probably have better luck finding an open-minded steady girlfriend."

"I know. But I ended a long-term thing this past winter. Not really ready for anything serious yet."

Another point for Bern, that he'd had a grown-up, normal-person relationship. More proof that he was just as new to all this kinky stuff as they were.

Still, the topic wasn't spurring their chemistry, and she knew there was a man sitting ten yards away, who was itching to see some physical boundaries bent. And they were hers to bend, as Bern couldn't be expected to make the first move, not with somebody's husband watching him.

So Sam uncrossed her legs, letting the instep of her high heel brush his calf.

He took the hint and stepped closer, his knees just breaching the V of her thighs.

Intruder, she beamed to Mike. *Intruder between your wife's legs.* However barely.

Bern stooped a little to say, "I'm not nervous at all anymore." His tone was dark, not particularly innocent. The shadow of a smile played just behind his lips, and Sam imagined kissing him. She could now, if she wanted to. *He* wanted it, she thought, and her body did as well. It was only her brain that needed a push. She took a deep swallow of her wine.

"I'm still a little nervous," she admitted. "But it's nice."

"Tell me about yourself." He spoke the words as though they were far more scandalous ones. Ones like, *I can't wait to get you home and bury my cock inside you*. He was doing just as she'd asked: making this look as tawdry as possible for their one-man audience.

Boldly, she put her fingertips on his side, as though he'd just suggested something sinful. *Ooh, firm.* "What would you like to know?"

"Job?" he asked, switching his beer to the other hand so he could settle his cold fingers over her warm ones and press her palm flat against him. She rubbed him with her thumb, and something about the soft cotton or the hard muscle shot straight to her sex.

She cleared her throat. "I'm an actuary."

"That's something to do with insurance, right?" The slow, easy way he said it . . . God help her. He could probably read her the obituaries and she'd still get all itchy with want.

"Something, yeah. It's exceedingly dull to anyone who doesn't like numbers and statistics." She bit her lip coyly, hoping the move didn't look cheesy.

"But you do?" he prompted. "Like numbers and statistics?"

"I do. I like finding patterns and interpreting data. I was also captain of my high school math team. Are you turned on yet?"

He grinned, and it transformed his face. He smiled with one side of his mouth more than the other, making him seem at once friendly and unsavory, like a con man. "I think I just came."

Sam laughed, then took a sip of her wine, savoring the taste, watching the garnet liquid swirl in her glass before she raised her chin to look him in the eyes. "What about you? What do you do, Bern Davies?"

"I'm an electrician."

She blinked. "Really?"

He nodded. "Large-scale commercial stuff. I work for a contracting outfit that does office and retail renovations and refurbs."

"Well, you're in the right city for that. And I guess that means I can't ask you to come over to fix how the lights go dim in my apartment when the microwave's on high."

He licked his lower lip. "I'd prefer to be asked over to tend to more interesting tasks. Though while I'm there, I guess I could take a look."

Just then, the man seated next to Sam was greeted by a friend or date. "Here," Sam said, and offered her stool. It was a perfect opportunity to move their talk a bit farther from the crowd at the bar. To remind herself how tall Bern was, and to give Mike a better view of that fact.

They relocated, and she leaned against the wall beside the jukebox. She forced her eyes not to seek Mike, though her peripheral vision told her exactly where he was and how perfect a vantage point he had. Bern took her cue, standing close enough for the toes of their shoes to touch, his black leather ones flirting with her pointy-toed heels. She imagined the items jumbled together on the bedroom carpet, her and Bern jumbled together across the comforter.

"You know, you never answered my question from the first e-mail," he murmured.

She dredged the memory but came up short. "Which question was that?"

"About what your husband gets out of this whole . . . arrangement."

"Oh, right."

Again, that mischievous smile curled his lips. His head dipped only a few centimeters, yet the move seemed to cast her in a shadow, a similar darkness passing over his expression. "So what's in it for him?"

"Well, I honestly can't explain it much better than he could. He's not a weak man at all, and he's really assertive in every other aspect of his life. But he's got an incredibly high-pressure job, and for some reason, the fantasies seem to take him out of all that. I think deep down, his worst fear is that he's going to fail, that he's not man enough. He's going to find out he's not the alpha dog and then he'll get torn apart by the rest of the pack. So when we pretend he's not capable of keeping me faithful or pleasing me in bed, that's him confronting his deepest fear. But also living through it, so it loses its power over him. And for whatever reason, it turns his crank."

"Wow." Bern blinked, staring at the wall above her shoulder. "That's fucking interesting."

She smiled. "Isn't it? Took me ages to feel like I understood it. And he doesn't really feel like he understands it at all. But it resets something in him when he's feeling really stressed from work, and it turns him on like nothing else does. Like it opens up some vein of naturally occurring Ecstasy in his brain."

"Can't argue with that. That's what the idea of having someone watch does to me."

"And I think . . . I dunno, I think there's another side to it. A way different side, where he's actually really smug and full of himself."

"Oh?"

Sam felt herself blushing, unsure about sharing the thought, as she had no clue how attracted to her Bern might really be. But she decided to trust all the cues his body was offering hers. "Yeah. He thinks I'm . . . He thinks I'm really sexy, so there's some part of him that likes the idea of another guy getting to enjoy me for an evening, all the while knowing that he's the one who gets to keep me."

After a thoughtful pause, Bern grinned. "That may be the sweetest, filthiest, most fucked-up thing I've ever heard."

Sam laughed. "That's my husband. Sweet and filthy. I think also . . . You know when you first meet a girl, but she's not your girlfriend yet? There's some kind of competitive drive, keeping you on edge. Whatever chemical's happening there, I think that's part of it, too. If he pretends other men still have a chance with me, or could take me away, he gets a hit of some aggressive male hormone."

"Nice that he doesn't take you for granted, I guess."

"No, definitely not."

"And he's watching us right now, right?" She could tell from Bern's tone, the idea excited him. His voice had the nervous, giddy edge of a kid hoping they were getting away with something.

"He is. But I'm not supposed to 'spot' him. Though if he weren't liking what he saw, he'd have let me know by now."

"Well." Bern was dying to crane his neck and find out who the mystery voyeur was, she could sense it.

"Don't look," she warned. "We're doing such a convincing job so far."

He leaned a little closer and there was that smell again—that personal scent more alluring than any clandestine cologne sample. He might only be coming so close to be compliant, following her and Mike's script, but she felt a selfish thrill from his mere proximity. She reveled in the heat coming off his big body, could practically feel his weight on top of her.

"So what's in it for you?" he asked.

She sipped her drink, stumped by the question. She'd never bothered posing it to herself. "Well, it's his kink more than mine. So the first reason is to treat him. But he's never pressured me to take it this far—I was the one who proposed all this. I guess what I get out of it is the pleasure of blowing his mind."

"Wow."

"It took a while for us to wind up here, believe me. Took a long time to trust that it really was something my husband wanted, that he wouldn't regret it and end up resenting me, or that I'd end up feeling guilty, worried I'd done something I could never take back. Or resenting him for getting me to do something I never really wanted for myself."

"But now you think maybe you might want it? For yourself?"

She studied him openly, her gaze skimming from his eyes to his throat, down his torso, and back up his gorgeous arms. Her logical brain didn't have a ready answer to that question, but her body chimed in. "Yes, I think I just might."

Mike's head was so flooded with conflicting chemicals, he feared he might actually pass out.

Adrenaline, as his possessive instincts begged him to cross the floor and staple the guy's throat to the wall with his hand. It blended with some secretion from his kink gland to create the most violent, maddening testosterone, the stuff snaking like lava through his veins, sending blood to his cock and heat to his chest. All the primal male switches inside him were flipped on, all the valves open. Made him want to fight and fuck and scream and come, all at once.

His brain and body were on fire, and it felt fucking phenomenal.

He sipped his beer, breathing deeply, trying to get used to the scene. It was what he'd been wanting in theory for months, and the pleasure was brutal. The jealousy was different with an actual, real man triggering it, and with his wife allowing the kind of contact he'd only ever fantasized about. Because he'd always trusted her implicitly.

He'd be lying if he said he wasn't angry at her, standing so close to this other man, smiling and laughing, acting as though she weren't married. His rational brain reminded his primitive one that she was doing this for him, and after ten minutes or more, the truth of it solidified and he felt the aggression disperse, eaten up by the excitement.

The reality of this situation turned him on more than he'd even *hoped* it might, and that frightened him.

It was his kink, not Sam's, so if he felt this conflicted, how must this feel to her?

She didn't look conflicted. If her piqued reception to that man's flirting was merely an act, she'd sweep the Oscars.

Jealousy stirred his cock, to see her looking at another man that way. Those wry smiles had been his for the past five years, only his. That lip bite. That focused attention. The instincts kept flip-flopping in his head, but one thing was constant—the pounding erection between his thighs.

The guy was perfect. Tall, handsome, easygoing. His hair was dark, his face unshaven. Anything that created a contrast between him and Mike was a plus. Though the sentiment caught like a splinter in his heart, Mike hoped the attraction Sam was exhibiting was a hundred percent real.

But Jesus, he was in over his head, treading water to keep from drowning in all these feelings. Jealousy, rage, fear.

But no, don't focus on the bad stuff. Surrender to the physical sensations, and never mind labeling them. She was doing all this for him, and it'd be a waste to everyone involved if he held himself back from enjoying it.

So when the waitress came around, Mike ordered a whiskey on the rocks and settled into the warmth it opened in him, settled into the buzz of the bar. Settled into the fire pumping through his veins at the sight of his wife laughing at another man's joke, the casual touch of familiar fingers on a stranger's arm.

I want to kill that cocksucker, Mike thought.

But I want to watch him fuck Sam about ten times worse.

CHAPTER FIVE

Samira couldn't say which was more drunk-making—the wine or Bern.

Or the fact that Mike hadn't given her the signal, implying that he must be cool with what was happening.

Sam was cool with it. Hell, she was hot from it.

She hadn't expected that. She'd come here hoping for a signal that she could do this, for Mike, expecting the pleasure she might take from the experiment would come mainly from blowing his mind. Before finding herself at this moment, she'd been hoping to maybe feel intrigued by Bern, or at least receptive to the idea of sleeping with him. She'd been hoping for a *lack* of misgiving. Never had she thought she'd get this turned on. Yet here she was, a little weak and a little warm from this new man.

They were still standing by the wall, and no one was near enough to overhear what they said. Still Bern leaned close, speaking in private tones that made even mundane facts sound like seduction. He told her about his dog; his work-in-progress Colonial in Carrick that he was fixing up; how he liked to volunteer with Habitat for Humanity a couple of times a year, wiring new and repurposed homes for low-income families. Between that hushed, deep voice, that sweet-dirty accent, and those penetrating eyes, the words streamed into Sam's ears and her overheated brain translated them through the filter of his body language.

I can't wait to fuck you.

You won't believe how thick my cock is.

I'm gonna make you scream my name in your husband's bed.

"But it could be worse," he was saying, and Sam had completely lost the thread of the conversation. Her gaze had dropped to his arm, flexed from holding his beer. This must be the inverted version of the hazard men ran into all the time, trying to speak to women with deep cleavage.

She nodded, hauling her attention a couple of feet higher, to his face.

He laughed. "I'm totally boring you, aren't I?"

"No, no. Sorry."

"Tired?"

She smiled. "I was thinking about sex, actually. Wine does that to me." *So do tall strangers with pleasantly shaped shoulders, it would seem.*

Was that a blush behind his stubble? "Well."

She sipped her drink, trying to hide her persistent smile.

"Does that mean I stand a chance?" he asked.

The question had her standing up straighter, the knowledge that he must be as into this as she was flooding her equally with pride and nerves. "I wasn't sure what to expect when I met you. I didn't know if I'd be a little attracted to you and maybe willing to round it up for the sake of the mission . . . but even if I'd gotten my hopes way up, you'd have surpassed them."

His expression brightened. "Really?"

She nodded. “I think you’re very handsome. Even handsomer than the picture you sent. And I spent a lot of time looking at that picture and warning myself not to get my hopes up too high that you’d look like that in person.”

“Well. Good.” He squinted dramatically. “You’re not as out of focus as you’d led me to believe, but you’re still passable.”

She swatted his arm, faking offense. “Wow, thanks.”

His tongue flirted with the corner of his lips just a moment, the heat in his eyes going from warm to downright scorching. “I think you’re incredibly sexy. Way sexier than I’d let myself expect you might be.”

She flushed with relief. “Good. We’re on the same page, then.”

“So you think there’ll be a second date, or whatever this is?”

“That’s entirely up to my husband, but I’d like to.”

Sam took a moment to assess what she was feeling, making sure she was lust-drunk, not plain old wine-drunk. Nope, this high was all Bern. Bern, and Mike’s unseen, watching eyes. She put her hand to his side again, loving the heat of him, the feeling of trim muscle shifting softly under her palm. Again, he laid his own hand over hers, fingers rubbing her knuckles. He tapped her glass with his, a little toast to celebrate that the attraction was mutual, perhaps.

“So if it does happen,” he asked, “it’ll be at your place, right? Or a hotel . . . ?”

“Our place. In our bed.”

“Ah, of course.” She sensed another blush behind that stubble, and if she wasn’t mistaken, his lips were darker, fuller. Her own felt the same. “And when would I actually get introduced to him?” he asked.

“You know, I’m not sure. I’m not actually sure you do, not until he ‘catches’ us. Though if that’s not okay with you, we can figure something out.”

“I think I’m down with whatever you guys have planned. Just

curious. Part of me thinks it's pretty low, getting with some guy's wife without even shaking his hand . . . Then another part remembers the whole thing's sort of fucked, so why worry about the etiquette?"

"He wants realism," she said. "So the more mysterious and impersonal you stay to him, the better."

"Sure. You know, for all I know, you're actually a single woman with a pretty crazy kink of her own."

Sam laughed. "That'd be a twist, huh? But I assure you my husband's very real, and very much watching us."

"Can I ask you some more personal stuff?" Bern leaned in closer as he said it, and Sam suddenly wanted to taste the beer on his lips.

She stroked his side through his shirt, tempted to touch his chest, his belly, but not finding the nerve. "Go right ahead."

"I'm not real set in my ways, sex-wise. And I know this is like a performance for him, basically. Like live-action, made-to-order, designer pornography."

She nodded, struck by the aptness of that analogy. "Yes, I'd say that's exactly what it is."

"What sort of sex do you think he wants us to have?"

"Well, obscenely hot sex. Sex for an audience."

"Showmanship?"

She laughed. "That's a good way to put it. It doesn't *have* to be a porno-level performance, completely overdone and corny. But dirty talk, for sure. He'll want a lot of that. A lot of me talking about how good you are, and how . . . you know. How big you are, and how much better you are at sex than anyone I've ever been with."

"This is going to be great for my ego."

"Think you can do that? The talking? Ideally you'd be really smug and kind of a jerk, and make me tell you how much better you are."

"I bet I could. I'm not inhibited. Not that I've ever done it with anybody's man watching . . . but yeah. I can be a cocky asshole. Short of actually making you feel, I dunno—demeaned."

Sam smiled. "A lot of women would feel demeaned by the entire arrangement."

"But not you?" Worry drew his eyebrows together.

She shook her head. "Like I said, I was the one who offered to make it real. Before now, it's all been games."

Concern gave way to curiosity. "Oh? How so?"

"I go out with a girlfriend after work, come home late, making excuses. That sort of thing. He accuses, I 'confess.'"

"Turbo-charged sex ensues?" Bern supplied.

"Pretty much, and during it I tell him all about the made-up guy. Now, if you become a part of it, he gets to watch it for real, instead of just imagining. So make a big deal of yourself, if that makes sense."

He smiled, the gesture warm and a touch confounded. "Makes as much sense as anything else about this proposal."

Neither spoke for a long moment, their gazes flicking across each other's faces. In that silence, Sam fell into a little trance, awed to realize she might do things with this man. Touch him. Kiss him. Have sex with him and explore the beautiful body promised by his fitted tee. She could imagine so easily having encountered him under innocent circumstances, at this same bar, out with a friend. This tall, handsome man with a low, soft voice and that sinful drawl. He could have offered her a drink, and she'd have told him thanks but no thanks and flashed her wedding ring, and felt all flattery, no regret. And maybe later she'd have remembered him as she walked home, and bitten her lip, indulging in a moment's guilty pleasure, imagining what he might have been like in bed.

But they were beyond imagining now.

And with that thought, this mission changed. Before, her pleasure had been Mike's. Now she felt a desire separate from his kink, a current wired directly between her body and Bern's.

"Are we allowed to kiss?" he asked.

Cheeks burning with pleasure, Sam nodded and slid her hand farther around his side. She heard the little thud as he set his beer on the jukebox, then his mouth was lowering, closer, closer. A hot, thrilling sensation squirmed in her middle, and she hoped Mike was feeling this same pleasurable agitation. Then Bern's mouth brushed hers, soft and uncertain. Big fingers, cool from his glass, touched her jaw, and he pressed his lips to hers.

She heard and felt a soft sigh escape his nose to warm her own, and she tilted her head.

You're kissing a man. And he's not Mike. Guilt and excitement mingled, a potent mix.

Yes, she was kissing a man, and he felt so different. Unnatural, but not in a bad way. His lips were soft and a touch hesitant, but he hadn't spent the past five years getting trained in the art of kissing Sam as her husband had. If Bern made it to their bedroom, he'd be playing the role of the self-assured, gruff jerk. Let him be uncertain here. This was the time and place for doubt.

Though, strangely, Sam felt none, herself.

No tap on the shoulder or clearing of a throat stopped them, so after half a minute she trusted that Mike was enjoying the show, and she joined the kiss for real. She slid her hand up Bern's ribs and over his chest—firm and warm. She laid her palm on his throat and kissed him back, showing him what she liked. He was a quick learner, and his respectful contact changed, mouth growing bold.

She stroked his jaw, wanting to feel his beard. She'd dated a guy with a goatee during grad school, but she'd long forgotten this soft scratchiness after all her years with Mike.

Bern tasted different as well, nothing to do with his beer. His skin would taste different, his sex would smell different, his sweat, his come . . . Her pussy tightened, intimate muscles clenching at the notion.

She wondered then how Bern was supposed to treat her.

Not as though he was in love with her, surely. Not *un*affectionate, but not overly fond. Maybe even a touch callous. She didn't think there was room in Mike's fantasies for mutual respect, for kind smiles and caring. Bern wasn't meant to treat her poorly, but he *was* supposed to defile her, essentially. He had to both worship and use her, and this kiss felt like neither of those verbs. It felt sexy and exploratory, borderline romantic. But for now, that was okay. The mere fact that a strange man was kissing her ought to fit the bill for this first outing.

Bern's tongue slid against hers, sure and brazen. It told her, yes, he could do this. He could drive if they gave him the keys, and she'd be more than a willing passenger—she might just be an eager one. If they weren't at a bar, in plain sight of the entire room, she wondered what she'd do. More than she would have guessed. She might even slide her palm down his front and cup him between his legs, and find out if he met Mike's most key criterion.

His fingertips pressed softly at her jugular for a couple of heartbeats; then he pulled away, straightening. He made a funny little noise, a *whew*, like he was overheating, then grabbed his beer and took a long drink. Sam smiled and sipped her wine.

He leaned an arm along the top of the jukebox, his posture at once matching his accent: pure, casual charisma. When he spoke, it sounded as though lust had dropped his voice half an octave. "Well, I didn't notice anybody punching me in the head, so I guess your man approves, huh?"

"I'm assuming so."

"That was . . ."

She waited patiently, wondering what adjective Bern would find.

"That was something," he finished.

She smirked. "Just 'something'?"

"If we were on an actual date, that would've been hot. I mean, it *was* hot, just with a shadow looming over it."

"While you waited to see if you'd get punched in the head?"

"Pretty much."

"Will it be hotter if there's a next time, with you knowing there's no punch coming?"

"Oh yeah, I'm sure it would be. Though the threat wasn't without its own weird appeal."

She laughed. "Do you think you'd like there to be a next time, if my husband's up for it?"

He looked thoughtful as he sipped his beer. "I would. What would the next step be?"

"It'd probably start like tonight, you and me meeting and having a drink, but then I'd bring you home. I don't want to go super far the first time, but you know. Mess around. Third-base-type stuff, or whatever feels natural."

"Where would he be?" Bern asked.

"He'd be at the bar, watching like tonight, then head home before us. We have a bathroom off our bedroom. He'd watch from there with the door cracked, with us pretending we don't know he's there."

"Huh." Another long, pensive stare into the middle distance.

"You don't have to commit right now, of course. And obviously I have to talk to him first."

"I *want* to say I'm up for it . . . I don't know how I'll feel tomorrow, and right now I'm jacked up on adrenaline, so it's hard to be sure. Maybe we can all think about it for a couple of days, make sure we're all still into it."

"Would you like me to let you make the next move?" she asked.

"If you guys know right away you want to take it further, go ahead and let me know. Please. That'll make my decision way easier."

"Okay, I will. And vice versa. If you know right away, feel free to tell us."

"Deal."

Sam drained her wine and Bern asked, "Can I walk you to your car, or . . . ?"

"We took a cab. We weren't sure how tipsy we'd need to get to make it through this evening."

Bern laughed and nodded at her empty glass. "Hey, only one round. Guess I don't require the thickest beer goggles."

She smiled. "No, you were a very pleasant surprise."

"So were you. And a cheap date to boot."

"Cheaper than you know—I'm paying the tab."

"No way. That'll wreck the perfect job we've done, making it look like I'm wooing you."

She made a face, hesitating.

"Come on. You've got to let me pay. Plus, it's not like I'm some saintly sex surrogate in all this. There's as much in this for me as there is for you both."

Weird, but Sam hadn't thought of it that way. She wanted to please Mike so much, had gotten her hopes up so high and was so relieved by the reality of Bern, she felt as though he were doing them a favor. That he needed to be thanked profusely. Like they'd hired him.

But of course he got something out of this. He'd answered their post for a bull, but they could easily have answered his request for an audience. She smiled to herself, excited by the prospect of realizing two men's sexual fantasies in one fell swoop. As for Sam, she'd be given a taste of forbidden male fruit, something she'd forfeited happily enough when she'd said *I do.* Hopefully she'd be getting pleasure, if Bern was as good in bed as she was prepared to pretend he was.

She touched his arm, a grateful gesture. If they went through with all this, they'd become quite a few things to one another—conspirators. Partners in orchestrating Mike's fantasy. Lovers, of course. Friends, it was starting to feel like to Sam, though not of the simplest variety.

After Bern settled the tab, she asked, "Would you walk me out? My husband and I are going to take separate cabs on the way back . . . You know, part of the role-playing. I want it to look like you're taking me home."

"Of course." Proving himself the consummate acting partner, Bern offered his arm and a cocky smile. She had to glue her eyes to the door with all her will to keep from looking at Mike, barely ten feet to the left in her periphery, but she managed it.

Sam called for a cab. The cool spring air and relative quiet enveloped them, and everything felt very different. More real, more delicate. She realized in a breath, she had her hopes up for all of this to work out. It made her vulnerable, the feeling of going on a date with a wonderful man and praying he'll call you back, that he'll *like* you back, but not wanting to float too high above the earth, only to crash back down if he didn't reciprocate.

She felt something else, too—guilt.

Not from what she'd done inside, but what she was doing now. It seemed selfish to still be linked to this new man's arm once their performance had wrapped. If Mike couldn't see it, who was it for? If it was for Sam or Bern or both of them, was that okay? Where did the kink end and actual adultery begin? Those delineations were Mike's to draw, and without him watching she felt uncomfortable enjoying Bern's company. She slid her arm from his.

"You can head home, or wherever," she said. "My cab should be here soon."

"Then what? He finds one of his own?"

She nodded. "I'll text him, tell him I'm running late, waste enough time that he can beat me home. We'll pretend I kept him up waiting while I was out flirting with you."

He smiled. "I am so jealous of whatever totally fucked-up sex you two are going to have when you get home."

She laughed. "Thank you. If all goes well, maybe you'll get to partake someday. Oh, and thanks for the drink."

"No problem. Hope to hear from you soon." He didn't kiss her good-bye but laid a hand on her upper arm and gave it a friendly, gentle squeeze, one that left goose bumps in its wake. "Take care."

"You, too."

Sam watched him stroll to a pickup truck and climb inside. He lowered his window to prop his elbow on the door, and she returned his lazy wave and watched him pull onto the quiet street.

A long, ragged, loaded breath tumbled from her lungs when he finally turned out of sight.

Her cab arrived shortly. Sorry, I'm running late, she texted Mike from the backseat. On my way now, I promise. Home in 30. She was still role-playing, and she could swear her heart beat a million times while she waited for his reply, terrified he'd hated every moment of the bar, that he was angry and disappointed and traumatized by the realization of his kink.

Her phone buzzed. She pressed the little green word-bubble icon with a shaking thumb, held her breath as she read Mike's text.

Just getting into bed. Come home soon. Please.

His lie flooded her with relief, telling her where his head was.

She'd have the cab take her to their neighborhood's wine and spirits store, then browse long enough to be sure Mike beat her home, as they'd planned. He'd be under the covers when she got in, acting as though he'd been there for ages while she was out. He'd interrogate her as she undressed and she'd deny, deny, deny, then finally fess up. She'd tell him every nasty thought she'd entertained about Bern since she'd shaken his hand, and no doubt come up with some new ones while she and Mike fucked.

Then she imagined Bern's hand in another context. Her brain took a stab at picturing him alone, back in his bed, stroking to the thought of her and Mike watching him. The vision drew her breath short and tensed her legs. She'd conjure it again in an hour when Mike reclaimed her.

She smirked to herself, watching the lights of Pittsburgh streaking past the windows. The city felt vibrant and colorful as they drove through downtown, its streets like throbbing veins delivering life.

Tonight she'd altered the bounds of her marriage forever, and there was no going back. They'd made a crease that could never be ironed out, and more were likely to come. Folds, turning pretty paper into origami, shapes emerging, seam by seam, his instructions, her hands, two dimensions becoming three.

They might end up with a perfect swan or a torn and crumpled wad, but either way, they'd find out together.

CHAPTER SIX

The front door bolt snapped downstairs, and Mike hastily set aside the book he'd been browsing. Or rather, the book whose pages he'd been staring at while his brain buzzed with memories and fantasies and conflicting thoughts.

He left on the light but turned onto his side, pretending to have nodded off. He listened to soft sounds below in the kitchen, then the guest bathroom. He wondered what, if any, accessories Sam would add tonight—a taste of latex between her legs or the slick evidence of lube, something to deepen the erotic, electric jealousy already sizzling in Mike's body.

Her heels clicked down the hall and up the stairs. The floorboard squeaked, then her steps went silent as she entered their carpeted bedroom. Mike sat up and leaned against the headboard, feigning bleariness. "There you are."

A faint smile, its guilt pure pantomime, he trusted. "Here I am."

"That must have been some bridal shower," he said, improvising.

She didn't miss a beat. "You know how us girls get about that stuff. We ended up at a bar across town for cocktails."

"But you had a good time?"

"Oh yeah, great time." She yawned as she took off her necklace and kicked her heels beside the dresser. He admired her slim waist and lush hips as she shed her jeans and stripped away her shirt, ditched her bra, and pulled a long tank top over her head. It hid details Mike had long ago memorized—the mole just below her left butt cheek, the twin dimples above, the scar from her appendectomy. No man knew her body as well as he did, and no man ever would. Though perhaps one might enjoy the chance to take a tour.

"What did you get up to?" she finally asked, combing her fingers through her hair.

"Ordered Chinese, watched some TV. Read a bit, nodded off."

"That sounds relaxing."

"Would've preferred to spend my first real night of vacation with my wife."

"Sorry, no boys allowed at bridal showers. No straight ones, anyhow."

"Yeah, of course."

"Well, I'm bushed." She tossed open her side of the covers and got underneath.

Mike settled next to her, stroking her arm. "I was kind of hoping . . . you know. We could kick off vacation week with some you-and-me time?"

"I'm really wiped out, honey. Sorry. Tomorrow, though. I promise." She rolled onto her side, away from him.

Mike edged closer. There was no cologne tonight as a catalyst to spur their script forward. He ran his palm down her waist and settled it on her hip. "You sure I can't change your mind?" He slid his hand forward to the front of her panties. She promptly pushed it away.

"Don't," she said, overly brusque.

"Why not?"

"I told you. I'm tired."

"Can I maybe just touch you while I get myself off?" He edged his fingers under her waistband and she pretended to try to pull his hand away. His fingertips found her wet. Condemningly wet. *Good girl.*

"Well," he said.

"Don't."

"You sure you don't want to? Feels like you do." He took his fingers back and put them to his lips as she watched, tasting the bitterness of latex and lubricant, just as he'd hoped. He frowned even as his cock pounded, and he made his voice stern and cold. "Sam."

Her eyes were wide with fake fear or innocence. "What?"

"Who was he?"

"Who was who?"

"Who do you think? The guy you clearly fucked tonight."

Her mouth opened and closed, then she slumped in defeat. "It doesn't matter."

"Doesn't it? Do our vows not matter, either, then?"

Sam rolled her eyes. "I just met him. At the bar, and all the girls were heading home. He bought me a glass of wine." And fuck, Mike could picture that scene perfectly now. Picture the man, his rival.

She sighed. "I didn't mean for anything to happen."

"But something did. *Again*, Sam? Jesus fucking Christ."

"Just a quickie, back at his place. Don't be angry—it didn't mean anything."

"Means something to me. Your husband." Mike dropped the anger from his tone, leaving only hurt in its place. He let her know that Act I was over, the accusation done. Time for Act II—humiliation.

"It won't happen again, I promise. It was just one of those things. He was just . . . I couldn't help it."

"What's his name?"

A pause. "Bern."

Oh yes, Bern. It was nuts how much sharper the edges of Mike's kink felt, just knowing she hadn't made that name up. It cut him to ribbons, knowing exactly what the guy looked like, and exactly what he looked like flirting with Sam, standing between her knees. It made the jealousy and anger stronger, but it did the same to the pleasurable feelings, and his misgivings stood no chance of winning out.

Maybe he was a pervert or a head case, but goddamn, he wanted these things. He wanted her to fuck that man. Deep in his heart he feared their charade would become reality—she really would favor some stranger over Mike and he'd lose her. He'd lose her, and it wouldn't be the actions of the cruel, heartless woman she pretended to be for him. He'd lose her to a man she liked more, and it'd be Mike who'd shoved her into his arms. He felt his cock soften. Sam sensed the change and she turned over, eyes full of sincerity and concern, their game paused.

"Mike?"

"Sorry. My head got the better of me for a second."

"Tell me."

He sighed. "The jealousy. It feels different when there's an actual guy involved. Not night-and-day different, but more real. With way higher stakes."

Her gaze dropped to his chin and she ran her fingertips along his collarbone. "You know I'd never actually leave you for some other guy, though, right?"

"My brain knows that, yeah."

"I can only be honest with you . . . Tonight was a turn-on. He was a turn-on, and so was the thought of the three of us taking things into this room someday."

Mike swallowed.

"But you know what else was hot about it?"

"What?"

"Knowing you were watching. And thinking that what I was doing was getting you off. Thinking about how maybe taking things further would, like, blow your mind. You were right there in my head, as much of a part of it as he was. I was flirting with him, but I hoped it was driving you just as crazy."

He smiled at that, all these things he'd needed to be told without even knowing what words could articulate them. There was nothing wrong with craving reassurance. He'd be inhuman if he didn't need a *little*. He kissed her forehead. "Thanks. That's nice to hear."

"And, incidentally, you're sexier than he is. He's hot, but let's be honest—you're the man I married, and I didn't settle."

"Good."

She stroked his chest and arm, hands admiring in their familiar, flattering way. Her brown eyes met his. "You feel like making regular old married-people love? Just you and me and nobody else?"

Just Sam, he thought, kissing her lips. He ought to let her know more often, she was enough, without their games. She was plenty. She was a feast.

"I'd like that very much, Mrs. Heyer."

CHAPTER SEVEN

Bern woke late on Sunday, finally dragged from his sheets by the plaintive whining of his dog.

"You're spreading it a bit thick with those pathetic eyes," he told her, pulling jeans up his legs and finding a clean shirt. After a pit stop he laced his sneakers, grabbed Molly's leash, locked the door behind them, and headed for the park.

The day was cheerful, the air springy, the sun warm and watery behind a thin wash of clouds. The city felt worlds away from the place he'd shut his door on the night before, everything feeling fresh and . . . innocent. Kids playing, moms chatting, fellow dog owners standing around patiently with their plastic baggies.

Innocent, unlike Sam and her indecent proposal.

It was too soon after waking for him to get all horny about the idea, but there was a noticeable lack of misgiving in Bern's brain and gut.

He wanted the arrangement to go ahead. He didn't want to get wound up fantasizing about it, in case Sam or her husband decided to pull the plug. But his decision was made. He'd ended a relationship because he hadn't felt satisfied sexually. It had been a hard decision, breaking up with someone over sex. Sex wasn't everything. Sex mellowed in any relationship . . . though with them, it had never truly blazed, no matter how much he'd tried to stoke it. His ex probably thought he was a world-class shit, and maybe justifiably so, but something inside Bern had always been nagging, simmering, begging him to unleash it. After three years together, he'd had two choices with his ex—break up or propose. And he'd known he couldn't sign up to spend the rest of his life feeling like his needs were being only half met. That he was only really getting to be a watered-down version of who he wanted to be in bed.

He pulled out his phone and found Sam's number, then paused. Would it be weird to send his verdict as a text? Was an e-mail better, maybe, or was brevity key? Probably didn't matter. They were all just digital words, and that was what the doctor ordered—a phone call, he felt, would be too intrusive. But was this too soon? Was it like a date, where he was supposed to wait a couple of days lest he look too eager?

Then, all at once, he decided he didn't care.

Morning, he wrote. Just wanted to let you guys know I'm down for whatever might come next. Hope to hear from you sometime. Enjoy your Sunday. Bern.

He tossed the *sometime* in there, hoping it sounded casual, no pressure, whatever. Hoping *he* sounded casual, when really it felt like something substantial was riding on all this.

There was a chance that fulfilling his desire to be watched could blow the sex center of his brain clean open and change his life. That's what kinks did to people, right? If falling into step with the thing that most turned your crank wasn't crazy hot, crazy satisfying, why else would people take such crazy risks to scratch their itches? Trolling the adult personals had shown him his so-called kink was about as vanilla as they came. If people risked permanent scarring or arrest or death by asphyxiation to realize their fantasies, the payoff had to be worth it. He hoped he'd find out for himself. And he hoped Sam and her mysterious husband would find out, too.

He loitered for a few hopeful but ultimately fruitless minutes, in case an eager text came back from the ether to get his hopes up. But nothing. They might still be asleep.

They might have changed their minds. Jesus, he hoped not. Sam was gorgeous, and their kiss had driven him crazy. He wanted her, no doubt, and he wanted her husband watching. In Bern's mind, someone was always watching. He needed that fantasy—those eyes on him—as truly as he needed friction.

So he jogged his dog around the park a few times, until both of them were panting. There was laundry to be done and groceries to buy, errands to run and his mom to call before the workweek intruded. He had to put Sam and her plans for him out of his mind, lest he catch himself checking his phone every two minutes like some kid with a terminal grade school crush. Even as he thought it, he pulled the device out, feeling a phantom call buzzing in his pocket.

Nope, nothing. *Cool your jets, Davies.*

Easier said than done.

"And you're sure?" Sam asked, glancing from her phone's screen to where Mike stood in the kitchen, stirring pasta sauce. It was just after six, and she'd read that text so many times that day, she'd memorized every pixel.

He smiled dryly. "How many different ways can I say it? I'm sure. Go for it. See if he's free some weeknight."

"You don't want more time to deliberate?" It had been less than twenty-four hours since their first meet-up, after all.

"No, I don't. Do you?"

"No," she admitted. She wanted this, Mike wanted it. Bern wanted it, so said the text that had woken her with a chime that very morning. "Okay." Her heart was bouncing around between her ribs, hands shaking as she crossed the room and plopped onto the couch. She opened Bern's message and hit REPLY.

"'Hey,'" she dictated as she typed. "'We're up for taking things to the next level. Are you free some night this week? We're on vacation, so anytime works for us.' Sound okay? Not too desperate or creepy?"

"Sounds perfect."

"Right. And . . . sent." She set the phone on the coffee table, chest clenching with who knew what emotion—fear, excitement, a touch of guilt.

Mike brought bowls of spaghetti to the breakfast bar and she got up to join him. He always ate standing up, on the other side of the counter, to make up for how much of his workdays were spent sitting in cars or in front of a computer.

"Thanks." Sam twirled noodles on her fork, then promptly dropped the thing with a clank as her phone jingled. She looked to Mike with wide eyes.

"Go ahead."

She pushed her stool back and jogged to her phone, a red numeral one staring at her from the corner of her message app. She opened the text as she sat down again.

"'If you could meet up early, around six, I could do Wednesday or Thursday,'" she read. There was more—I'm not expected to sleep over, right? I work early, plus my dog has needs.

No, he wouldn't be expected to stay the night. He was expected to love her and leave her. But Sam didn't read that bit out loud, thinking she'd start keeping those boring logistical bits between herself and Bern.

"Either of those days work for me," Mike said, spearing a slice of sausage.

"Let's do Wednesday. Meet him at the same bar at six, then you beat us home so you can hide and watch?"

"Sounds good to me. How will you get back?"

"I could just let him drive me. If you're comfortable with that."

He gave it a moment's consideration then nodded. "Sure."

She tapped out a new text with the instructions, plus a note that no, Bern wasn't expected to sleep over. They ate in near silent anticipation, interrupted by another cheerful chime.

Sounds like a plan. See you Wednesday at six, missus.

Mike cast her a curious glance.

She set the phone aside, faking nonchalance. "Nothing. No one."

She caught a smirk flash across his face before he covered it with an imitation of skepticism.

"Just Michelle, asking if I wanted to meet her for dinner on Wednesday after work. No husbands allowed," she added quickly—too quickly—and turned her attention wholeheartedly to her dinner, trying to look as evasive as possible.

"Oh. Okay."

"You can live without me for a night, right?"

"I can . . . It's not just one night, though, lately. You've been going out a lot—"

"It's my vacation, too, you know," she cut in. "And I can't remember the last time I saw Michelle." Actually it had been two years ago, right before Michelle had moved to Seattle. And what a good friend Michelle was! What a perfect, unsuspecting wingwoman for Sam and Mike's deviant sexual escapades.

"Well," he said heavily. "I'll miss you that night. But girls' time is important, I guess. Go out and have your fun."

She smiled, feeling perfectly sinful. "Thank you. I'm sure I will."

"Sam." Bern stood from his seat at the bar and they shared a brief hug.

Just that little sample of his strong body had Sam's humming. She stepped away, flushed, and rubbed his arm. "Hello, stranger."

They weren't strangers anymore, though—she could feel it in their embrace. She took in his scent and the shape of his body, and all the nerves she'd felt when she stepped through the bar's front door disappeared. Bern right here before her, Mike somewhere behind her, watching. The two men had her blood pumping this hard, and damn, it was thrilling.

"Thanks for meeting me again," she said. "Can I get you a drink?"

He waved the offer away, and she realized what a silly idea it was. She may have orchestrated this evening, but she wasn't its hostess. Bern was her official alpha male, and he must be allowed to lead. He was going to seduce her, hands firmly on the wheel.

"Cabernet, right?"

She remembered all her erstwhile fantasy men, all the drinks she'd pretended to have ordered for her. "You choose."

The bartender came by and Bern gave him orders Sam couldn't hear. She felt her eyebrows rise with some surprise when Bern handed her a glass of red wine.

He shrugged an apology. "I don't really know anything about cocktails, sorry. I'd hate to order you something horrible."

"This is perfect." And it was. She sipped the dry red and it tasted how the evening felt, dark and ripe. Rousing. Familiar now, the taste of her would-be lover, here in *their* bar. This man who knew what she drank.

"Is he here?" The low hum of his deep voice warmed her blood as surely as the wine would.

She nodded. Bern may as well glimpse the man who could very well be watching them fool around by the end of the night. The man who was lending Sam out for Bern's pleasure, essentially. "He's at a table, to the left of the door. Black T-shirt."

Bern's gaze left her face a moment to search. He turned back, blinking madly. "Really?"

She smiled at that. "Really. Is he not what you'd expected?"

"He looks like what your ad was asking for."

"Looks like," she allowed. "But in his head, when we're playing, he's different."

"Must be. He looks like a . . ." He stole another glance. "A bouncer."

"He's in law enforcement."

Bern spoke through a laugh. "Fuck me."

She grinned and took another sip. "That's the idea."

"Have a seat," he said suddenly, but he didn't join her. Sam sat with her back to the bar and Bern stood between her knees, like last time. But tonight she'd worn a dress—a plum-colored jersey A-line, nothing showstopping, yet it felt luxurious as her bare calf glanced Bern's clothed one. A warm shiver trickled down her arms when she imagined him stepping forward, driving the fabric back, pressing himself hard against her center. She hoped Mike was watching, and that a similar thought had his cock growing heavy and hot, any pang twisting in his heart purely part of the game.

Bern spoke softly, leaning in so she could hear and making the air between them feel close and intimate. "So when you take me home tonight—or when *I* take *you* home to your place—how will it work? He leaves first so he can be ready to watch us?"

She nodded. "We've got a signal worked out. I'm supposed to put a specific song on the jukebox, and that's his cue to head out."

"What song?"

She grinned. "Springsteen. 'I'm on Fire.'"

"A classic."

"That song makes me shockingly easy," she admitted.

"Good to know."

She took a deeper swig of her drink, hot plumes inching through her veins in thick pulses. She needed a decent buzz for when the time came to leave with Bern, that chemical permission slip that let her ignore the troublesome voices trying to undermine her resolve. She was on the highest board, in her suit and goggles with the cameras poised to capture her dive. She'd be damned if she'd back out now . . . but that didn't mean the jump should scare her any less.

Bern's brows knitted. "Can I ask how long you've been married?"

"Together five years, married three."

"What's it like?" he asked, eyes narrowing with curiosity.

"It's very . . . reassuring. The more comfortable I get with him, the better I know myself. And the more I like myself."

"That sounds nice."

"It is. It may not be terrifically thrilling, but it's . . . It feels great, like a squishy old couch you can't wait to sink into after a long day." She laughed. "I'm not really making it sound very exciting, but I like it. I recommend it."

"You don't think it sounds exciting, being married to someone who wants to get up to crazy sex shit with you?" Bern asked in an elevated whisper.

"Oh, well, yeah, you're right. I take it back. It *is* pretty exciting. I guess I was thinking more about lazy Sunday mornings."

"Not lurid Wednesday nights, out picking up strange men?"

She raised her glass to that.

"Am I driving us later?"

"If you don't mind."

"Nope, not at all. You worried about any neighbors spotting me, sneaking into your place?"

"Nah. You could easily just be a friend of ours."

"A friend who shows up and suddenly there's loud sex coming from your place ten minutes later?"

She laughed. "Ten minutes? A girl likes some wooing, you know. Aren't you Southern men supposed to be all about the courting?"

"Okay, okay. Twelve minutes. Never let it be said I'm not a gentleman."

She sipped her drink. "As for the loud sex, I can't worry about what my neighbors might think. I can't think too hard about any of this, or it'll pull my head out of the . . . well, the performance."

"That's fair. Forget I mentioned it."

"So, are you excited?"

"Of course I am."

"Have you indulged your own kink at all before?" she asked quietly, gaze on the tempting V of skin and tease of soft-looking hair peeking between the two open top buttons of the navy henley he wore. Its collar was fine but she reached up to fuss with it, just for a chance to touch him. "Being watched?"

"No more than most people probably have, I guess. Mirrors. Video camera, a couple of times when I was younger, before the Internet made that seem like the worst idea in the world. But my ex got custody of that footage when we broke up, and I'm sure she destroyed it."

"Probably wise. Have you ever—I don't know—done it in front of an open window?"

"Not really. Well, once on vacation we did it on the hotel balcony, but it was night and I doubt anyone could see. I haven't ever dated a girl who was into that stuff, and I'm not so obsessed with it that I made it a requirement."

"Maybe you should. It's really fun, being with someone kinky. I'm glad I am."

He smiled. "That's pretty charming of you. Though it seems like for every kinky or kink-friendly woman, there must be like fifty kinky guys. I think it's important to be realistic. Though I do want to explore it more. I never really let myself prioritize it before. But all that got me was sexually frustrated, and feeling like an asshole for breaking up with perfectly nice girls who just couldn't go there. And hadn't known what I really wanted, from the start."

"If it makes you feel any more hopeful," she said, "your kink is pretty easy to accommodate. Just don't fall in love with a girl with body image issues, and roll it out early on, and I'm sure you'll at least enjoy tons of hot mirror sex."

"Yeah. We'll do our wedding registry at a home goods store—full-length mirror, ceiling mirror, mirrored headboard, one of those angled three-panel deals they have in dressing rooms . . ."

"Cheval," she offered. "Magnifying? Hmm, maybe not."

"Fun house."

Sam dissolved into giggles from the visual. "That might *give* a girl body image issues."

"But it'd make my man-business look huge."

"Then tiny. Then huge, then tiny," she teased, imagining the effect.

Bern cracked up, and had this been a regular date, it would have been the moment when Sam thought, *I could really fall for this guy.* As it was, it was the moment she relaxed in her mission and trusted her desires, and set her worries free for good.

"Okay, no fun-house mirrors," Bern said. "Oh hey, you guys

should invest in a one-way mirror, if you get good at this cuckolding thing. No more peering through door cracks."

"Oh yeah, that'd be awesome to explain to a contractor when it goes in. *Or* our landlord."

He made a disappointed face. "All the more reason to become homeowners."

They chatted for a long time, long enough for Sam to have a second glass of wine and for Bern to finish nursing his one beer. Around seven she got change from the bartender and wandered to the jukebox, downloading the signal song from the digital catalog.

She had to wait through a few queued tracks, but when the synth of that familiar opening pulsed through the speakers, it felt as though all the lightbulbs turned red, the thermostat cranked to ninety. Somewhere by the door, Mike would be leaving bills on his table, heading out into the cool night air, climbing into her Focus, and taking the short way home.

Sam smiled as the song wound down, and Bern looked to be suppressing his own grin when she shrugged into her jacket and shouldered her purse. He held the door for her as they left.

"We should take a long route," she said.

"Sure." He unlocked her side of his truck's cab. "Just get me pointed in the general direction."

She told him the street and glanced around his vehicle as he got them on their way. Pretty tidy, though clearly he worked out of this truck. There were papers and bits of hardware scattered here and there, and a parking pass with the logo of a renovation company dangling from the rearview mirror.

It was a quiet drive. Not an uncomfortable silence, but pensive.

The curtain was about to go up, and they were two actors, holding their breath in anticipation of their opening night. Sam wanted to please her audience. She and Mike had settled on another signal, for when the actual show was under way. If the plug needed to get pulled, he'd simply flush the toilet. That was Bern's cue to get his pants on and get the hell out, and Sam's cue to start panicking over whether she and Mike had irreparably damaged their marriage.

She hoped she'd be able to enjoy whatever Bern had to offer without her ears being perked, straining for the swirling sounds of *red alert, abort, abort.* Her own excitement felt skittish—hopeful but hesitant. It was one thing to get turned on kissing a good-looking stranger in a bar. Who knew if she'd feel any of that once they were in Sam and Mike's bedroom. In their *bed.* Christ, she hoped she would. This was starting to feel as though maybe it could be for her as much as it was for Mike. She'd gotten into it, eager to blow his mind. But since she'd kissed the man currently sitting just to her left, she'd started to think maybe she could go there, and as more than just a wildly indulgent partner. As a plain old red-blooded woman, too.

The silence began to feel heavy. She reminded herself of her role. Tonight she was a selfish, heartless, dissatisfied wife, and Bern was the man she'd chosen to bring home and have some much-needed fun with. She reached across the cup holders and set her hand on his thigh. He cast her a quick glance, swallowed, and smiled as he looked back to the road. She gave his leg a squeeze, liking the flex of his muscle as he switched between the gas and brake, the authoritative movements of his arm as he shifted gears. Was it just her, or did he seem to be driving a bit quicker all of a sudden?

In a heartbeat, Bern yanked up the curtains and flung them headfirst into their script. "And you're sure he's gone out?"

She fell into the game easily after all these months of practice. "He won't be home for a couple of hours, at least."

"Great."

Her palm grew damp from the heat of his thigh, the truck's cab at once smaller and warmer. She felt guilty flirting with Bern without Mike there to witness it . . . but it was all in the service of the performance, so she tried to set the guilt aside.

Dear God, how did people manage to actually *cheat* on each other?

Think about sex, she ordered herself. She stole a long glance at Bern, his profile stern with concentration as he drove . . . or stern with the effort of not steering them off the road, if her hand was proving a distraction. What might Mike be hoping to see them do tonight?

A big deal had to be made of Bern's cock. That was a given. His sexual superiority was at the heart of the scene, so she'd be praising him profusely, for both his physical attributes and his skills at making her feel good. Was she allowed to give him tips or instructions, Sam wondered, or was he meant to just be naturally perfect at everything?

Or was she supposed to fake it and act like he was utterly amazing, even if he wasn't?

They reached Sam's block just as the last of the daylight faded. He parked right between her Focus and Mike's PBP sedan, apropos of everything. Sam's heels were loud on the sidewalk. Their bedroom faced the street, and it took all her effort not to glance up and check if Mike was watching from the window. She came within a breath of taking Bern's hand before she realized what a scandal it would look like to a neighbor, and wrapped her fingers tightly around her purse strap.

She was steps, seconds, breaths from changing the shape of her and Mike's sex life, forever. Whatever happened tonight, for better or worse, their marriage would never look quite the same.

CHAPTER EIGHT

Sam's heart was pounding, thumping like a bass drum as she led Bern up the front steps. Her keys jingled as she fumbled with the lock, but she shot Bern a look of well-faked mischief just before pushing in the door.

She switched on the light and he looked around. Originally she'd hoped first and second bases could go down in the living room. It seemed a fitting setting, the bedroom such a bold leap. But there was no good place for Mike to conceal himself downstairs, and in the bedroom there was both the closet and the bathroom.

"Can I get you anything?" she asked. "Beer or wine?"

"Are you having anything?"

"I might have a splash of wine."

"I'll have the same, thanks."

She led him down the hall, and he wandered around the living room, inspecting the book and DVD shelves while Sam poured two small measures of merlot. He met her at the counter and they toasted with a clink, then took turns using the half bath.

"Would you like the tour?" Sam asked when Bern reappeared.

"Sure."

"It's short. Kitchen and living room, obviously." She waved her arm around. They carried their glasses down the hall and up the stairs, floorboard creaking as they reached the landing. She led him past her and Mike's room to the next door.

"This was the guest room that my husband turned into an office," she said, waving limply at the space, as though any reminder of the man bored her to tears. "He spends more time in here than the bedroom, that's for sure."

"And is that the bedroom?" Bern asked, pointing.

She gave him a sly look and slipped into her seductress voice. "It is. Would you like to see it?"

"Yeah."

She led him inside and turned on a reading lamp.

"Very nice."

"Thank you." Sam drained her wine and set the glass on the dresser, kicked off her heels by the door so everyone involved would be reminded how tall Bern was. Gently, she took the glass from his hand and set it beside hers, harnessing all her willpower to keep from glancing at the dark crack of the bathroom door—Mike's peephole.

She ran her hands up Bern's biceps and over the rounded balls of his shoulders, admiring. She caught him swallowing before mirroring her boldness, sweeping his arms around her waist and pulling her closer. They hadn't kissed in the bar that night, but when he lowered his mouth to hers, it felt like the easiest thing in the world.

No hesitance, like their first meet-up—he knew his role and seemed eager to play it. His tongue was bold, the kiss deep and dirty, making her brain misfire, and she wondered what else he could do with his mouth. The brush of his short beard was hot in its newness, as sexy as the taste of her and Mike's wine on this man's lips. She stroked his neck and shoulders and upper back, followed the gentle curve of his spine to the hard swell of his ass.

She freed her mouth, licking her lips. "You look good." She let her gaze roam his body from feet to face. "Why don't you get comfortable?"

He eased off his shoes in two fluid moves, suddenly holding her elbows and walking her backward to the bed. She felt her hair bounce as her butt plopped onto the mattress, and smiled up at where he stood between her knees.

Staring down at her with a smirk, he stripped off his henley and tossed it to the floor, revealing a light gray undershirt and some of the nicest arms Sam had ever had the pleasure of exploring.

She crawled back as Bern got to his hands and knees on the bed, bracing himself above her, looking down with some wonderful threat glinting in his eyes.

"When was the last time you got fucked?" he demanded.

Her pulse spiked. "Maybe a week ago," she lied.

"With him?"

She nodded. "Dullest two minutes I've suffered all month."

"You fake it for him?" Ooh, he was good at this.

"I don't even bother. I just wait until he falls asleep and I take care of myself."

"Oh yeah? And what do you think about?"

She grinned indulgently and stroked Bern's braced arms. "A man like you."

"Like me?"

"Yeah. Big and strong. Big all over . . . like I hope maybe you are." As Mike hoped as well.

Bern slid them across second base, dropping his hips and driving up her dress to press his erection between her legs. Whether he was big or not, she couldn't tell, but he was stiff, no mistaking it.

"Well."

"Been hard since we first started talking at that bar."

Though it felt like a sharp upping of the stakes, Sam spread her thighs wider and hugged them to his waist. He accepted the invitation, rubbing against her with slow, teasing motions of his hips. His breathing grew harsh just as hers did the same.

What are you thinking, Mike? She wished there were a psychic feed from his brain to hers, and that he could beam her reassurance and instructions.

She wanted to trust what was happening. It felt good and hot and *right*, though that was no guarantee Mike was feeling the same. Was he hard, too? Was he touching himself? Which ached worse in this moment—his cock or his heart? *Cock*, she prayed. And she could make it hotter by ignoring her fears and embracing her part.

She slid her palms to Bern's rolling hips. "I bet you're a great lay."

"Find out."

"I hope to . . . but not tonight. Save something for next time."

"Don't save too much," he warned. "My cock's so hard. I hope you're not going to send me home hurting."

"I wouldn't dream of it."

He lowered to his elbows and kissed her, his hips slowing to match the pace. She wrapped her legs a bit higher around his waist, liking the feel of him. But on the whole, it felt too tender. Without having articulated it to herself before, she'd always known Bern was here to act as Mike's sexual rival, and though it was all just play, he shouldn't cross the line between sex and affection. Seduction was one thing, but she didn't want what they were doing to resemble romance.

"Keep it dirty," she whispered between kisses.

"Sure."

He righted himself, sitting on his heels, and peeled away his shirt.

Bern was hot in a tee and jeans, but stripped to the waist he was *obscene*. Big, but not beefy-big. Lean, but not slender. Just . . . *yikes*. Mike kept fit for the sake of his job, but she suspected Bern did so for more superficial reasons. Normally that might strike her as vain, but just now? No complaints. Not a single one.

She wanted to run her fingers down the trail of dark hair that ran from his chest to his navel, to cup the bulge between his thighs and watch his expression change. She wanted to touch the muscles that flanked his hipbones and feel the contours of his abdomen and the flat plane just below. Wanted to ease his waistband down and feel the crisp curls hidden there, learn a few more things about the nature of prematurely graying hair.

"You look great," she said, admiring him openly.

"Bet you do, too. Maybe you could take that dress off. Gimme a show."

"Maybe I could."

He moved and Sam got up from the bed, smoothing the garment. Bern sat expectantly at the foot of the mattress as she walked around to stand before him, the scene in perfect profile to their hidden audience.

This little striptease was Bern's show, but she objectified him in return. *Damn, what a body.* He was out of her league, frankly, but the way he looked at her . . . She'd *never* felt this hot in her twenties.

It was a jersey shirtdress, with buttons running all the way down the front. She undid them slowly, bottom to top, then let the item fall to her feet. She was wearing a matching bra and panties—ones that Mike had picked out for exactly this moment—warm gray with black lace trim.

Bern hissed a word—"Nice," perhaps, or, "Yes," obscured by a heavy sigh of approval. Heat shot through Sam's middle. Mike never failed to make her feel desired, but she'd forgotten the thrill of a new, strange man's approval, how electric this could feel.

She took a step closer, standing between his knees and inviting him to touch her. His fingers skimmed her sides, hips to ribs, then traced the lace bordering the top of her panties. He slipped one finger just under the material but didn't pull them down, merely drew his knuckle back and forth, back and forth, across her lower belly. A low, happy grunt answered her when she combed her nails through his hair.

She was secretly pleased when he didn't ask her to strip naked or do the job himself. Instead he stood, took her face in his hands, and kissed her. A deep kiss, a handful of sensual, needy laps that did the job of twenty minutes' foreplay.

The room seemed to spin as he stepped back, his mischievous smile returning. She admired his body as he stroked her hair, neck, shoulders. *What's Mike wanting to see?* she wondered, curious if Bern was wondering the same thing. If either of them could guess, it was her.

She sat on the mattress, tugging Bern close by his belt. He smiled down at her, running a hand across his hard belly. The hand slipped lower, over his buckle, then lower still to cup his straining erection.

"Show me." She tugged at the waist of his jeans, her eagerness no act.

"You wanna see?"

"Yes."

He rubbed his bulge with a slow, lazy rhythm. "Say please."

"Please."

"Say it again."

"Please. Let me see."

He unbuckled his belt with a practiced motion, freed his button, and lowered his zipper. For a taunting minute he kneaded himself through the dark cotton of his underwear, the long, explicit strokes showing her that yes, he was as big as they'd hoped for.

"Please. Show me."

First he showed her a smile, dripping with cockiness. Then he pushed his waistband down and let her see him, bare and hard and thick, his head flushed, his scent potent and exciting.

For a long moment she merely stared, frozen in the knowledge that she was being presented with a cock that didn't belong to the man she'd married. Then Bern spoke, breaking the spell.

He gave himself one slow, thorough pull. "That big enough?"

"That's plenty." Above and beyond. Bigger than her husband. Bigger than any man she'd had before him, for that matter.

Did Mike like what he saw? Had this man's cock given him that pleasurable punch in the gut he craved, a gulp of that scary-strong cocktail of jealousy and lust? Did it get him five times drunker than their dirty talk about other men's dicks could ever hope to?

"Touch me," Bern said.

She grazed the underside of his length with her fingertips, then again. She measured his girth with her fist, squeezed to feel how stiff he was. As she explored him, she imagined that hard thickness pushing inside her. Mike might be in the room for that moment, or pretend to walk in. She swallowed, overcome—turned on, undeniably, but overwhelmed as well.

"I love it," she said, remembering her role. *Worship him, dum-dum.*

"This what you've been missing?"

She admired him with a greedy stroke. "It's perfect."

"Maybe you want to suck me," he said.

"I do." Her reply was automatic, but chased by a worry—was it too soon? Though when would going down on a new man not feel like a leap? Now was as good a time as any.

"Here." He took her hand and coaxed her from the bed, having her kneel before him on the carpet, the two of them still in profile to their unseen audience.

He murmured a long, pained "Yeah" as she spoiled him with strokes meant to rouse all three of them.

Bern played his part well, with the calculated calm of a career philanderer. But this close, she felt the tension in his body, the energy practically vibrating from him. Two men were having their fantasies realized tonight, and she wondered what Bern was most tuned into—the nearness of her lips or the presence of her husband's eyes.

She brought her face close, letting her breath steam the dark, taut skin of his head. Her other hand she dropped to his hip, lest she obscure Mike's view. A shiver enveloped her as Bern combed her hair aside with his fingers, drawing it into a sloppy ponytail. The weight of his hands urged, edging her lips closer.

"Taste me."

She let her lower lip brush him and his cock twitched. A firmer order from his guiding hands and she took his crown in her mouth, closing her lips around his heat.

"Good."

She imagined it was Mike who'd uttered that happy syllable, approval whispered from the dark of the bathroom. Another inch slipped between her lips, another. When he was slick with her spit, she sought a rhythm. *Don't service—worship*, she reminded herself, and let her mouth do the job of her eyes and hands and words, handling him like the lust object he'd been cast as.

"Fuck."

His sensuality gave way to a darker tone—she felt the shift in the way his fingers gripped her hair and urged her motions. His sounds were as hot as any other detail about him—guttural, muttered nonwords, grunts and sharp inhalations. She longed for different ones, the kind that would echo the tempo of his hips as he fucked her. *If* he fucked her. Jesus, please let him fuck her.

That final thought struck her, woke her up.

I really do want this. Every bit as much as Mike wants it for himself.

"Fuck, that's good. Nice and deep."

She moaned around him, and she wasn't acting anymore.

"You're so hungry for me, I can feel it. What's wrong—he can't stay this hard for you? Or you just want a nice big mouthful?"

Rhetorical questions, resounding accusations to stab holes in Mike's ego.

"You like that," Bern said, stroking her hair. "You like sucking that fat cock."

She did. It wasn't a hardship, moaning like a porn star around him, but as exciting as he felt, it was incidental. Size mattered only as a novelty and for how hot it might be getting Mike. It was the power that had her high—the knowledge that she held the keys to two men's deepest desires.

"More." It was a statement, not a request—Bern's hips had begun making demands. He took her mouth only deeply enough to intimidate, not to gag. He slid a hand between his thighs to fondle his balls and she could see his wrist and arm trembling faintly. She nudged his hand aside to do the job for him.

"Yeah."

She gazed up at his flexing abdomen, his tight chest, the shadows of his strong arms. He swallowed, then their eyes met. His mouth dropped open with a silent moan, and for a moment, she owned him.

Watch him and he's yours, she mused. And she kept her attention on his face for the rest of the act, until he eased her fingers away and slid from her mouth, panting.

Bern took a seat on the edge of the bed and she moved her attention to his thighs, memorizing his skin and muscle while he collected his wits. At length, he let out a long, delirious sigh.

"Were you close?" she asked, looking up to meet his eyes.

He grinned. "I can go all fucking night. But I like variety."

Liar, she thought. He'd been closer than he wanted to admit. But she liked the fib. She liked knowing how hot her mouth or Mike's gaze had gotten him.

"Bet you like variety, too, huh?" he asked.

She smiled. "You have no idea how much." Neither did she—but she was learning fast.

"Well, you've got me, tonight."

"That I do."

"Why don't you tell me all the things you're dying to do with me?"

"Where to start?" She weighed him in her hand. "Let me just enjoy you. Stand up."

He did, and she lavished him with hungry touches—enough to tease but not to torture—fascinated to explore his new, beautiful body. Mike's was just as wonderful. Better in many ways, as she knew it so well, how to please it, and felt assured that it knew how to please hers in return. But Bern was a thrilling new toy.

She stroked his belly and hips, backside. His skin was warm and taut, the hair sprinkled across his chest and down his abdomen darker and denser than Mike's. Between his legs it was darker still, but shot through with the same silvery gray that decorated his temples. Sam wasn't sure why she found that so appealing, but it turned her on, undeniably. She ran her fingers through the curls and his cock tensed in reply.

Not wanting to be cruel, she gave his length a couple of gentle pulls, keeping him stoked, then moved her touch lower, cupping his balls again. He responded with a sucking breath and a grunt, and his hand came to rest softly on the back of her head once more. Sam had never heard a single one of her girlfriends ever express any enthusiasm for this bit of the male anatomy, but she had to say, Bern had a great set, as balls went. Tight and heavy, compact.

"I love how you smell," she said.

"More than how I taste?"

Pretending to have forgotten that flavor, she gave the beading head of his cock a slow lap. "I like both," she decided.

"Maybe someday I'll let you find out how my come tastes." His words were confident but the tone beneath them strained. His words tightened her, too, and Mike, surely.

She smiled up at him. "I hope so."

"Maybe you'll let *me* find out what you taste like," he added.

"You only have to ask. You can have anything you want."

But he didn't ask. He simply slid her fingers from his cock, took her hands, and urged her to trade places. He dropped to his knees on the floor, nudging her thighs wide. His hand slid under her butt, coaxing her closer to the edge, and she had to lie back to keep from slipping off. Unwilling to be robbed of a good show, she propped herself on her elbows, watching the concentration tense his features as he slid her panties from her legs and took her in. He brought his face closer, closer. She imagined Mike in the dark bathroom, standing if he wasn't already, not wanting his view obscured by Sam's thigh.

A warm breath heated her lips. She'd been aching for ages, her clit untouched all that time he'd spent being spoiled by her hands and mouth. His nose glanced her, sending a shock of pleasure up her body.

"Yeah." Another nuzzle, and she held her breath at the sensation. His tongue traced her lightly, drawing a sigh from her lungs. She lay back against the mattress, letting her arms trail above her head as she surrendered to whatever he was going to do to her.

The head he gave was nothing like Mike's. Her husband's tongue was fast and ingenious, mastered at teasing her clit with rapid, fluttering flicks, and he knew how much pressure she liked from years of getting her off.

Bern was the opposite. He gave her folds deep, firm, languid kisses, punctuating every few laps with a nip at her clit. He was as slow and decadent as caramel, and though the contact didn't stimulate her in the expert, efficient way Mike could, the sheer dirtiness of those penetrating strokes of his tongue had her toes curling.

"Wow," she murmured. He wasn't better or worse than Mike, only different, but that wasn't the message she was supposed to be conveying. "You're so good."

His mouth left her so he could speak. "Better than your husband?"

"I never knew how good this could feel."

She felt him penetrating—his fingers, not his tongue this time. He moaned. "You taste so sweet. When we fuck I want to eat you for an hour, until you're screaming for my dick. Begging."

"I'm close to begging now."

"That's what you think." He added a third finger, filling her with a hot, curious ache, a need to know how his cock would feel, how fast or rough he might fuck. "You have no idea how bad I'll make you want it."

She made a little noise, a cross between a sigh and a laugh. "I love your threats."

"Not threats. Promises."

"Even better."

He lowered his mouth once more as his fourth finger slid inside, offering the first taste of that pleasurable, stretching pressure. He closed his lips over her clit, the contact hot and hungry. Sam snaked a hand over her belly and ribs to cup her breast, letting her wedding band scrape across the tightening peak of her nipple through the satin.

She teased herself as Bern pleasured her between her legs, hoping maybe she could come. Everything felt good, but it was so different as well, too distracting in its newness. She had a noisy, analytical brain, and she couldn't get off unless she was truly relaxed, so she couldn't say if it was in the cards for tonight. But Mike needn't know that.

She let Bern spoil her for another five minutes or more, let his muffled moans and grunts fill her ears and tried to let fantasies about him fill her head. She tried to relax enough to climax, but it wasn't to be. Her orgasm would have to be as manufactured as her contempt for her supposedly inept husband.

"Yeah," she muttered, threading her fingers through Bern's messy hair. She let her leg muscles flutter, rubbed his back and shoulders with her feet, curled her spine, mewled and whimpered. "Keep going." She said it again and again, then his name. The latter fell strangely from her lips, feeling like a shoe slipped on the wrong foot, but she repeated it over and over for both sets of eager ears. "Bern. Bern."

It was a finely faked orgasm, complete with clenching and writhing and twitching and a homely, authentic guttural moan at the crescendo. *An award-winning performance*, she thought as she pretended to unfurl from her release, chest rising and falling with hitching breaths. Bern gave her clit a final lap, and she bucked, no need to feign oversensitivity. She'd never thought *any* time was an appropriate one to fake an orgasm, but this circumstance seemed a legit exception to the rule.

Bern slid his fingers from her, and a hot pang shot through her as he licked them clean.

"Good?" he asked.

She grinned. "I think you could have guessed that for yourself."

"What's my reward?" He climbed onto the bed, pushing her legs together and straddling them as he scooted closer, finally kneeling astride her thighs. She watched his fingers curl around his cock, clit pounding with frustration.

"Just about anything you want," she said.

As his fist tightened and began to stroke, his gaze jumped all over her body. "Take your bra off."

She did as instructed.

"Nice. Lemme watch you play with them."

Sam ignored a pang of self-consciousness, focusing on the show he was offering her as she kneaded her breasts for him. The tendons in his forearm stood out as he masturbated, and she imagined him doing this every lonely night since Saturday, thinking about her, or merely thinking about being seen.

"You look good," she murmured.

"Yeah. You like watching me?"

"I do." She couldn't decide which she liked more—watching or listening. His voice and body were tied when it came to rousing her. "I can't wait to watch you fuck." *And hear it.* Maybe she had a kink of her own, after all. She wanted to listen, as surely as Bern wanted to be watched, it would seem. Wanted to know what he'd say as he got close, or as he took her, and how he'd say it. Wanted that voice right at her ear as she got there herself, next time.

And she could admit, she wanted a *next time.*

Her words did something unmistakable to him, sinking him into a deeper level of arousal. His hand sped alongside his racing breaths.

"Let me see your hips move," she said.

He knew what she was asking for, keeping his fist still and thrusting his cock into the grip. Sam wished she had Mike's view, wanting to see the flex of his side and back and ass. She suddenly adopted Bern's mirror fetish.

Before her eyes, he reached the end of his rope. Wild moans spilled from his throat and she imagined those sounds even closer, right by her ear as he came apart, inside her.

"Where do you want it?" he panted, his meaning clear.

She pondered her options, fevered from the change in his voice—that smooth, sugary accent had gone from sultry to filthy. His body only seemed stronger, the more turned on he got, but his voice . . . She sensed weakness there, surrender, and felt powerful in turn.

As for his question, Mike was a hips-and-legs man, so let Bern desanctify that territory. "Right here," she said, stroking her upper thigh, just below the crease.

He edged back a few inches. His hand sped and she admired his face, his expression reckless, cheeks flushed. *A desperate man is the most fascinating creature in the world*, she decided, watching this strong alpha male torn to pieces from wanting.

"I wish my husband could see this," she said. "Show him exactly what I'm missing."

"This," Bern mumbled, strokes harsh and graceless.

"Yeah. That cock."

"Oh . . ." He dropped forward, bracing his weight on one arm as his hand pumped. His release arrived with a strangled sound, hot come lashing her skin, slipping down her hip. Three spasms, four, and he was gone, a strong man all at once limp and reeling. *Marvelous.*

He collapsed beside her on his back, chest working like a bellows, eyes clenched tight, as if he were in pain.

She gave him a minute to catch his breath, stroking his arm lightly. He opened his eyes to gaze into hers, and a delirious smile overtook his lips. A chuckle escaped him as he buried his face against her throat.

When he pulled away he asked, "That scratch your itch?"

She nodded coyly.

He reached down, watching as his fingers rubbed his cooling come into her skin. Idly she wondered, *Has Mike come yet? Has he even touched himself?* As much as she liked and appreciated Bern and his role in all this, she wanted him gone soon, so she could take the temperature of her marriage, check it for scrapes, and bandage any parts that may have been banged up during tonight's charade.

"He'll be home soon," she said.

Bern nodded. After a final lazy moment he took the hint, leaving the bed to find his underwear. Sam followed suit, pulling on her panties and clasping her bra. She got her dress back on, thinking a stray neighbor didn't need to see her saying good night to Bern in her underthings. Her hair was probably condemning enough. She combed it with her fingers as he buckled his belt and checked his pockets for his wallet or keys or phone.

"I'll walk you out." She waved her hand for him to precede her into the hall and downstairs.

Bern swung by the half bath, and then they loitered at the front door. Sam's inclination was to kiss him good night, but she wasn't completely confident in the gesture, so she rubbed his arm through his sleeve instead.

"Thanks so much for coming by," she said, beaming a grateful, humble smile at him.

"Thanks for inviting me. Really." He swept his fingers through her hair once, then seemed to think better of the familiarity, what with their audience now out of the loop. "If you guys want to keep going with everything, just know I'm down for it."

"I know how to reach you."

He nodded, then straightened, distancing himself from her as he flipped the dead bolt open. "Thanks again."

"You too. Drive safe."

He offered a wave, as good a parting message as Sam could have come up with herself. She returned it, smiling until she'd closed the door on his back. As she locked up, her heart tightened like a knot, hope weighted with fear.

Let him have loved it, she prayed as she started up the steps.

Please, God, let him have loved it.

CHAPTER NINE

Sam flipped off the lights and headed back upstairs. Mike's name begged to burst from her lips, but she didn't know for sure if they'd still be role-playing, if she was allowed to acknowledge that he'd been watching this entire time . . .

Her pulse was everywhere as she entered the bedroom—in her throat, pounding in her chest, and still thrumming between her legs, from Bern. Then as her eyes met Mike's, her heart froze all together. He was leaning against the doorway of the bathroom, wearing jeans and a T-shirt, and an intense, focused expression she couldn't begin to read.

Say something. Please.

He didn't. She didn't dare flash a smile or say a word, just stood inside the door, hands clasped before her. After a long pause, he approached. He stopped in front of her, face still inscrutable, his gaze scanning her up and down.

"I wish you'd say something," she murmured, wrecking any illusion he might be enjoying. "I need to know how you're feeling."

Still, he didn't. He said nothing. Instead his hands rose, fingers tangling in her hair, and when he kissed her he felt a foot taller than the man who'd just left, his mouth driving every memory of Bern's body and contact straight out of her head.

If she'd expected anything from her first kiss with Mike in the wake of the night's events, it would have been neediness. Uncertainty. But there was pure, fierce possession in the stroke of his tongue and the press of his lips. She held his shoulders and welcomed it. Surrendered to it.

He ended that muscle-melting kiss after a thorough minute. Surprise had tamped down everything she'd felt, messing around with Bern, but as Mike stepped away, all the hot, antsy longing flooded back in, a fever consuming her body all over again.

He took her hand, rubbing her knuckles and glancing her wedding band. In a calm, neutral tone, he said, "Thank you."

She couldn't suppress a smile of relief. "You're welcome. Did it feel how you wanted it to?"

He led her to the bed and they lay on their sides, facing each other with their knees locked. He stroked her hair and spoke to her collarbone or throat. "It felt . . . It felt like everything I feel when we're just talking about it, but times a hundred."

"But it wasn't too much?"

"It wasn't easy. The jealousy always hurts. And it hurt deeper than I ever would have guessed, this time."

She frowned, a pang twisting in her chest.

"But the way the jealousy gets me hot, it did that just as deep. Jesus . . ." He laughed and shook his head, clearly at a loss for how to articulate it.

"Just tell me you don't regret it."

He shook his head again, then leaned close to kiss her, softly this time. Sweet and brief. "I don't regret a second of it. Do you?"

"Only if you had. So no."

With reassurances tendered, Sam relaxed. She didn't have the emotional stamina to launch back into role-playing, and she sensed Mike didn't, either. She wanted him to ease the ache Bern had left in her body, but only on an authentic Sam-to-Mike level—no games.

"So what was the hottest thing about it?" she asked, tracing the seam where his arm lay against his ribs.

"The stuff you guys said. And just seeing another man touching you. All the weird stuff that gets me off. Watching you enjoying another guy, more than me. Or pretending you do."

"So we did a good job?"

Another laugh, candid with over-the-top disbelief. "Oh, you did a great job. And I'll never tell him to his face, but he's fucking *good* at this. I felt like we ought to be paying him or something."

"Yeah, I was pretty impressed, myself."

Mike smiled slyly. "What else about him impressed you?" He stroked the side of her breast, bringing a tight, tingling heat to her skin. He wanted a little taste of their game, but luckily nothing that demanded she pretend.

"I think he's really attractive," she said.

"He a good kisser?"

"Yeah. Different than you, but nice. It was strange, being with someone new after five years." God forbid if Mike ever wanted a similar chance—she'd be loath to grant him one, hypocrisy be damned. "He doesn't know me anywhere near as well as you do, obviously, but it was kind of sexy that he didn't. And that I didn't know what he likes."

Mike scooted lower on the bed and brought his mouth to her cleavage, his words steaming her skin between glancing kisses. "What about when he went down on you?"

"Way different, but it felt really good. Can I be honest with you?"

"Of course."

"I faked it."

His lazy kisses paused for a few thoughtful seconds. "Did you?"

"Yeah. It felt great, but he doesn't know my body the way you do, and it didn't seem like the scenario called for me to be giving him pointers, you know? I thought it'd be hotter to pretend he was utterly blowing my mind. I thought your fantasy would have him be just . . . perfect."

"So he didn't get you off?"

"No. But it was really hot. I wasn't faking *enjoying* it."

He'd gone quiet and still, and she stroked his hair, waiting as he examined his thoughts. She knew him well, and perhaps three times a week she watched this process—watched his expression go blank while he considered a choice that needed making or a piece of news that demanded digestion, turned a development around in his mind and decided how he felt about it.

After a minute's silence, her curiosity elbowed her patience aside. "Is that disappointing, or a relief, or . . . ?"

"I guess *relief* is the right sort of word. Or, I dunno . . . pride. I like that, knowing he can't actually please you the way I can. Not right out of the gate."

"Of course he can't. You've been perfecting that art for years."

"As long as it was still hot for you."

"Incredibly hot. And in no small part because I felt you watching." She traced his ear, then his jaw. "I was dying to know if you were touching yourself or not."

"Not really. I had my hand clamped over my dick most of the time, and I really wanted to, but I was afraid I'd come after three strokes and then the watching wouldn't feel good anymore."

She smiled to herself and raked his scalp with her nails. "So you've really been suffering this whole time."

"So bad it hurt. Like, fucking physically hurt."

She slid her hand between them to palm him through his jeans, finding him stiff, making him stiffer with a couple of soft squeezes. Her own sex roused in response, pleasure gathering in her body like an angry fist. She was right back where Bern had gotten her, and here with her was the man who knew how to bring her home as no other ever had. "Did you want to watch him fuck me?"

"Yeah." He was distracted, voice breathy. "But I'm glad you didn't. Not tonight. But yeah, I wanted to see it."

"Did you like watching me go down on him?"

He shifted and swallowed, exhaled heavily against her neck. "Yeah. That was as hot as the talking."

"He was as big as we'd hoped."

"I know. I liked watching you touch him. And suck him. Did you want him? Want him to fuck you?" He was speaking more quickly now, his breath growing short.

"I did, but not yet, like you said. But I loved his voice when I was turning him on. I think that was the hottest part for me."

It was a relief to be speaking frankly about the experience, to be able to talk dirty about it with complete honesty, no cruel part to play. It told her maybe this kink really was a gift she could give to Mike, without it feeling like a burden to bestow. Steadily, she was coming to see that there was more in this for her than the simple granting of his darkest wishes.

She kissed his chin, then whispered, "I loved making him moan and knowing you were watching." And it'd be a thousand times sexier the next time, knowing for sure Mike was enjoying himself. The next time . . .

"I kind of hope I get to fuck him," she admitted, a sheepish smile probably audible in her voice.

"I kind of hope the same thing."

"So does he. Or so he said when I walked him out." She slid Mike's zipper down and freed his button, stroking his erection through his underwear until he was panting. "You think you'll be in the same room next time?"

"I think maybe we could pretend I walked in on you guys. Maybe he could be a cocky dick about it, and you could make me watch, like he was going to show me how you needed to get fucked."

Her body jolted at the notion, Mike's kink sinking another barb into her sexuality, reminding her it was steadily becoming her kink, too.

"He'd like that. He wants to be watched."

"Wants to be watched while he fucks another man's wife."

"Lucky us."

Mike laughed at that. "True. How about you and me, right now? You up for it?"

Sam's turn to laugh. "I thought you'd never ask. I'm dying over here."

He left the bed to strip naked and Sam slipped out of her dress and underwear once more. She felt another hot jolt, knowing Mike was about to find her soaking wet, and that this time it really was from thoughts of another man, just as he loved to pretend it was.

He sank inside her from above with an easy, deep push, both his body and voice shuddering from the contact.

"He did all that," she said.

"I know. And with his mouth."

True. She was slick with her own desire, and with Bern's spit. Mike had never given her reason to think he wanted direct contact with the man they might find to fill the role of their bull, but he did seem to fixate on all that damning evidence.

"If he and I fuck, do you think you'd want to do what we talked about? Using a female condom so he can, you know . . . leave his mark in me."

"In theory, yeah."

She'd read plenty about the rituals cuckolding practitioners favored during the reclaiming process. Once the humiliation was done, the husband would be overcome by competitive urges and want to cleanse his woman of the other man, replace the intruder's come with his own. Even clean it away with his mouth, in some cases. She didn't know what Mike might want to do, but none of the popular options turned her off. And even the things she didn't think Mike or Bern were up for—the ultimate humiliation of the defeated, outmanned male going down on his rival, tasting his wife on another man's cock or being made to swallow his come—actually turned her crank a little.

But that stuff was the big leagues. Let them get some practice playing this game as amateurs before they tried going pro.

Still, she imagined those things as Mike took her. She studied his mouth and theorized about selfish things, about watching him service another man. About him being made to lap another man's trespass from between her legs.

Not so selfish, considering what I'm doing for him.

Just as Mike's jealousy warped under the heat of his arousal, the taboo, too-far aspects warped for Sam, becoming her most potent triggers. After all, Mike was never more worked up than when he was fantasizing about being demeaned by a competitor. Maybe one day she'd watch him slide his lips down a man's cock, see another's release glistening on those lips. The idea made her pussy clench and heat, a change not lost on Mike.

"What are you thinking about?"

"Just about all the stuff that might happen, if we took things further. *When* we take things further."

"Tell me." He leaned back so he could tease her clit, also giving her a gorgeous view of his body working.

She wouldn't tell him *exactly* what she'd been imagining. Baby steps were always the best practice. "Just about what you might do, after he was done. To reassert yourself."

"There's stuff I want to do, but I think I might have to get drunk the first time."

"Like going down on me, after?"

"Yeah. Exactly. I want it, in my head, but it might take a couple of shots of bourbon to actually get my brain to shut up long enough for me to actually do it."

"That's what alcohol's for."

"That wouldn't be too nasty for you?"

She shook her head. "No, I think it'd be sexy."

His thrusts sped at her proclamation. For minutes on end they simply fucked, Mike's taunting fingers teasing her in time with his driving hips. Eventually he broke their silence.

"Did you . . ."

"Did I what?"

"Did you clean yourself up, where he . . . you know."

"No." Bern was still there, basted into her skin. Mike's territory.

He said nothing at first, just took her with a slowing, pensive intensity. Surely pondering how his thighs were pressed to the spot where another man had soiled her.

She stroked his short, soft hair, dying of curiosity. "What are you thinking?"

He grunted a wordless sound, looking overwhelmed.

"You can tell me anything."

"I was wondering . . . what he'd taste like."

So exactly the answer she'd been hoping for. "He'd probably taste like another man, violating your wife."

He muttered a "Yeah," body slowing ever more with distraction.

"You can find out, if you want. I wouldn't be grossed out."

"No?"

"No. I'd like it if you would, actually."

He didn't accept the invitation right away. For another minute he made steady, pensive love to her, both of them surely tangled up in the idea that had been broached. Eventually he slid from her without a word, moving not down the mattress, but to the floor, where he knelt facing the bed.

"Come here," he said softly.

She scooted to dangle her legs over the edge, and for a long moment he stroked her calves and thighs, unfocused gaze seeming to hover at the spot where Bern had branded her. She could sense him needing a nudge of permission, so she put her hand to his ear, stroking, coaxing, inviting. Still he didn't take the leap, so she brought them back to the fantasy.

"You going to just let some other man leave his mark all over me?" She said it tenderly, the sweetest accusation.

He brought his face close, searching for a scent, perhaps. He kissed her thigh first, two inches or more from the spot. Another kiss, closer, and then right there—a tentative glance of his tongue chased by a more forceful lap. Sam could see how he changed from the way his back tightened, tensing with pleasurable jealousy or aggression. Stroking those muscles, she imagined this territorial ritual taken further still, Mike's tongue banishing all trace of his rival from deep between her legs.

When he'd laved her clean, she tugged at his arm and he joined her on the bed.

"He's gone now," she murmured, and he did as she hoped, picking up where they'd left off. He looked stern and cool as he took her, but she smiled her affection up at his face, then drew him down for a kiss. If any trace of Bern still lingered on his lips, she couldn't find it. When their mouths broke apart, she let her hands continue the tour, stroking his powerful arms and back, palms riding his undulating hips as he claimed what was his. Only his.

"Mike."

He moaned his reply, eyes closing.

"I love you so much."

"I love you, too." He sounded pained as he said it, but a happy pain.

Sam snaked an arm between them to tease herself, eager for the release that had been simmering inside her for so long. It took little more than her fingers' deft friction and the spectacle of Mike unraveling above her to bring it all to a boil. She succumbed to an orgasm more deep and violent and animalistic than she'd ever have found the creativity to fake, a smaller tremor not far behind.

Mike kept his pace through her pleasure, determined.

"He couldn't do that to me," she told him, voice wavering.

"Only me."

"Only you." Perhaps Bern could be taught to make her come, but it'd take a lifetime for him to ever get close to knowing her as well as Mike did. She admired her husband's body, thinking she'd never felt him this hard before. She made a circle with her forefinger and thumb, squeezing his shaft where it drove into her.

"You're so big."

"Yeah?"

"Of course. You're perfect." She could tell him that now, and it felt good after all the make-believe. She was thankful there was still room in their sex life for praise and appreciation. It would hurt to feel she couldn't ever watch him with open adoration when they fucked, lest she pop the bubble of his fantasy.

"You make me *feel* big, when you look at me like that."

She kept her gaze on his cock as it disappeared again and again inside her hand and sex.

Relief bloomed inside her as the haze of the orgasm lifted. She'd given him what he'd wanted, and he'd liked it as much as they'd hoped. She'd liked it, and here they were, still enough for each other, just the two of them. She released his cock to cup his jaw with both hands, staring right into his eyes.

"Come for me, Mike."

"I'm close."

"Good. I want you to do what he can't." She meant come inside her, bare, as Mike well knew. It was much too soon to say whether their three-way chemistry might prove strong enough for Bern to join them regularly, and be allowed that ultimate trespass.

"Turn over." Mike's impatient hands guided the actions as she got to her hands and knees.

Jesus, she'd missed this. It had been Mike's favorite position before the games had begun, perfect for a possessive man. He pulled her roughly into his thrusts, ownership resounding in every slap of skin and grunted male breath. In no time at all she could feel him losing control. The hammering of his hips forced her thighs wider, wider, until she lay flat on her belly, Mike sliding his hands beneath to cup her breasts, coming with a flurry of wild groans.

Kisses punctuated the spaces between his panting breaths, peppering her shoulder blades and the nape of her neck. She nudged him and he turned over, closing her in his arms as they'd done hundreds of times before. She felt his cock softening at the small of her back, felt his heartbeat pulsing at her spine, felt his come breaching her lips to wet her thighs. She smiled.

"Have I mentioned lately what an awesome wife you are?" he mumbled, sounding wasted.

"Probably. But you're always welcome to say it again."

He kissed her instead, a firm press of his lips to the crown of her head.

Sam sighed and flexed her toes. "I'm so glad that went well."

"Me, too."

"I wonder if he liked it."

Mike's soft laugh warmed her hair. "It sure looked like he enjoyed himself. Plus how could he not—he got to fuck around with *you*."

"You flatterer." After a long pause she added, "I can't believe vacation's already half over. Though no one can say we haven't been making the most of it."

"You know what I think?" Mike asked, shifting so she could twist around and face him.

She kissed his chin. "What do you think, Detective Heyer?"

"I think you should give him a call tomorrow. Or e-mail him. See if he's free this Saturday night."

"I'd be awfully insulted if he had a better offer."

"Better than us? Impossible."

She grinned at his confident tone. "We'll just have to find out. I'll ask him tomorrow."

"You know what else I think?" he asked, voice turning low and seductive.

"What's that?"

He kissed her nose. "I think we ought to order a pizza. I'm fucking starving."

CHAPTER TEN

Late Thursday morning, Bern felt his cell buzz in his pocket. A dozen times in a given workday he might feel a new call or text stir at his hip, but rarely before this week had he been one to drop what he was doing to check whose name was gracing his phone. He eased the heavy spool of cable looped over his shoulder to the ground.

A little envelope winked at him from his screen. He opened it, pulse throbbing in his throat. A hopeful smile tried to hijack his lips as he saw Sam's name at the top of the text, but he bit it back. No need for a coworker to bust him and ask what girl had clearly put such a shit-eating grin on his face.

Hello again, he read. Thanks for meeting up last night. We both had a great time, and were wondering if you might be free to hang out again this Saturday, around eight? Let me know!

He hit REPLY. Hello yourself. Saturday at eight sounds perfect. At the bar, or your place? Tell me if I should bring anything. *Wine, condoms, camcorder, whatever.*

Her answer came only a minute later and he pursed his lips to quell another smile.

Just your charming self. See you at our place at eight. E-mail if you need the directions.

The rest of the day passed in a horny blur, with Bern distracted by what was likely to go down on Saturday. He had been wiped out this morning, and not merely from skipping dinner, fucking around with a stranger's wife, getting to bed late, and starting the workday at seven. By the time he'd made it home, all the relief of his orgasm had faded to nothing, and he wound up lying awake, replaying everything and theorizing about what might come next until past midnight, abusing himself with the embarrassing, boundless enthusiasm of a teenager.

Now he was . . . what? Fifty-eight hours from who-knew-what.

If he got his way, who-knew-what would consist of enjoying Sam's gorgeous body again, and getting spoiled not only by her attention and the theoretical attention of her unseen husband, but maybe an actual, live, visible audience. Better than any mirror, and much safer than some video beamed off into the ether. And though it had never occurred to Bern that he might enjoy fucking somebody else's woman while the guy watched, lately it was all he could think about.

Maybe he and Sam were alike in that respect—they'd gotten snagged by her husband's kink like a snatch of catchy music, or a craving for a certain food once the aroma wafted past. Felt like he'd fallen under its twisted spell, and now he'd never come out of it unless the wish got granted, the curiosity satisfied.

Fifty-eight hours, he thought, hefting the cable back onto his shoulder. In fifty-eight hours all his borrowed fantasies might come true. Until then he'd be like a kid on Christmas Eve, dying of impatience, waiting to sprint down those steps and tear open his presents.

This was going to be a long-ass end to the workweek.

Sam barely touched her dinner on Saturday evening. She'd made chicken soup, and made it early so they'd have plenty of time to digest. Made it with less salt than usual so she wouldn't feel bloated, picked it because it promised she wouldn't wind up gassy or sleepy. Still, she spent much of the meal letting it spill from her spoon back into the bowl, barely half a serving making it past her lips. Mike's hand crept across the breakfast bar to take hers. She thought he'd been watching the news playing behind her on the TV, but when she looked up, his face was full of concern.

"You okay?"

"I am. I'm nervous, but not bad nervous. Just all keyed up." She pushed the bowl away. There were too many butterflies in her stomach, no room for soup.

Mike left his side of the counter to rummage in the freezer. He shut the door and handed her an ice-cream sandwich. She had to smile at that. "Thanks."

"Gotta keep your strength up."

The ice cream tasted more right than the soup: decadent, in keeping with the evening. Chicken soup—what had she been thinking? Save the comfort food for the flu.

In a couple of hours' time she was going to sleep with a relative stranger while her husband watched. Why on earth was she letting herself get worked up over gas and a bit of water weight? She licked grooves into the sides of the sandwich, as she had as a kid, licked deep enough that the soft chocolate cookie sheets could be sealed together like a ravioli. Only then did she let herself bite in and enjoy both textures together.

Mike did the dishes and stowed the leftovers, giving Sam the luxury of taking a long, thorough shower, scrubbing and shaving and exfoliating all her nooks and crannies. Each and every one was on Bern's personal menu for the evening.

She used the expensive lotion her mother had given her for her birthday . . . surely not with these preparations in mind. It smelled good, like vanilla and rum. *Bern's dessert*, she thought as she plugged in her styling brush. She got her hair as shiny and perfect as she might for a wedding. Funny, when the only vows involved in tonight's festivities were the ones she and Mike planned on desecrating.

"Looking good."

She jumped at his voice, then rolled her eyes at herself for being so wound up. She stowed the brush and met his gaze in the mirror. "Thought I'd make an effort."

Mike came in and leaned on the counter as she did her makeup. "Can I get you a glass of something?"

"Oh God, yeah. Please. Wine. A big one."

He laughed and disappeared, returning with her order. Sam took a gulp and finished up her mascara, plucked a stray brow. Mike followed as she went to the bedroom. He sat on the bed and watched as she got dressed—deep blue underwear, a casual, silvery gray dress with beading along the bust. She auditioned a few pieces of jewelry, settling on a black pearl necklace. Plus her wedding ring, of course, which she shined on her hem.

"You go to all this trouble before our dates?" No true jealousy edged Mike's tone, just a playful chiding.

"Yes, I did. More, in fact—I was still into waxing back then."

He rose and stepped close to run his palms down her sides. "Damn, you look good."

She smiled at him, smoothing his T-shirt along his firm shoulders, stroking his arms. If he was a leg man, she was an arm girl.

"What about you?" she asked. "You get yourself all gussied up special for me back when we were a-courtin'?"

"Do extra reps in the gym count?"

"Oh my, yes." She squeezed his biceps, her favorite of all his fine features.

"Then I did indeed."

"What time is it?"

Mike checked his cell phone. "Twenty minutes."

"Hooo." She shook out her hands and let loose a deep breath, willing the fearful excitement to stay at a manageable level. She shouldn't be this worked up. After the last time, she knew Mike was truly into it, as was she. As was Bern. Still . . .

"Jesus, I'm nervous."

"That's good. Pretend you're nervous about me coming home and catching you with him."

"I could." She straightened her shoulders. "Yes, I will."

Tonight, Mike would once again be hiding in a bathroom, this time the half bath in the downstairs hall. Once Bern arrived and things were getting hot and heavy, he'd sneak upstairs to the bedroom threshold and watch for a bit before asserting himself. Or before Sam pretended to spot him, caught in the act—whoever found the balls to break through the fourth wall first.

They headed back to the living room and Mike poured himself a bourbon. Sam was tempted to drain her glass and have another, but chances were Bern would want a little something to get loose, and if she joined him, she'd be three sheets to the wind and probably trip trying to get her dress off. Or tip over and clock her head on the corner of the dresser, leaving Bern and Mike to suffer a very awkward introduction as they waited for the ambulance.

At eight-oh-two, the bell rang.

All the relaxation Sam had found in her wineglass fled like a frightened bird.

Mike kissed her cheek. "See you soon." He headed for the bathroom, leaving her shaking in her heels, ever the unprepared hostess. She walked to the front, pausing at the mirror in the hall, checking her teeth for wine blackening, hurrying on. What must Mike make of all her clomping from the closed bathroom?

A knock at the door emptied her brain. She strode to answer it in a state of eerie calm. The door swung in, and there he was.

Dear God.

Had ever a man been made who looked this good in jeans and a work shirt, hair tousled, face unshaven? Flowers and a bottle of wine accompanied him.

She smiled and accepted the tulips. "Hello. And thank you."

"Hello yourself."

Now get inside before a neighbor sees you wooing me.

Bern did as her brain begged and she locked up behind him.

"You look amazing." He wasted no time, leaning down to kiss her, slow and seductive. Heat moved through her at the taste of his mouth, lust snaking low, hot and heady. After a wooze-inducing moment, she managed to pry herself away. She took the wine from him, body tugged in two clashing directions—arousal and anxiety. But she could feel the nerves easing. She'd underestimated this man's ability to draw out her sensual, slinky side.

"Would you like a glass?" she asked, holding up the wine.

"Sure." He followed her to the kitchen and gestured for the bottle. "Let me."

She found him the corkscrew and two glasses, busying herself with arranging the flowers in a vase. She stage-whispered, "He's in the first-floor bathroom."

Bern nodded and slid her glass across the counter, leaning in on his elbows. “So. When’s he due home?”

Game on. “Not for a couple of hours.”

Looking smug, he toasted the notion with a clink of his glass against hers.

“It’s been ages since I’ve been brought flowers.”

“That’s a shame.”

And a lie. Mike had sent her roses at work not even two weeks ago to celebrate a small promotion she’d earned. Man, had he ever gotten laid that night.

“It’s been ages since he’s given me a lot of things.” She looked straight into Bern’s eyes and sipped her wine.

“Maybe I can make up for some of those shortcomings tonight.”

“Maybe.” She gave him a wicked grin, anxiety gone. She wished he were wearing a necktie so she could draw him across the counter and kiss him. Not that Mike could see. Studying Bern’s shoulders and chest through his T-shirt, a wave of gratitude swept over Sam, leaving her momentarily misty. She got to have *sex* with this man. Some husbands might spoil their wives with a trip to the spa, but she got to indulge herself with another man’s body. A gorgeous body. A more enticing, decadent weekend getaway she couldn’t imagine.

Bern set aside his glass as she rounded the counter. She stroked one hand over his arm, sipped her wine with the other. “This is very nice,” she said, gaze moving all down his front.

“It’s Chilean.”

She grinned. Neither of them really believed she was speaking about the vintage. His warm palms slid down her sides to her hips, the sheer size of them thrilling her.

“You look great.”

“Thanks. A bit overdressed, maybe.”

"I don't mind." His eager gaze moved down her body and up again. "You look like a present, waiting to get unwrapped." *He* looked exactly like what he was—an electrician sent to rewire her with his rough, capable hands.

Their mouths came together, hers eager and his hungry. She felt the glass being coaxed from her fingers and heard it find the counter, then he was walking her backward into the hall.

Between deep laps of his tongue he growled, "Goddamn, you smell fucking amazing."

She squeezed his arms. "You feel amazing."

"He's in the bathroom?" he whispered, right against her mouth.

"The one in the hall."

And he led her right there—pushed her up against the closed door, rattling the inch of wood that separated them and Mike. *Oh fuck, don't let the latch fail.*

She raked his back with her nails, let go a breathy moan for both men's benefit. The length of his body pressed against hers, his lips too high to kiss but his throat a welcome substitute, as was this pleasant, loomed-over sensation. She tasted no cologne, no aftershave, just skin and the faintest trace of his sweat. His fingers were in her hair, his mouth above her temple, close enough that his ragged sighs heated her scalp.

"Been thinking about you all week," he said.

"You, too." She lapped at his jugular, stroked his hard shoulders.

"What about?"

"About what I didn't let us do last time."

"And tonight?" he asked.

"Anything you want."

"Tonight I just want to be inside you," he growled, loud enough for Mike to hear. One of his palms slid down, along her shoulder blade, waist, hip, then around, knuckles brushing above her mound.

"You can certainly have that," she said, dizzy.

"It's all I've been able to think about."

"Me, too. That, and how good you felt in my mouth."

He made a wonderful noise, a sigh blended with a grunt, then stooped to kiss her neck, a bold hand rising to cup her breast. Hot breaths steamed at her throat. She drew her nails through his thick hair, remembering his tongue's slick, deep caresses, the last time she'd held his head this way.

"Are you hard now?" she asked.

"Find out for yourself." He stepped back a pace and took her hand, laid it brazenly along the fly of his jeans. Goddamn.

"We ought to do something about that," Sam said, cupping him.

He led her up the stairs. It felt odd for another man to take charge in her bedroom—finding the light switch, kicking his shoes off where Mike's sometimes sat.

Again, his height gave her a forbidden thrill, and his body made dark promises as he backed her toward the bed. She sat with a little huff and he stood between her knees, hands sliding down her bare calves and slipping off her shoes. Then he tugged at her hips, bringing her butt to the edge of the mattress, her crotch against his fly as he stooped. She was drunk in an instant from the bossy way he held her in place, from the greedy friction of his hard cock against her soft, sensitive folds. She wanted to hold those powerful arms but couldn't quite reach, so she held his wrists instead, lost in the fascinating gleam in his eyes as he stared her down.

"That feel good?" he asked.

"Amazing."

"You been missing me?"

She focused on his slow, pumping hips and the thickness of his thighs in those jeans. "You have no idea."

"You wish you'd taken things further last time?"

She shook her head. "Only if there wasn't a second time."

"Lucky you, then. You wanna see me?"

"Always."

He stood up straight, unbuckled his belt, and lowered his zipper. With a peek of black cotton and a practiced motion, he exposed himself, the cock that Sam—and Mike—had thought of and theorized over and dirty-talked about a hundred times since Wednesday night's festivities. He stroked himself for a few beats, a little show Sam recorded for later enjoyment.

"You do that this week, thinking about me?" she asked.

"Every night." His hand seemed to tighten, though his pulls slowed.

A floorboard creaked, the familiar noise rousing her as much as Bern's touch might, flushing her entire body, hot as a heat wave. She knew Mike was watching now, just outside the door.

She swallowed and met Bern's gaze. "Show me how to touch you."

He held himself still as Sam sat up. She took his hip in one hand, his warm, stiff flesh in the other.

"Nice and tight," he instructed, fingers closing around hers to show her the grip he wanted. "Not too fast."

"Is that how you fuck? Slow?"

"Sometimes," he muttered, voice all at once shallow and strained.

Mike is watching, she wanted to tell him. She tried to convey it with her eyes, somehow, but Bern's attention was on her hand.

"I like it fast, usually," she told him. Fast and a little rough. She liked her man wild and strong, and tonight, Bern was her man.

"I can do that, too. I can give you whatever you've been missing."

"I bet you can."

He slid her hand from his cock. "Move back. Get your dress off."

She scooted up the mattress, then managed to peel the garment away and toss it to the floor. Bern stripped to his shorts, six foot something of toned, sexy stranger standing at the foot of her bed, erection straining at black cotton.

His weight bucked the mattress as he crawled to her, drawing her onto her side, claiming her mouth with his as he stroked her breast, her arm, her ass. In turn, Sam surveyed his hard abdomen and the curve of muscle framing his hipbone. She edged her fingertips back and forth along his waistband for a few moments before sliding her palm down his ridge.

"Mmm."

She'd seen him before, felt his heat in her hand and mouth, but he felt so new, still. New and exciting and the best kind of wrong.

He moaned. "Fuck, you're sexy."

She glowed at this compliment, coming from a man she objectively considered a level or two above her on the sexiness continuum. But the conspiracy they shared made her feel exotic and rare, her kink cred getting her on par with his sheer hotness.

He slipped his big hand inside her panties and she gasped. His rough fingertips shocked her bare, sensitive clit, tickled her curls. Her nerves adjusted and the touch went from alarming to intriguing to maddening in the span of a few shallow breaths.

"You're wet," he said, stroking the seam of her sex. "Wet for me."

"From thinking about you before you got here, too." And from thinking about the other man whose fantasy they were realizing.

He brought his mouth to her neck, licking and kissing her there. "Tell me what you want."

She squeezed his cock tighter, wriggling her other hand from under his shoulder to fist his hair. "I want to use you," she whispered, then raised her voice a bit, thinking of Mike. "And I want you to use me. And show me everything he's been denying me."

"Like what?"

"That's what I'm hoping you'll show me."

"Show you?" His tone was curious and she knew what he wanted to hear.

"Yeah, show me. I want the lights on so I can watch you fucking me."

His hips bucked, thrusting his dick into her grip.

"We can move the mirror, if we want." She nodded toward the full-length mounted to the outside of the bathroom door.

"Dirty." It was an accusation, warm with wonder and excitement. "But maybe I'll just let you have that wish."

She released his cock to push his shorts down his hips and ass, exploring that firm flesh. Mirror indeed . . . He'd look phenomenal from the side, fucking. She said a silent prayer that this affair might continue, that the three of them would reach some level of trust where they could actually record these encounters. Mike would love that. The idea had always seemed too risky to Sam before, but that had been back when Bern was a hypothetical entity, a gamble. Now that he was a real man, hard and hot and intense, she wouldn't mind having footage to commemorate this fun, filthy chapter of her surprising marriage.

Mike could hold the camera, she thought. That would jerk his crank like crazy, being relegated to the humiliated helper role. *You getting all this?* Bern might demand. *Got a nice clear shot of me fucking your wife?*

An order sprang from her lips unbidden. "Get on top of me."

He did, knees planted wide between her thighs. She pushed his shorts down another inch or more, ran admiring hands over his ass as he stroked his bare cock against the crotch of her panties, hot skin dragging against damp satin.

She sensed another presence—Mike's shadowy shape in her periphery, at the threshold. It set her heart pounding, but the nerves morphed to excitement. She'd let him speak when he chose to, let him watch for as long as he liked. Let him catch her, not the other way around. Let him enjoy the show until the desire drove him to intrude. After that, who knew what might come?

CHAPTER ELEVEN

Bern was going to have a heart attack if he didn't get inside her.

He'd *never* felt this hot before, the need pulsing like a violent, physical urge. Like the point of a knife pressed to his throat. He had to have Samira, and soon. No, now. Now, now, now. Make her husband watch. He could sense the man already, feel his attention. It lit him up as bright as the friction.

He stared down at Sam. "I want you."

She returned his gaze, smiling. "Good. You get me."

It was all the permission he needed. He backed off to drag her panties down her legs and ditch his own shorts. Crawling up her body, he made a quick stop to press his mouth and nose to her folds, to smell and taste her, a final dose of anticipation before the big moment. Her nails drew hot lines across his shoulders. *She wants this as bad as I do.* He was that eager and more, but if she was playing it urgent, he'd play it casual.

"He'll be home soon," she said, tugging at his arms.

He's already watching. Bern grinned at her and she raked her fingers through his hair.

"All this time you've already gone, not getting fucked the way you need it," he said. "You can wait another minute while I enjoy myself."

To demonstrate, he gave her sex a deep, firm lap with his tongue, then another, a dozen more until he felt her heels dig into his back and heard her whimper.

He crawled the rest of the way up her soft, warm body, until he was braced with his hands beside her ribs. "Was that really so bad?"

She bit back a grin, stroking his chest. "Not *so* bad."

"How did you want to . . ." He glanced between them demonstrably.

Her surprised expression said the formality of protection had slipped her mind, but she reached for a box on the side table. Bern watched with interest as she got herself prepped with a female condom. He'd never used one before. Of course, for the purposes of the fantasy, he knew they were supposed to pretend it didn't exist. For all their audience was to believe, Bern would be bare inside her, desecrating that most personal of spaces. It was all about his bare cock. And Bern was all about the attention, after all.

A lube bottle stood at the ready as well, and Sam slicked a squirt of it down his shaft, drawing an involuntary grunt from his chest.

"Ready?" He whispered it, centering his ridge against her lips, teasing in long, slow drags of his heavy cock.

"Yeah."

Again, he made her wait. He'd make her wait until she begged him. Surely their one-man viewership wanted that as much as he did.

She rubbed his arms, attention locked between their bodies. "You feel so good."

"So do you."

"I want you."

He smiled. "Ask me nice."

"Please."

"Nicer than that," he said, lowering to his elbows to kiss her neck and collarbone.

"Please, Bern."

He nipped at her throat. "Tell me what you want."

"Your cock. Inside me. I want you to make up for everything I've been missing out on."

He pushed back up, staring down at her for a long, searing moment, watching her eyes dart to his, back between their bodies, up again. Goddamn, she was beautiful.

Finally, he angled himself and gave her a taste.

She sucked in a breath, gaze on his cock. He glanced down as well, exciting himself as the next inch disappeared inside her slick, hot folds—she wasn't faking wanting any of this. Flushed and tight with desire. The pleasure was intense already. Dangerous, when he'd come here to give a command performance.

He eased out, then back in, the heat of her shutting his eyes. "Yeah."

"More."

He gave it this time, burying himself halfway then slowly drawing back out, back in again. Holy shit, he was fucking somebody's *wife.* The idea had his cock aching.

"You're so big."

"You been missing that?"

"I've never had anyone as big as you."

He decided to believe that was true—all the better for embodying his role. Then he wondered about the third party who'd be joining this game any minute. Bern had seen him across that bar, and he was bigger than his kink suggested—taller, and built. If the man took himself out and jacked off to everything that was going down, Bern might discover for himself if Sam was lying or not. Though the selfish prick in him hoped she wasn't.

He smiled down at her. "This what you've been missing?"

"So much more."

"Tell me."

"I want it rougher than he can do," she said. "And for longer."

Heat flashed up the length of his body. "I can give you all that. Whatever you need."

"Show me."

Fuck, those words. Hot as a hungry mouth on his cock. He slid deeper—all the way—earning himself a happy, excited noise and a fresh scrape of her nails.

"Feel good?" he asked.

"Amazing."

"Nobody's ever had you this deep before."

"Never."

Please, God, let that be true. "How do you want it? Slow?" He gave her long, explicit thrusts, making a spectacle of his length. "Or rough?"

"Let me get used to you first. But after that, hard and fast."

Bern got used to her as well, savoring the feel of a new woman, her sounds and smells. And this particular woman had put on a white dress and given herself to another man for keeps, yet here they were, she and Bern. The thought made him feel too many things—guilty and excited and a hundred shades in between. And above all, wicked.

"This what you've been needing, honey?"

"And then some." Those nails rasped his arms. "Fuck, you're big."

He didn't think he could hear that too many times. He ought have her record it, for him to listen to when he jerked off. Maybe make it his ringtone. "Am I thicker than him?"

"Yeah. Thicker than anyone I've had."

Again, that fever burned his skin. "Harder?"

She slid her hand between them to give him a squeeze, an extra sharp pulse of pleasure blooming. "Definitely."

The time for slow savoring was over. Bern leaned back, bracing his palms on her thighs, hips speeding. What a fucking view.

For a minute or more they merely watched—watched his hard, bare cock claiming her swollen pussy in deep, greedy strokes. His breaths grew shallow, heart beating hard from the taboo as much as the effort. From the audience.

Watch me, you twisted, freaky head case. Watch me fucking your wife. It got him panting to think it.

His exhalations grew ragged, like grunts now. What did they call him in the parlance of the cuckolding scene? The bull. Fine with Bern. He felt more animal than man, powerful and reckless. And a red cape was waving in his head, thanks to Sam's eyes and her unseen husband's.

"You like watching me, don't you?"

"I do." She stroked his thighs, her gaze caressing the rest of him.

"Lemme watch you, too. Touch your breasts."

She did as he asked, palming them, passing her thumbs across her nipples and drawing them to points.

He swallowed. "That's good. Looks almost as good as when you sucked my cock the other night."

"I'll do that again, if you want."

"Maybe." But not yet. Her pussy felt too good. Maybe in a couple of minutes it would *really* feel too good, and he'd have to stall lest he give away the fact that all this crazy pleasure just might get the better of him. Already the arousal was making him dim, clever dirty talk no longer waiting on his tongue. The animal wanted out, and Bern opened the gate. Moans and grunts spilled from his mouth, spurred by the feedback burning between what his eyes saw and what his cock felt, and all of it intensifying tenfold, just knowing that a stranger was watching.

Fuck, he needed a distraction. Something to cool him to a less combustible state. Getting Sam off could do nicely.

He slowed his hips and found his balance, one hand still on her thigh, the other spread over her mound, thumb on her clit. The contact seemed to zap her, drawing small bucks from her body for the first few strokes, before she began to move with him, hips urging the friction.

"Bern."

"Feel good?"

"Yeah."

"You wanna come on my big cock?"

"Yes."

He circled the spot, slow and light. "Say please."

"Please. Make me come."

"When I decide to let you, you'll come. Not a moment before."

"He'll be home soon." She said it breathily, like a whisper, but loud enough for their audience to hear. "You have to leave before then."

"You think he won't know? You think he won't be able to smell it in his own bed?" Bern demanded, hips slowing even more, strokes growing long, making what was happening between their bodies as obscene as he could. "Think he won't see these sheets soaked with another man's sweat and come?"

Her eyes shut. "Bern."

"Look at me."

She did.

"Like he won't smell the sex leaking down your thighs and wonder who got you so wet?" he went on.

"I'll change the sheets," she panted, hands rubbing his arms in a frantic, thoughtless rhythm.

"He'll see it on your face," Bern said, making his voice cruel. "He'll wonder who got your cheeks flushed and your lips swollen, who had your head pushed into that pillow and your hair all messed up."

"We have to hurry." Her hands slid to tug at his ass, and he slowed further. "Please."

"Please what?"

"Faster."

He dropped to a glacial pace, letting them both savor the drag of his cock as it slid from her lips, then the luxurious heat as he drove back in, filthy-slow.

He found the right rhythm, timing the thrusts with the teasing of his thumb. The hands that had once caressed her breasts for his entertainment had given up that cause, and he watched her fingers play with her nipples in subtle, small tweaks, unmistakably for her own pleasure. Sexier than any show by miles.

His voice caught on a moan and he cleared it, feeling the craziness of need descending hard and fast. "Sam."

"Sam," came a sharper voice from behind them.

In the moment that Bern muttered, "Fuck," he wasn't faking the panic. He went ice-cold, even with his cock buried in Sam's hot body. He heard her echo the sentiment beneath him, both of them going dead still. Adrenaline pounded, his pulse ticking in his ears.

Be a dick, his mental script coached. He turned his head slowly, keeping his expression stern, annoyed. He stopped short of true eye contact, staring instead at the man's chin. His cock throbbed, hard and loud as a gong, it seemed. He felt more naked than he'd known possible.

And it felt fucking amazing.

"Mike," Sam said, no embarrassment or shock in her voice—more like exasperation. Unlike Bern, she was prepared for this moment, still perfectly in character.

Her husband was just as Bern remembered—tallish, built, with a no-nonsense face, honest blue eyes aimed at Sam. There was hurt in those eyes, and Bern wondered if that was acting or actual—if maybe the hurt and jealousy got the guy off.

"Sam" was all the man said. His posture was tight, an invisible holster seeming to draw his shoulders back, straighten his spine. But then he changed, all at once defeated.

Bern felt Sam's hand on his side, rubbing. Eager to look away from Mike, he stroked her thigh in return, watching his fingers.

"I never meant for you to find out like this." She wasn't apologizing. Just stating facts. If anything, she sounded as though her fun had just been spoiled.

Her touch made Bern's cock twitch inside her. He'd been so hijacked by chemicals, he'd lost track of his extremities. But there he was, still hard, still into all this. He glanced at Sam's husband for the briefest second, just about positive the guy was hard behind his jeans.

"Why?" Mike asked, sounding far more sad than angry.

"You know why." Her hands coaxed Bern with rhythmic tugs. He obeyed, beginning to thrust again. It was different with their audience *right there.* Still hot, but goddamn, he felt stripped. And *goddamn*, it felt good. Like he was on fire, the man's gaze kerosene.

"In our bed?"

"I need things you can't give me." Sam spoke to her husband, but she kept her attention on Bern, caressing his stomach and chest.

"I try to give you everything you ask for."

"Try and fail. I need more."

Bern read it as a cue to take her a bit quicker, a bit rougher, in long strokes to exaggerate his length. She moaned her approval.

"And this guy can give you that?"

"He can," she said, flashing a fond, smug grin at Bern. "If you want to know what I need, grab a seat and watch what he can do."

The word *watch* electrified Bern as it always did, and he lost a few seconds, reality seeming to rematerialize as Mike returned from the hall with a desk chair.

"Right there," Sam said, directing her husband to set it beside the bed, close to the side table so the view of what was happening between their bodies would be prime. Front row.

"Show my useless husband what I like, baby," she said to Bern.

First things first, Bern thought. He slid all the way out of her and cupped his balls, displaying his cock. Sam stroked his length with an adoring hand, her touch and Mike's attention massaging some pleasure center deep in Bern's brain, making him crazy.

"You can never give me this," she said to Mike. "And no matter what you tell yourself, size does matter."

"Sam—"

"He feels so good. Big and thick and deep."

She let Bern go and he buried himself to the hilt. Sam groaned her approval, and his body electrified at the sound, pride blooming in his chest. The live audience had him blazing, a zillion times more intoxicating than a girlfriend watching in a mirror had ever done. And a mirror had always done plenty, before.

"Where were we?" Bern asked, finding his voice.

She grinned, seeming to like his notion to treat her husband as though he were invisible. "I can't remember, since we were interrupted. Refresh my memory."

He put his thumb to work on her clit, hips pumping his cock into her, deep and steady, pulling out nearly all the way, sparing Mike nothing. "You don't remember this?" he teased her.

Another smile. "Maybe I just wanted a reminder."

"Greedy."

Her smile changed as his body demanded more, lips becoming a disbelieving little O shape. Her cheeks were stained deep pink, and Bern felt another burst of pride, knowing her excitement was no mere performance.

"Good," she murmured. If having Mike here gave her any anxiety, she didn't show it. Jesus, where did a guy need to go to score a wife like Sam? A pang of sharp appreciation jabbed him, almost reverential, and he suddenly wanted to savor this remarkable woman, make the most of the time he got to enjoy with her. It did something intense to his desire, doubling his determination. He began to fuck her harder—primal, competitive urges driving his body.

"Yeah." She stroked his arms and shoulders.

"You like it rough?" Bern asked.

"Yes."

Abandoning her clit for the time being, he dropped to brace his elbows at her sides and took her, fast and wild. He felt surprise in her body for a few moments, until she caught up with the demands his cock was making. Her warm, soft thighs hugged his waist, inviting him to drink his fill.

He smiled down at her, their faces so close. "You like that?"

Wordless panting affirmed his question and she gripped his arms tight, nails biting.

"You missed getting fucked like this, didn't you?"

He caught a "Yes" behind her gasp.

"I'll spoil you rotten," he promised, rising to hold himself up on his palms, hips still hammering, each thrust still long and deep, offering glimpses of his driving cock. "I can fuck for hours. Bet your husband can't do that."

"No," she murmured, gaze glued right where everyone wanted it to be.

"You feel that?" Bern punctuated the words with a series of mean thrusts, the sharp slap of skin on skin.

"God yeah."

"That's what it feels like, getting fucked by a man."

Eager hands ran down his sides, making a show of exploring his hips and ass in contrast to his feverish thrusts. Bern eased up, letting the scene turn slow and sensual for a minute or more. He needed the break, frankly—a chance to cool the friction that had his cock screaming, begging him to turn his promise of longevity into a bald-faced lie.

"I can fuck for as long as you want me to." He stared her dead in the eyes.

"I bet you can."

"I'll make you come more times than you can count. Leave you limping tomorrow."

He thought he caught a smile on her face for a moment, then it was swallowed by a moan as he pushed deep. Beyond the physical pleasure was the more abstract sensation of another person's eyes on him. Bern felt it, as sure as he felt Sam's slick heat or the pressure drawing taut in his belly. It stoked him as friction never could, making him blaze.

Watch me, asshole.

There was an aggression to the thought, one at odds with his rational feelings about Mike. In reality, he was grateful to the man. But playing this part, he gave himself over to the contempt, let himself feel a hundred feet tall.

Was he allowed to make eye contact with him? Bern was tempted to aim a cocky-ass glare at the guy, but maybe he was supposed to be ignored. He'd err on the side of caution and ask Sam about it ahead of time if he got invited back for a repeat performance.

He pondered the logistics and likelihood of the idea, to cool his body a few needed degrees.

It'd be the perfect arrangement, if they wanted Bern to come back. He'd get laid—with an audience, the thing he coveted most, and with someone he really liked, but without the complications and pressure that came with an actual relationship. Sam would presumably get her rocks off, and her husband's mind would get blown in the peculiar way he preferred. Win-win-win. Plus, give it time, and who knew—maybe they'd want to tape it. Then Bern would get hard on a new level, thinking about them watching the footage. Watching him. The gift that kept on giving. Maybe if Mike ever traveled for work, they could cam for him, let the man pretend it was a hidden camera or something. The possibilities were fascinating when these two particular kinks collided.

Smiling down at Sam, Bern decided she was the prettiest thing he'd seen in ages. Pretty and passionate, and goddamn, she loved her husband. Bern might only be some side dish, an amusement sourced to complement Mike's desires and satisfy Sam's parameters. But he felt like he'd hit the fucking jackpot, having stumbled into this chance.

With a final fond grin, he slipped out of his thoughts and back into his body, back into a reality that was as good as any fantasy he'd ever put himself to sleep with.

He held her gaze, feeling the fire smoldering in his own. "Bet you're just dying to come on my cock, aren't you?"

Can a man die of sexual frustration?

Mike didn't think so, but if anyone was in a position to find out, it was him. The palms resting flat on his thighs were damp and hot. *All* of him was hot, like he'd caught a fever. He couldn't stop swallowing. His right hand fought conflicting orders from his cock and his head.

Touch yourself. It's your fantasy being acted out on that bed.

No, don't. You'll come in five strokes and you might feel different after.

But Jesus, he hurt. If he'd ever been this hard, he couldn't remember it. It was so exactly perfect—Sam's familiar body, owned by the masculine spectacle that was Bern's. Mike didn't want the man, himself, only the concept of him, the size and force of a built, hung man, owning what Mike's heart knew to be his own.

There'd been an incident, years before, when he'd found out a girlfriend had cheated on him with her ex. Mike had been about twenty-two, and though the relationship hadn't been serious, he'd been crushed. They'd broken up, gotten back together the next summer, but Mike never quite got over the infidelity. Not because of the shattered trust or the jealousy, though. Because for about six months, the only thing he jerked off to was imagining his girlfriend with some other guy. It was crazy, what that did to him—made a knot of his heart, an aching, squeezing pain that got crossed with his sexuality, and made his cock throb like nothing else ever had.

He and that girlfriend had wound up breaking up the second and final time because Mike had become "too intense, sex-wise." Guilty as charged—he probably hadn't handled it the best, but Jesus, his whole world had been on fire.

The fantasy had gotten put on the back burner for a long time, through periods of bachelorhood and a couple of girlfriends who simply weren't the types Mike could imagine cheating on him. Too sweet; no naughty, selfish gleam in the eye. Then he'd met Sam.

She didn't come off as heartless or anything of the sort, but she had that sly little smile, a touch of mischief in and out of the bedroom. She was whip-smart and analytical, and in dark moments, he'd imagined her turning that penchant for planning toward selfish scheming—deceptions. Then he'd fallen in love with her, and he'd known if she wasn't the one, nobody was. But could he live the rest of his life never getting as hot as he had at twenty-two, when his ex ran around on him?

He'd started looking for signs, started reading too much into Sam's late nights at the office . . . not to be a controlling dick, but because he was playing a game with himself. Getting worked up, imagining her fucking around on him. It wasn't fair to her, though, letting her think he really did distrust her. It had taken him ages to find the balls to tell her the truth, and he'd been gambling with more than he was prepared to lose. But holy fuck, look what the truth had gotten him. Where it had taken the both of them, plus this stranger.

The guy was perfect. Younger than Mike, taller, and better-looking, he imagined. Bigger dick—longer and thicker, just *more*. It didn't take much mental effort for Mike to diminish himself in his head, to concentrate on all the ways Bern Davies had him outmanned. Not least of which was the way Mike's wife was moaning beneath his hammering body.

Mike knew *exactly* how her pussy felt, and he hoped this shithead realized how good he had it. He shoved the thought aside, focusing a hundred percent on the fantasy. It'd be a crime to waste the live show.

One thing he *hadn't* anticipated was the smell. Sex infused the room, and some animal filter in his brain knew that it wasn't the usual scent. That was some other man's stay-the-fuck-away chemical signals. A scent that made Mike see red, except then the red blurred, rejiggering a possessive synapse in his brain, linking it to the one that got him hard—a crossed circuit he wouldn't trade, not for anything, not anymore.

"You're so fucking good," Sam groaned. If she was faking it again, he'd never have guessed.

"You wanna ride my dick?"

Fuck yes, please.

"Yeah."

Mike watched as his wife straddled her new lover, her gaze holding Mike's when she sank down on that rival cock. "Fuck."

Bern echoed the sentiment, his intruder's hands closing over her hips. The guy was in for a treat—Sam was great on top. Mike had a hell of a view, could see her face, see her breasts, see each inch of

Bern disappear as she rose and fell, see the indentation of her flesh where this strange man's fingers pressed.

"Good," Bern muttered. "Ride me. Ride my dick."

Mike's mouth went dry and his hand twitched, cock begging.

Sam found her pace, and after a minute or more she finally turned her attention to Mike. Her face told him everything his fantasy fed on. Scorn in her eyes, revenge in her smile. *Talk to me*, he begged. He might have to speak first. But as his lips parted and closed uncertainly, she took those reins, intuitive as always.

"Like what you see?"

He swallowed, throat tight and sore. "Sam. What the fuck? How can you do this?"

She slowed, but didn't stop, and to Bern of all people, she said, "Sorry."

"Sam," Mike repeated. "What the *fuck*?"

She went still, hands caressing Bern's chest idly. "I didn't mean for you to find out like this, but he gives me things you just can't."

"I'd give you anything you asked for," Mike murmured, mesmerized for a moment, feeling almost out of his body. Christ, they'd never played their game like this before.

"There are some things you just can't offer me." She raised her hips, Bern's cock slipping free. She walked backward on her knees and Bern sat up, propping himself on straight arms, spreading his thighs.

"You could never give me this." She held Mike's gaze, taking Bern's length in her hands. Mike wondered if the man could feel her wedding band on his skin. Sam stroked his cock and balls, admiring, flaunting. Mike's own hands were curled into fists at his sides.

"I'd buy you toys," he told her.

A huff of derision. "They can never compare to a real man. A real man with a big dick, who knows how to use what he's got." She dropped to her elbows, taking Bern in her mouth. That in itself hijacked Mike's blood pressure. But when he saw the other man's fingers tangle in her hair, he thought his body might rip clean apart, leave him in a sparking, mangled heap on the bedroom floor. Somehow he held it together, even as he watched Sam's capable lips slide up and down, watched her cheeks hollow with the exquisite sucking that had been Mike's alone until recently.

Startling as a gunshot, Bern met Mike's eyes, and spoke to him for the first time. Two simple words, cocky and cruel, to reach across the room and strike him dead in the heart. "Taking notes?"

Mike shuddered, hate and lust short-circuiting his brain and body, every impulse a hot, conflicted jumble. He wanted to kill this man . . . but not as bad as he wanted this man's come slicking his wife's sex.

If he shot in her mouth, would I kiss her?

The very thought was a shock—the sort of question he'd been avoiding asking himself, since that first night. Since the first time he'd tasted this man on his wife's skin—the first time he'd ever tasted any man, period.

In truth, yes, he wanted to. He ached for the *insult* of it, more than anything. But he didn't think he could, not while the guy was still there. Not the first night. Maybe eventually.

Maybe eventually, he'd share that kiss with her, and perhaps even more . . . eat her out and be forced to taste what another man had left. They'd certainly fantasized about it enough, and role-played it. Mike liked that part, the way his brain flipped, halfway through the game. He'd start out cowed by humiliation, but as the imagined seed was licked away, the dynamic would change, possessiveness kicking back in, and he'd get hot from thoughts of reclaiming her. Sometimes the role-playing stopped short and they just fucked like beasts, Sam letting him see how riled he got her.

"Suck that cock." It was Bern speaking, giving voice to Mike's own thoughts. "Suck me good and I'll make you come so fucking hard." He gathered Sam's hair in his hand, guiding her bobbing motions. "Good. That's good . . ."

But soon enough, he let her go. Sam sat up.

"Hands and knees," Bern told her.

Sweet fucking Christ, yes, please.

That view. Side-on. Before Sam had even fully settled into the position, Bern was taking her. If the guy liked getting watched, well, happy birthday, asshole. Mike kept his face stoic, but everything happening before him struck him as viscerally as a kick in the guts.

Strange hands held her hips, fingertips digging into the soft flesh there, and with each stroke came a flash of bare, flushed cock and dark hair, a rough grunt.

Mike wanted to touch himself. So fucking badly. He didn't think his dick had ever *hurt* like this—like a cruel hand had his balls in a fist, twisting. Add to that the jealous flames licking up and down his body, and this had to be akin to madness.

"Goddamn, you're hot." Bern's body sped, one hand resting on Sam's lower back, the other dangling at his side as he watched, the pose full of cocky porn swagger. But it was better than any porn Mike had ever seen. His deepest desires made real, this show his alone to enjoy, with all its smells and sounds and the heat of two fucking bodies. His wife.

"You like it hard?" Bern asked.

"Yeah." The second the word left her lips, the sex went from rigorous to rough. Mike's hand twitched, begging to relieve his cock.

Bern grasped Sam's hips, kneading her flesh in time with his driving length. "Bet you feel amazing when you come."

She moaned her reply and craned her neck to watch him.

"Maybe I'll just find out for myself." Bern stooped closer, riding her tighter, looping an arm around so he could touch her clit. To make his job easier, Sam pushed up from her elbows and braced herself on her palms.

It was surreal, watching this man fucking her the way Mike might, on the nights when his kink wasn't center stage. It stung for real, but only for a second. It was perfect, of course, the idea that this shithead was giving Sam the kind of sex Mike knew she liked most.

"Bern." Her voice was stilted from the motions. "Jesus."

"Yeah, you like that? You like that nice fat cock?"

Mike flushed hot as Sam said, "Yeah."

"Why don't you come for me, show me just how much you love it?"

"I will."

Will you? Really? She'd faked it that first time. Would tonight be different? He honestly had no clue if he wanted that. He wanted her pleasure, and his kink wanted evidence that he really was outmanned. But a selfish, honest bit of him still hoped Bern couldn't get her off. Once the guy was gone, Mike would give her anything she asked for, make her tremble around his dick or against his tongue or fingers, to hell with the game for a change—let them both remember how good they were together. Just the two of them.

You're wasting the show, worrying about it.

Fucking right he was.

He pushed the self-analysis aside and drank in the scene taking place before him. *For* him.

Their bodies were hugged too close for Mike to glimpse that most explicit point of contact. In its place he fixated on the sound—animals rutting. In his bed. Bern's triceps twitched with the strokes he gave Sam's clit, and her own hands were fisted around the covers. She looked crazy in the hottest way possible, her pretty face flushed, lips parted, wild eyes aimed at Bern over her shoulder. How he adored that look—the one she always wore when she'd had a couple of glasses of wine and dulled her inhibitions. The one she wore on the nights when she asked for it hard and fast.

She'd claw him if they were face-to-face. Drag her nails down his back and arms, a pain Mike knew well and loved. He longed to move to the mattress, sit beside her and touch her hair, run his thumb across her swollen lip. He wanted to take a turn, take over. Take her back. As always, the uncertainty had him panting.

Bern's free hand shifted to the small of her back, something possessive in the way he pressed his palm to her skin, like he was pinning her down, asserting his strength. Mike's cock was on fire, screaming to assert a few needs of its own.

"Fuck." It was Sam who said it, and he knew what it signaled. She was close. She'd said *Fuck*, but what it meant to Mike was *Don't you dare stop.* She probably didn't even know she did that.

She's not faking it.

He swallowed. Good. Let her come apart with this stranger inside her. Let the guy do the same, and leave Mike to scrounge for whatever pleasure was left to him. Table scraps from another man's feast.

"Yeah." Bern kept his hand working, hips speeding as he surely realized she was coming. Mike could see excitement in his strained features—excitement Mike had felt any number of times himself, in this lucky bastard's exact position.

She muttered, "Fuck me," but it came out breathy. She was already there.

Bern let loose a long, low groan, a sound of satisfaction, but not release, Mike didn't think. Not yet.

Where will he come? And how might Mike banish him, afterward? His face and throat burned, skin flashing hot at the question.

Their bodies slowed, and Bern stroked her back with both hands, gazing down with something approaching affection. "Good?"

A satisfied sigh answered him, and she turned her head to grin drunkenly at him.

He gave her butt a soft whap. "On your back."

She did as ordered and Bern knelt between her thighs, taking her deep and swift, bracing himself upright with his palms on her knees. "Want you to watch when I come."

Her hands ran up and down his belly. "Happily."

She wouldn't be the only one.

Strange, pleasurable, scary feelings gathered in Mike as he studied the scene. An insecure bit of him wasn't comfortable with exactly how hot it got him to watch another man—a strong, built man—fucking his wife. But Sam had asked him once, *Would you still be turned on if I weren't there?* If it were just a man that he was watching? And no, he wouldn't. Not at all. The reassurance lowered his hackles, soothing an impending identity crisis. Attractive men didn't get him hot—competition did. And the fear of failure, for whatever reason. But it was true, Sam was always there. Without her, there was no fire to stoke.

And here she was indeed, those slender hands that had been exclusively Mike's for all these years, caressing this stranger's chest and sides and ass, egging him on.

"You look good," she told him.

"Hope you'll think about this the next time you let your husband fuck you."

Mike swallowed a moan.

Sam smiled up at Bern. "You know I will."

"Maybe someday you can tape us."

The need racking Mike's cock doubled at the thought. A video of Bern fucking Sam . . . God, he'd love that. The perfect porn, and he could watch and pretend he'd hidden a camera, caught her messing around behind his back. No copy for Bern, of course. Too risky. And recording it at all was risky in this day and age, but goddamn, some gambles were worth it.

"Maybe your husband could help," Bern added, his voice unmistakably more hoarse than before. He turned his head and shot Mike a second's mean glance. "Maybe we'll make him hold the camera."

Sam gave a wicked little giggle, her cruelty as hot as the smell and heat of their bodies in Mike's bed.

Bern dropped lower, palms set beside Sam's shoulders. He took her roughly, flesh pounding flesh, and dragged a harsh moan from her lungs. "Bern."

"Yeah. You like that."

Yes, she does.

She gripped his ass, following or urging the motions. "I love it."

"Want me to give it to you? Shoot you full of my hot come?"

Mike held in another pained sound, teeth grinding.

"Please."

"Good. Beg me. Beg me and I'll let you have it."

"Come for me, Bern. Inside me. Please."

"I can feel it," he said, nearly seething. "I'm gonna give you so much. Spank me."

Without a second's pause, she slapped his ass.

"Yeah. Again."

She spanked him again, rubbed the reddening spot, then gave him another.

"Yeah." His head rolled back, hips racing so fast the motions seemed to blur. "Oh fuck, here I come."

She slapped him again, three more times until he froze, groaning long and loud and shameless through the spasms. Mike nearly lost it himself, so close it hurt.

Bern stayed braced above her, back rising and dropping as he caught his breath.

Get the fuck out of my fucking bed so I can fucking come, asshole. Mike held the words in, certain he was on the brink of an aneurysm or heart attack.

After a maddening minute, his swear-riddled prayer was answered.

"I better let you deal with your husband," Bern said, as if Mike were a dog that needed walking.

Sam nodded up at him with an exaggerated frown. "Yeah."

They disentangled themselves, both bodies damp with sweat in the low light. Bern dressed quickly, and Sam slipped into her bathrobe.

"Thanks for coming by." She stood on her tiptoes and they kissed. "You have no clue how badly I needed that."

"Anytime," he said, then shot a mean look at Mike. *Any time you turn your back, my dick's in your wife*, his glare seemed to say. Mike would have appreciated the sentiment if his sexual frustration weren't begging him to strangle the man to death.

Though his fantasy had been realized tonight, Mike couldn't wait for the door to close behind their guest. He could claw his own skin off, he was so worked up. Sam walked Bern out, and Mike was stripping his shirt before he even heard the dead bolt click downstairs. By the time Sam was back in the bedroom, he was down to his shorts, and even those felt like a straitjacket.

They both paused where they stood, gazes locking.

Sam smiled, eyeing his erection. "I was going to ask if it was good for you, but I guess that's my answer."

Her comment killed the role-playing, but Mike didn't care. He could appreciate her wanting to know that her real-life husband was okay with everything that had just gone down, and like the last time, he was too fucking hot to keep the games up, himself.

Dropping her robe and crossing the carpet, she came to wrap her arms around his waist, belly brushing his cock. He planted a kiss on her forehead, wanting to do way more than that.

"You're not too sore, are you?"

She smiled up at him and shook her head. Her fingers twined with his and she led him to their bed.

"I still have the condom in."

"Good."

A little laugh answered him, but he was burning up, body in too much of a crisis to register much more than the need to come.

Sam lay down as he stripped away his shorts. Just the swipe of the fabric against his cock made him buck. He got her thighs spread with his knees, pausing a moment with his crown poised at her lips. He felt the slickness there, knowing only a small measure was lube. That was the enemy there—for real this time—easing his way. Making him insane.

"I'm gonna fuck his come right out of you." The promise came out like a death threat, his voice hoarse and crazy. He shivered as he heard the words, surprised he'd uttered them. Eager hands stroked his arms and he took the plunge.

A sound like he'd never made before ripped from his lungs, a groan of pain and fear and disbelief. The sex version of a primal scream. And why shouldn't it, when he was fucking his mate, her sex still dripping from a rival?

Beneath him, Sam was engaged but quiet. He hadn't let her know what he wanted from her—which Sam his mind wanted, his kind wife or the callous actress. He didn't know, himself. He didn't really care. Another man had been with her tonight, and that was enough.

"I loved watching you with him," he said.

Her grin was full of relief. "I'm glad."

"Did you enjoy yourself?"

"I did. I came tonight."

Mike's hips sped, unbidden. "You liked how he fucked?"

"He's good. He doesn't know me like you do, but it was exciting to enjoy his body."

"You like his cock?"

"I do."

"More than mine?" He took her slowly, calling attention to the equipment in question.

"Honestly?"

Shit, did he really want to know? "Yeah, honestly."

"I like yours more." She stroked his chest and neck. "But he's hot. New and different."

"He's bigger than me."

"Yeah, but it's the man that matters, not the size. And both of you turn me on. Did you want me to pretend I liked him more?"

"Maybe." Yeah, he did. The assurances were appreciated, but his body wanted to get back to the conflict that'd had him burning up, watching the two of them.

"In that case, I was only trying to make you feel better."

"Oh?"

A sly smirk. "He's way better than you. And bigger."

Another hot jab in the arousal synapse of Mike's brain. "I'm gonna fuck you till there's nothing left of him inside you."

And he did. He owned her like a beast, screwing until the friction shifted, lube burned up and the condom began to drag on his skin. He pulled out, fumbled with the lip of the thing until Sam intervened and did it for him. He made a hurried trip to the bathroom, to soap and rinse his throbbing erection, then he was back with her, above her. He sank deep in nothing but Sam's own slick folds.

"What got you this wet?" he demanded.

"Him."

Mike's climax rose, the point of no return looming close on the horizon. She felt so fucking good—warm and swollen and slippery, familiar. Bern hadn't felt her like this, he told himself. Only Mike got this.

For now.

Just as he was about to rush headlong into the final stretch, Sam slipped a hand between them to play with her clit. Shit, he should have offered to do that. But he'd gone nuts with lust. He prayed he could hold off long enough for her to come.

"I'm close," he admitted.

"Me, too."

"What are you thinking about?"

She didn't answer right away, pursing her lips on a reply as she remembered they were playing again. "Just about how good he felt," she said. "Big and rough and strong, and how he made me come so easy."

He had, too. Another man had felt her climax, felt that hot little hug around his cock. Made her shudder, and maybe recognized that fleeting glimpse of momentary crazy in her eyes that Mike loved so much, and maybe even appreciated it as much as he did. Jealousy nudged him ever closer to the edge, his hips pounding, dick aching. But he couldn't beat her to the punch, not knowing that Bern had gotten her off. No fucking way.

"And how good he looked when he came," she added. "When he shot inside me."

"Come for me," he ordered.

"Mike."

He'd slipped them from their games without even realizing it, but it was exactly where he wanted to be.

"Jesus, Sam." If it weren't for her busy hand, he'd have dropped to his elbows, slid his forearms under her back and held her tight as he hammered himself home. She'd cradle his head as she always did, and there'd be nothing left of the world except the two of them, Mike and Sam. Mike and the most wonderful woman he'd ever met.

"Come for me, baby. Please."

The hand gripping his shoulder was hot and damp, the other racing between their bodies, between her legs. He gave her his cock the way she liked best, fast and hard and controlled, though the friction was dangerous. He felt his own orgasm coming, already in motion and impossible to stop, a train bearing down with its whistle shrieking. Then he felt it—the tug of her body around him, the subtle squeeze of her climax. The second her fingers left her clit, he shoved his arms beneath her back and chased his own release—bolted down the track and let the momentum demolish him.

"Sam. Fuck."

Pleasure had never come so near to pain—a searing, screaming rush that swallowed him whole, a rush so intense it left no room for relief, only obliteration.

Mike came back to reality blinking, panting, reeling, as though from a punch.

There was Sam, beneath him, her hands grazing his back. There was her smile, and all around and against him, her warmth. He buried his face against her neck, smelled her skin, tasted it on his lips between gasping breaths.

He felt her tremble, followed by a tiny laugh.

Unsteadily, he pushed up to his elbows to stare into her eyes. "Yeah?"

She nodded. "You're so sexy."

He laughed himself, and flopped to his side. Here they were in their room, though it would never be quite the same, would it? Strange new memories had taken root, and they'd have to either choose to tend and harvest them, or else tread amid the dead husks of regret. But what was there to regret, if this kink really could serve the both of them? It had grown on Sam, he knew that much. And now that she really was getting off with another man, not merely pretending she had . . .

He rolled onto his hip and kissed her cheek, her shoulder, her arm.

She stroked his hair. "Happy?"

"Incapacitated."

"That'll do."

He nestled his chin on her shoulder and studied her face. "Are *you* happy?"

She nodded against the pillow. "Did I earn my Wife of the Year trophy tonight?"

"Tell me it wasn't that much of a hardship."

"Yes, such a trial. Two guys, two orgasms . . . I've got it so bad."

"*And* I do dishes and laundry," he said.

"Yes, you're a very complex man."

"A man with a complex, you mean."

She smiled, tracing his ear with her thumb. "Being kinky isn't a mental illness, you know. If anything it's a superpower."

"And you're definitely happy we went through with it?"

"Very. Are you?"

"Yeah." He swallowed. "Yeah, I think so."

She frowned.

"No—I mean, I don't regret anything. It's just hard to say it makes me *happy*, since . . . you know."

"Since it's the ugly feelings that get you off?"

"Yeah. Happy's like . . . contentment. Security. I can either choose happiness or being out-of-my-mind horny, where this thing's concerned."

"Are you satisfied, then?"

"Yes." He could say that with certainty. He was deeply, utterly satisfied. And in the dark little cracks where the happiness couldn't shine, those were the shadows he'd dig around in, stoking the strange flames that flickered in his body and brain.

"Good," Sam said with a lazy sigh. "That's all I wanted to know."

"I wonder what he thinks of us."

She laughed. "From what I've gleaned, he thinks we're like some crazy old rich person who keeps throwing fistfuls of money at him. He doesn't get it, but he's not complaining. I suspect he's perfectly happy playing tourist."

"Think we'll do this again?" he asked.

"That's all up to you."

"Actually, it's all up to you."

"I think we'll have to disagree on that one. But if you want this again and he's game, I'm honored to oblige." She leaned in and kissed his forehead. "It's awfully fun. Why shouldn't we keep doing it until it's not fun anymore? I mean, it might take ages to find another guy I—or we—have the right chemistry with."

"True." Goddamn, she spoiled him.

"And if the chemistry keeps working for all of us . . ."

"There's lots of other things we could do."

She nodded. "Ditch the condoms. Maybe tape it."

"Yeah."

Infinite other "maybe" scenarios. Maybe a real three-way, with Mike allowed to enjoy her while she sucked Bern's cock. So many options. So many that he better not start drafting his wish list and jacking up his hopes. Plus, something just as good was right here in his arms—his wife, all to himself.

He squeezed her tightly, sad their time off was coming to a close. Though luckily he'd snapped a thousand mental photos, each a perfect postcard of their vacation.

The thought put him to sleep smiling.

CHAPTER TWELVE

With everyone's work schedules back in full swing and no meet-ups possible for two weeks, creativity was required to keep the three-way embers stoked and glowing. So with Sam's permission—and by proxy, Mike's—Bern took to texting her. Quick, incendiary missives, typically between dinner and bedtime. Some that welcomed her reply, and some merely to keep her edgy for him, she bet.

Can't stop thinking about you. Ask me over.

That had been the first one. Mike had been lying next to her in bed. She'd answered, He's home. Wish I could. Same as the next evening—

Tonight?

No, not tonight. Soon, baby. It's killing me, too.

And the night after that—

Is he home? I'm dying for you.

Mike *had* been home, of course, lying right next to her as usual. The issue at the moment was actually that Bern was going away—leaving for a big construction job in the middle of the state for a week—otherwise he'd surely be fucking her brains out that coming weekend while Mike watched. As soon as he returned, Sam's period was due to arrive, so sadly nothing epic was happening until the weekend. They'd arranged the next time, though, Sam and Bern, in a text exchange full of real, giddy urgency, instead of pantomime conspiracy.

In all seriousness, he'd texted, when can we get together again? I'm not dying but I AM eager :-)

She'd replied with a smile on her face. Us, too. And they picked a date, one that no one was all that pleased with.

Man, that sounds like forever from now, she'd told him.

Christmas wouldn't be as special if it happened every week, he'd written back.

You don't actually believe that, do you?

Not for a minute. I could fuck you every night and it wouldn't be enough.

She'd grinned. Filthy man.

Sam marked their upcoming rendezvous on the calendar on the fridge with the loaded code name *Girls' Night*, and she bet Mike got hard every time he glanced at that square. These scandalous texts were mere treats to tide them all over.

Mike was in on the texts, of course—in fact, he probably enjoyed them the most of everyone. When he asked who was messaging Sam, she'd lie, then find some reason to leave the bed and give him a chance to grab her phone, to "catch" her.

Is he home? Bern had asked, that one night. I'm dying for you.

He is, she'd replied, pulse quickening. Are you hard?

You have no idea. Want to see?

Show me.

Five minutes later, he'd sent the first photo—so much more erotic than Sam ever would have guessed. Sexting had always struck her as tacky before, so often manifesting as harassment, or the jurisdiction of impulsive kids. But when Bern sent her a photo of his hand wrapped around his cock, other thumb tucked under the waistband of his shorts, holding them down . . . her first reaction had been a shocked suck of breath, chased by a wave of arousal. Her gaze had jumped between his ready cock and that gruff fist, and she couldn't say which was hotter. Her next reaction had been to wonder how he'd taken the thing, with both hands occupied.

Don't wonder how, just be glad he did.

A new text had pinged a moment later, drawing a sigh from Mike—feigned annoyance. Sam knew that sigh for what it was—impatience. And excitement.

"Sorry. It's Michelle. She's chatty."

I should be inside you, she read.

She typed back, How?

In your pussy. Deep.

Yes, you should be. But what will you do instead?

Stroke myself. Tell me how.

She bit her lip and wrote, Slow and tight.

She'd left the covers to brush her teeth, and been all but jumped by Mike when she came back to bed. He'd given it to her rough and fast and wordless, a smile hiding just behind his lips.

And so it had gone, all through the time while Bern was away.

He was due back in Pittsburgh tonight, and had mentioned he wasn't getting home until late, so Sam wasn't holding her breath on getting another digital gift. They'd be seeing him on Saturday night. She could wait four more days, as much as she'd come to savor those little teasing tastes of him. To say nothing of the resulting trouncing from Mike.

Though considering whom she was dealing with, she ought to have known better.

Ping.

She grabbed her phone from the bedside table just as she was undressing, Mike's curious—and warming—attention not lost on her.

Hey beautiful.

Hey yourself. Uncanny timing—I was just getting undressed. Did the Wang Signal go off?

Undressed? You driving over here naked? That's awful bold.

She smiled.

Cute. It's late and he's here. Afraid you'll have to take care of yourself.

Afraid so. Tell me how, he wrote, the words now a familiar refrain.

Any way you want . . . as long as you tape it for me.

No reply came, and though Sam got under the covers wearing a coy little half smile, her nerves hummed. That was a loaded challenge she'd just laid at his feet, and she was as jittery as she was excited to find out if he ran with it.

"Michelle again?" Mike asked.

"Yeah." She kept her voice airy—distracted and distant.

"Everything okay?"

"Mm-hmm . . ."

"Okay."

Sam grabbed her book and moved her eyes across the same page a hundred times, taking nothing in.

Half an hour later, a chime shot her pulse into overdrive.

Check your e-mail.

The video was in her in-box, the attachment labeled, *What You Reduce Me To.*

She swallowed, face hot. Her phone was on mute, and she hit PLAY with her heart thumping in her throat. On the little screen, Bern's body loomed large, his skin lit brightly against a dark room. He must have used his computer, and she squinted into the shadows, curious what his home looked like. All she could really make out were dark covers and light pillowcases, and of course Bern, kneeling wide before the camera, on his bed. Her belly clenched and heated, and her cheeks burned to be watching this, lying just a couple of feet from her husband. She hit PAUSE and leaned over to find her earbuds from the side table drawer.

"What are you doing?" Mike asked.

"Just a thing I want to watch. I won't make you listen while you're trying to read."

"I don't care. What kind of thing?"

"A *Daily Show* segment."

"Oh, I'll watch with you."

She ignored him, plugging in the cord, angling her screen away from him with a very real bolt of guilt, and hit PLAY.

She turned up the volume, and at first there was no sound, not aside from the faintest hush of Bern's breathing. He was shirtless, wearing either workout pants or drawstring pajama bottoms. With both hands he touched his chest, abs, hips, thighs, before bringing them back up to trace the shape of his erection behind the fabric. Sam swallowed. If this had been some anonymous, hot guy on the Internet, she doubted she'd have registered more than a passing, reflexive thrill. But he'd taped this for *her*. And there was no doubt in her mind, this man was hard from thinking of her, excited to perform for her.

He eased his bottoms down, exposing himself. For nearly a minute he taunted them both, grazing his length with measuring fingertips before fisting it. She watched his face, and his gaze as it moved between his hand and the lens, his stare hot and edgy, aimed right at her. He had to be out of his mind with excitement, knowing he'd be seen doing this.

He stroked himself, slowly, then quicker, grip looking tight, biceps clenched. Breathing turned to panting, turned to moans; his voice roused her as much as his body. He murmured things, things she could only catch snatches of, hot little tastes like, "Yeah," and "Watch me," and "You missing this?" His free hand was restless, cupping his balls, rubbing his belly, circling his chest. As he got closer, it settled in the crease of his thigh and hip, seeming to press there, rubbing with distracted, thoughtless motions. Sam's mouth was dry, breath short. Arousal was humming hot and hungry between her legs.

"Fuck." On-screen, his eyes shut, lips a tense O. "Yeah. Fuck."

And he came—came for her, it felt, right on his clenched belly, shaking fingers making a mess of him.

Despite everything he'd just shown her, despite how personal, how intimate it felt . . . watching his face as he came down from the insanity of the lust felt twice as raw. He tugged his bottoms up to cover his cock, then leaned to the side to grab a hand towel. He smiled at the camera, chest and stomach still rising and falling fast as he wiped his skin clean. "Hope you enjoyed that little show. Hope you can't get to sleep now, wishing you were over here with me, instead of stuck there with him. I hope—" The distant barking of a dog cut him off, and he doubled over for a moment, abs hitching with a silent chuckle as he straightened. Another bark, and he turned to laugh-shout, "Molly. Shut it." Then to the camera, "Anyhow, that's what you're missing, Samira. Call me when he's gone some night, so you can get me there yourself, okay? Sweet dreams." And that handsome face went blurry and bright, leaning in close to the glowing computer, killing the camera.

Sam's heart was pounding, but only half from the private show. If she could only watch five seconds of that video ever again, it would've been his smile, and the way his muscles had tensed from laughing when he'd scolded his dog. And that realization had her hands trembling, as she admitted to herself, she had a crush on him.

Duh. But the clarity of the thought was so sharp and so sudden, it stung. She should be hot for him, that was fine. If she could come from his touch—his mouth or hands or cock—all the better. But a crush? Why did that scare her so much?

Because Mike doesn't get hard imagining my crush.

No, Mike didn't fixate on soft things—first kisses, private and tender touches, the subtle trappings of romantic interest. For that matter, neither did Bern, she assumed. She was feeling something that belonged only to her, with no place in their games. She'd imagined having sex with any number of men she'd never, ever touch—strangers and celebrities and wholly fictional men—in the five years she'd been with Mike.

But I've not had a crush on a one of them. Nothing this warm and soft and . . .

Stop it.

When she took the earbuds out, Mike asked, "You okay?"

"Oh yeah. Just . . ." She made a frazzled noise, feeling every measure of it. "I think I'll take a bath."

"It's after ten," he said, watching her kick away the covers.

"I know, but I'm all wired." Let him think it was a ploy, let him think she was pretending to sneak away, to touch herself under the guise of the bath. In reality, she *was* wired. *Only because no one's ever sent me homemade porn before.* Not from Bern's smile. Not from hearing him say her name . . .

And not just *Sam*, either. *Samira.* Mike used her full name when he was worried about her; to check that she was okay. Bern wielded it in a far more mischievous way.

The hot water dissolved the bulk of her worries, leaving a simmering buzz of arousal. By the time the heat waned, she knew full well that Mike would have watched those same few minutes' debauchery she had, and she was eager for the sex that awaited her. He'd be thinking of the things that excited him—the threat of the man his wife lusted for. Of that man's size, his confidence, his words. He wouldn't dwell for a moment on his smile or laugh, or the silliness of him shushing his dog. He'd fixate on the blunt, aggressive aspects, the dynamics that vibrated on his male wavelength. Those subtler seductions wouldn't even register.

And they shouldn't. And they *wouldn't*, not outside of those few minutes' panic. It was late, and Sam was overthinking her reaction. And policing herself for something entirely natural. *I mean, God forbid I have a crush on the man I'm getting off with.*

Mike had changed since their games had become reality, though not in any of the ways she'd imagined or feared. She'd worried he might grow jealous or possessive in a capacity that felt more angry than lustful. Or that he'd become insecure in everyday life, not merely while he was mired in his role, or turn genuinely distrustful of her. Or hateful toward Bern. But she'd been wrong.

Mike was changing in a dozen soft, surprising ways. He'd never been stingy with affection, but now she caught him touching her fondly at odd, sweet moments. He smiled at her more, the gesture sometimes sheepish, sometimes hungry, but always warm and conspiring. Gratitude suffused him, and she felt it in his touch and saw it in his eyes, tasted it in the needy, eager way he kissed her.

While they'd never stagnated or even cooled much toward each other, she hadn't felt this . . . this *infatuation* humming from him since they'd first fallen in love. She hummed for him as well, as surely as she hummed for Bern. It brought to mind a term she'd come across when looking into the whole cuckolding thing to begin with, one used in the polyamory community. *New relationship energy.* That honeymoon glow you could only get from a new lover, or in Mike's case, from a wife he was suddenly viewing through a mind-bending new lens. Through a kaleidoscope, through a chemical high.

She stood from the bath and toweled off, feeling light and loose. Mike would be in bed, hard as hell and wound so tight it had to hurt. Bern was a few miles away, probably sleeping soundly, she thought, smiling as she dressed.

She shut off the light and fan and padded into the bedroom, finding Mike reading. Or pretending to read.

"Good bath?"

"Very nice."

He watched her climb into bed, his gaze surprisingly mild. Had he not taken the hint? She'd left that video open on her phone just for him.

"Three more workdays," she said, switching off her lamp. Three more workdays and it was the weekend, sure. But three more workdays and their next encounter with Bern was going down. *Christmas countdown*, she thought, recalling his analogy.

"Three more," Mike agreed, turning onto his side to stroke her bare arm.

She smiled at him. "You feeling amorous, Mr. Heyer?" She was on her period, but that never stopped them.

Gaze on his grazing fingers, he said, "I watched it."

"Oh?"

Were they playing? She didn't think so. If they'd been playing, Mike would be acting hurt. She felt her stomach sour, dread coiling inside her.

He met her eyes. "Did it turn you on?"

Truth only. "Yeah. It did."

"And that's what he wants most. Somebody watching."

She nodded, feeling cold. Scared.

"Let's get a camera," Mike said.

Like a knot tugged free, Sam's entire body fell slack from relief. "A video camera?"

"If you're comfortable with it."

"It's sooner than we'd planned to go there—only our fourth date, or whatever you could call it . . . but I think I'm ready, yeah." Her only real misgivings about taping the sex were those of vanity—she was far more nervous about seeing her naked body on-screen than she was about the video getting out. Mike would be careful, and Bern got off on being watched, so there was more in it for him if they kept it for themselves.

"You *think* you're ready?" Mike prompted.

"I am." She smiled. "A little shy about seeing my naked ass on camera, that's all. But that, in exchange for simultaneously fulfilling two gorgeous men's greatest fantasies?"

"Think about it for a couple of days. If you still feel okay, maybe we'll do a little shopping on Saturday morning."

And maybe she'd get to send Bern a text to the tune of, *You must have been a good boy—looks like Santa brought you a camera.* Man, would that ever get him off. Then she pictured the theoretical video, of Bern's gaze burning into the lens, his performance as much for their eyes as it would be for Sam's body.

"I already know my answer," Sam announced.

"Yeah?"

"Yeah. Don't forget we'll need a tripod."

CHAPTER THIRTEEN

Samira squinted as the sun dropped low, zapping her through the kitchen window. She checked the clock. Twenty minutes to eight—*shit.* She abandoned the remaining dinner dishes in the sink and jogged down the hall and upstairs, through the bedroom and into the bath. Mike was brushing his teeth, and she elbowed him aside.

"Hang on, hang on." He leaned over to spit and rinsed his brush. "Okay, all yours. Jesus, you're wound up." He said it lovingly and tousled the hair she'd spent twenty minutes styling.

"It's my cinematic debut," she said, smoothing what he'd mussed. She pulled her makeup bag over and got to work.

"Anything else that needs doing before showtime?"

"Just the last of the dishes."

"On it."

He left her alone with her performance anxiety.

She shouldn't be this nervous. It was only Bern. Well, not *only* Bern, not like it was *only* stay-in-with-a-movie-and-pizza date night or something like that. But she knew him, in a way. In a few very, very intimate ways, and she trusted their dynamic.

Only tonight was different. She'd texted him from the car as she and Mike had pulled out of the Best Buy lot.

Just bought a little surprise for tonight.

Sam had waited a patient forty-five minutes while Mike had deliberated the choices, and she'd eyed each one like it was the fourth witness they were going to invite into their scandal.

Bern's reply had come just after they'd crossed the bridge. Oh yeah? Tell me more.

Well, it's two parts, really. And one of them is a tripod.

She'd held her breath, butterflies swirling. He hadn't replied until after they arrived home and Mike had been opening the camera's box.

Ping.

Sorry. Head exploded.

She'd laughed.

"That him?"

"Yeah. I think we just broke him."

Mike's smile had been grim, but not mean. "Long as he appreciates how good he's got it."

"He does."

And even after two encounters—and two weeks of their X-rated pen pal arrangement—the man's imminent arrival still gave Sam schoolgirl jitters. He was sex and mischief all rolled into one tall, muscular package. She trusted him with a very big secret, one that could hurt her and Mike much worse than him, should it get out. It gave him actual power. And she liked it.

She finished her makeup, head filling up with ideas about what the camera might catch tonight. She eyed it as she walked through the bedroom, making a mental note to not leave it perched on the tripod like that when the cleaning lady was due to come. *Like she hasn't seen weirder shit. Well, maybe not weirder than the shit she might discover if she actually watched the video.*

Everything felt different this evening, the stakes higher. There was the camera, but there was *more*. She could sense it.

All this time, Sam had taken her own pleasure from fulfilling two men's wishes, but she was growing curious about things that neither of them had yet owned. It felt as though it was only a matter of time before Mike would take a more active role—if nothing else, masturbating while he watched her and Bern together. Given the chance, maybe their arrangement might evolve into an actual three-way, and maybe Mike would let Bern see exactly how blurry the edges of his kink were, its humiliation aspects drawing the two men closer. Would Bern want to see what Sam had—Mike lapping away what he'd left on her skin? Could he take his role that far, or were there limits to his showmanship?

She couldn't guess, but boundaries were forming, ripe for fucking with. She'd fantasized about the next obvious step, about Bern looking Mike right in the eye and saying, "Your wife looks good getting fucked by a real man, doesn't she?" In her mind, Mike didn't reply, and Bern went on. "I can't help but feel bad she's cheating on you with me . . . Go ahead and rub one out. Watching us is probably hotter than anything you've managed with her."

She wouldn't be surprised if Bern took them there. He was quickly becoming the conductor in these encounters, and she bet he'd only grow bolder with time. He'd settled capably into his role as wife-defiling alpha male, and seemed poised to take a more active approach to the defiling of Mike—in orders and cruel words, if not physical contact.

She hoped he would. She wanted Mike drawn into the encounters as a whole body, not just a set of eyes. Tonight he might hold the camera. Soon, perhaps, he'd let Bern see how far his kink drew him into its shadows, let him watch that first step of the reclaiming, as he cleaned away the offense. And she hoped they'd take it even further, in time. She wanted to watch those two strong bodies, so adept at pleasing her, inching closer and closer, the darker these games grew. Mike had already tasted Bern on her skin. Would he taste the man himself? Would Bern let him—

The doorbell rang, putting an end to her theorizing and announcing the handing over of supremacy from one man to another. She pecked Mike on the cheek as they passed on the stairs—her heading for the front, him to his office, where he'd hide until he was ready to walk in on them.

She waited until he was out of sight, then opened the door.

Christ, this man floored her. That familiar, sly smile had her heart thumping, skin heating. Funny how having an infatuation with one man didn't diminish her love and attraction for another. Sam was fast becoming a monogamist's nightmare.

"Hey." Bern shut the door behind him and leaned in to kiss her cheek.

She accepted it with a squeeze of his shoulder. "Hey yourself. Good to see you. In person, that is."

He gave her a thorough looking-over. "Not half as good as seeing you."

"Wine?" she asked, leading him to the kitchen.

"If you're having some."

"I am."

Bern watched as she opened the bottle. "I make you nervous, still?"

"Barely at all," she said, smiling. In fact, this was her first drink of the night, a testament to her growing comfort. "And only nervous in good ways." She poured two measures of red and they toasted.

"I could always take or leave wine before I met you," he said, studying his glass. "Now I catch myself craving it."

She grinned. "That's because it tastes like foreplay."

He laughed. As his smile faded, his eyes narrowed with a thought. "So I've been here twice now. And you keep asking me back."

Sam spoke quietly, in case Mike was in the mood to keep the game's infrastructure hidden. "We have indeed."

"So is what I've been doing working for you? Both of you? Need me to be more of a dick, less of a dick, anything like that?"

"I think you've been a perfect dick, so far. And I hope you'll be able to keep it up when he joins us."

"That happening tonight?"

"I think so, yeah."

"And I should just keep up the current dick levels?"

She laughed. "Or maybe even ramp it up further, if you could. I mean, be how you have been toward me, but you really can't be too cocky and mean toward him, I don't think."

"He really likes that, huh?"

She grinned. "Oh yeah, he loves it."

The pensiveness left his face and he returned her smile. "Good. And you're fine with it?"

"Definitely. We invited you over to be a show-off and an asshole, so, by all means." She studied him with her eyes narrowed, full to the brim with mischief.

"Yeah?"

"Lights, camera, action, tonight."

She watched Bern's expression change. He took another sip, eyes unfocused.

Their arrangement was like a big game of kinky hot potato, power getting passed among the three of them. Right now it was hers, and it felt good, like slipping into a killer dress. She'd never felt this sexy before in her life. And though she'd never have the body of a twenty-something again, at thirty-six she had two men panting at her feet and the experience to know what to do with them.

"Can't wait," he said softly. "So you guys are comfortable with that?"

She nodded. "We'll be keeping the tape. Or the file or whatever. No offense, we do trust you, but with us being married, and Mike's job, we'd be way more fucked than you if it wound up on the Internet."

"No, that's fine. Of course." He took another sip, nodding thoughtfully. "Plus, you know me—"

Yes, she supposed she did.

"I'd get way more out of you keeping it," Bern said. "Out of you guys watching it. Just text me when you do, maybe."

"Easy." She clinked her glass against his, feeling smug and happy as a well-fed cat. "That's why this is all such a perfect arrangement."

An arrangement, yes. And arrangements ended, but when?

Not soon, Sam hoped, though they couldn't go on forever. Bern was a good guy and an honest one, she believed, and she imagined that if he started dating someone else, he'd have the courtesy to break things off with her and Mike. So they'd lose him someday, and probably because *he* chose to end things. It gave her a pang, sharp with sadness and, yes, jealousy. Bit ironic, that. But she couldn't imagine finding another man who fit the bill like Bern did, and knowing it couldn't last was like knowing summer vacation would end with the start of school—an inevitability to be dreaded for the fun it ruined.

Caught up in the thought, she drained her glass more quickly than she'd intended. Such worries had no place in her head tonight, though. Why spend every decadent bite of a slice of cheesecake worrying about one's hips?

"You seem a little . . ." Bern trailed off, but his expression said he sensed her tension as plainly as he could taste the wine.

Her lips were ready to spew forth her insecurities, but she held them back. *He's your lover and your guest, not your husband. Not even your boyfriend. Zip it, and remember who this man is to you.*

"You said you weren't nervous," he teased.

"I'm not. Just wound up, what with all the new stuff we get to do tonight."

His expression brightened, only to darken as he smiled. He took a step closer, leaning on the counter and staring down at her, looking tall and hungry and devious. She thought he was going to have them toast yet again, but he merely brought the back of his hand to hers, rubbing their knuckles together. A funny bit of contact, familiar and affectionate. Sam swallowed a much-needed breath while Bern finished his wine.

When he spoke, it was scarcely more than a whisper, hot words falling from his tongue to heat her skin. "I wanted to ask you about something."

"Anything."

"When I leave here . . . like, every time I've ever left after we hang out . . ."

"Mm-hmm."

"I'm already hard again before I'm halfway home."

Oh, she liked where this was going. "Okay."

"I'm just saying, if you guys ever wanted round two, all you have to do is ask."

"That's very impressive."

"You deserve as much credit for it as me," he said. "I've been a sort of one-and-done kind of guy, since I hit my thirties. Until you."

She glowed like a hearth. "It'd be a shame to waste it, then."

"But I wanted to ask, in case, I dunno . . . I'd be lingering too long."

"I'd be more worried that *you'd* be weirded out after you came. You know, like sobered up and maybe unnerved by my husband being there."

"Hadn't given it a second thought." He smiled again, the gesture different from any Sam had seen him wear before. Not shy—sheepish maybe, happy-guilty. "I like that he's there," he added.

"Yeah?"

"I don't think I'll ever understand what he gets out of me being with you, but I get an audience, you know? It's like, I get your body, and let's be honest, we're pretty good at fucking each other."

She blushed. "Hear, hear."

"But him being there . . . I dunno. It takes everything and makes it five times hotter. No offense."

"No, not at all. That's a lot like what he said to me, after the first night you and I messed around. Like the fantasy had always gotten him hot, but seeing us actually *together*, it was like cranking the volume way up."

He leaned in close, making Sam feel pleasantly small. "You want to get things started, maybe?"

She rubbed his sides then took a step back, nodding, tugging at the hem of his shirt to tell him to follow. She led him down the hall and upstairs. By the time they reached the bedroom threshold, the lead had changed, Bern now guiding her backward by the shoulders, plopping her onto the mattress with a gentle push. His attention flashed to the side, just for a moment—to the camera on its stand. Sam watched his throat work as he swallowed, and smiled to herself.

"Would you mind if I taped us?" she asked him coyly, as though she couldn't guess. "Give me something to remember you by, the next time your job steals you away."

"He could find it," Bern warned, but his real reaction was evident in his parted, flushed lips, his slitted eyes.

"A chance I'm willing to take."

"For you," Bern said, stroking her cheek with his thumb, "anything."

"Good."

He left her to investigate the camera, seeming to get the hang of it easily. He crouched to check the frame, and Sam saw the little red light blinking. *Showtime.* She shot the lens a smile, then turned her attention to Bern, who came to stand between her legs once more. He loomed, broad hand brushing over the front of his jeans. "When's he back?"

"Not for an hour, at least." Right as she said it she heard that telltale creak, that old floorboard announcing Mike's arrival at the threshold.

"He caught us once." Bern's gaze followed her hands as she stroked his thighs. "Twice would just be cruel."

"Serves him right, him seeing what he's been denying me. I ought to make him watch the tape—he could use the pointers."

Bern smiled, looking amused by her cruelty. He cast the camera a moment's hot stare. "We should at least give him a good show, then."

CHAPTER FOURTEEN

Mike was burning alive, every heartbeat pumping lava. He braced his shoulder against the door frame, so overheated his muscles felt weak and his mind foggy.

Sam and Bern were kissing on the bed—that man's strong body braced atop her soft one, his hips moving with subtle strokes and her hands exploring him in return.

Mike knew those hands, and the admiring way they moved over Bern's back and arms. *She's turned on.* She wanted this man, as much as she wanted Mike.

Outside this space, Mike trusted that his primacy was secure.

But inside this space . . .

He sank into his role, into his fantasy. Neck-deep into the humiliation and pain of discovering he was being outmanned, behind his back. And in his bed.

"Lemme see you," Bern told Sam as he got to his knees between her legs. She peeled her shirt away while Bern stripped her skirt. The way he drew her legs up to get the thing off . . . the way he held them once the fabric had fluttered to the floor, with her ankles resting on one of his shoulders, stroking her thigh with a slow hand . . .

Mike's own hand drifted. His palm was damp, catching on the cotton of his T-shirt as he touched his chest, his belly, then settled it over the front of his jeans. Even the muted touch needed to adjust his erection made him suck a breath; he was so hard and needy he felt faint.

Taste her, he wanted to say. He'd felt this urge every time the man had come over—the desire to dictate. To be a director in these matters, as much as the victim. That was an aspect of his kink he'd never registered before. But it made sense. For years he'd been fantasizing about being cheated on, and it was his imagination, after all, that controlled the other man's actions. But Bern was real, and once the games were under way, he took his cues from his own cock. The lack of control only buried Mike deeper in that helpless sensation he craved.

Bern watched as Sam got her bra off, caressing the legs he held to his chest. He stripped her panties next, spreading her wide as he lowered himself, fully clothed, against her. Sam gasped beneath him. She'd be feeling his fly against her lips, his belt buckle at her mound. Bern didn't kiss her, but locked those powerful arms beside her ribs, staring her down as his hips and ass moved in slow, controlled waves, stroking his excitement against hers.

Mike palmed his cock, ran his fingertips along his zipper. He wanted air on his baking skin; air and friction. His mouth was dry, lips nearly chapped. He licked them, and again he thought it—*Taste her.* He wanted his wife's fingers in this man's dark hair, his head between her legs. Wanted all that, and Sam's eye contact as it happened.

Before him, Sam was tugging at Bern's shirt, her feet curled and rubbing at the backs of his thighs.

Impatience tinged her voice. "I need to see you. Take your clothes off."

"Don't you like this?" Bern exaggerated his thrusts, and Mike was pretty sure he was smiling.

"You know I do. But I want to watch you." She stroked his chest, then his arms. "You're so fucking hot. Let me see you."

He submitted, tugging his shirt up and away. Sam's hands were greedy as the motions resumed, taking in every square inch of his flexing back. She held his head, jacking Mike's pulse. *Taste her.*

Instead, Bern gathered her in his arms, drawing her up with him. He knelt and Sam wrapped her legs around his waist, her arms around his shoulders. Face-to-face, chest to chest. He held her ass, his fingers pressing into the ripe flesh there. His thrusts mirrored the motions he coaxed from her, and Mike wanted Bern's clothes gone as badly as Sam must—wanted him naked and the two of them fucking. He wanted to see it all, every explicit detail. Every inch of the cock that had him outmanned, every muscle in the body his wife craved more than his. He wanted to memorize the effortless way this strong man held and handled his woman, and Sam's moans as that cock claimed her.

"I want you," she said. "I *need* you."

"Tell me."

"Your cock. Now. Please."

"Worried he'll come home?"

"I don't even fucking care," she seethed, nails racking Bern's back. "Let him see. I just need you inside me. Now."

"You wet for me?"

Mike shivered. How many times he'd said those same four words to Sam, he couldn't possibly count.

"You know I am."

"Better check for myself."

Taste her. Mike fisted his hand at his side, no longer trusting his own self-control.

Bern lowered her to the covers, and their eyes locked as he opened his belt buckle and lowered his zipper. He grabbed her hand, pressing it to the cock now framed by his spread fly, hidden by his shorts. Sam's mouth was open, and her lids took on that heavy look that Mike knew only too well. If he were closer he'd hear her panting, faint and hungry, as Bern worked her hand up and down his erection.

"Feel that?" he murmured.

"Yeah."

"Good. You think about that while I'm eating your pussy."

Mike didn't see Sam's reaction—his own eyes shut reflexively in that instant, a wave of excitement taking his breath away.

When he opened them, Bern was pushing his jeans and shorts down. He stepped out of them, stripped his socks, then kicked his clothes aside and dropped to his knees.

He grasped Sam by her thighs, sliding her to the edge of the mattress. He dove in as though starving, drawing a noise of surprise from her. Just as Mike had wanted, she held his head, slender fingers threaded through black hair.

"Fuck, you're good."

He was different as well, more vigorous and aggressive than the last time Mike had watched him do this. His entire body was in the act—back and sides flexing, hips pumping. And he sounded wild, the motions punctuated by a grunt now and then. Sam's legs were spread wide, heels digging into his back. Mike ached to be closer, to see it all.

"I need you," Sam said, sitting up, running her fingers roughly through Bern's hair. "Now. Please."

He looked from his task, gaze on Sam's as his tongue delivered one, two, three final laps. "Do you, then?"

"Yes, now."

One hand went to his cock, his triceps flexing as he stroked. He was hard and ready as he stood. "Got what you need?"

Sam moved up the bed to get the condom in place. It was easy enough to edit it out of the fantasy, but Mike selfishly hoped they might eventually find occasion to forego them completely.

Bern moved to kneel on the bed, still stroking himself as Sam got ready. Mike watched him with the strangest mix of lust and revulsion, in unsettled awe of this physical manifestation of his own most potent wants. This man made his deepest sexual wishes come true, as surely as Sam did. A man he hated, yet by proxy desired. Nearly his lover, in a way, but his enemy in another.

With Sam on her back, Bern took an ankle in each hand, easing her open, feasting his eyes. "Goddamn, you look good. You ready for me?"

"More than ready."

He braced his hands, brought his hips to Sam's, and she guided him home.

"Fuck." He slouched from the sensation, shoulder blades jutting.

Sam tugged at his ass. "More. Please."

"You feel so fucking amazing." He eased back, then drove a little farther. "God yeah. Tell me how."

"Deeper. Slow to start."

Bern gave that, and Mike felt sweat slicking his own back.

"Faster," Sam directed, touching Bern's face. There was wonder in her expression, a look Mike had basked in a hundred times or more. It burned him in too many ways to see it now.

Bern's shaft was dark and slick, now owning Sam in long, relentless strokes. Mike wanted to mimic those motions with his hand on his cock . . . fill his fist with his own aching flesh, fill his eyes with the spectacle of their bodies.

Their grunting voices mingled, as hot as any of the physical action. Mike drank in the scene, owning his part. He'd come home early from work to find the woman he loved getting pounded by a hung, handsome stranger. Well, not a stranger, no—he'd caught them before, after all. In the bar, and right here in his bed. This was no one-off threat anymore; this was his *rival*, and Mike couldn't measure up, not in any way. He'd gotten a ring on Sam's finger, that was all. A token, paled by the pleasure and excitement this intruder was bringing.

The man Mike was playing tonight, how would he frame this? How would he take this pain and manifest a segue . . . ?

Maybe this is for the best. If I let her get her needs met with him, she might be satisfied enough to stay with me.

He cleared his throat, drawing two pairs of eyes to the threshold.

Sam looked away. "Shit."

Bern slowed, then stilled, buried deep. His chest rose and fell with labored breaths, and his head dropped back, a cocky gesture packed with contempt. "Well, goddamn, look who it is. Guess we meet again."

"Get off my wife."

Bern smiled, and Sam's fingers gripped him hard by the hips. She said, "Don't deny me this, Mike. I deserve pleasure."

"And this asshole gives you that?"

Her hands kneaded the enemy's body, admiring the muscles of his hips and ass. "He does."

"And I don't?"

She held his stare, cold. "You don't really want me to answer that, Mike."

Bern slid out, then back in, slow. "I think our fun's over," he told Sam.

She squeezed his arms. "Don't you dare." She kept speaking to Bern but looked to Mike. "Keep going. He should see what he drives me to. What I need, what he can't give me."

"This can't keep happening, Sam—"

"Don't deny me this," she said again. "I need this. I need *him*."

After a pause, Mike said, "Never again."

Catching the permissive tilt to his voice, Sam smiled. "Just this one last time." Her legs hugged Bern's waist, urging him. With a final glance at Mike, his thrusts resumed.

"You can watch again, if you want." Sam's gaze flicked to the chair they'd left there, for exactly this purpose. Mike feigned uncertainty for a beat, then walked to it with an air of resignation, though inside, he was about to catch fire.

"The tripod seems a little unnecessary all of a sudden," Bern said to Sam, then met Mike's eyes squarely. "Since you're here, grab that camera. Get a nice shot lined up. Maybe I'll watch it later, so I can see what it looks like from your perspective—me fucking your wife."

Mike rose to get the camera, tripod and all, arranging it between his knees with shaking hands. He'd have held it as ordered, except he didn't want a second of this show flattened, reduced to two dimensions through the viewfinder. If this scene were an oil painting, he needed to see the real thing, not the print.

"Let's give him a good view," Bern said to Sam, pulling out. He moved to sit at the edge of the bed, legs spread, erection looking obscene, gleaming from the condom's lubricant—from Sam, his imagination supplied. "On my lap." Sam came around to straddle his thighs. She was no wisp of a woman, but Bern clasped her hips and eased her down onto his cock like she weighed nothing. She sucked a breath, then turned to meet Mike's gaze over her shoulder.

"Good?" Bern asked her.

Her dark eyes shut and a smug smile curled her lips. "You have no idea."

And they had no idea what a spectacular view Mike had—explicit, as Sam rose up and dropped back down in slow strokes, aided by Bern's hands.

"Yeah. Ride that cock."

"You're so fucking big, baby."

Mike flushed—in his cheeks and between his legs. *Keep telling him that.*

"Want it a little faster?" Bern asked.

"Yeah."

Of Mike he demanded, "You getting all this?"

A rhetorical question. Mike swallowed, hands antsy atop his thighs. Christ, he needed to touch himself. He'd jumped off a lot of diving boards recently in the name of his kink, but each new one still demanded a show of bravery, a leap of faith. And sometimes, a nudge from Sam. He settled a palm over his screaming cock, through his jeans, squeezing faintly. Even that had him panting. *Look at me*, he willed her. *Tell me to.*

It was another fevered, endless minute before she did. Another glance over her shoulder, another evil smile, then—

"Turns you on, doesn't it?"

He didn't reply, frozen when Bern's stare met his.

"Does it get you hard, watching me fuck your wife? Or have you just forgotten what it's supposed to look like?"

"Go ahead," Sam told Mike.

His fingers went to his belt buckle, opening it. Then his button, his zipper . . . One last choked breath, and he eased his jeans and shorts to the tops of his thighs, cock springing free. He held his palm to the underside, not stroking, merely cupping—even that threatened his longevity. His entire body was pulsing in time with their motions. He was too close already, teetering on the edge, scared of the drop. He couldn't guess if his pleasure might turn to pain, to see them together with the insanity of lust stripped away.

Bern was kissing Sam's neck, teasing with his lips and tongue and soft bites. Mike got lost watching those subtler violations, and for a moment, anger subsumed lust. So strange, how the penetration didn't threaten him, yet this did, somehow. He let the rage dull his excitement, then froze altogether when Bern's eyes opened, aimed at Mike's hand.

He wondered what on earth the man was thinking. And the authentically jealous side of him hoped the asshole was surprised. *You're bigger, but not by much.* That little moment's taste of power twisted his excitement, darkened it. And suspended in those few seconds' intensity, Mike felt something shift between the two of them, this rivalry taking on a much realer edge, if a harmless one. *Before you get any ideas, asshole, just remind yourself I only* pretend *not to please her. You're the sex toy. I'm her husband. She's mine and she's fucking amazing.*

And it was that thought that got Mike's fingers circling his cock, caressing, if not stroking. In his line of work, there was a lot of figurative dick-measuring that went on, as colleagues jockeyed for position and as the good guys and bad guys sized one another up. Right now that clash of manhood felt literal and very, very real. And also hot in a sharp, unsettling way.

"Show him how hard you make me come," Sam murmured, her voice cleaving the male tension.

In a breath Bern had flipped her over, onto her hands and knees. In profile, Mike watched the enemy sink deep in a smooth, long stroke. One hand held Sam's hip, the other reaching around to tease her clit.

"Yeah, just like that."

Her words had Mike's hand tightening around his cock, and in a dozen strokes, he knew he'd gone too far. The pressure was tight, arousal gathering like a thunderhead, unstoppable. *Come*, he willed her. At least let him see that much while the lust haze kept it all safe.

"Just like that," she groaned. "Don't stop."

Bern took her harder, his far arm flexing in time with his fingers' motions. "What'll you think about when you come, baby?"

"Your dick."

"What about it?"

"Fuck . . . you're big."

"Nice and deep?"

"Yeah."

"Nice and thick?"

She nodded frantically, voice lost in a groan.

"Yeah, you think about that."

And shit, Mike was thinking about it, too. He held on until Sam's face told him she was there herself, needy tension straining every feature. When her moans grew jagged, Mike fisted himself tight and jacked himself home. In his head he heard the things Sam would say, were it just the two of them. *Yeah, come on, baby. Do it. Show me.* This time she said those things only with her eyes, as her long hair swung to the beat of Bern's punishing body. Those eyes shut just as Mike's orgasm arrived. It rocked him in wave after wave, the crest of it nearly painful, the ebb pure white relief.

Mike came down, slowly and not completely. His cock was pulsing, only half limp, even after that revelation of a release. He'd come in his fist and on his shirt. He stripped his tee and wiped his hand and crown clean with shaking fingers.

Bern slowed behind Sam, only his gleaming skin giving away the effort. He regarded Mike carefully, it seemed, a mix of curiosity and caution on his face.

Mike dropped his shirt to the floor and hiked his jeans and shorts back up, searching his body for panic, or revulsion . . . but finding neither. He felt sex-drunk, and behind that, still turned on.

"Well," Bern said. He pulled out, giving Sam's hip a little slap, spurring her to turn onto her back. She did so with a sigh of greatest satisfaction, then let her head drop to the side to look at Mike. Her eyes widened. She'd not seen him come. And to judge by her expression, she'd not expected him to.

"I think your husband likes to watch," Bern told her. He was kneeling astride her legs, cock in hand. "You think he'd like to watch you suck me?"

Mike sensed in an instant what that question was. It was the ball being passed to Sam, and she, in turn, passed it to Mike.

"You don't mind, do you? After all that, I think he's earned it," she added, stroking Bern.

Mike could've shut it down then, with an unequivocal *Get the fuck out of my house.* He would have, if his excitement weren't already building all over again, that curious heat gathering deep in his belly. Instead, he heard himself say, "Just make it quick."

Sam smiled, biting her lip, and there were two layers to that grin—the one that belonged to the cold-hearted bitch, and the one that belonged to the woman who played her. Their games had survived to see the other side of Mike's release, and it delighted her.

"Go and sit," she told Bern, reaching back to pat the bed's edge.

He got into position and Sam dropped to her knees, just as he'd done for her. She stroked his thighs and Mike checked the camera, angling it to center them in the frame. Between his legs, he felt his cock growing warm and heavy. Fucking crazy. Like he was twenty all over again.

Sam clasped Bern's cock, her gaze moving to Mike and the camera just before her lips closed around him. He watched, mesmerized, in awe of the two of them. In awe of his own reality. Sam took Bern deep, dropping the man's head back. His arms were braced behind him, every muscle looking taut and on edge. Strong and helpless at once.

Voice strained, he asked her, "You like how I taste, don't you?"

She answered with an eager moan, still working.

"Yeah, you do. You love that dick. You love tasting me, don't you?" Suddenly he turned, eyes burning straight into Mike's through the viewfinder. Bern swallowed and, panting, he asked him, "What about you?"

Mike could only blink, brain going blank with shock.

Bern slid himself from between Sam's lips. "On your back."

She did as commanded and he climbed on top, sinking deep once more.

"Fuck, you're wet." He looked back to Mike. "You ever eat your wife's pussy?"

A tremor rattled through Mike, setting his hands trembling atop his knees. "Yes."

"Tastes good, doesn't she?"

Mike didn't answer. He could sense the next question, one that terrified and intrigued him equally. What scared him most was that he was the only one who could answer it. Sam would never decide for him.

Bern pulled out and shifted to lay alongside Sam, stroking himself. "Why don't you come over here and taste what your wife's left all over my dick?"

CHAPTER FIFTEEN

Anticipated or not, the invitation struck Mike like lightning. It was so brazen, so . . . confrontational. So *soon*, it seemed. And it was a question that demanded action or refusal, not limp, grudging obedience. It put Mike firmly in his place as the degraded victim in all this, and it scared him.

Scared him because he was tempted. Scared him more so because it underlined how this was no longer his show to orchestrate. Bern had stolen his reins tonight, and Mike wasn't sure he was ready to embody his part so completely.

Sam was still playing. She turned so she could stroke Bern's chest, but she didn't meet Mike's eyes. And he knew why—it was too much pressure. If she wanted him to submit to it, she wouldn't tell him so. The ball was entirely in Mike's court. *Fuck.*

He eyed Bern's cock, trying to pinpoint what would change if he submitted. What it said about his own sexuality. Sam had a far better perspective on it, wisdom always at the ready. What would she tell him?

You don't want to suck a man's cock any more than you wish your wife would actually cheat on you. We explore stuff when we're playing, but it's just a game. I'm not unfaithful and you're not bi, not for keeps. Not once the curtain drops. But it's your script to read from. Your choice.

His choice, and all of this was his idea. His wife had broken her vows and slept with another man to please him. This upping of the stakes was nothing compared to that. And he'd tasted this man's come on his wife's skin before. Was the reverse really such a far leap?

Well, yes. It was. He tried to imagine doing it, guessing at what he'd feel. Humiliated and intimidated, demeaned. And with that, his cock stiffened. He eyed the camera's screen, and adjusted it to center the bed with shaking hands. It'd capture whatever it captured, and surely anything it missed would be etched indelibly onto Mike's memory.

Bern stroked the base of his cock as Mike took a step closer. "Thought you'd say yes. Stay there," he ordered, sitting up. "Get on your knees."

Mike swallowed and did as he was told, holding his breath as Bern rounded the bed to stand before him, erection at eye level. Mike swallowed again. The man smelled of sex—the familiar scent of Sam, plus his own musk, at once arousing and repulsive and *infuriating*, short-circuiting every primal male instinct at work between Mike's ears.

"Taste her," Bern said, still gripping his base.

This was the closest Mike had ever been to another guy's dick, and it was scary. To head off a germinating sexual identity crisis, he reminded himself what this was—the symbol at the heart of his kink. The knife that stabbed him in the heart and, in turn, got him so insanely hot. But it lost its edge without a woman close by. He looked to Sam, and she read his mind.

She left the bed and dropped to her knees beside him. With a smirk, she reached for Bern's shaft, stroking him with slow, lazy pulls. "Scared?"

Mike said nothing.

"He's already had your wife," she said. "Is your mouth really so much worse?"

His lips parted but no words came. Lust was beginning to crowd away the nerves, but not completely.

"Want me to show you how?" Not waiting for an answer, she leaned in to trace the underside of Bern's cock with the tip of her tongue. His flesh twitched, and Mike saw a bead glistening at his slit. *You'll taste more than Sam*. But what he'd be tasting didn't matter. Only the sensations mattered—the complete and utter debasement. He shifted closer on his knees.

"Open up," Bern said.

Mike did, glad he wasn't being asked to use his hands. He wasn't being asked to service this man, only to be degraded. A task he could handle.

Bern held his cock, sweeping his head across Mike's lower lip, then along the upper one.

"Smell that?" he demanded. "You smell your wife on me? Or maybe that's not something you'd even recognize."

Sam ran her hand up Bern's thigh and cupped his balls, admiration in the gesture.

"Taste her," Bern repeated.

And Mike leapt. He shut his eyes as his tongue met the smooth skin of Bern's head. He offered a few timid licks, and though it was mostly lubricant that greeted him, he imagined it was Sam—that intimate flavor he knew from hours of feasting. The rival taste was there as well, strange and strong. But what wasn't there was regret or panic. Be it via his eyes or ears or mouth, Mike wanted to be demeaned. He craved it.

His role wasn't cock worshipper, though—it was that of the loser husband, and he felt no need to pleasure Bern or prove anything in the skill department. He'd take orders like the obedient little cuckold he was, and the next one arrived shortly.

"Take me in your mouth." Bern's normally deep and confident voice was shaky, and it occurred to Mike in a flash that the guy had never done this with another man before, either. Seemed so obvious now. It didn't breed a kinship between them, but it banished the very last of Mike's misgivings. He parted his lips and let Bern ease his cock over the lower one.

"She's all over my dick," Bern breathed. "I know you love cleaning away whatever I've left on her. Now do the same. Clean me up. Make it so you can pretend like I've never fucked your wife. Never fucked her better than you could ever dream of doing."

Mike met the challenge halfway, opening his mouth wider and letting Bern push inside. The sensation frightened him, nearly as though the man's cock were a gun. He realized in that ugly moment what a cowardly fetish his was, the way he'd been practicing it, leaving all the physical submission to his wife. Now *sit back and watch* had become *drop to your knees and open your mouth*, but even behind the fear, the humiliation had his own cock rousing.

"Close your lips," Bern said, barely a murmur. "Make it tighter."

Mike did as he was told. Took what he was given—not deeply, but the two or three thick inches Bern fed him was plenty.

"You taste your wife on me?"

Mike moaned. He tried to imagine he tasted Sam, but Bern's scent and flavor were intense, primal and intimidating, so starkly male. Mike shivered when a gruff hand cupped his head, fingers splayed in his short hair. For half a minute or more, Bern dictated. Not too rough, but bossy. Bolder. He gave more, and Mike gagged.

"Good." And it was over. Bern slid out, and when he spoke his voice was stiff and stilted. "Bet you were worried I was gonna give you more than just a taste."

Mike said nothing and kept his gaze on Bern's legs. He shivered when the man ran his fingertips through Mike's hair—a brief, patronizing gesture.

"Saving my come for your wife," Bern said. "You want it, you'll have to eat it out of her cunt."

And would I? Mike wondered. He wasn't sure, but more than likely, he'd find out before the night was over.

Sam's breathing was short, high in her chest. It felt as though a fire were consuming her.

Only a couple of weeks before, she'd felt this same fever as she'd violated her vows and taken a new man's cock in her mouth.

She'd felt all that and more, watching Mike do the same.

Never could she have imagined that would turn her on—not as much as it had. Before tonight, there had been a taboo appeal to it, a curiosity. Now? Jesus, maybe she did have a kink of her own. She'd be thinking of that moment a thousand times in the coming days . . . and amending it. Imagining Mike getting drawn into the act, not merely surrendering to it. His hands on Bern's hips, or his fingers wrapped around the base of Bern's cock. Of both men getting caught up. Of Bern taking it all the way, and of Mike drinking him down.

She flushed all over, ready for whatever Bern wanted next. For the first time, she felt truly, fully immersed in this game. Fearless and utterly eager.

Her eyes met Mike's, finding them edgy. Electric. She knew he must be seeing just the same in hers, and prayed she'd feel it when their bodies came back together, after Bern had gone home. She moved back to the bed when Mike returned to his chair.

"How was he?" she asked Bern, her casual words undermined by the breathy lilt of her voice. She might as well have said, *That's the hottest fucking thing I've ever seen.*

Bern glanced to Mike or the camera. "He could use a few pointers."

She smiled. "I'd be happy to give him some."

"And what about me?" Bern asked, crawling close, looming large, erection brushing her mound as he straddled her thighs. "You happy to give me a little something?"

"Anything."

He smiled right back, the gesture one thousand watts of sultry Southern charm. "Spread those pretty legs, then."

She bit her lip. "Yes, sir."

Bern shifted his knees and she did as she was told, all but seared by his gaze as he took her in. "You ready for me?"

"Always."

Bern craned his neck to address Mike. "Don't stop rolling, now."

Mike's only response was to part his lips, but Sam could read him like a book—that was arousal glazing his eyes, and darkening his cheeks and throat and ears. He'd come, he'd stepped beyond his comfort zone, and he was still in it. Still turned on. The three of them were up to their necks in the game now, and in it deeper than Sam had ever expected they'd go.

Yet here they were. Every one of them ready to see what came next.

"Take me," she told Bern, tugging on those thrilling arms.

"Ooh, I like when you give the orders."

Do you, then? A tempting notion. "Get inside me. Show him what I need."

Another hot smile. "Well, yes, ma'am." He steadied his cock and took her deeply in a single thrust.

"God yeah." She gripped his hair, not faking an ounce of the desire burning inside her. "Lemme see you lose it."

"What's the rush?" He took her slow and deep, and for the first time, Sam was eager to watch that video. That ass, those hips, the muscles edging his ribs . . . all that in profile, working for her. Her own fantasies were coming into focus tonight, in so many ways. She'd always imagined that if she had a kinky side, she'd know it. But it had taken seeing Mike on his knees, live and in person, to set her on fire. She never could have guessed her reaction. Just as she never could have guessed the way indulging in another man's body could deepen her feelings for her husband. She'd worried if anything, it would have dampened it. But no. Since their guest had arrived, sex had gone from a warming hearth to a blazing wildfire. A thought burst through the haze, one that slapped her in its clarity.

Don't ever leave us.

Fuck, that was some dangerous thinking. That was attachment talking. She chalked it up to the intensity of the emotions in the room, and fell back into the moment.

"I like it fast," she said, holding those slow-pumping hips. "You know that."

"He not rough enough for you?" Bern asked, glancing at Mike.

"Not like you can do it. Show him."

And he gave her what she'd asked for, driving quick and hard. "Get on your hands and knees."

She did as she was told.

"Good."

But after a minute, Bern's punishing body stilled, then stopped. He spoke to Mike, three little words shifting the room's entire atmosphere. "Come over here."

Sam searched her husband's face for trepidation, but it was impossible to locate behind the humiliation act. In any case, he was obedient. Suddenly the weight of three people dipped the mattress.

"Can you find a fucking clit?" Bern demanded, every inch the brash, wife-defiling shithead he was here to play.

Mike didn't speak, but he knelt and edged close to Sam's side, one hand on her back not far from Bern's, the other sliding under her belly, familiar fingertips alighting on her clitoris. Sam shivered and moaned, shocked.

The pleasure was insane. It went far beyond a hard, skilled cock and a set of fingers that knew her as well as her own did. There were the smells and heat of two men, the disparate pitch of their breathing, mismatched moans at her side and back. But the psychological high was as potent as any physical aspect of what was happening. She'd never felt so much at once. Like an object of adoration and worship, like a prize desired by two hard, panting male animals.

Could Mike feel Bern? He was taking her so deeply, did Mike get the glance of Bern's balls against his knuckles with every impact?

"She loves that dick," Bern muttered, and Sam tensed right up to the edge of orgasm at those words. Not from the crassness of them, or his tone, but because something about it . . . He was talking to Mike, not her. There was a sharp dichotomy at play, a *them* and *her*. She was being pleasured by two men. Served and used at once.

"Fuck," she groaned. "Don't stop."

"Not till I feel you come, baby." Bern, of course. Mike's voice was no more than a low hum of a moan. Together, Bern's words and Mike's sounds—they were something entirely different. So much more, as though one plus one made a hundred.

The pleasure built with every pounding thrust from Bern, every incendiary stroke of Mike's fingertips. From the sensations and so much more. In a flash she imagined the wake of this encounter, of rolling over and kissing each of these men in turn. She was drunk on the moment, on the boundaries they'd obliterated. She'd never known sex could be like this. It *couldn't* be like this one-on-one, no matter the lovers or the bond they shared.

Dangerous thoughts.

It was only the orgasm that drowned them out, her worries flattened in the face of the pleasure as two men, two voices, four hands became her entire world.

"God yeah. Baby, don't stop." She spoke to the both of them, and it was the both of them she moaned for when the climax hit. The moment she came down, Bern took over.

"Get that camera," he told Mike. "Bring it close." To Sam, "Turn over, honey."

They both obeyed, and when Sam flipped onto her back she could see Mike's hands shaking around the camcorder. But he did as instructed, aiming the lens right at the action as Bern took her. It was quick, rough, even frantic, and he was there inside a minute.

"Here I come. Here I come, Sam."

His hips froze, pressed hard to her backside as he released. She heard and felt him go slack, heard him gulping deep breaths. Warm hands caressed her thighs and hips for a few moments, then he slipped his softening cock from inside her. She could feel his come on her lips, and her thoughts and curiosities changed immediately. She knew what *she* wanted—the same as what Mike wanted, in theory. Tonight, nothing excited her more than these two men, together, in every way possible.

She collapsed against the pillows, her exhaustion all real, no act. Bern was sitting farther along the mattress, leaning back on his palms and catching his breath. Sam looked to Mike, finding his expression stony . . . though she thought there might be a glimmer of excitement or curiosity there. She propped a leg up and let her hand drift to her tender, swollen folds as she mentally edited out the rim of the condom. Mike's eyes widened as two fingers stroked her lips, surely glistening with what his rival had put there. She laid out the bait and left it up to Mike to take it or not. She thought she knew their guest well enough now to feel comfortable inviting Mike's pleasure to begin, even after Bern had come. And if he wasn't, she trusted him to make a graceful exit, play the part of the selfish, sated man and dismiss himself if things took a turn he didn't care to witness.

She could sense all these same questions and hypotheses flying around in Mike's head as well. His eyes darted, but they kept flitting to where her fingers flaunted his enemy's seed.

Take me back. Take back what's yours.

Just as she began to think it wasn't to be, a final nudge was given. By Bern.

"Your wife's gonna feel me dripping from her cunt for hours," he said, voice steady once more. He looked to Sam with a mean smile. "Bet you'll like that, won't you?"

"Anything to remind me how good you fuck."

"That's my girl."

Ooh, you're good.

Then suddenly Bern was on his feet, gathering his clothes. The relief hit her like a cool breeze, a gasp of fresh air she'd not realized she needed. He'd set them up, taken them further than she'd even expected, but he was letting the two of them finish the story.

"I'll see myself out. Call me next time you need a decent fuck," he told Sam, buckling his belt.

"Way more than decent. And drive safe."

He came over and they shared a quick kiss on the mouth, Sam's fingertips skimming down his arm as he pulled away. He left them for good without so much as a glance at Mike.

When she heard the front door click shut downstairs, she let her fingers continue their display. Mike crossed to the bed and sat beside her.

"It's still warm," she said through a sigh. "What he left inside me."

"You're my wife. I don't want another man's come where mine belongs."

"Too bad for you, then. Unless you want to do something about it . . . ?"

A glint of determination shone in his eyes. Sam held her breath as he moved, parting her legs and getting to his elbows and knees between them. Her arousal blazed back into brilliant life, and faking apathy became more challenging.

"Can you see what he's done?" she taunted, slicking more evidence of Bern's trespass along her folds. "I've been dying to taste him. Maybe you could do the job for me."

Mike smelled her first, a deep, heady sampling of the scent of her and Bern's sex. As he brought his mouth closer she felt the warmth of his exhalations on her clit. She raked her nails through his hair, wondering if it triggered any memory of Bern similarly touching him. She did it again, softer and more affectionate.

"Go ahead. Tell me how good he tastes."

Mike's tongue glanced her pussy and she had to fight to cover up the fresh waves of pleasure that spread through her, to keep up her role as bored wife. This was all too amazing and fucked and perfect to be her sex life.

Finally, he managed a firm lap. They'd acted out this moment dozens of times, but it had to be different. Doing this had to put another wrinkle in Mike's definition of his sexuality. Same as that hot, loaded moment when he'd taken Bern in his mouth. But once the line had been crossed, she could sense the change in him. He'd jumped. It was done. Now he was free.

He caressed her with deep licks, the contact feeling so like Bern's style, that languorous savoring. She held his head as he did the deed, her insides curling into a tight, hot ball of excitement. When he finally seemed to be satisfied that all traces of the other man were gone, he edged up her body and claimed her mouth.

She could taste Bern there as well as herself.

At her waist, Mike was fumbling with his pants.

"Take it out," he murmured, and Sam stripped the condom.

Mike got himself free and sank inside her, the zipper of his jeans scraping the soft skin of her inner thigh. She didn't think he'd ever felt this hard—and he'd come barely twenty minutes earlier. The humiliation was done for the night, the reassertion process begun.

She murmured his name.

"You came for real tonight?" he asked. "Both times?"

"I did." And she might again, if he gave her the chance. But as it was, his pace was frantic. His body slapped hers, graceless and aggressive, needy. She had to wonder, was he reclaiming more than his primacy? His manhood, perhaps, in the wake of what he'd done? Whatever the reason, it was as hot as any camera-worthy performance Bern could offer.

Camera. She looked to the side, finding it back on the tripod, red light still blinking. As Mike's eyes shut, as they always did when he was racing to the finish, she turned to stare that lens down and smiled. An evil little look to tell the viewer, *I know exactly how good I've got it.*

Though how and when *it* might come to an end, she couldn't begin to guess.

CHAPTER SIXTEEN

How did you feel about it?

That was the question Sam was dying to ask both men, in regard to Saturday night. Asking Mike first seemed only right, though finding the chance was tricky. He was woken up by a new and demanding case at five the next morning, one that kept him out late for the next three nights and had him too burned out for intense conversations about their sex games once he was home. It also left Sam on her own, with too many memories and not enough feedback to know where everyone stood. She could only vouch for her own feelings, but at least they were loud and clear and utterly unconflicted.

I want to see that again.

Mike and Bern, touching. She wanted to watch the video, badly, but it felt like the first viewing ought to be for her and Mike, together. So she settled for the film in her head—rewatching again and again, and imagining the two men taking things further than they had, replacing Mike's uncertain receptivity with something hungrier, and replacing Bern's brash contempt with a taste of awe. Reversing the roles, making Bern the shameless instigator, on his knees, Mike ever the overcome and uncertain one, surrendering to the act and ultimately loving it. The aggression of the actual night she kept, but doubled the lust. She hadn't gotten so lost in fantasies since she'd been a teenager, though she also knew the high would deflate if she found out Mike regretted that act that had left her so hot.

A hundred times she toyed with e-mailing Bern, asking him what he felt about it. They hadn't talked or texted since the big night, and she couldn't say why. Because they'd gone too far for his comfort? Because he was waiting to hear from her first, and was worried about the same thing—that it had been too far for them? She had her own answer for him—*hell no, that wasn't too far*—but not Mike's. And so the silence lengthened, gathering like a dark cloud to dampen her burning mood.

It wasn't until Wednesday evening that she got a chance to sit down with Mike for some unwinding time. After a long shower, he sank with a sigh onto the couch, head dropping back in relief and exhaustion.

"Well done, Detective Heyer." She handed him a beer and turned the oven down to warm. Dinner would keep while she got some answers. She poured herself a glass of wine and joined him, curling her legs up and resting them on his thigh. "It's so good to have you home at a decent hour."

"Fucking amazing to *be* home. Jesus, that was a gnarly bust."

"Need to talk about it?"

"Christ no. Let's talk about anything *but* that. How's your week been?"

"Work's quieted down, which is good. Haven't done much in the evenings, though. Mostly just been coming home and being a lump, but it's been nice . . . I've had a lot on my mind. Since Saturday."

Mike's gaze cooled, expression difficult to read. "Oh?"

"I, um, haven't been talking with him—texting, I mean. I didn't want to keep things all ramped up until you and I talked. About how you feel about everything that happened."

Mike smiled, and that simple gesture brought Sam's breath back in a quenching rush.

"Was my coming twice not enough of an endorsement?" he teased. "Or do you mean because of . . . you know. What I did. To him."

She nodded. "Just tell me you're not traumatized."

He shrugged. "It was out of my comfort zone, but that's kind of par for the course with the entire arrangement, right?"

"True. Did it . . . did it turn you on at all, or the opposite?"

"Neither. It was just . . . I don't know what the right word is. Like, scary, but without any trauma, I guess. I dunno. Same as when I've tasted what he . . . You know what I'm saying."

"But it's not your thing."

Mike laughed softly. "Sami, this entire adventure we've been on is *my thing*. And that stuff's all part of it. I don't know how to describe it, since you don't have this weird desire that I do. There's stuff I like to feel that doesn't automatically connect to my dick. The fear I feel when I imagine you cheating on me, and the discomfort from when he and I overlap, physically . . . Those things don't feel good, except they do. They hurt, but then it's like it ferments into something hot. Am I making any sense?"

"Yeah, you are." And she realized with pleasure that she'd never heard him explain his kink so articulately before, or perhaps with such ownership or awareness.

"The bad feelings feed the good ones," he said. "It's like a punch in the stomach, but chased by more than an absence of pain. By more excitement than anything else gets me feeling."

She licked her lip, nervous to share her own turn-ons. A silly hesitation, considering the taboos he'd owned up to. Then again, it had taken him a few years to open up about those, and he'd been scared when he first began to share, to say the least.

"What is it?" he asked.

"When you guys were both with me, at the end . . ." She laughed. "Holy crap, that was hot."

He squeezed her upper arm, smiling. "Good. For me, too."

"And also when you and him . . ." Why was it so hard to say some of these things, after everything they'd planned and orchestrated? She sipped her wine. "When you took him . . . in your mouth."

"You liked it?"

A blush burned in her cheeks. "That was so *fucking hot*." She laughed again. "I hadn't expected it would be—not like that. I haven't been able to stop thinking about it."

"Well. Good, I guess."

"I hope that doesn't weird you out."

"Tell me *my* turn-ons never weirded you out." He smirked, knowing all too well that they had. They'd made her reconsider their engagement, after all.

He shifted to better face her, and took her hands. "If we see him again, and that happens again . . . I was up for it, last time, even if it freaked me out a little. But knowing you're watching, and that it excites you, even a fraction as much as watching you and him together excites me? I could maybe even learn to like it, knowing that."

She was still blushing, but she felt humbled now, not embarrassed. "Oh. Well, good."

"And if you talk to him, you should tell him that, too."

"Maybe."

Mike paused, brow creased, attention on their hands.

"What?"

He looked up. "I don't want to go much further with him, though. Me and him, doing things. Third base is my limit."

She nodded. "Sure."

"Just wanted to put that out there. Maybe tell him, if it comes up. We blurred a lot of lines this weekend, but I need that one to stay crystal clear."

"I'll tell him. I mean, if he even wants to talk to us, still. He's been conspicuously quiet."

"So have we. Maybe he doesn't want to look too eager."

"I hope so. I'd like to keep going. I was wondering how you were feeling about the next step—ditching the condoms and everything." That next step in making Mike's fantasies a reality was a biggie, and it demanded a lot of everyone. Demanded trust from Sam and Mike, but arguably asked even more of Bern. She wasn't sure how or when to bring it up. Maybe an e-mail, once they were communicating again. *Any chance you like us enough to get a blood test and be monogamous for a while?* Hard to guess. They'd begun talking only a month before, and Mike was the one who fixated on the fluids, not Bern. And for all Sam knew, she wasn't Bern's sole lover at the moment. He was built and striking and charming. His answer could so easily be, *Flattered, but you're not my only arrangement. Sorry.*

That thought had her resolving yet again to keep this in perspective. It felt kind of ridiculous, asking a man to commit to them for a few weeks or months, to be *faithful* to them because of what got Sam's husband off.

But it just might get Bern off, too.

Unlike Sam, Mike didn't seem too burdened by the question. He merely shrugged and said, "Up to him. I trust your female intuition—and your instincts. It's a calculated risk, but if you think it's one worth taking, I'm with you."

"He'd have to basically be monogamous with us. It's a lot to ask, but I will. Fingers crossed we're worth staying faithful to, huh?"

Mike laughed. He picked up his bottle, eyeing it with surprise. "Jeez. Haven't even tasted this."

"Dinner?" Sam asked, standing. She felt twenty pounds lighter with this talk accomplished.

"Will it still be good in an hour?"

"Sure. You not hungry yet?"

"Would you like to maybe watch the video?"

Sam felt her brows rise. "Right now?"

"I've been thinking about it all week. Yeah, right now."

She eyed her dwindling glass. "If I refresh this, then yeah, I think I can handle watching my naked debut. In here?" She nodded to the TV.

"I was thinking upstairs. Watch on the laptop."

"All right, then. Get it set up and I'll meet you in ten minutes."

He smiled. "It's a date."

Bern eyed the clock. Ten after ten. Past his bedtime on a work night, yet here he was, lying awake, staring at the ceiling. Again.

Sunday, Monday, Tuesday, Wednesday. Four days now, and not a peep from Samira.

That can't be good. Did it mean Saturday night hadn't been what they'd hoped for? He'd felt so goddamn cocky when he'd left, positive that had been a command performance. Had one or both of them felt creeped out about it, after? Or, God forbid, during? The only off tension he'd sensed had been when Mike had gone down on him, but that had been so quick, and the guy had gotten hard again, after. Was it from being so close, when they'd fucked Sam together? He kept defaulting to it being some homophobia issue. The most obvious explanation.

Unless they had a fight or something. Unless Mike was worried Sam might actually be feeling more than she was supposed to, maybe—

Brrrzzz. He reached for his phone so quick he knocked it to the floor. It slid to a halt with its screen lit up, and there it was, a new message alert.

He scrambled from the covers. *Be her. Be her.*

It was.

Be good. Be good.

Hi! she'd written. An encouraging start.

Bern sat at the edge of the bed and a new message appeared.

Long time no text. Okay if we chat a little? she asked. If not, no worries.

He typed back, Of course. Want me to call?

Brrrzzz.

Sure.

He pulled up her number and hit TALK, heart beating quick.

She answered immediately. "Hey, you."

"Hey. What's up?"

"I kind of wanted to call and take the temperature of everything, I guess. Since we haven't talked since Saturday."

"I'd been wanting to do the same, but I figured I better let you guys make the first move. Just since it was so intense last time."

"Yeah, sorry about that—about the wait, I mean. Mike woke up to a break in one of his cases, and he's barely been home except to sleep. I didn't even know myself exactly how he felt about Saturday until tonight."

"And?"

"And it was awesome."

He grinned, flopping back across the bed. "Oh yeah?"

"Yeah. We both think so. Did you have a good time?"

"It was fucking crazy. And yeah. I had a great time. We took things pretty far, I thought. Were you two cool with all of it?"

"You mean when he put his mouth on you?" she mumbled, sounding a touch shy.

"Pretty much. I knew that stuff was sort of at my discretion. I wasn't sure if I called it right or not, taking us all there."

"You did fine. Mike's okay with it—a little uncomfortable, but that kinda goes with the whole scene, you know?"

"And you were fine with it, too?"

A pause. "I was more than fine with it."

"Oh?"

"I'd always been fine with it, in theory, but when it actually happened . . . Holy shit, that was hot."

Bern laughed. "Well, good. That makes it hotter for me, I guess." Knowing she was watching, and that it excited her? Fuck yeah, that made it hotter for him. He might prefer her own mouth on his dick, but he'd take her watching eyes just as readily.

"So all that stuff," she said, "feel free to take it that far again. But not much further—not unless Mike changes his mind. I think we butted right up against the edge of what he's comfortable with."

"I'm kinda with him there. But cool—good to have some boundaries spelled out."

"And good to hear you sounding like you might like to do it again . . . ?"

"Absolutely. Just name a night."

"I'll have to look at my schedule tomorrow, but I'll text you. Maybe this weekend, if you're free?"

"Friday or Saturday night can work. Monday I go out of town for a few days, so Sunday's not ideal."

"That should work. And actually, I wanted to float one other thing past you."

"Shoot."

"It's a lot to ask—let me say that up front. But would you consider ever making a commitment to us? Not super long-term," she added quickly. "Just for a month or two, enough to make it worthwhile for the three of us to feel comfortable forgoing the condoms?"

He blinked, surprised. "Oh. Jeez."

"I know, it's a lot to ask of you. You should absolutely say no if it's too much, and we don't need to know right away or anything. But Mike's so into the whole fluids thing . . ."

"Sure." Bern knew that shit was key to the whole cuckolding scene—he'd even read some articles about sperm competition syndrome, intrigued to have found a biological explanation for Mike's kink. "You must be on birth control already," he said.

"I am, and I'm religious about it."

"I figured."

"And also, if you did decide you were okay with all this—and no pressure—we'd pay for your blood tests, obviously."

"Now, that's just silly. But whatever the case, it's intriguing, I'll give you that. And I'm not sleeping with anybody else right now, so it's not a crazy request. Just feels weirdly . . . serious, you know?"

"It feels a little like I'm asking you to go steady with us."

He had to laugh. "Kinda, yeah. Anyhow, I'll think on it. And I'll see you this weekend, it sounds like."

"I sure hope so. I'll text you which night, after I check the calendar."

"Cool. And, um, should I go back to texting you like we were while I was away?"

"That would be very nice."

He grinned from ear to ear, glad she couldn't see. "Will do, then, Mrs. Heyer."

A theatrical gasp. "I never told you my last name."

"It's on your mailbox."

"Oh, right. Not all that scandalous anyway, huh?"

"Not since the topic of blood tests came up, no."

"Anyway, nice to hear your voice again, Bern. We'll see you soon."

"Sam, wait."

"Yeah?"

He licked his lips, feeling hot just asking the question. "Did you guys watch it?"

"Yeah, we did. About an hour before I texted you, in fact."

"And?"

A giggle answered him first, then a little sigh. "And it's pretty fucking hot."

"You guys fuck, after?" His hand drifted down to settle over his rousing cock.

"We didn't even make it to the end."

"So it's almost like I was there with you, in a way." He warmed all over.

"It was. And we were talking afterward, and Mike was thinking that some weekend when he's stuck working, he'd like us to make another one—you and me. Like he'd set up a hidden camera, to catch us."

Just him and Sam, and a camera. "Keep talking and you'll give me a heart attack."

She laughed again, lighting him up and bringing his cock to full attention. "Anyhow, ideas for the future."

"You've given me plenty of ideas for right after we end this call."

"Have I, then?"

"You want pictures?"

A warm little laugh. "I want video. But I'll take whatever you feel like sending."

All at once short of breath, Bern said, "Night, Samira."

"Good night. See you soon."

"Sooner than you think."

Another quiet huff of a laugh. "Bye."

"Bye."

He ended the call, and headed straight for his laptop. Lights, camera, action.

CHAPTER SEVENTEEN

They saw Bern that Friday, and again the following Thursday, then Saturday . . . At least once a week for the next month. It was nearly July now, and Mike could sense the changing seasons in intimate ways—in the scent of their sex and sweat, in the light that lingered between the bedroom blinds late enough to paint Sam and Bern's skin gold as the games began.

Things had changed among the three of them, too, slowly and steadily. They'd grown comfortable with one another, but not in a way that cooled their collective heat. On the contrary. It was Mike and Bern who'd needed to get good with their own dynamic, and they had. Mike could touch the man without much hesitation at all now, and he'd . . .

And he'd learned to suck cock. Like, properly. Not with the limp receptivity of that first time, but with obedient purpose.

He shivered at the thought, caught as always between arousal and unease. But that was his kink in a nutshell—most any kink, really. Skating along that sharp edge that separated power and helplessness, control and surrender, pain and pleasure. He desired Bern, in a way, as much as he hated him in another. That man's cock was the ultimate symbol of what got Mike hot—the usurping of his wife. And with the trust now feeling implicit among the three of them, he could drop to his knees and take that man's orders, provided there still remained a trace of Sam in the act. And Bern never failed to deliver that.

You taste her on me?

Come over here, honey. Show him how I like it.

You know what you're sucking? That's the cock that's gonna fuck your wife tonight.

He'd gotten used to the weight of Bern's hands on his head, used to the smell of him, even to the rhythm he liked. Insanely intimate. The only thing they hadn't done was have Bern finish with Mike, and they likely never would. Cuckolding was all about the rival's intrusion, the marking of the woman. It was a primitive head trip with paternity all twisted up in its core. It wasn't quite right if Bern didn't come inside Sam, and if Mike didn't remedy that violation.

At the end of the day, it wasn't a kink he'd ever have chosen for himself. But you didn't get a say, did you? And Mike was willing to bet most men didn't experience the level of gratification he did when he indulged this strange facet of his sexuality and psyche—this intense, orchestral merging of his fears and aggression and his body's most basic drives. He bet other men's sex lives were like "Mary Had a Little Lamb" pecked out on a toy piano. His was a full-on symphony. Who could care how fucked it might look from the outside?

He eyed the clock, thinking he'd better finish his coffee and get to the station. Sam had the day off, to balance a string of late nights earlier in the week, and she was out jogging now. Mike's day should be fairly dull. A case had just wrapped and he had mostly paperwork on his plate; a quiet enough Friday to round out the week. And that night, he and Sam had their guest coming over.

Guest? Or maybe something more akin to a partner of sorts.

Bern had committed to them, after all—gotten his blood test results a few days before, as had they. Everyone was good to go. Bare.

Mike felt a heat wave move through him at the thought.

Quit it. He'd never get through the day's admin if he allowed himself even a moment's meditation on the things that might happen tonight.

He drained his mug, grabbed his keys, and headed for the door. *Bring on the longest eight hours in history.*

"Try it now," Sam told her phone, and hit the RECORD button on the laptop.

After a pause, Bern said, "Oh! Hey, I see you. Say something, so I can see what the delay's like."

Sam turned around to face the camera on its tripod. "Something."

Another pause. "Three or four seconds, maybe—not that it matters. Nice work. Even if you did need to call an electrician."

"Only to test the connection, smart-ass." Sam hit STOP on her computer, and the camera's red light went dark. It had taken two hours—not counting the two trips to Best Buy to find the right cable—but she'd succeeded in getting the video camera to function through the computer. The entire point of which was tied to the evening's appetizer course.

It was four thirty, and Mike would be wrapping work in an hour or so. Bern and Sam were going to be starting the night off on their own, but with Mike watching the feed on his phone, via a chat application. Sam had tried simply using the laptop's webcam, but the video came out dark and bluish, and the sound sucked. In the end, it had been worth all the trouble. They'd be pretending that Mike had planted the camera to bust Sam and Bern in the act. A bit of a twist on the usual come-home-early-and-catch-them routine.

"I'll head over, if it's not too early," Bern said.

"If you've got nothing better to do, go for it." Sam liked when they had time to chat before the sex took over. It helped her ease into her role, loosened her up. And over the course of the past few weeks, she'd come to see Bern as a true friend, not merely a purpose-made playmate.

"Be there in thirty, then. Need anything?"

"Whatever you feel like drinking."

"Cool. See you in a bit."

"Bye."

Nice. The camera was due to begin rolling at five forty-five—Mike was planning to drive home, then watch from his parked car before coming in. Sam smiled, imagining him shielding any visible excitement from the neighbors with a strategically positioned briefcase.

She was already groomed and ready to go, and once Bern arrived the two of them would have a half hour or more to hang out before the performance began. Maybe that made her hopelessly female, but Sam felt foreplay began well before any touching did. She wanted her lover's warm, easy smile, and to be asked how her day had been in that disarming Kentucky accent. Wanted their glasses to clink before their lips ever met.

She tidied the living room, feeling happy and relaxed when the bell eventually rang.

As always, Bern just about filled the door—six feet-plus of tall, sturdy man, his handsome face always such a knock to the senses.

"Why, hello," she said, feeling flirtatious, leaning in the jamb and blocking his way.

"Hello yourself."

She could see on his face, he wanted to kiss her. Passersby wrecked that option, of course.

"Invite me in?"

"I dunno. What have you got there?" She nodded to the paper-bagged package in his big hand.

He unwrapped it, holding up a bottle of Malbec. Guileless man that he was, the price tag was still on it.

"Eighteen bucks? You may absolutely come in, then." She stepped aside and he brushed past, bare arm glancing hers.

"Hope that wasn't sarcasm."

"I usually buy the big utility jugs that cost half that much, so no, not at all." She took the bottle.

"You look great."

"Thanks." She was wearing jeans and a T-shirt dressed up with a long, funky necklace. "Nothing too fancy today. I'm in a three-day-weekend state of mind."

"Doesn't stop you from looking hot," he said, toeing off his shoes. "No work for you today, then?"

"Nope. I put in forty hours, easy, by midweek. I earned it." And maybe a couple of months previous, before the force of nature known as Bern Davies had entered their lives, the old Samira would've worked the full week anyhow. Her erstwhile priorities looked awfully boring, in light of these new extracurriculars.

"What about you?" she asked. "You get off early?"

"Not strictly speaking, but my schedule's seven to three on this new project. Fine by me, even if my dog's not impressed with the whole six-o'clock-walk situation."

Sam led him to the living room and poured them each a glass, the scene feeling familiar and easy as the arrival of summer itself.

"So," Bern said with a poorly stifled smile. "No condoms tonight." Not a question.

"Looks that way." She set her glass aside and put her hand on his forearm—just a little taste of flirtation. As much as she felt comfortable with, with Mike not yet watching. "But you get a say, of course."

She knew Bern's answer already. They'd had a delightfully filthy exchange when Sam wrote to confirm their tests had come back with a big thumbs-up, same as his. What had that e-mail from Bern said, the one that'd had Mike yanking Sam's top off before they'd even staggered from the computer to the bedroom? *I'm gonna fuck you so good, I'll have you begging me to shoot you full of my come. Bet your husband will like that—tasting just you and me when he eats you out after.*

Her pussy heated all over again just remembering those words.

"Can't wait." Bern nodded to her glass and Sam picked it up so he could clink them. "Cheers to that, huh?"

"And how." They drank.

"How long have we got?" he asked.

"Before we kick off the fun?" She eyed the DVD player's clock. "Almost a half hour."

"Good. That gives me plenty of time to grill you before we get down to business."

Sam's smile surely only expressed half the pleasure that was warming her body. She'd come to find this man no less than fascinating in the two months she'd known him, and she'd stopped overthinking the crush and given herself permission to revel in it.

"Grill me?" she asked, flattered to imagine he might find her even half as intriguing. "About what?"

"Anything." He laid his arm along the back of the couch and crossed his legs. "I have no doubt you're just as interesting as your fucked-up husband, but precisely how, I'm not yet sure. But I want to find out."

Sam blushed. "What's brought that on?"

He smiled, the gesture a touch guilty. "A few of my coworkers have started asking questions. Apparently I must look like a guy who's been getting some."

She laughed. "Busted, huh?"

"Guess so. Anyhow, they asked who the girl is, and I kept it real vague. But the more they rib me, the more I can't help but realize I don't know all that much about you. I mean, we know each other real well in some ways, but not the basics."

"I'm afraid my sex life's easily the most scandalous thing about me, but by all means, grill away."

"Does your family live close?"

She shook her head. "Newark."

"Oh. You a Jersey girl?"

"Born and raised."

"Hence the Springsteen fetish?"

"You got it. I moved to New York City for college and started my career there."

"How did you wind up in Pittsburgh?"

She smiled at the memory. "Mike. We met totally randomly, when I was here visiting friends. I fell for him in, like, one night. Packed up my life and moved in with him less than a year later."

"Wow."

"I know. Very fast, especially for me. It was the first serious relationship I just leapt into without analyzing it to death. None of my friends and family could believe I hadn't even made a spreadsheet with the pros and cons of moving away."

"How'd you guys stay plugged into each other, while you were long-distance?"

"Lots of phone calls and e-mails, and one of us would travel to see the other, every other weekend. The distance never really registered, we were so into each other."

He smiled, eyes crinkling. "That's awesome. And did you know right away what he's into? Kinkiness-wise, I mean."

"No, not at all. He didn't tell me until . . ." She paused and took a deep breath, thinking she'd shared her body with this man, so these little bits of her past weren't so precious, surely. They were secrets, in a way—aspects of her marriage she'd not shared with anyone before, but Bern was different. And it was nice to talk about these things with a friend. There was no one else she could confess them to.

"If I'm being too nosy, just say."

She shook her head. "He told me after we'd been living together a year or more. It almost drove us apart, actually."

"Really?"

"In a way. He already knew that got him hot—the thought of getting cheated on—but I had no idea. He went through this intensely jealous phase after we got engaged, and I threatened to break it off if it didn't stop, and he came out with it. The sexual stuff."

"And you were okay with it?"

"Not right away, no. At first I was incredibly hurt. And just . . . confused. I'd never heard of cuckolding before, or known much about kinkiness at all. I was a tiny bit relieved, too. I mean, at least he didn't really think I was capable of cheating on him."

"Sure."

"Once the shock wore off, I wanted to be all open-minded and rational about it. I knew in my brain, he can't help what turns him on. But I didn't like it at first—not at all. It still felt terrible, having been the focus of all that suspicion, getting viewed as someone who'd actually done something wrong, you know? I definitely wasn't ready to act it out with him."

"But eventually you did."

She nodded and sipped her wine. "Eventually. When I told him

I wasn't sure I could stay with him, he immediately knocked off the jealousy crap. We spent a lot of time talking about the cuckolding—as a kink, not an actual thing we ever planned to do—again and again over the next year or so. It stopped stinging, and as I read more about it, I started to find little parts of it where I thought, *Oh, okay, I can see how that's kinda hot.*"

"So how did we wind up here?" Bern asked, nodding down at their legs.

"Mike and I started playing around with it about two years ago. Once or twice a month I'd indulge him, pretend I was cheating on him. I'd stay late after work, like I told you, and send him suspicious texts, and come home smelling like men's cologne samples."

Bern laughed, that noise that lit her up like nothing else.

"And other things. I'd let him catch me wearing needlessly sexy underwear. And I keep a box of condoms around, and sometimes I'd open one up and rub it between my legs. So he tastes it."

Bern swallowed, eyes going a touch glassy. "Clever."

Sam nodded. "It's been fun, and I've gotten more and more comfortable with it. It's always been something I do for him, like a treat, but over time I started finding something in it for myself, too. It's like . . . It's almost like I found out he was secretly into guns, right? And I was horrified at first, then started thinking about why he enjoys them; then I start going to the shooting range with him to try to understand. Then I catch myself looking forward to it, and even having fun. It's his thing, but now it's mine, too. It's not just a favor or a treat anymore—not the way it was at first."

"No?"

"I caught myself thinking up scenarios of my own, not just asking what his fantasies looked like and trying to replicate them. And the more I imagined being attracted enough to other men to cheat, the more I could admit to myself, hey, I *am* attracted to men other than the one I married. I don't think women always like admitting that to themselves. We get so beaten over the head with the Mr. Right fairy tale, like true love can override biology. Which is bull, of course."

"Huh. I never thought about it that way."

"For the sake of getting into my role, I spent a lot of time making up these fantasy men I was sleeping with, and in time, I started to wonder what it would be like to sleep with somebody else, for real. Could I ever actually go there?"

Bern smirked. "Bet I can guess the answer."

"Still, it took a marathon's worth of baby steps to get here."

He leaned back in his seat and took a deep drink. "That's really cool."

"Yeah. Yeah, it is."

"Hope I meet somebody as open-minded as you someday, when I'm ready to settle down again. You guys seem to have it all figured out."

"Oh God, not remotely. This experiment's just gone shockingly well. We've been lucky. But if you want some awesome, kinky marriage someday . . . I dunno. When you meet someone you really like, just be honest about what turns you on. And let your partner *see* how much it turns you on. Mike's kink didn't do anything for me on paper, but when I started humoring him, playing along, and saw the way it set him on fire? That was a power I wanted to have, once I got a taste."

"If you and I were together in some alternate world, how would you indulge my kink?"

She sipped her wine, considering it. "It'd be easy in some ways—buy a load of mirrors, abuse Skype now and then. If you needed more, like you decided you really wanted to put videos out there into the larger world, even just of yourself . . . that would be trickier to get on board with."

"Really?"

"I think so. It sounds ridiculous, given the way Mike's been sharing me with you, and the way jealousy's all wrapped up in his kink, but I'm more possessive than he is. It would take some major effort for me to get comfortable with the idea of other people being allowed to watch my partner being sexual. I guess I'm greedy that way."

"I could see that."

"You ever think about doing that?" Sam asked. "Putting yourself out there for strangers? I know confidentiality's important to you, but there's plenty of ways you could disguise your face, or just keep it out of the shot."

"Sure, I've thought about it. And not only when I'm single and don't have my own partner to watch me. There's something about it being taped and viewed . . . something risky, maybe. That excites me."

Sam nodded, the notion resonating. She'd only been playing at getting caught, but the adrenaline did have something to recommend it.

"It sounds super fucking vain," he went on, "but the idea of maybe being out there, in video form, and imagining someone saying to their friend, *You have to watch this guy*, or of doing it live, and letting the person on the other end of it tell me what to do . . . I've got loads of fantasies about it, but I've never taken that leap. I almost did, right after I ended my last relationship, but I couldn't pull the trigger for some reason. It felt too sleazy at the time. Like, *So this is what I broke us up over? So I can jack off for some stranger on the Internet?* When I saw your ad, it didn't feel so selfish anymore. I mean, look what *you* were willing to do for him."

"You've still got time to try those other things, online. I can understand how it felt cheap at the time, but if it does for you what our games do for Mike, you'd be crazy not to. Plus, I'm sure you'd earn yourself a heck of a following."

"Especially if I'm comfortable telling myself all my viewers are women. And pretending to believe it."

She laughed. "Oh, true. It might take some suspension of disbelief. And for now, I'm happy to continue making the *massive* sacrifice it requires to indulge you, and be the sole audience for your one-man shows."

"What a saint you are," Bern teased, his smile sharp and hot.

"What a saint *you* are, so selflessly stepping in to be the gasoline squirted all over Mike's and my sex life." She bit her lip, feeling just a touch off base as she gave voice to her next thought. "Is it almost as good as knowing you're being watched, knowing there's some couple across town, talking about you while they're having sex?"

His cheeks pinkened, if she wasn't mistaken, his gaze darting away for a second before pinning hers again. "I'd say it's a tie."

A laugh fizzled in Sam's throat. There was something in his eyes . . . something loaded, and a little hazy. A look she knew well from any number of first kisses, first dates. That muted hunger of attraction. It should come as no surprise, given everything they'd done to each other, and everything he was here to do with her tonight, and yet . . .

He wants to kiss me. And she wanted to kiss him—she felt the tug as she might with a man she'd never even touched before. Curiosity and magnetism. She wondered if it shone in her eyes, too. Bern's lids looked heavy, and his lips were parted.

Don't you dare.

But she should've known he wasn't the kind of man you dared.

Those lips came down to hers, and they were hot. Full. Their noses brushed, and this could have been a stranger, for all the uncertainty she felt. Her hands rose, fingertips met by his stubble, the heat of his skin and the firm shape of his jaw filling her palms.

When they kissed for Mike, it was a cocky, aggressive act. This was far softer, slower. Intimate. Wrong—and not in the good way.

Kill it now. But in her few seconds' hesitation, he intensified the kiss, and instead of stopping him, Sam angled her head and invited him deeper. This tasted like so much more than Malbec.

He was making her all warm and foggy, winding her up.

She put her hand firmly on his chest. "We should stop." Christ, her voice was all husky and low. She cleared her throat. Bern covered her hand with his, pressing it tight—but only for a breath. Then he seemed to catch himself, and let her go. She linked her fingers carefully atop her thigh and willed her heart to slow.

"Yeah." He nodded, gaze on her hands. "We should."

"If it's not for his eyes or his ears, it's . . . I don't know exactly why, but it doesn't feel right."

Another nod, yet she didn't sense much conviction when he said, "Of course."

She stood and grabbed their empty glasses, and made her voice light. "It's just about showtime, anyway. No reason we can't misbehave for the camera."

Bern got to his feet, slipping a hand down the front of his jeans to adjust himself. That alone got Sam's pulse spiking. *I've got way too much power over these men.* A position she'd never imagined she'd find herself in, back when she'd just begun to picture how the realization of Mike's kink might look. Before the games had begun, her fear had been that she might feel exploited. Not bullied but coerced by her own need to feel like she was *enough* for him. She'd worried back then that she might feel manipulated, even though, in reality, she was fast becoming the ringmaster.

And if she had any doubt of that, Bern held his arm out and said, "Lead the way."

CHAPTER EIGHTEEN

As they headed up the stairs, Sam said, "So, we're pretending like he's hidden a camera tonight."

The whiny floorboard creaked under Bern's weight. "But he's joining us later?"

"Yeah."

No reply, and at the threshold of the bedroom she turned to find him smiling. "What?"

"We're all through with the condoms tonight, right?"

She nodded, biting her lip. "That's right. Unless you've suddenly changed your mind?"

"If you knew how much I hate needles, the fact that I got the tests done would tell you how in I am." He stepped close, thighs brushing hers, chin at her temple. She felt his fingers in her hair and the heat of his breath as he spoke. "You know what I can't figure out, though?" he murmured.

"What?"

"So I get to fuck you bare tonight," he said, and her pussy gave an eager squeeze.

"Yes, you do."

"But I can't decide what I want to do to get you wet for me."

She shivered. "It won't take much."

"My mouth, maybe." The mouth in question brushed a soft kiss against her forehead, and Sam could nearly feel his tongue between her thighs, taunting with its deep, savoring laps. Then she imagined his cock there, no condom, no lube. Only skin on skin, just her and him. She swallowed.

"Or maybe we should just go ahead and find out," he said, so soft it was barely a whisper. A current of intimacy crackled between them, one that felt dangerously disconnected from Mike. He ought to hear every word, she thought—every nonlogistical one. Unspoken rules dictated that he read their e-mails, watch nearly every moment they were together, or at least be given a chance to do those things. To deny him access to her and Bern's sexual relationship felt too much like actual infidelity for Sam's comfort.

You're thinking way too hard about it. Mike likes feeling jealous and left out. Now be a good little wife and fuck this hot man.

Well said.

"Wait here a sec," she told Bern. "I'll hit RECORD before I turn the lights on, so my dicking around in front of the camera doesn't wreck the illusion."

She padded through the dark room and opened her laptop, dimming the screen as far as it went. She double-checked it was Mike's username she was contacting, then hit CHAT. From the top of the dresser, the camera's light turned red, its lens aimed at the bed. She hurried back out to Bern.

"Showtime."

She barely heard the growl of a "good" he uttered before his mouth was back on hers, a hundred times hungrier than before. Bossy hands held her head, and he walked her backward into the room, knocking the light switch up to illuminate it all for Mike.

He broke their mouths apart and ran gruff palms up her sides, cupped her breasts. "Been thinking about you all day. Every bit of you."

She grabbed his belt in both hands, mirroring his aggression. "I haven't *stopped* thinking about you since last time."

"What've you missed most?" he demanded, his pushy body crowding her to the edge of the bed, forcing her to sit.

"How good you make me feel." She fisted his collar and drew him down on top of her, wrapping her legs around his waist. She could feel the stiff insistence of him and it curled her fingers into claws against his back. He locked his strong arms erect at either side of her ribs, staring down at her as his hips began to roll.

"Can't wait to get inside you," he said.

"Good. I want every inch of you."

"Deep?"

"Deep. And bare." Just saying it now gave her a thrill, and from something more than simple taboo. Something possessive. *You're mine*, she thought, holding his stare. *Nobody gets you except me.* Not forever, but for now—and that was more than enough. Hypocritical though her excitement was, she couldn't deny its potency. She'd thought her days of calling a new man hers alone were over, but as always, Mike's desires rewrote her perceptions of what sex could be. Who *she* could be, as a sexual person. As a woman.

And this woman got to call this gorgeous, strong, eager specimen of a man hers.

And not just him.

Outside, Mike was parked on the street, and, having not received a text with any changes to the plan, Sam could only assume he was watching everything that was happening, on his phone. *He's mine as well.* Man, was she spoiled. But she didn't take it for granted—not for a single moment.

There were things Samira wanted tonight, when Mike joined them. She wanted both their bodies against her, front and back. No double penetration—just the hot, naked skin of two ready, rowdy men pressed close, two voices breathing quick and hard, their fingers brushing as they touched her.

Bern freed a hand to reach down, toying with her necklace before slipping it over her head and setting it aside. "Let your hair down."

She slid off her elastic and tugged her braid free.

"Yeah, good. I love your hair."

"Now you—take your shirt off."

Bern sat back, and Sam watched with awe as he obeyed. All that lean, flexing muscle that made him look so gorgeous in a well-fitted shirt—straight-up heart-stopping in the flesh.

"I could stare at you for hours." She ran her palms over his abs and chest, watching his muscles twitch and tense from her touch.

Their bodies came together, Sam's legs hugging Bern's ass and his hips pumping slow.

"Too many clothes," he panted after a hot minute.

"So fix it."

And he was on his feet, grabbing her ankles, pulling her bodily to the edge of the mattress. Sam laughed and got busy undoing her fly. She shed her shirt and he tugged her jeans away, then she sat up. She didn't want to miss a minute of the show. She wanted to watch him as surely as he was dying to get watched.

He undid his belt with slow, precise motions, and lowered his fly. Sam studied the dark hair that trailed from his navel to the band of his shorts, the way that line grew denser and darker. His jeans dropped and his thumbs went to his waistband. "Don't rush," she said, letting him see the way her eyes feasted.

He cupped his straining cock, then stroked, making a show of himself. "Don't rush? That go for the night itself?"

"Absolutely."

"When's he due back?"

"Don't know, don't care." She looked up, meeting his gaze. "Plus, is it really so bad when he catches us?"

"I like getting you all to myself . . . but no, it's not so bad. I don't mind showing him how to please you."

"Or you," Sam countered, electrified as always to imagine the men touching each other. Or watching Bern's cock disappear inside Mike's mouth. "I say let him catch us."

Bern was still stroking his erection through his shorts, accentuating its obscene outline.

"You like being watched," she mused.

"You know I do."

"You like being photographed, too?"

Oh, that easy Southern smile. "Bet you already know the answer to that."

"You'll have to settle for my eyes tonight, but I'll add it to the menu for future use."

"You wanna see me now?"

She nodded, then curled her finger to tell him to step closer. When he did, she rubbed his hard, thick thighs and gave his taunting hand a front-row audience. "Show me."

"You said no rush."

"I lied. Show me."

One thumb slipped behind the waistband, easing it down to expose the base of his shaft, and that dark V of hair shot through with silver. Impatient, she reached out to finish the job herself, but Bern caught her wrist in a firm grip.

"You're eager tonight."

No doubt. At times this man felt like a controlled substance, one Sam didn't a hundred percent trust herself to be left alone with. "I want you."

"You'll always get me. You'll always get this," he said, and pushed that black cotton down to expose himself. Six times she'd been with him now, yet the sight of him still thrilled her as it had that very first night.

And this night was different. What she saw was precisely what she'd get when Bern took her. The condom's whisper-thin barrier felt like a wall coming down, making all of this so undeniably real. In this realm of negotiated three-ways, losing the protection was strangely like telling someone *I love you* for the first time. The physical manifestation of stakes being upped intensely. Of attachments being declared and promises made.

There had been high stakes before—their identities and privacy, and Bern's risk of having a part in the accidental dismantling of a marriage, should Sam and Mike not have weathered the storm these games could easily have unleashed. But this new boundary . . . *I trust you*, this move told Bern. *We trust you. And we want you all to ourselves, at least for now. We want you. Do you want us back? Enough to be faithful?*

And he'd told them, yes, he did. Christ if that didn't mean something to Sam, something so beyond the bounds of Mike's kink and its preoccupation with fluids . . .

Bern moved her hand to his cock and she clasped him, charged with more than lust. With gratitude and awe. And something darker. She gave him the strokes she already knew he loved, and desire spurred her to go further—to rush to the floor to kneel and close her lips around him.

"Fuck yes. Sam."

Outside, in his car, Mike was watching. And he'd know exactly what this felt like. This room, this floor, her mouth, Bern's cock—every angle of it, every role. She took him deeper, aggression hijacking her excitement. A few times in her past, she'd felt this same drive. Aided by alcohol and the scary thrill of new attachment, she'd felt this fuel burning in her blood, driving her to fuck a new lover so good he'd never want another woman. It had been years since she'd felt it—not since she and Mike had still been new to each other—but it came back to her in a rush.

He felt so right in her mouth. Familiar but forbidden, the same as his voice and scent and the rhythm of his pounding body when it claimed hers. Same as his name in her messaging app or her in-box. Everything about it.

Christ, I love this man.

Whoa. Shit.

Not actually, of course. That was the wine and conspiracy talking. And thankfulness, for everything he'd done for her and the man she *truly* loved. She loved Bern as she might a good friend. A real and powerful love, but not what she felt for Mike.

Just lust, intensified. Lust on fire—nothing more. She returned her attention to the physical, and got lost where she needed to be, between their bodies, until—

"Sam."

She froze. That was no overwrought murmur from Bern, but the stern sound that announced Mike's arrival in the festivities. She freed her mouth but held Bern firmly as she turned to meet her husband's eyes. Her worries had had her rooted too deeply in reality, and she struggled to pick the right emotion to feign—ambivalence, annoyance, pity? Bern came to her rescue, tilting her face so she met his eyes.

"Keep going," he said.

She stroked his cock, but didn't take him back inside her mouth.

Bern's gaze jumped coldly to Mike. "You again."

"I'm getting really fucking sick of finding you here."

"Your wife's got needs. I meet them." Bern looked down at Sam, his annoyed expression saying he thought this conversation might go on for a while. "Go ahead and get on the bed, honey."

"Don't you fucking call her that," Mike cut in, but the strength in his voice was already waning. "I've been taping you both, you know. I've seen everything."

Not everything, Sam thought, cheeks warming as she moved to kneel on the mattress behind Bern. *Not that kiss.*

"Hope that tape's still rolling," Bern said to Mike. "More footage for you to get pointers from."

"You can't come into my home and talk to me like this."

Bern's posture hitched, as though with a silent laugh, and Sam imagined he was smiling now. "You can't pretend you're really that offended," he said to Mike. "You have fun when we all get together, too, don't you?"

Mike's expression shifted officially from angry to unsure, and his gaze sought Sam's.

"It get you off to watch a better man please your wife?" Bern asked.

That's pretty much exactly the idea.

Mike didn't respond, and Bern turned to Sam. "Touch me. Show him what you need that he can't give you."

Sam moved to the edge of the mattress and reached around to stroke him. She made the pulls long and indulgent, and watched Mike's face. The predictable subtleties were there—the wariness in his brow, the glazing of his eyes. All the contradictions that constructed his sexuality, written on that handsome face.

"Mike," she said. "Come here."

He did, looking nervous. She could bet why, but that wasn't what she was after tonight. She told him, "Take your clothes off." Her hand stilled on Bern's cock and she asked, "There's no reason you both can't make me feel good, is there, baby?"

Bern answered after a pause, turning around. "I guess not. But you said he can't please you."

She glanced at Mike, who was stripping away his shirt. She took in the body that she wasn't supposed to admire, excitement deepening and those worries finally dissipating. "He can take direction."

Bern smiled down at her, seeming to give in. "Like I could say no to you."

She grinned right back. She could laugh to think she'd ever worried this role would demean her. Exploited? Try spoiled. "It's what I want."

"How?"

"Lie with me," she told Bern, and the two of them stretched out on their sides, facing. She heard Mike's belt hit the floor. "Mike, come behind me."

He did, and it was everything she'd fantasized it might be. The solid heat of two strong men against her, and the filthy feel of two hard cocks—Bern's bare one at her mound, Mike's against her ass, still covered by his shorts. Bern slid an arm beneath her and one above, and freed her bra clasp. She shivered to imagine how that might look and feel to Mike—to watch another man unwrap her with such brazen entitlement. The pitch of his breathing told her she guessed right. That it made his blood boil in precisely the way he liked best.

"What do you need, honey?" Bern asked.

"You. Always."

"Inside you?"

She kissed his mouth. "Yeah."

"Better get your panties off, then."

Sam could read Bern's mind in that instant, and smiled to herself as she realized this man served Mike as much as he did her. He planted little invitations like that one, knowing exactly what the move would do to his seeming opponent.

Sam took that segue and rolled with it. She craned her neck and spoke to Mike. "Would you?"

He said nothing, but his mouth was just behind Sam's ear, and she heard him swallow. He edged along her body and pushed her underwear down her thighs, her calves. Sam slipped her feet free and turned her attention back to Bern. "Get me ready?"

She rested her top knee on Bern's hip, giving him access. His fingertips tickled her curls and found her clit. Her leg twitched and he smiled.

Sam reached her hand back to run her nails through Mike's hair. "You, too. Get me ready."

Bern's fingers felt good, but the pleasure heightened tenfold when Mike's touch joined the game. He reached between her legs from behind, the edge of his hand brushing the length of her sex. With them both working at the same task, she was struck by just how well the man at her back knew her body. He touched her with a smooth, subtle perfection, knowing every spot to hit, the exact pressure and friction. She wanted him to slide those fingers inside her as he had countless times, to tease her into hysterics with the promise of his cock.

And what she really wanted, deep down, was for their cuckolding dynamics to burn away, just for one night, and for each of these men to reveal themselves for who they were. She wanted Bern to watch

Mike fuck her as he did when it was only the two of them. She wanted her husband rough, and smug, and showing off to Bern as boldly as their guest did to Mike. She wanted both of them baring what they actually felt, openly. Two excited men, eager to please her, and no callous-wife part to play. No parts at all. Just for one night.

Ask them. They'll give that to you.

"Now you're ready," Bern whispered, dipping inside her, his fingers surely touching Mike's. Arousal flashed the length of her body at the idea. And he was right—she was wet, and from her own thoughts as much as from their two pampering hands.

"Show me what you want," he said.

Sam slid her hand between their bodies to stroke him, her touch sloppy with distraction from what both men were doing.

Bern's lips were at her forehead, and he exhaled in a huff. "Yeah, you want that, don't you?"

"Always."

"Maybe your husband would like to help me give it to you."

Sam wasn't entirely sure what he was implying, but she liked where this was going.

"What d'you think?" Bern asked Mike. "You wanna give me a hand?"

And between her legs, Sam discovered what Bern meant. She felt him take Mike's hand and put it to his cock, making him guide it to Sam's lips. She wanted to see it all, so badly, but her raised leg blocked the view. She pictured it instead, feeling hazy.

The butt of Mike's hand stroked her just before Bern's smooth crown found her folds.

"Yeah," Bern breathed.

"You let him do this?" Mike asked, barely louder than a whisper. "Fuck you, unprotected?"

I do now. "I need to feel him. With nothing in the way."

Bern moaned, his hips driving him deeper. "Yeah, you need to feel this."

While the actual absence of the condom was negligible, Sam felt the difference starkly.

You're mine, she thought, kissing Bern's throat. *Maybe not forever, but for now.* She felt his silent groan against her lips as he began to thrust.

"She loves it bare," he said to Mike. "She loves my come."

Sam blushed, the sensation winding her tighter.

"I'll get rid of you the second you're gone," Mike said.

"Oh yeah?" Bern was panting. "Bet I can guess exactly how. Bet you know how I taste even better than your wife does, don't you?"

"Fuck you."

Bern laughed softly. He held Sam's hip, taking her deeper. She longed for Mike's hand on that same spot, and for their fingers to touch. Anything that united them physically. Anything that further merged the *three* of them—that was what Sam craved. Mike hungered for the threat of a rival, Bern for an audience. Sam wanted more. An enmeshment. A bond. She'd ventured into this situation intimidated but hopeful, prepared to pay much more than mere lip service to Mike's kink. Now here she was, sealed between these two men's bodies, feeling consumed and adoring it.

She'd never seen this coming. Not for a second.

Mike shifted and his hands closed around her breasts, the sensation curling her spine, driving her ass against him. Sometimes he'd take her from behind, on their sides just like this, and those fingertips teasing and toying could make Sam come without her clit ever being touched.

Tonight it was a different man's cock rushing in and out of her, and the experience was electric. Bern's shaft rubbed her clit as Mike spoiled her breasts, and they were everywhere—their scents in her nose and their groans in her ears, their hard bodies framing her soft one. Pleasure, multiplied, and like a flame doubled by the presence of a mirror, Sam burned brighter than she ever had before. She stroked Bern's back with one hand and laid the other over Mike's fingers, feeling his knuckles dance as he teased her nipple. Moans were rising in her throat, and she let them flow.

"You like this?" Bern murmured. He said it softly, but Mike could hear it as easily as Sam could. "Two men?"

"It's amazing." So amazing she could be drunk, or high. Too good to believe.

"You deserve it," he told her.

"And you spoil me."

"Every chance I get."

"I like . . ."

"You like what?" Bern prompted.

Sam turned her head to look at Mike, then back to Bern. "I like the both of you. Having both of you, as you really are. All games aside."

And that was the reality she wanted to be in when she came tonight. Plugged in and present with these two men, all pretense and drama stripped away. No more barriers, not of any kind.

I just fucked with Mike's script.

Yeah, she had. But in a way, she felt they'd role-played as far as they could. Mike could only "catch" them so many times. If simply getting to watch Bern fuck her still ate him alive in that way he so loved, the theatrics seemed a formality.

"Just as we are?" Bern echoed, slowing.

"Yeah." Again, she looked to Mike, needing reassurance. If she'd wrecked his fantasy, she couldn't tell—he looked stoned on arousal, and his cock was as stiff and ready as ever.

Bern stilled completely. "You mean I finally get to find out how you guys fuck, just with each other?"

Sam blinked, surprised the exhibitionist was so eager to watch. She couldn't guess his reasons—simple curiosity, or maybe a touch of that insecurity that got Mike so hot? Did he want to see what his dirty texts and photos and videos and real-life performances drove them to, when he wasn't around? She couldn't say for sure, but there was no denying the eagerness in his voice. "If that's something you want, I'm game. Mike?"

"Is that what *you* want?" he asked her.

"Yeah. It is." She'd seen Bern fake a dozen things for them—cruelty and cockiness and every mean shade in between. She'd love to see what else that gorgeous face might project, with the artifice set aside. Would she see fascination there, as he watched them, or blind lust? Even a touch of jealousy? That would be a reversal indeed.

Bern slid out. "Show me, then."

CHAPTER NINETEEN

Bern sat up, kneeling on the bed. Sam's heart was beating hard, and from more than just lust. She turned over and looked into Mike's eyes, seeking any sign that she'd steered them too far from the heart of his kink. None greeted her; only the intensity of sexual excitement.

She kissed her husband—the man she'd kissed thousands of times before, yet never like this. She made it deep, and fierce, and grateful, her teeth catching his lip and her palms curling with possession around his neck. His hair brushed her fingertips, so soft and subtle after Bern's longer waves. He tasted different—he'd had a swallow of whiskey when he'd come in.

"You feel good," she said, hooking her leg around his hip, welcoming the stiff press of his erection still trapped behind his shorts.

"Not half as good as you." He dragged his palm lightly over her breast, drawing her nipple tight and her breath short.

"I want you."

"Tell me how."

She smiled at those three little words, ones he'd whispered and moaned and used to order her any number of times these past five years. Ones she'd gotten very used to reading in Bern's texts as well.

"On your knees, with your hand."

Mike knew what she meant. Sam rolled onto her back as he shed his underwear. He knelt between her thighs, allowing only three eager strokes of her hand before he moved it aside and slid deep. She shut her eyes and smiled, loving this familiar moment, and when they opened, she held Mike's gaze, then Bern's. Their guest's lips were parted; he licked them as though thirsty.

She looked to Mike. "Show him what I like." A frisson moved through the room at that order, everything inverting in one hot moment.

Mike took her at a taut, controlled pace, with that rough little slap each time their bodies met. This was Sam's favorite view during sex—Mike's gorgeous torso, upright, clenched and undulating as he thrust. He laid a hand across her mound, thumb on her clit, and the contact arched her back and curled her toes.

"Good." She squeezed his arms, just as she might Bern's, and feasted on the sight of her husband's body. It was the most free she'd felt since these three-way games had begun, letting her new lover finally glimpse behind the scenes, and see her husband for who he really was.

Bern's gaze was on her, moving from her face to her breasts to the point where their bodies met.

"Can I touch myself?" he asked.

"Of course." Let him be watched, even as he was the audience.

Sam was burning up, and from so much more than the friction of Mike's fingers or the rush of his driving cock. From everything her eyes could take in, every sound in her ears and every scent suffusing the room. From the flex of Mike's abs and the tops of his thighs as he owned her; from the spectacle of Bern's fist making slow work of his startling cock. From the reality of her own sex life, in this bright, blazing moment.

Her hands were on her breasts, deepening the pleasure. "I'm close, baby." She said it to Mike, but it was meant for the both of them.

"What do you need?"

"Just this. Don't stop."

"Rougher?"

"Yeah."

He delivered, his thrusts racing, body meeting hers with a force that had her orgasm intensifying to a foregone conclusion. She looked to Bern, finding fire in those blue eyes.

He told her, "You're so fucking hot."

"You, too." She dropped her attention to his pumping hand. "Keep on giving me that show."

"Whatever you need."

She looked to Mike, finding his expression absent—from arousal, not dispassion. He was too close to stay plugged in without losing himself. She knew that hazy, far-off look so well.

"Get me there, baby," she said, already on the brink.

A dozen hard thrusts did the job, and when the crescendo struck he dropped to his forearms, pushing his dick deep as she rode the spasms.

"Sam."

She came back to reality to find her fingers denting his biceps, and felt the crazed expression plastered across her face. She sighed loudly, then glanced at each man in turn with a smile.

Mike lowered, as though doing a push-up, and kissed her forehead. "That's my girl."

She nodded, utterly wasted. "That's me."

"What now?" Mike whispered, loud enough for Bern to hear.

She swallowed, struggling for clarity and considering the logistics. Bern had to come next, if she wanted to indulge Mike's reclamation fantasies. "Him," she said.

Mike eased out, that slick friction tensing her anew. In a breath, Bern was in his place. His cock felt cool as he pushed in deep, taking her breath away. Never had the fact that she was with two men struck her so hard.

"How do you want me?" he asked, taking her slow and steady.

"However you like it."

He gathered her legs, holding her crossed ankles to his shoulder. His hips bumped her ass with every thrust. He liked this position especially, she bet. Him upright, performing, holding her like an instrument. She liked it as well. Liked feeling mastered.

Mike was at her side, stroking her arm with his fingertips. He had to be close, if he didn't dare touch himself. Sam leaned over to kiss him, then moved his hand to her breast—more for Bern's benefit than hers.

A thought struck her. *Good God, this is on tape.*

The uncontestably hottest night of her life, and she had the homemade porn to prove it. She nearly laughed aloud, giddy at the thought.

Bern swore through a moan. "I shouldn't be this close already."

Her heart danced at that proclamation. The thing she wanted most had both of these men teetering on the edge.

"I *want* you close," she said, and urged his thrusts with a hand on his side. "I want you to lose it, inside me."

His eyes shut and his head dropped back, a sign Sam could recognize well, now. "Yeah."

When's the last time you got to do this? she wondered. With his last serious girlfriend, likely, but that had been months ago. She selfishly hoped he hated condoms, and had suffered through the necessity of them with any interim lovers. She hoped this was a treat for him, a gift worthy of his fidelity.

"Fuck, I'm coming. I'm coming, honey."

"Do it."

"Get ready. Get ready for me." He dropped her legs and Sam gripped his shoulders, drawing him down. He raced into his pleasure, eyes blazing, hips furious. With the deepest groan, he froze, buried to the root. His body rocked in three clenching waves, and Sam was lost in the moment. His skin shone, slick in the lamplight, and she doubted he'd ever looked so sexy. She smiled and touched his face, letting her fondness show—letting both men see it.

Bern pulled out and sat beside her, expression dazed. She wondered if he'd go now, too sobered by his orgasm to want to watch what came next. But no.

"Let me see." He spoke to Sam, but she knew the words were meant for Mike. He wanted to know what went down after he normally took his leave.

Sam was curious herself, how Mike might want to remedy the violation. She expected his mouth, and was surprised when he knelt between her legs once more and slid inside. That moment was beyond explicit—she was wet from so much more than her own arousal and climax. She felt Bern's spoils slicking the space between them, and Mike had to as well.

"You feel me?" Bern muttered—that was the only word for it. Nearly derisive, the way he asked it.

Mike shut his eyes, fucking hard and fast. "Yeah."

"Just try to get rid of me," Bern said, and his attention was on Sam's face.

Mike was there inside a minute, his orgasm rocking him as a punch might, shock on his face as surely as relief. He closed his panting body over Sam's, moaning softly into her hair.

She stroked his back and head, and breathed the both of them in, those pungent, mismatched smells that now marked her sex life.

Mike caught his breath and moved to the side. Bern mirrored him and Sam sighed loudly into the air between them, then giggled.

"Holy shit," she whispered.

"Oh good," Bern said.

Mike added nothing, just kissed her throat and hummed a happy noise. She kissed his temple in reply, then turned to look at Bern. "Thank you."

"You are so fucking welcome."

She grinned. "That was awesome."

"Good. You deserved every second of it."

Only one orgasm, yet she felt completely annihilated, spent to the point of oblivion.

"I'm gonna leave you two alone," Bern whispered. "I'll show myself out."

"Okay."

He kissed her lips one last time and left the bed. Sam listened to him dressing and traced Mike's face with a fingertip.

Muted footsteps grew faint, then disappeared down the stairs. The click of the dead bolt, then the lock as he shut the door behind him.

She buried her face against Mike's neck. "Mmmm . . ."

"Oh yeah?"

"Oh fuck yeah."

He laughed, and they fell into a peaceful silence. Sam felt sleep creeping up on her, until Mike drew her back into his orbit.

"Was it different?" he asked, sounding perfectly awake himself. "Having him inside you? Bare?"

She nodded. "Yeah. It was sexy. Felt extra forbidden. Sort of . . . dangerous. And dirty."

"Could you feel it when he came?"

"Yeah." That was a lie, of course. But Sam's mother had always said a kind lie made a fine compliment, so surely a lie that turned your lover's crank was a valentine. "I felt it. It felt hot when he came."

Mike swallowed. "What was the hottest thing for you tonight?"

She stroked the swell of his shoulder. "Having both of you, just as you were. It felt like I was the one getting indulged this time . . ." She frowned. "That's not quite the right wording. I get indulged plenty when we're acting out your fantasies."

"But this was yours. Yours to direct."

"Yeah. You love imagining I'm cheating on you. I guess I just love feeling that desired by two men. And feeling . . . shared. Like, in the dirtiest way possible."

Mike laughed. "Always."

"We can go back to it being about the cuckolding, of course. I sort of wrecked the continuity tonight. But we can always go back to you two pretending you've never met. Back to the days when I just randomly brought someone home."

"The soap opera parts of it don't matter to me—the narrative. Not the way it did at first. Just seeing you with another man is plenty intense. *Tonight* was intense, even with all the humiliation stuff gone."

"Yeah?"

"Absolutely. Part of me was pretty fucking proud, in fact, showing him I know how to please you."

She smiled. "Me, too."

"Maybe I'll change my mind, but if we want to try making these get-togethers about something else—about you getting to be with us both, however you want, or about whatever he might be wanting . . . I'm happy to take us all off the script. See where this goes as a straight-up threesome."

"I would be, too. And I'll talk to him. See if he's on the same page."

"Though I think we're back to surveillance fun, for next weekend," Mike said, winding Sam's hair around his finger.

"Oh, right. I forgot." Mike was going to be in Philadelphia for three days, for a statewide narcotics summit. "So just me and him, if that's okay."

They'd not done that yet—just Sam and Bern the entire time, and Mike watching via live feed. She'd been wondering how it would be afterward. How she and Bern would say good night once the show was over. If he'd stick around for a drink, or be gone as quickly as when he was here to play Sam's heartless piece on the side. She thought back to this very evening, thinking she'd better have her boundaries in order. In the middle of getting ravaged by a hot electrician was *not* the time to try to get one's head on straight about propriety.

"Works for me," Mike said, letting her hair spool from his finger in a long curl. "And I'm sure it'll work for him. You guys just do whatever you want."

"Oh, speaking of cameras . . ." She left the lazy comfort of the bed with a grudging groan to shut the laptop. "So, Saturday night?"

"Yeah. The meetings are supposed to wrap early that night. I'll grab a quick dinner and be free by seven."

"Fingers crossed your hotel Wi-Fi is nice and fast," she teased as she lay back down beside him, rubbing her thumb across his stubbled chin.

He smiled, bent his head to kiss her knuckles. "Amen."

CHAPTER TWENTY

Bern was free the coming Saturday, and plans solidified through a handful of texts.

Can't fucking wait, he wrote that Monday.

Us, either. See you around 6:30.

With Mike leaving for Philly on Wednesday morning, Sam's week would feel endless, even if the anticipation always sweetened these dates.

She waded through the workweek, her normally stimulating job no longer holding a candle to the dynamism of her personal life. No fewer than three of her coworkers asked her if she was feeling okay. She assured them she was.

"Just spacey. One of those weeks." *Just horny out of my ever-loving mind, thanks.*

Saturday arrived, along with the usual happy jitters. Mike texted around noon with a bit of a letdown.

Hey, pretty, you jinxed us. Just tried watching YouTube and the connection here sucks donkey balls. Why don't you guys tape yourselves tonight and e-mail it to me?

"Boo," she said to the living room at large, then typed, Aww, that stinks! But okay—I doubt your heart could handle the buffering. And the show must go on, huh?

Fucking right. Plus, this way I can grab drinks with a few of the guys after the last meeting wraps. Love you. See you before bed, I hope . . . ?

Banging another man? Absolutely! xoxo

Except just a few minutes shy of five, a phone call chimed. Sam greeted her mother cheerfully, expecting the usual family gossip, but it was a different sort of news that followed. Sam felt the weight of the real world come crashing down around her, as painful and sudden as a shot in the heart.

She hung up with tears streaming, wetting her shirt collar and slipping between her breasts. It was all she could do to tap out a shaky text to Bern. Something just came up. I have to cancel tonight—I'm sorry. I'll explain soon. She set her phone aside, throat so tight it ached, eyes raw.

Mike was probably still having drinks. Going to call you later tonight, she texted. Try to be free after dinner. She'd try his phone at seven, when she and Bern had been due to hit RECORD for him. It might interrupt his social plans, but she needed to talk to him so badly. Needed him here with her, as the news left her feeling suspended, the earth crumbled away from beneath her feet. She gripped the counter's edge, rocked by a sob, and moaned into the emptiness.

Seven couldn't come soon enough, though the wait would give her time to compose herself. She'd take a bath. That would—

The doorbell chimed.

"Oh fuck." Her phone said it was six fifteen, so it could only be Bern. She rubbed her eyes with the heels of her hands, but there was no way he'd miss that she'd been crying. She'd showered after a long run but not gotten around to changing or doing her makeup before the news had struck. It didn't matter now. It felt as though nothing mattered anymore.

She twisted the bolt and opened the door, her sheepish smile quivering. "Hi."

"Hey." He paused, his own smile wilting. He had a bottle of wine under one arm. "Are you okay?"

She laughed, feeling mixed up and freaked out and ridiculous. An utter mess. "Not at all, no. Sorry. I texted, but you were probably already driving."

"Did you need to cancel?"

Sam nodded. "Yeah. I just got some bad news. I'm not really feeling very . . ." And she trailed off, voice swallowed by a warble. "Sorry," she gasped.

"Hey, it's okay. I should've checked my phone. I didn't mean to intrude . . . Maybe you should sit down a sec." He stepped inside and shut the door.

She wiped at her runny nose with her wrist and they walked down the hall to the living room. Sam sank onto the couch cushions. She reached for a tissue but the box was empty.

"Hang on." Bern set the wine bottle on the breakfast bar and disappeared inside the bathroom, returning with a roll of toilet paper. "Here."

Grinning in embarrassment, Sam accepted it. "Thank you." She blew her nose. "Are you feeling seduced yet?" she joked, heart loosening by a degree when Bern smiled.

His gaze was mild, calm. Kind. "Can I ask what happened?"

"You can, but only if you're prepared for me to have three dimensions."

He looked troubled at that, eyebrows drawing together. She'd never seen him wear that expression before.

"I mean, only if we want to wreck our group fantasy," she said, "by you seeing me as more than just your . . . whatever you think of me as. Kinky fling partner? We've managed to keep everything all fun and games before now. I'd hate to drag it down."

"You're my lover, Sam, not a blow-up doll. You've had three dimensions since the first time we talked on the phone. You've had about six since what happened last weekend. And if my acting like a friend to you feels too intimate . . ." He laughed again, softly, voice dropping to a near whisper. "Sam, your husband's sucked my dick. You think a little crying's going to scare me off?"

She had to smile, tears still slipping free. "When you put it like that . . ."

"So what happened?"

"My cousin died."

"Oh God, that sucks. I'm so sorry."

Sam nodded. "Thank you. I haven't seen her in years—she lived in Tehran, like most of my dad's family does. But she used to visit every summer when we were kids."

"You guys were close?"

"I'm two years older, but she was always more sophisticated and worldly than me, so it felt like we came of age together, sort of time-lapse-style."

"Can I ask what . . ."

"She was walking, and I guess someone ran a red light. Just one of those freaky things."

"Shit. That fucking sucks, Sam." He paused. "Wish I had something more poetic or comforting to say. But mostly that just really sucks."

Sam laughed, fresh sobs rising. "That's all that can be said about it, really. So thanks . . . Anyhow, I'm just dealing with that. My mom only called around five, so I'm still in shock."

"Sure. Want me to go, or stick around and distract you?"

"God, I dunno." She smoothed her hair back, curls wild and fuzzy from air-drying. "I'm such a fucking mess tonight."

"I'll at least stick around for a bit. It's no good being on your own right after you get news like that."

"I don't really feel like talking about it."

"Sure. We'll talk about other stuff, then."

She dabbed at her eyes. "Like?"

"Like anything . . . Like when did your dad come here? To the States?"

"In his early thirties, with my mom. He's an engineering professor."

"Really? My dad's an engineer. Or was—he retired a couple of years ago."

"Oh?" Sam mustered the energy to make small talk. It felt nice, actually. A relief. "Let me guess—electrical engineering?"

"No, structural. Rail and bridge infrastructure."

"What about your mom?"

"She teaches high school English."

Sam considered that. "Is that how an electrician came to write his e-mails and texts with such studious capitalization and punctuation?"

Bern smiled. "Yup, that's her fault."

"So how'd you get into your field?"

"It's a pretty boring story."

"Boring sounds nice, just now." It beat *sad*, certainly. "Tell me."

"Well, my parents are hard-asses," he said, "and if I was going to college, I had to pay my own way. I didn't want to do farmwork, which is most of what there is to do where I'm from. I tried driving delivery trucks but hated that. My dad got me connected with a contractor friend, and I just . . . I dunno, I really liked it. I did menial work for a couple of years when I was eighteen, nineteen, and thought the electrical stuff looked the most interesting, so I got certified. Then I apprenticed for a guy I knew from that contracting company, worked a few years, and realized that all that time, I'd been saving money for this education I was supposed to get, except there was no other field I was all that interested in. I was happy doing what I was, and getting paid well for it. So. Here I am."

"Here you are," she agreed, and her gaze dropped from his eyes to his chest, to his long legs, his strong hands. It wasn't a lustful scrutiny, just a momentary rush of . . . something softer. Something humbling. Gratitude to have him here, acting like a friend. *Being* a friend. Being three-dimensional, just as she'd feared becoming to him.

Why wouldn't I want that? I don't really want to sleep with the idea of a man. I want to sleep with a human being. A hot, charismatic one with undeniable skills in bed and a very, very open mind. A kind one, too, who made her feel human in return.

Even if he didn't feel like comforting and distracting her, even if he wished he'd gotten her text and saved himself the trip . . . even if he'd go home disappointed that he hadn't gotten laid, he was doing everything a friend would. Setting his wants aside, treating her well. And it was undeniably calming. Her body hurt less. Her heart had loosened some, and that choking sensation had faded along with the initial shock of the sad news.

They chatted more about their upbringings, about Sam's college years, about the small town where Bern had grown up, about Pittsburgh. When the conversation hit a natural break, she sighed, feeling lighter.

"Little calmer?" he asked.

"Yeah." It was hard not to feel calm around this man. His voice alone was like a nightcap.

She reached out and touched his hand. Funny how intimate—how *bold*—that felt, after everything else they'd done. Bold but pleasant. "Thanks," she murmured. "I'm sorry you got your time wasted tonight, but it was nice to not be alone with myself for a little while."

He smiled and turned his hand over, circling her wrist loosely in his fingers. "My time wasn't wasted. I don't think people can do the things we have with and for each other without qualifying as friends, Samira. And anyone who thinks it's a waste of their time, hanging out with a friend who's having a shitty day . . . well, they deserve a punch in the side of the head."

She laughed, rubbing his palm with her thumb. "Good point."

"I brought wine, and my night's all freed up. You want to watch TV or a movie or something?" He paused, seeming to reconsider. "I mean, unless that's weird. Unless Mike would be uncomfortable with that."

Mike. She wasn't certain if she'd ever heard Bern speak his name before. And she had to give the matter serious thought. What would Mike want? For his wife to sit home alone with her grief, if the alternative was for her to get her emotional comfort from his sexual rival? There was a line buried in here somewhere, a blurry one. But she also doubted that Bern had any designs on her apart from fun and sex. He wasn't trying to move in on her, or on Mike's role as her partner.

She told Bern, "I think he'd rather I had the company."

"You can check with him."

She considered it, but he was probably still out, and she hadn't told him precisely when to expect her call. "He's having drinks with colleagues right now."

"Glass of wine while we wait?"

Sam thought about it. "You know what? He thinks you're coming over tonight to fuck me. If he's going to have an issue with us hanging out fully clothed, as friends, on a night when I really don't feel like being alone . . . ? That's an argument I'm willing to have with him. So, executive decision—sure. Let's watch a movie."

"Right, then. You pick, I'll pour."

Sam knew a lot of things about Bern Davies's tastes, but none of them helped her as she scrolled through the offerings on Netflix. He seemed like an action-movie kind of guy. And she could go for some mindless explosions and stunts just now. "How about I pick three, and then you decide between those?" she called.

Bern was at the breakfast bar, busy with the cork. "Just pick. I'll watch whatever."

"That's too much pressure. I'll choose three."

"As you like it," he said, and walked over to deliver glasses and the open bottle to the coffee table.

"Okay," she said, eyes narrowed at the screen. "This new superhero thing is option number one."

"Already saw it. Kinda sucked."

"See? I told you choices were important. Okay, how about something older, then?" she asked, scrolling. "I've never seen *Commando*."

"A classic."

"Okay, *Commando*, or . . ."

"*Commando*. Hit PLAY."

"Bossy," she scolded, but did as he said.

Bern took a seat and filled the glasses. Sam got comfy, sitting cross-legged and pulling the afghan over her lap. She wasn't cold, just vulnerable, and the weight of it was comforting. Same as Bern's arm might feel if she leaned into it . . . but she didn't dare. She was studying that arm as the studio logo appeared, and he noticed.

She turned to the screen. "Sorry. You have distracting arms."

"Are you flirting with me?"

"No, just being honest." She glanced down at herself and laughed. "Wow, you're really peering behind the curtain tonight."

"What do you mean?"

"I got that bad news before I could pick out some clothes or do anything with my hair."

"I think you look beautiful."

She snorted. "This is what I'd wear to clean the house."

"Well, you must look beautiful when you're dusting, then."

She smacked his shoulder. "You Southern men."

"What about us?"

"What's the term? Honey-dripper."

He made a face, the picture of innocence. "Never. I just call it like I see it."

"Do you get teased by the other contractors for that accent?"

"Sometimes. I had this one guy who was always calling me 'Rodeo.' I tried to tell him I've never been on a horse in my life, but he wasn't hearing it . . ." He trailed off, looking thoughtful.

She nudged him with her elbow. "What?"

"How were your parents, when you hooked up with Mike? Are they traditional about stuff, like wanting you to marry a guy from the same background?"

She shrugged. "I think my mom was, but she never came out and said it. My dad couldn't care less. He's really into the American melting-pot concept, not traditional at all. The only thing I know we did that disappointed them was not having kids."

"That's officially off the table, huh?"

Sam nodded. "We've always been ambivalent. And, I mean, we've had little moments where one of us is suddenly intrigued by the idea, but we've had way *more* moments where we're positive it's not for us. And parenthood isn't a decision I want to go into half-assed, you know?"

"Sure."

"What about you?"

"I dunno. I want to say yeah, I'd like kids someday. But I'd have to get married, and at the moment that's really not high on my priority list."

"You've got time."

He made a face. "I'm thirty-six. Gimme four years to meet and fall in love with the right woman, and I'm already looking at forty-year-old dadhood."

"Forty's nothing these days. Especially for the guy. Now me—if I changed my mind tomorrow, my eggs are already on the fifty-percent-off day-old shelf, halfway to the Dumpster."

Bern laughed and winced at once. "Harsh."

"It's true!" She leaned forward to top off her glass. "I'd get all those weird looks from people, like, *Gray hair* and *pregnant?* And my mom would be sending me links to articles about every terrifying older-mother birth defect there is. But you—you'd just get teased by people, like, *Uh-oh, Bern, looks like your bachelor days are over!*" She poked him in the arm. "In *fact*, you'd probably get thrown a party to celebrate your virility or something. All while my ovaries are being serenaded with a funeral dirge. You hit forty and you get put out to stud. I hit forty and I'm off to the glue factory."

He shook his head, smiling. "You're fucking insane."

Sam sank back in her seat, vindicated. "It's all true. Don't bother trying to deny it."

"Drink your wine, crazy lady."

She took a big sip, realizing the heavier feelings had lifted enough that she could register the alcohol's warm tingle. She hadn't taken any of the movie in, and when machine-gun fire flared, Bern lowered the volume.

He said quietly, "It's nice to see you smiling again."

Sam nodded. "When you get news like that, it's hard to remember there's other ways to feel, aside from just . . . agonized."

"You need to talk more?"

"No. Thank you. I feel sort of numb about it just now, like I've used all my sadness up for the night. I'm sure I'll be a wreck again tomorrow, but for now, I think I can just sit with it. Let it sink in, in the back of my head, while I let other stuff distract me."

"Good plan." Bern regarded her for a long moment, gaze slipping from her eyes to her shoulder. His hand came up to touch her hair, giving one curl a soft tug and watching it spring back. "I like your hair like that."

"Tell me you like it the other way, too, because it's embarrassing how long it takes to get it to look that good."

He smiled, the gesture etching little lines under his eyes. "I do. But it's neat to see what it looks like, left to its own devices . . . You know when you've been dating someone for two or three months, and you're getting pretty comfortable with each other, but you still make a decent effort every time you have a date?"

She nodded.

"Then suddenly they get the flu or something, and you get to see what they're like at their worst. Looking like hell, and no charm at all, all needy and everything?"

"And?"

He grinned. "I *love* that. I love the first glimpse I get of a girlfriend when she's just a wreck."

Sam laughed. "You're sick."

"No, really. I dated this one girl for a few months, and she was great, but I *never* saw her without full makeup on. We fall asleep, she's wearing makeup. By the time I see her the next morning, she's redone it for the day. I mean, I don't really care what a woman wants to do to her face, but it was starting to feel weird. Then she got mono, and it was kind of awesome."

"You're horrible!"

"No, I'm telling you. She was way too pooped to do *anything*—which sucked, of course, except I was just, like, fascinated to look at her with no makeup on. She had all these little freckles I'd never seen, and her eyelashes looked so . . . delicate. It felt like I was reading her diary or something."

"Well, okay, that's sort of sweet." Yet something sour squirmed in Sam's middle—jealousy. It didn't warrant feeding, of course. She was married, and Bern was her lover, nothing more. Why the hell should she care if he still harbored fond feelings for some ex-girlfriend? If anything, it should commend him. "Why did you guys break up?"

"Oh God, I can't remember. This must have been ten years ago."

Yet he still remembered her naked eyelashes. *Jesus, would you listen to yourself?* Whatever. This entire crazy affair had Sam feeling as mixed-up as a teenager. It stood to reason she'd revert to a younger woman's irrational emotions now and then. Perspective was the key. Be psycho, but with self-awareness.

Bern smiled, leaning in, eyes darting.

"What?"

"I'm just looking at you."

"At my delicate eyelashes?" She batted them.

"Yeah. And everything else. Did you used to have a pierced nose?"

Sam blushed, touching the spot. "Yeah. In grad school. I could never quite carry it off. And the spot's never quite faded." She scrutinized him right back. "You've got little wrinkles here," she said, tracing the lines at either corner of his lips. "But they're way deeper on this side. From that shit-eating Southern grin you wear when you're about to get away with something."

He showed her that grin now, the one that gave him a single dimple.

"And you have two perfectly white eyebrow hairs," she added, stroking them with her thumb.

"I don't doubt it." His voice was soft and low, nearly lost to the drone of the TV. Sam watched his lips form every single letter, something shifting between them, unmistakably.

She read the truth in his stare, and felt it echoed in her own. *I want you.*

In a blink, in a breath. A wanting that had been there always, beneath the surface, and now the harder feelings of the evening had melted away to let it break through. And it did, like a sleeping creature coming to life, spreading its wings, hungry and ready to hunt.

That force rose inside her. As though by magnetism, her hand came up to cup his jaw. She didn't kiss him; not yet. She brushed her thumb over his thick stubble, studying the contrast of white and silver and darkest brown. His blue eyes looked dark as well, and they watched, wary but hot. Her curious touch moved to his mouth, thumb tracing his bottom lip, then the top, finally, boldly, running along the seam between them. They parted and she could feel his breath—hot. He smelled of wine. It didn't seem right that he should ever taste of anything else.

"What on earth are we doing?" she asked, holding his face.

"Whatever you want."

"I don't know what I want."

"I don't believe you."

Sam swallowed, scared and excited. "I don't—"

"Just tell me what you need me to be," he whispered, "and I'll be that."

CHAPTER TWENTY-ONE

Tell me what you need me to be. I'll be that.

Sam swallowed, hazy all over. Of course he would. That's what he'd done all along—been who they wanted. The lover Sam could break her marriage vows with; the rival and the intruder to realize Mike's fantasies.

So what did she need right now? To feel good. To escape the pain and heartache for a little while, and be sheltered by the heat and size of this man's body. By his desire and her own. Only it wasn't right, not like this.

But one thing can make it right.

"I can't kiss you unless we record it," she whispered, gaze jumping between Bern's eyes and mouth. "It wouldn't feel right if he couldn't watch."

Bern nodded. He had to know, as she did, that this wouldn't end with just a kiss. She gave his lip a final stroke then got up. As she crossed to the corner to grab the laptop, she registered her clothes again. Drawstring pants and an old tee—if Bern wanted to see the real Sam, he sure was getting what he was after. No dress, no makeup, mismatched underwear, and puffy eyes. Yet he seemed to like her. Before things had grown heated, he'd seemed to want to be here, as a friend as much as a lover. Seemed to *want* her, still, even when things weren't all fun and games.

The movie went silent and she turned to find Bern setting the remote back on the coffee table. She propped the laptop open beside it, aimed it at the couch, and hit RECORD. She joined Bern back on the cushions and whispered too quietly for the computer to pick up, "Just pretend it's a hidden camera again."

"Sure."

Good. Because the alternative was to make this a show, and Sam didn't have a performance in her tonight. Moreover, she didn't want to share Bern's attention with the camera—she wanted his eye contact all to herself. And knowing Mike would get just as hot over a "secret" tape as he would over a cocky, show-offy one, she trusted it wasn't a selfish need.

She touched Bern's face as their mouths met, and everything bubbling inside her came to a head. Desire eclipsed sadness as his tongue stroked hers, and a deep breath became a groan in his throat. Her fingertips rasped against his stubble. He'd shaved that morning, but she'd bet his five-o'clock shadow routinely asserted itself by half past ten. She liked that about him. She'd dated mostly clean-cut, academic guys before Mike, and had since realized she liked her men blue-collar and a touch rough—rough around the edges and a bit rough between the sheets, too. She'd thought those more pedigreed guys had been her type—intellectual overthinkers like herself, guys with expensive shoes and strong opinions about restaurants. New York men with advanced degrees and the soft hands to match. It had taken one chance meeting in a dive bar with a Pittsburgh cop to change her tune forever.

She'd been in town that weekend for a friend's engagement party, and her flight home had been canceled due to some mechanical issue. She'd gone back to the hotel for the night, ended up at the bar across the road, and ultimately wound up taking Mike back to her room. Ten months later, she moved in with him.

And five *years* later, here she was, feeling a very similar persuasion of lust-wonder, exploring an electrician.

I just need a fireman and a mechanic, and I'll have the set.

Bern's hand was strong and broad, fingers splayed possessively along her jaw. His other arm lay along the back of the couch, idly toying with a lock of her hair. The heat between them had crowded out the sadness, filled in all the isolation she'd been adrift in before he'd arrived. A temporary respite, but she'd take what she could get, for as long as it might last. She stroked his chest through his shirt, picturing the bare skin she'd come to know well these past couple of months.

He was wearing a work shirt, and she freed a button, then another, each and every one. She slid her hand inside to feel the heat of him through his tee, the thump of his heart. Her kisses wavered as his hand closed around hers and moved it down—over his hard belly, then pressing it to his even harder erection. She squeezed him through his jeans, earning a low moan and stealing control, if only for a breath.

"I want you," he said. "So bad."

"Do you?" Hungry for proof to underline those words, she undid his fly and exposed him.

"You see how bad?" he whispered.

Sam nodded, swallowed, spoke too quietly for the computer's microphone to possibly hear. "I never thought I'd ever be with another man, after I married him. And not like this." She stroked his bare cock, wondering if he even knew what she meant. It was undeniably different now, without the condoms. Not the sensations, just . . . She wasn't even sure. The way it blurred the few lines left among the three of them. If Mike wasn't to be the only man who got to have her, she'd have assumed he'd at least be the only one who got to come in her, like that. And if Bern got that, too, and this sex felt so intimate and personal . . . What was still Mike's?

Our love. Our home, our day-to-day life, my family. Those were a lot. Those were huge, but she couldn't help but feel that this was wrong somehow, even with the camera running.

In her gut, and in her heart, it was just the two of them.

It'll be his, too, when he watches the video. But did she really believe that, or merely want to, for the sake of permission?

"What do you need tonight?" Bern asked, his hips shifting, pushing his cock into her strokes.

"Just to feel good." Emotions rose and tightened her throat. *Just to not feel bad, for a little while. Take me there.* Too much to say aloud without risking tears. Mike didn't need a video of Bern rocking his sobbing, hysterical wife on their couch. That was an intimacy too far, even set against all the carnal things they'd done together.

"Here," Bern said. The next moment he was on the floor, kneeling before her, coaxing her legs over. She let him slide her pants and underwear off in one slow, gentle motion. His attention was on her skin as he stroked her calves and thighs. There was reverence in his eyes, and his gaze was as soft as she'd ever seen it. She wondered for a brief, dangerous second, what kind of a boyfriend this man would make. He'd so embodied the brash role they'd written for him, it hadn't occurred to her he could be this tender.

That same scratchy stubble she'd caressed was on her thigh now, a sharp tease to contrast the soft lips trailing kisses up her leg. When he tugged at her hips, she scooted closer, opening up for him. Her fingers tangled in his overgrown hair, and she led his mouth right where she needed it.

A soft lap, another. Deeper, deeper, until he was giving her those hungry strokes she'd been fantasizing about since their very first night in bed together. He gave head like it was a feast. Like it was for him. Mike gave head like he was treating Sam, and he knew exactly what she liked. But there was an undeniable thrill to being consumed, to feeling like this act was something she was giving a man, and not the other way around.

She fisted his hair gently. "Feels good, baby. I like how deep you get."

He met her gaze. "I'll show you deep."

"I bet you will."

"Not till I make you come." Bern went back to work.

She loved how he looked from this angle. His eyes were shut, lashes dark and long, brow drawn in concentration or excitement. She studied the streaks at his temples, more silver than gray, she decided. Studied his fingers, and the soft dents they made in her thighs, and his nails . . . Tidy nails, clean for a man who spent his workdays on building sites.

Words dropped from her subconscious, brightening the space between them. "You're so sexy." He gave her more, his nose glancing her clit as he tasted her with long, filthy sweeps of his tongue. Her words had spurred him, but they scared her. Not the words themselves—she was supposed to be objectifying him. No, it was the way she'd spoken them. With more awe than lust. She needed to make this dirty, and fast.

"I need your cock, baby."

"Do you, then?" He showed no signs of stopping.

"Please. It's all I can think about."

He slipped a hand between her legs, two thick fingers sliding deep as his mouth moved to her clit. She gasped from the penetration, and all at once her fretful fib was true—she needed his cock, now. Needed his excitement driving into hers in the rawest, darkest ways, erasing everything outside of the sex.

"You're wet," he murmured, fingers pumping. "Wet enough?"

"Yeah. I'm ready."

"Want you as wet as I can get you, first. Wanna earn this."

"You have. Just . . . please. You. Now."

He quit teasing. Had he heard in her voice how badly she needed him? Needed his body inside hers, but simpler things as well. His face. His words. The weight and heat of him above her, and the blissful, relentless motion of his hips as he rocked them both into oblivion.

When he stood, Sam lay back. He shed his work shirt, peeled away his tee, pushed his open jeans down his thighs. He stripped naked for her, then joined her on the couch, lowering that thrilling, beautiful body to hers. He held himself up on one arm and angled his cock between her legs, easing in halfway, backing off, edging deeper. He made a wondrous sound, a sigh mixed with a moan, and framed her chest with his forearms, settling in.

"This what you need?" he asked, and began to thrust.

She shut her eyes and dunked herself in the sensations for a long moment. "Yeah. That's exactly what I need."

His pace was quick, but not rushed. "You miss this when we're apart?"

"Every minute."

"Me, too. I love it inside you, this way," he whispered, slowing, making her feel how right—how *wrong*—this was. Just their skin and nothing more, just her excitement and his.

In the back of her mind, she knew he shouldn't be whispering, but she loved his voice this way, so soft and personal. Hers. She loved these words that made a sacred place of her body, and not for the sake of defiling it.

"You feel so fucking good." Again, so quiet. Spoken louder, brasher, those words could have fulfilled Mike's script for the two of them, but whispered this way, they hummed like a secret. His voice grew quieter still when he pressed his mouth to her throat, exhaling in a hot rush. "Soft, and warm—"

"Don't whisper. He should be able to hear."

But for once, Bern didn't do as instructed. There was no way the recording caught it when he told her, "There's things I want just between you and me."

"It can't work that way."

"Only words, Sam. What he wants brought me here," he murmured, and nipped at her neck. "I say the sorts of things he wants to hear, fuck you how he wants to see us. I'm his porn star, taking his requests, but I'm a man, too. I don't ask for much. Just a few harmless words."

Were they harmless, though? If the things he was saying weren't hurtful to Mike . . .

It's not letting him hear that's hurtful.

Or would not allowing Bern to voice them be just as hurtful? He wasn't their whore, after all. He was their lover, and his needs mattered.

She whispered back, "What else?"

Bern moaned, and loud enough to be heard. He took her hard and quick with long, deep thrusts, before settling back into the steadier motions.

"I think about you," he breathed. "About what we've done. And about you watching us doing those things. Watching the movies."

She clawed his back, making him buck.

"Tell me you've watched."

"I have."

"Tell me . . ." He panted, sounding all at once overcome, his powerful body growing graceless and heavy. "Tell me it was real, the times I've made you come."

All but one. All but that first night, when he'd been too new, too novel to truly let go with. "It's real."

"Oh . . ." His heavy breathing left her skin slick where his lips teased her jaw. "This is his fantasy you're realizing. Him watching us, and you taping me—that's mine. What's yours, Sam?"

"I . . . I get to sleep with you."

"That's still his. What's yours?"

Her fantasies . . . They were so simple, so *blah* compared to Mike's and Bern's. Sometimes when she made love to Mike, she imagined he was someone else: a celebrity, or a character from a movie or TV show or book. Someone not unlike Bern—an exemplification of exquisite maleness. Like any woman, she fantasized about the lovers she had assumed she'd passed up forever in exchange for the security of monogamy. She'd explored that variety from the safety of her imagination. And now, in reality. On her couch.

"This is his *and* mine," she told Bern, fingers tangling in his hair.

He held her stare, and something in that look said he didn't believe her. But all he said was, "Then I better give it to you good."

And he did. The sex grew rougher, quicker, needier. Lit by the glow of the computer, Bern's face was set in stark concentration, his teeth nearly clenched and his breaths coming in low grunts to punctuate each thrust. Sam felt every ounce of that aggression. It echoed through her, but she felt her own ferocity mirroring his. She wanted him. She loved the way he wanted her.

She wrapped her arms tight around him, hugging his strong, long body close, urging his hips with the greedy motions of her own. Messy sex, with the most obvious views blocked from the camera's watching eye. Not porno-hot or choreographed to incite. Just two people who wanted each other in the homeliest and most urgent ways, two bodies giving and taking and sweating and aching together.

"What do you need, Sam?" He practically breathed the question, surely just a groan to the microphone.

"This."

"What else? Tell me how to get you there. Because I can't last forever."

"Make your angle sharper, so—yeah. Just like that." He'd raised his hips a little higher, so the base of his cock brushed her clit with every stroke. "God yeah. Exactly like that." She threaded her fingers through his hair and held on tight, eyes shutting. She let the room become a concept, a dark, warm space populated by their mingled breath and heat and noises. She felt release inching closer with every push of his body, like he was forcing her to the edge, stroke by stroke by stroke.

"Make me come," she whispered.

He gave it to her faster, strokes shorter and rougher.

"Yeah. Like that."

"Come for me, honey."

"I will. Don't stop."

All it took was a half dozen more pushes, and she was there. And so was Bern. He didn't slow when her moan announced her orgasm—he raced home beside her, his own groan turned staccato by the frantic hammering of his hips. And with no chance to come down, Sam felt an aftershock rising up.

"Don't stop," she begged when his release had his hips locking. "Don't stop, don't stop."

With a pained gasp he obeyed, thrusts hard and uneven. Sam held his neck and arm, nails digging, and rode a second shorter, sharper orgasm. As it crested she released her grip, and Bern stilled. He was softening inside her, and his body loosened to match.

"Holy shit."

Sam nodded, lost for words. She stroked his damp back and he caught his breath, racing exhalations steadily deepening against her throat. But as the fog of the orgasms lifted, so did the relief they'd offered.

Sam felt sober instantly—backhanded by reality.

She glanced to the side, to the digital green light that said her computer was recording.

Mike can't watch this.

Good God, what had she been thinking? She *hadn't* been thinking. She'd let her attraction mute her good sense and set Mike's rights and feelings aside to meet her own momentary, impulsive needs.

If he watched, he'd see that the sex had been different. No doubt of it.

He'd notice how Bern hadn't once looked at the camera. He'd notice there was no dirty talk . . . not the cocky kind, meant for his ears. He'd notice that Sam hadn't even bothered to take her shirt and bra off—that the show hadn't been on her mind, but the sex certainly had. He'd notice that Bern the exhibitionist had been almost completely absent, and that Sam had just slept with someone entirely new.

"Fuck."

Bern raised himself up on straight arms, expression darkening from bliss to worry. "You okay?"

She sat up, forcing him to his knees. There was a naked man on her and Mike's couch. She stood and clamped a hand between her legs, fingers met by the spoils of everything they'd just done. "No, I'm not sure I am."

"You thinking about your cousin?"

"No. I'm thinking about Mike." She hurried to hit STOP on the computer, feeling ridiculous—shirt, no pants, hand making a dam between her thighs. "I can't let him watch this. That was way too . . ." She turned, finding Bern holding out the toilet paper roll. Dignity abandoned, she dabbed between her legs, then pulled on her underwear and pants.

Bern stood, and she hated the hungry way her gaze sought his chest and belly as he hiked up his shorts and jeans.

He tugged on his tee, and as the collar fell into place to reveal his face, Sam found his brow gathered in worry. "That was . . . It was intense, yeah. And probably not what he's expecting to see."

She shook her head, panic rising.

"Sit," he said gently.

She did, feeling that wetness along her sex and a pang of shame.

Bern crouched before her. "It'll be okay."

"Will it?"

"I know, that wasn't . . . that wasn't right, was it?"

"I don't think so, no."

"We've been making porn for him before," Bern said, attention on Sam's fidgeting hands. He took them, but she slithered her fingers free.

"Don't."

"Sorry."

"That was . . . like *lovemaking*, wasn't it?" she asked, body flashing hot, then ice-cold.

He nodded.

"I mean, not that we're in love," she added, unwilling to even entertain that idea. "But you know what I mean. That was intense, and emotional, and just way too different. That . . ." She met his eyes, fear tightening her chest. "That was just for us, wasn't it? There was no room in that for Mike at all."

Bern wore an expression she'd never seen on that handsome face, and it dunked her in ice water. He agreed. And she had to wonder, had he known as she had in the back of her mind, that what they'd done was wrong? Had he suppressed that glaring fact for the sake of lust? Or had he known all along that he'd let things get as intimate and private as he had, and chosen to go there regardless? She wasn't sure she could handle knowing which was the truth, and focused instead on the crisis at hand, the unerasable mistake they'd just made.

"I can't show Mike that."

"Will you tell him it happened?"

"I have no idea. I feel like . . . I feel like I just cheated on him. For real."

Bern's gaze retreated, moving around the room. "I don't really know what to say. I'm sorry, I guess—"

"Don't. Don't be sorry. Neither of us meant for that to happen the way it did. Right?"

"No, not like that."

She chose to believe him. "We got carried away. We were doing exactly what we had his permission to, just sort of . . ."

"Doing it all wrong," Bern offered, with a hint of a sheepish smile.

"Pretty much." She wished she could mirror even a sliver of his levity, but she didn't feel it. Who had he just betrayed, after all? A man he'd known for a couple of months, while the solidity of Sam's entire *marriage* felt damaged.

Bern touched Sam's feet, and she let him. "I didn't mean for this to happen. Honestly. This isn't what I stayed for tonight. I only wanted to be what you needed."

"And you were. I just feel really guilty about what my body decided I needed. Jesus, in all our planning, I never saw this coming." *Did I? Fuck if it hadn't felt natural. Maybe even inevitable. Fuck, fuck, fuck . . .*

"It's an emotional kind of night," he said, squeezing her feet. "Nobody could expect you to just slip into the role or whatever, given everything that's on your mind."

But they wouldn't expect her to fucking *make love* to her supposed sleazy piece on the side, either.

"I'm sorry, Sam. Maybe I should go. Let you get to bed, and maybe you'll feel a little less freaked out in the morning?"

Say yes. Tell him to go. That was her brain's contribution. Something softer and more dangerous whispered, *Ask him to stay. The last thing you want to be right now is alone.* Frozen by the choice, she said nothing.

On the counter, her phone buzzed and chimed. Then again—a call, not a text.

"Fuck. That's him." She let it ring, rubbing her face.

"I don't know how your marriage works," Bern said slowly, "but I don't know that you need to tell him, necessarily. Not if the truth would hurt him."

"I've never had a decent reason to lie to him before . . . and I don't know that I could if I wanted to." Or if she even wanted to. *Truth only. Always.* Her body chilled to imagine it. Please, God, don't let her have ruined Mike's kink for him—or, far worse, his trust in her. "He'll believe me, that it was just impulsive. Just my emotions getting the better of me."

Bern nodded.

But yes, you'd really better go. Because how could Mike believe that him staying, after, could be blamed on impulse? Bern, sleeping in their bed? No, that couldn't happen. By some twisted magic, Bern could fuck Sam, but sleeping beside her? Way out of bounds. There was no ambiguity on that count.

She stood. "You need to go. I'm sorry. You've been so lovely, but we have to call it a night."

"Sure." He carried their glasses to the breakfast bar. "I'll show myself out. Just . . . just be kind to yourself, okay, Sam? We didn't plan this, and you've had a fuck of a shock today."

She nodded, then turned away, busying herself tidying the coffee table. She slapped the laptop closed.

His quiet good night was the last thing she heard before the door clicked shut down the hall. She eyed the clock, feeling alone and cold, worse than before he'd arrived. So many different kinds of hurting.

It was eight thirty, and Mike had probably just seen her text when he'd called. Before then, he'd surely been hoping for an e-mail by ten—not only hoping, he'd have been *hungry* for it. And she had none fit to show him. Instead she'd have to call and disappoint him, tell him, *I'm sorry, but something terrible's happened.*

And when he asked her what she meant, God only knew if she'd tell him the whole truth behind why she was crying.

CHAPTER TWENTY-TWO

Mike hit the road at four the next morning, with the sun not even a promise yet in his rearview mirror. He'd slept only a couple of hours, waking around two and never really falling back to sleep. He *couldn't* sleep, not knowing Sam was back home, alone and grieving.

He'd seen her through only one other loss like this one—her grandfather. The man had been eighty-five, though, and ailing. This was her cousin, a woman she'd grown up with, a woman even younger than her—how did you even process that? Mike's job may have left him cynical about violence and death, but he could still hurt for his wife. He ought to be with her now, drawing her a bath, cooking their meals, walking with her, patiently sitting through movies he'd normally veto.

I should have been there last night. He should have been there when she got that phone call, ready to close her in his arms the second she hung up. Instead she'd spent that horrible evening all on her own. And after all that, she'd thought she'd owed him an apology—like he even cared about the video and their games, once he'd heard the news. Like his sexual desires held any sort of candle to the loss of a loved one.

The five-hour drive from Philadelphia seemed to go on forever, though in actuality he made excellent time, stopping only for coffee and gas. He was pulling up along the curb just shy of nine, the summer sunshine misleadingly cheerful, and his heart feeling leaden as he mounted the front steps.

He pushed the door in. "Sam?"

Nothing. She might be sleeping in, exhausted from a long night of crying. "Samira?" He jogged up the stairs, but found their bed empty. She couldn't have driven to Newark to see her parents—she'd have told him. Her pajamas were folded sloppily atop the dresser, and Mike found the bathtub bone-dry, which was odd. Sam almost always showered first thing—

"Oh, duh." He went back downstairs and found her running shoes missing from the bin by the door. "Nice detective work there, Heyer."

She felt up to a run—that was a good sign. His heart lightened by a few degrees and he headed to the kitchen to start a pot of coffee. A big one. Could be a long Sunday. While he was at it he turned on the TV and Sam's Pandora account, and cued up her Roberta Flack station. It was the one she always defaulted to when she was blue, and he wanted everything about this day to be easy on her.

A rattle drew his attention as he dropped two slices of bread in the toaster. Sam had left her phone on the counter, and a text alert lit up her screen. Mike glanced at it, curious.

Bern. He frowned, not sure why the man would need to contact her at nine a.m. on a Sunday.

Maybe he doesn't know why she canceled on him. He ought to cut the guy a little slack. But he still roused Sam's phone and read the message.

I don't know about you, but I slept like shit. What's going on over there?

Mike frowned, having only a vague sense of what that meant, and not liking it. As a man who spent his life taking the shortest and most direct route toward answers, the correct response was clear. He opened Bern's contact icon with a tap and hit CALL.

Barely a ring before— "Sam, hi. Are you—"

"It's not Sam, it's Mike."

A pause. "Oh. Hey."

"Sam's out. I saw your text."

"Right." Silence.

Mike couldn't blame the guy for sounding off—he knew he was using his on-duty voice, and Bern had yet to really meet Mike outside of the bounds of his kink. Those two sides of him were night and day. Still, he wasn't feeling very friendly just now.

"So you slept like shit," he said to Bern.

"I . . ."

"Sorry if my wife wrecked your big plans last night, but there was a death in the family. She probably *did* sleep like shit. So I'd appreciate if you put your own agenda on hold until she decides to contact you. She's got plenty on her mind already without worrying about your needs or mine or anybody else's except her own."

"Um, sure. Sorry. I'll just wait to hear from her."

"Good." Mike paused, realizing he was bullying the man who'd had no small part in actualizing his darkest fantasies. Balancing Bern in his mind as both rival and lover was a fucking head trip. Mike was a black-and-white sort of person, and he didn't know how to blend the persona and the man. How to parse the fact that he sometimes wanted to punch this guy in the face, despite having also sucked his cock.

"I'm sorry if I'm being a dick about this. I'm just looking out for Sam."

"Of course."

Mike heaved a heavy sigh. Best to let the guy know he was exasperated, not psycho. In all honesty, he didn't like speaking to him man-to-man. He much preferred their fabricated roles. "Okay. See you sometime, probably."

"Okay."

"Sorry to get in your face."

"Course not. Sorry if I was too pushy."

"It's fine. Anyway."

"Yeah."

Good God, was there anything more awkward than two male acquaintances trying to end a phone call? Finally Mike just said, "Bye," and hung up.

He rubbed his face, feeling like an asshole, and pushed down the toaster lever. He should've just let Sam deal with that—she'd have told Bern what happened, and he would have been sympathetic and polite, and she definitely would *not* have given their special guest star a poke in the eye just for doing his fucking job as a pushy third.

"This is why you're not in PR," Mike muttered, then turned at the sound of the front door opening. "Sam?"

"Yeah, hi. I was surprised to see your car. Welcome back. You must have hit the road at—" She'd been distracted, toeing away her sneakers, and Mike's fierce hug cut her off. She laughed and rubbed his back. "Hi."

"Hi, Sami." He let her go. "How are you?"

She shrugged, hair damp and curly at her sweaty temples. "Better after a run, I think. But stinky."

The smell of bread arrived with the distant sound of the toaster releasing. "You hungry?" he asked her.

"No. I think I'll take a bath. And maybe after, we could talk . . . ?" Her expression changed, tiredness giving way to worry.

"Of course. Whatever you need, I'm on it. And I'm making dinner."

She smiled and rubbed his arm. "That's sweet, but you don't need to. I could use a few distractions."

"Well, we can fight about it after your bath. Go do your thing."

She turned away to head upstairs, and Mike could tell her energy was tapped. She'd had just enough for that hug and welcome home, but now the grief had descended once more. He wondered if he ought to convince her to take the day off work tomorrow, or if the routine would do her good.

He ate his toast and listened as the water ran upstairs, then went quiet. He gave her a good fifteen minutes' uninterrupted soak before heading up with a cup of coffee for her.

He rapped on the bathroom door. "Brought you a present."

"Come on in."

Mike pushed in the door, finding her up to her neck and shoulders in good-smelling water. What that smell was, he didn't know—he only knew it came in crystal form, in a glass jar with silver Farsi writing on the label. She'd kept the lights off and lit a couple of candles at the edge of the counter.

"Wine would fit the scene better, but here you go." He set the cup on the rim.

"Oh, thank you."

He lowered the toilet lid and took a seat. Even with everything that was going on, it was hard to look at her—naked, with her long hair wet—and not feel lust stir. He shoved it deep inside his body and leaned in, elbows on his knees. "Anything you need or want today, I'm at your service."

"You're sweet." She didn't meet his eyes, her gaze lost somewhere on the surface of the water.

"That's my job."

"No, it's not. Your job requires zero sweetness whatsoever." She met his eyes, smiling faintly. Weakly.

"Goddamn it, I hate seeing you so torn up."

She sank a little deeper in the water, then sat up suddenly, wrapping her arms around her knees. The water clung to her skin and hair, sparkling in the low light. She met his eyes again, squarely this time.

"I need to talk to you."

"Of course."

"Not about my cousin. About something that happened last night, after I got the news."

Mike frowned, confused by her tone. She didn't sound sad. She sounded nervous.

"What?"

"I texted Bern to cancel, but he didn't get it in time. He showed up a little early, while I was still processing the news."

"Okay . . ." Mike's gut felt sour and raw, and he tried to remember what that text had said. *I slept like shit. What's going on over there?* "Tell me, Sam."

"At first, we just hung out. I told him he could go, but he was really nice about it. We talked, like friends, and watched a movie. Mostly talked. It was a nice distraction. But then it all sort of . . . changed."

"Changed? What do you mean? You tell me if he mistreated you, Samira." *And so help me I will wring the life from his body.*

"Things got . . . Things heated up." She looked to her knees. "I'd calmed down, and I felt like maybe if we fucked around, it would be a nice escape. It's hard to describe how I went from feeling so sad to needing that so much, but it just sort of happened."

He swallowed, throat tight. "Okay."

"I got the laptop out so we could tape it for you. I . . . I wanted to kiss him, really badly. I'm not even sure why . . . maybe just to feel something other than awful, I guess. But it didn't seem right if you weren't able to see it, you know?"

Mike nodded, confused now.

"So I hit RECORD and we . . ."

A hard heat rose inside him, utterly divorced from sexual excitement. She'd slept with someone last night and not told him about it. "And you taped it?"

"Yeah. But it . . ." A sob pinched her shoulder blades together, the water echoing a quiver in her body.

"Sam, what? Did he cross a line?"

She met his eyes, and her own were shining with tears. "No. I think I did."

"What do you mean?"

"It was different. It didn't feel like me and him, and you watching. It felt like . . ."

Mike went cold. "It felt like just you and him," he finished.

She nodded, pain written in her brow and lips and the set of her jaw. "It did. It felt like just me and him."

"How was it different from before?"

"I tried to keep it dirty, you know—talk for the camera, remember who it was all for. But it was tender. It felt like what I needed in the moment. Then it was over, and I said, *I can't show Mike that.* I knew the second we finished that I fucked it up. I fucked it up *so bad*," she said, voice breaking.

Mike didn't reply for a half minute or more, gone from hot to cold to numb, now. "Do you have feelings for him? Real feelings?"

When Sam didn't reply right away, panic broke through the wall, driving Mike out of the safety of his stupor.

"Sam?"

"I don't know." Or did she? He had to wonder, and perhaps the truth was part of what had her so spooked.

"Jesus . . ." He dropped his head, rubbed his temples.

"I *do* know I'd never, ever want to leave you, to be with him. But I do feel something. Something more than just the physical things I was supposed to."

"What about him? Does he have feelings for you?"

"I don't know."

Mike met her eyes, angry.

"I don't know, honestly. I'm not protecting him. He cares about me, as a person, I think. But I don't know what he thinks about everything—if he wishes we were something more."

"I want to watch the tape."

Her lips parted, but no words came out.

"I want to watch it. I want to see what it is that has you so torn up."

"I deleted it. I don't want anyone to watch it. Ever."

"Did you empty the trash?"

Sam's face fell, and Mike stood.

"I won't know what to feel until I see it," he told her as he turned toward the door.

The sound of rushing water told him she'd stood. "Mike, please."

"I have a right to watch it. You knew that last night when you decided to tape it in the first place." He left the bathroom door wide open and stalked through the bedroom, then downstairs, looking for her computer and finally finding it on a bookshelf. He opened it and typed in her password. They kept nothing from each other.

Nothing until last night.

He arranged the items in the trash can by type and found it—a video file with a time stamp from just after nine p.m. Sam appeared in the entryway, hugging her robe tightly around her body.

"I want to watch it alone," he told her.

She nodded, wet hair dripping on the hardwood floor, then

turned and let him be. He waited until he heard the floorboard over his head squeak, then opened the file.

It was dim and grainy, looking rough compared to the videos they'd made with the camera. He watched their two bodies, but more than that, he watched their mouths forming thoughts he couldn't hear. *Words only for them.* And he watched Sam's face as Bern went down on her, those eyes riveted to him, never once acknowledging their audience. The few snatches of dirty talk he did catch weren't for his ears. They were lovers' words, not actors', more tender than they'd shared in his presence, more intimate. And when they fucked, Mike's heart hurt, because he knew he had no place in it.

Anger moved through him, rushing and rising like a rough sea. But in time, what rose to its surface wasn't hatred or betrayal but sadness. Guilt. Shame, to not have seen this coming. He felt like a fool to have never guessed that the very thing that got him off could wind up manifesting for real.

He'd let his wife sleep with another man, knowing full well how she worked—that sex was emotional for her. That she'd never be able to sleep with a guy she didn't feel something for. Now that something had germinated and grown into an altogether different entity. One he had no part in. *I planted that seed and walked away. I don't get to be so fucking shocked to find that it's put out roots and vines.*

I'm a goddamn fucking fool.

On-screen, they came. Together. *"Don't stop, don't stop."* Those words had been Mike's alone . . . until now. He watched Sam stroking Bern's back, knowing exactly what those hands felt like, doing exactly that. It jabbed a fresh barb in Mike's heart, and not the kind that spurred his arousal. His fantasies were one thing, and this was another. This was real.

And it was all his fault.

"Fuck."

In the video, Bern asked Sam, *"You okay?"*

"No, I'm not sure I am."

"You thinking about your cousin?"

"No. I'm thinking about Mike."

Her arm loomed large in the shot a second before the screen went black. Mike blinked at it. Stoically quit the media player. Dragged the file back to the trash can and emptied its contents permanently. Shut the computer.

He couldn't say when, but Samira had crept back downstairs—he looked up to find her at the threshold to the hall, face as pale as he'd ever seen it.

"Tell me this," Mike said evenly. "Do you love him?"

She stood a little straighter, holding his gaze squarely. "Not the way I love you."

"But in some kind of way."

Her lips pursed. "I'm not sure, honestly. I feel something. Something that scares me."

"You and me both." He stood, checked his pocket for his keys.

Fear transformed her face, widened her eyes. "Are you going out?"

"You know exactly where I'm going."

"Mike, don't. Let's talk about it first. Give it time to sink in."

But Mike was programmed, personally and professionally, to default to action when he felt threatened. He needed to talk, yes, but not with Sam.

"Don't do this while you're angry, please."

About to pass her, he paused, their bodies nearly chest to chest. "I'm not angry," he lied. "But I can't breathe until I know what it is he feels for you."

And if that man gave Mike an answer he wasn't prepared to hear, he'd skin the bastard alive.

CHAPTER TWENTY-THREE

For easily the fiftieth time that day, Bern felt a phantom text buzz in his back pocket. He switched Molly's leash to his other hand and fished out his phone, hoping to see Sam's name in his messages. But no. Nothing at all. The not-knowing was torture. Not knowing how she was doing, not knowing if she'd told Mike what had happened—and if she had, not knowing how the guy felt about it. His stomach was in knots, anxiety like he hadn't felt in ages. In years.

At the end of the day, Bern really didn't know Mike Heyer that well at all; didn't know his temper, or how he might be with Sam, if she told him what had happened. If she didn't contact Bern by dinnertime, he resolved to call, to make sure she was okay. Just because a man was in law enforcement didn't mean he was some bastion of right and wrong . . . especially not when things got as personal as they had.

Molly was panting, and the day was shaping up to be a hot one, the sun harsh overhead. But all Bern felt was cold.

He couldn't stand the thought of Sam facing the brunt of the man's anger, not when last night had been his own fault, if anything. *He'd* shown up. He'd let things turn sexual, while Sam had been too mixed up and vulnerable to be making emotional decisions. He'd said those dangerous things to her while they'd had sex, and pretty much told her, *I want there to be things that are just between us. I want there to be an "us."* So grossly over the line, in hindsight, when he'd known the rules all along. But lust was more hazardous to common sense than alcohol—

He stopped short as his house came into sight. Sitting on his front stoop was Mike Heyer.

The dog whined, unhappy to have been choked.

"Sorry, Mol."

Bern didn't know where this was going, and he couldn't guess his own odds if things got physical. He lifted weights, but that was as much for vanity as anything else, whereas Mike probably had training in some kind of defensive combat.

He passed the guy's car, then his own truck, and called out a neutral "Hey."

Mike stood. Bern halted a few paces from him. Molly's ears drew back; she no doubt felt the tension. He stooped to rub her neck. "Chill." Looking up at Mike he asked, "You here to talk?"

A curt nod answered him.

"Inside?" Obviously—the whole of Carrick didn't need to be in on this. When Mike nodded again, Bern edged past him up the porch steps and unlocked the front door. "Just lemme feed my dog."

He filled Molly's bowl and closed her in the kitchen, then met Mike back in the front, in the den.

"You want a drink or anything?" Bern asked.

"No."

Goddamn, this guy was tough to read.

"Okay. Let's just talk, then." He nodded to the couch and was a little surprised when Mike sat. Bern took a seat opposite him on the edge of his recliner.

"Sam told me what happened."

Bern nodded. "She made it sound like she would. That was never in question, whether she thought you should know—"

"I don't need you to defend my wife's character, okay? I know her better than you ever will."

Bern sat back, annoyed and chastised at once. How old was this guy? Forty, tops. Yet Bern felt like some scolded teenager, busted for denting Dad's car. "Understood."

"You have feelings for my wife?" Mike demanded.

Bern took a slow breath, unsure what the best move was here. He'd never been a great liar, though. In time, he nodded. "Yeah."

"Tell me."

"I like her. A lot. If circumstances were different, I'd want to date her."

"You think you had a chance with her? At getting her to leave me for you?"

Bern shook his head. He'd not expected that would happen . . . though in truth he *had* entertained idle, wishful, selfish thoughts that somehow, it might.

"I was in this for exactly what you guys said you were after," Bern said. "Sex. Fun. In Sam's and my defense, I don't think most decent people could do what we have been, for as long as we have been, and not feel *something*."

He'd half expected for Mike to cut him off there, tell him to fuck himself for trying to defend Sam again, but the man just nodded, real slow and stoic.

Bern went on cautiously. "You guys went into this with a lot more at stake than I did, right out of the gate. Everything you feel—and I'm not pretending like I know what you feel, obviously. But all of that, plus however Sam felt about it. Nervous, I think. Hopeful. Plus the trust everybody had to extend to even go for it, myself included. The attraction." He laughed softly. "I mean, this wasn't one of us selling the other a used stereo. This wasn't some blind date, either. This was a fucking experiment, one that could've gone crazy wrong. But I don't think it has." He paused, inviting Mike to interrupt. When he didn't, Bern went on. "I think we did a pretty fucking awesome job, all three of us. If the worst thing that happened is that me and Sam wound up with feelings for each other . . . I mean, *shouldn't* we? I know you don't want her sleeping with somebody who sees her as nothing more than a body."

"You don't know me."

"No. But I know that much." Bern leaned forward, a thread of anger running through his nerves now. "You tell me that isn't true."

Mike said nothing.

Bern slapped his hands to his knees, wanting this done. "So what'd you come here for, Mike? What do you need to hear from me?"

"Do you love my wife?"

Bern laughed again, shaking his head. Goddamn if he even knew the answer to that question. "Honestly? I don't know. I feel something for her. If I felt this way for a woman I was regular old dating, I might be thinking that this could be something real. But it's not that fucking simple, is it? I'm a man. I have fuck-all clue what I feel, okay? But I want and like and respect your wife, and if all that adds up to something you can't trust, and you want to round that up to love, I can't stop you."

Mike's stone-cold eye contact finally broke, his gaze dropping to the carpet.

"This is fucked, man," Bern said. "This is exactly what gets you off, but the moment it goes off your little script, the second she's into it as more than just a favor to you—"

Mike's head snapped up. "You watch yourself, talking like you know the first thing about it."

"The first thing? You have any clue all the e-mails she and I wrote, setting this up just right? For you? I know all the logistics she worried about. I know how badly she wanted this to work. *For you.* I promised you guys I'd be fucking *monogamous* to you, to keep this going. Because it was a good goddamn thing, a thing *you* wanted. And I did, too, and Sam wanted to make you happy. Now maybe she wants it for her own reasons—emotional ones, as much as sexual. She wants it, outside of your parameters, and suddenly it's a goddamn crisis?"

"This was never about inviting you to get designs on my wife."

Bern cocked his head. "That's exactly what it was about. That's what cuckolding fucking is."

"We didn't invite you into our marriage to date her. To get emotionally involved with her."

"You didn't, huh?"

"No."

Bern stared him down. "Then exactly which of us is the prostitute to you? Me or your wife?"

He didn't even get a chance to stand before Mike was on him, fist around his collar and pressing into his throat. Bern went still, gripping the chair arms. He'd asked for this. He'd be the calmer man now, and wait to see where it ended.

"You ever call my wife a whore again and I will fucking break you."

"I never did." The words hurt to speak with Mike's knuckles jammed against his Adam's apple. "Which of us is denying her right to feel something for the man she's sleeping with? Which of us is reducing her to—"

"You were playing fucking *parts*," Mike spat. "And nowhere in that script did it say you were supposed to get a goddamn crush on my wife."

"We're human beings. We were bound to feel something." A livid, petty bit of Bern wanted to make this ugly. Remind Mike exactly which of them had sucked the other's cock in the name of his precious kink. But Bern felt too righteous—and too *right*—to fuck it up with that low a blow. "It was never part of the plan," he said. "But we're not robots. We can't just turn our feelings off."

Mike's knuckles stayed at Bern's neck, though the pressure had waned. They were reaching an impasse, but Bern felt he'd won somehow.

"Hit me, if that's what you came here for, Mike. Otherwise get the fuck out of my house."

Mike released Bern's collar and stood up straight, fists at his sides.

Bern stayed sitting, and with feigned calm he said, "You know I'm right." He hoped his voice belied the pounding of his heart. "And you know what this is, Mike, your coming here today? This is you losing track of what this has all been about, and taking shit too far. Same as last night was about me and Sam losing track and fucking up, taking shit too far. All three of us have crossed a line now. So you and me, let's quit with this shit and call it even. How about that?"

"Fuck you."

Bern stood, forcing Mike back a step, underlining which of them was bigger. "We made this bed precisely how you wanted it, Mike, now we're all fucking lying in it. This is *exactly* what you asked for. Don't treat me like a home wrecker when all I've ever done is grant your fucking wishes."

"You'd take her if you could."

Maybe that's true. But can you really blame me? "And isn't that exactly what gets you hard?"

Bern didn't see the punch coming. It registered as a flash of light and heat in his jaw—more concept than pain. The floor shifted under his feet, and he blinked to find his own hands splayed on the recliner, holding his reeling body upright. As the room righted itself, the pain arrived. Bern tasted blood and felt the tattered edge of his bitten tongue. He flexed his jaw as he stood up straight, and it throbbed but didn't scream.

"Go," he ordered Mike, and nodded to the exit.

Mike turned, strode to the door, and yanked it open. "Stay out of our lives," he said, and marched to his car without looking back. He pulled away with an angry rev and a squeal of tires, disappearing around the corner.

Bern shut the door and thumped it with his fist. "Fucking psycho."

Molly's nails skittered at the kitchen door.

"It's okay, girl." He let her into the den, crouching to rub her ears. "It's okay. He's gone."

Her tail wagged, if limply, and he stroked her neck.

"Everything's cool . . . Don't worry about that mean man. Sex makes us humans fucking rabid. Or love does. Or something."

She didn't seem to understand it any better than Bern did.

"Lemme put some ice on my mouth and we'll watch the Pirates game. How about that?"

Molly seemed to concur, following cheerfully when Bern walked to the freezer. He found an ice pack in the door and wrapped it in a handkerchief, holding it to his throbbing jaw as he sat back down and switched on the TV.

He pulled his phone out, checking the screen one last time and finding it blank. No surprise. He ought to just delete Sam's number now—no way in hell he'd be hearing from her again. He tossed the device aside and shut his eyes, welcoming the cold solace of the ice pack to numb the pain.

Breakups always stung, whether they came out of the blue, or hurt to deliver, or crept in like a slow rot. But Bern had never had one quite like this. This one tasted like blood, and the black-and-blue souvenir he had coming would last a week, easy.

But fuck the injury. Bern knew this particular breakup would keep on hurting long after the bruise faded.

CHAPTER TWENTY-FOUR

Sam was jogging for the front door the moment she heard Mike's key in the lock. The hour since he'd left for Bern's had been the longest of her life.

"And?" she asked, watching him push off his shoes.

He didn't answer. And that made her wonder what on earth Bern's answer may have been, regarding what there was between him and Sam.

"Mike?"

He passed her, heading down the hall. She followed him into the kitchen, confused when he opened the freezer. More confused still when he pulled out a bag of corn and walked to the couch.

"Mike, say something."

He took a seat, and Sam wedged herself between his knees to face him, sitting on the coffee table. "Talk to me. Please. What happened?" She watched him drape the bag over his right hand. "Oh God."

"I fucked up. A little."

"You hit him?"

"Just once."

"And I suppose he was asking for it?"

"In that exact moment, yes."

"But in general?"

He considered it, frowning. "Hard to say. Probably not."

"Oh, Mike . . . I knew I should have gone."

"It had to be me. Anyway, it's done now."

The bag's frost was melting, dripping onto Mike's jeans.

"Hang on." Sam got up to grab a dish towel and wrapped the corn in it for him. "Where did you hit him?"

"Jaw."

"Tell me you didn't break it."

"Guy never seemed to shut up, so I'd say no."

She shook her head. "He didn't say anything nasty, did he?"

"Not exactly."

"He didn't call me a slut, or threaten to tell everyone what we've been doing?"

"No."

"Then he didn't deserve that. You'd never punch *me* in the face, and I'm more responsible for what happened last night than he was."

Mike sighed, eyes shutting for a moment. "Until *your* wife develops feelings for another man, I won't ask you to understand."

"I guess this answers all those questions I had, about how far into reality your kink could actually cross before the threat stopped being sexy and just started being threatening."

"My kink is about sex. Sex isn't sacred to me, apparently. But feelings are."

"He can touch my body but not my heart. Is that it?"

Mike nodded once.

Sam heaved a sad breath. "Wish I could separate the two as tidily as you can."

He met her eyes at that. "He basically told me the same."

"And is it really so hard to understand?"

He looked to the floor, thinking about it for a minute or more before glancing up. "For me? Maybe it is. I can't imagine looking at another woman and feeling anything more than the smallest flicker of curiosity."

She touched his knee. "You're different, though, Mike. You're so hardwired for loyalty—it's right at the heart of your sexuality."

He frowned, like he'd never thought about it like that.

"You're almost pathologically a one-woman man," she went on. "I've always found that attractive about you. But most people aren't like that, I don't think. Loving one person doesn't stop us from finding others attractive, or even having crushes—harmless ones, usually. Ones we have no interest in acting on. But me and Bern . . . We acted first, and then the feelings followed. We fucked up, believe me, but we never meant to. He's never asked me if I'd leave you to be with him. Not even close."

A pause. "You *swear* that's true?"

"Absolutely. Never once has he made me feel like he wanted that—to replace you. Why? Did he say something to you?"

"He did."

Her heart stopped. "What, exactly?"

"That if things were different, he'd want to date you."

She frowned. "And was that all of it? That he'd date me if you weren't in the picture somehow?"

"You don't find that inappropriate?"

She shook her head. "No. Not at all. My feelings would be a little hurt if he didn't think that, frankly. Maybe I never spelled it out, before we started all this, but I want for the man we mess around with to like and respect me. I mean, don't you?"

Mike set the corn aside and scrubbed at his face. Through his fingers he said, "I don't even fucking know anymore."

She rubbed his thigh for a moment, then stood and grabbed her purse from the easy chair.

He looked up. "Where are you off to?"

She shrugged. "I dunno. I need to be doing stuff. I'll pick up some groceries or something. I'm *not* going to see him," she added, meeting his eyes over her shoulder.

"I didn't think you were."

"I'll be back. Hour or less." She couldn't quite make out what she was feeling, and staying so close to Mike's jumble of emotions wasn't helping. They both needed space, and a little time to process.

"Okay," he said softly. "Drive safe."

Sam shut the door quietly behind her and headed for her car. She didn't start it, just sat there holding the wheel and feeling her wedding band rubbing against its seam. She'd gone three years barely aware of that ring, it had become such a part of her body. As invisible as her knuckle or fingernail. Then last year, it had become something so much more loaded when she began removing it for their games. And a couple of months before, when she'd first seen Bern Davies's gaze catch on it. And last night, when she'd felt it click against his empty wineglass after she told him to leave. She almost wanted a new one now. This one had seen too much. Seen the rise and now the fall of their sex life 2.0—a glorious, thrilling ascent; a stumble, a fall, a punch.

Could be way worse. This could have wrecked her and Mike, and it didn't feel as though it would. Her regrets wouldn't fade quickly, but she wouldn't have the blood of their ruined marriage on her hands.

Still, this wasn't how it was supposed to end—their experiment with Mike's sexuality. They'd turned that contentious, thorny kink of his from something that upset him into something that took sex to a completely new reality. They'd let the beast free, and it hadn't ripped them to shreds. Instead Sam had poisoned the poor creature, and she didn't know if that thing that had fueled Mike's body like nothing else would ever recover.

He wanted me to cheat on him. In a way. With her body, in their games—in their imaginations. Then with her body, for real.

She'd always known the experiment would end, just not the way it had. In all her planning, she'd never thought to worry about this. *Call yourself an actuary, do you?* Hell of a job she'd done gaming the dangers, spending all her time getting spun up about privacy and discretion, about blood tests and leaked sex tapes.

Then again, her red flags always waved from amid the fields of cold, hard figures. She'd been out of her depth, up to her neck in a system whose dynamics she'd known nothing about, and with her marriage at stake. No numbers to go by, only gut feelings. Intuition. Good intentions.

And when have intentions ever *guaranteed a given outcome?*

Human error was always on her radar . . . yet falling in love had never entered the equation. If that's what this had been.

She looked to the house, and saw Mike's face framed in one of the small windows that flanked the front door. Her shoulders dropped . . . then squared as she realized what she needed to be doing.

Mike got his chance to end this thing that I started. And by all accounts, he'd fucked it up. His trust was a lot to demand after last night, but she swung the car door open and headed for the house. Mike let her in and she faced him in the entryway.

"I'm going to say good-bye to him." Even just saying those words aloud, something grated inside her. Saying good-bye to him . . . it felt wrong. As wrong as her actions of the previous night.

Mike's own reaction was instantaneous—a wince of surprise and disgust. "I don't want you to."

"I appreciate that. But this is complicated for me. I don't think you know what it's like to let someone into your life in such an intimate way, then to suddenly not be able to say good-bye. To end it for yourself. I won't touch him—not in any way. But I'll say good-bye to him, face-to-face. For maybe three hours now, he's been somebody you wanted to punch—and now you have. But for the past couple of months he's been as much a part of realizing your fantasies as I have. I'm going to tell him thank you for that, and apologize that it's all had to end the way it has. And then I'll never see him again."

"I think it's simpler, just letting it be done with—"

"I wasn't asking for your opinion, or your permission."

His expression hardened, then surrender smoothed his brow. "Fine. If that's what you need."

"It is. I'll be back in an hour and a half. If he's even home."

Mike nodded, and she turned back around and walked out the door.

She found Bern's address in her e-mail. The drive took less than twenty-five minutes in actuality, yet it also took three days, thanks to her impatience, and three seconds, according to her nerves. In a blink, in an ice age, she was taking her cue from the other vehicles on Newett Street and parking her car half on the sidewalk.

She eyed Bern's truck, and his house. So many intimate things she'd come to know about the man, yet she'd never seen his home. Her heart beat hard and her legs felt like water as she walked up the little concrete path to the front porch. Her steps creaked the boards and a dog's distant bark answered her.

"Molly," she muttered, remembering Bern's smile in that video he'd sent her, seeming like it was a million years ago. She pushed the bell.

His tall shape appeared through the door's pebbled glass. Dog nails clicked on the other side and she heard that deep voice say, "Down."

He cracked the door, his surprise evident in a heartbeat. "Sam." He let the door swing in, stooping to take hold of the Lab's collar.

"Hi."

"Hey."

"Look up a sec," she told him.

He did, and she studied his jaw. It looked swollen and red, and it would no doubt look ten times worse in the morning. "How does it feel?"

"Like an angry cop punched me in the mouth."

"I'm sorry. He didn't come over here expecting that to happen."

"Did you want to come in?"

She nodded.

Bern stepped back and Sam shut the door behind her. He let his dog go and Sam gave her ears a scratch.

Bern pointed to a bed in the corner. "Go lie down, Molly." She obeyed reluctantly. Bern crossed his arms over his chest. "He know you're here?"

"Yeah."

"And why *are* you here?" It wasn't anger putting that edge in his voice, Sam realized, but uncertainty. A lot was riding on her answer, and that scared her.

"To apologize for how everything seems to have ended. And to say good-bye properly. If that's okay."

His shoulders drooped.

You wanted to hear that I've come running to you, didn't you? And she'd be lying if she denied that her body wanted to cling to his just now. But in the bright and sober light of day, the temptation was powerless.

"Can we sit?" she asked.

Bern nodded to his couch and they sat with most of a cushion between them.

"I'm sorry about your jaw."

"I may have earned it, just a little."

"Well, it should never have happened. And it wouldn't have if I'd had a decent set of boundaries last night and not let you stay the way I did."

"We didn't know anything would happen."

Sam bit her lip, letting herself entertain a scary question. "Didn't we?"

Bern's eyebrows rose a fraction.

"I can't speak for you, but I can admit I fucked this up. You should have been a close-enough man. I should have liked you . . . been attracted to you, not *infatuated* with you."

"You should have settled for someone you weren't that into?" he asked.

"In the wake of what's happened, and feeling all this guilt, and regret? Maybe."

Bern laughed, sounding incredulous. "You should have stuck with some guy you could go through the motions with, so your husband could get his mind blown?"

"I don't know. But probably."

Another shocked laugh and he shook his head. "I think you deserve way better."

And in her heart, she knew he was right. The way she'd let things get away from her last night, that had been wrong. But feeling for this man, given everything she'd done with him, for Mike's pleasure . . . Bern was right. What felt wrong, truly wrong, was the way it was all ending now. And all because she'd fucked up, and lost track of priority number one, Mike's primacy.

She sighed, tired. "He never asked me for this, you know."

Bern frowned. "No?"

"No. I offered. I offered to role-play it with him, and I offered to make it happen for real. It was always meant as a gift, from me to him."

"One fuck of a generous gift."

She shrugged. "I'm not kinky like him." Or she hadn't been. Lately, she wasn't so sure. "I had a perfectly satisfying sex life from the moment he and I met, but he always had this secret thing he was yearning for—this thing he never asked to be hardwired to want. This thing he never got to experience outside his own head. I mean, his fantasies scared the crap out of me when he first explained them."

"Understandably."

"But like I said, he didn't choose those things. After I sat with them a long time I thought, if it took . . . I dunno, getting slapped in the face, say, for me to have really, truly satisfying sex, would he go there for me? And at first, no, he wouldn't have. He'd have been horrified, like I was when I found out he liked to imagine I was cheating on him. But if getting slapped could light me up the way the cuckolding thing lights *him* up? We'd have found a way to go there, if that's what it took to blow my mind. And I'd have felt like I was suddenly being served a feast, after always settling for scraps. Does that make sense?"

"You're talking to a man with a kink of his own. So yes."

"There you go. So when I quit being afraid of the things that excited him, I was ready to see what they might do to him. And it was fucking amazing, finding out. I even found a few little kinky seeds of my own hiding in there, the deeper we've dug into it. So this was never about me getting pushed, or submitting. He never pressured me, or guilted me, or even asked for it. He never made it feel like anything other than my gift to give him."

"You promise?"

She nodded. "It's been my hands on the steering wheel, from the moment we pulled away from the curb."

Bern stared at her long and hard, blue eyes narrowed.

"I can't decide if you look angry or curious," Sam said when the silence grew too heavy to bear.

"What makes it work, the two of you together? What does he give you that was enough to make you think, *I'm gonna marry this guy*?"

"That's so hard to say . . . Lots of things, really. He makes me feel secure and attractive, and he sees the things in me that I most want people to see. That I'm smart and fun. I can relax around him. And I dated a lot of guys I didn't feel that with before I met him. We just fit."

"Sexually, too."

She nodded. "He always fit for me that way. And since he came clean about his needs, I've been able to fit for him. With a little effort, and some nerve."

Bern nodded. He looked sad, she thought.

"Had you wanted to hear something else? That I had doubts about me and Mike?"

His smile was faint and unsteady. "Am I that transparent?"

Sam didn't think she'd ever felt so simultaneously flattered and uncomfortable.

"I want you," he said softly. "You have to know that. And yeah, for more than just the sex—not just because you realized my fantasies."

"Mike would say the same."

Bern's jaw was clenched, and she wondered how badly that must hurt. As much as whatever he was feeling had to hurt?

"I won't leave him. But exploring with you was incredible. I'll remember it for the rest of my life." *Maybe at times when I shouldn't. And hopefully, someday, Mike will want that. For me to remember you and fantasize about you. Just not any time soon.*

"So it's all over?"

She nodded. *It has to be, doesn't it?*

"You guys gonna look for another man to fit the bill?"

"I don't know. It's hard to imagine it just now." Though saying good-bye, burying this bond while it was still so vibrant, and vital . . . It was far harder to imagine that this was how things really had to be.

Another sad smile. "You telling me I was special?"

"Yeah, you were special, Bern. And it's looking like this could only have worked if you and I hadn't been *quite* so good together."

"That's some cruel twist, huh?"

"Yeah. It really is."

Though as Sam walked to her car a minute later, she couldn't help but wonder, *Does it really need to be?* It felt like a crime, when she and Mike had discovered more chemistry with that man than she'd ever bothered *hoping* they might. And just as they'd reached a point where all three were getting their wants fulfilled—Mike's curious appetites, Bern's desire to show off, and Sam's newfound craving for two men at once—now it had to end? Shouldn't *right now* be the point at which it all took off?

Except we fucked it all up last night.

But had they really? Permanently? And fucked it up how, precisely?

By being human beings. With feelings, and impulses, and moments of weakness.

So many times, for the sake of her role, she'd imagined cheating on her husband. She'd always been cruel in those fantasies, selfish, shameless. But now it had actually happened, in a way, and yes, she had been selfish, but not cruel. Vulnerable and mixed up. And while she didn't feel ashamed, per se, regret hounded her. Her actual infidelity hadn't fit Mike's script. It had been too quiet, too emotional, too real. Too human.

What had Bern said to her that had set these gears turning?

Something about how the alternative to their present predicament was to do all those things with a man she was indifferent toward. The way Mike looked at it, that was the only safe option, if they wanted to try this again someday. The thought turned her stomach.

And beneath the uncertainty lay sadness. Grief, to imagine losing all those vibrant new facets of her sexual self. To imagine she'd never again feel what she had, with her body worshipped by both of theirs.

I've given everything I have, accommodating Mike's needs. Last night I needed to feel those things with Bern. Not for keeps, but for a little while. With a man she'd performed a hundred filthy acts with, and yet true romantic attachment was too taboo to ever move on from?

Why did that smell so distinctly of bullshit?

Sam sat holding the steering wheel, staring straight ahead at nothing, as an unexpected emotion took shape in her chest, growing and solidifying with every breath.

Anger, or something like it.

And as she drove home, she assembled those feelings into thoughts, into an argument.

These sexual adventures had been worth gambling their marriage on, after all. Surely preserving them was worth fighting for.

CHAPTER TWENTY-FIVE

Mike paced the front landing for fifteen minutes or more, mind and heart racing, pulse pumping, body tight. When the sound of his own footsteps began to grate, he went to the living room to stare blindly at ESPN. He'd been pissed when Sam had left, but it mellowed quickly, leaving him feeling scared and stupid, ashamed of how he'd lost control. He squeezed his aching fist and let the pain humble him and cool his temper.

Beneath the jealousy and the anger lay sadness. They'd had it so good, these past few months. They'd ridden his kink further into the wilds than he'd ever expected, and now that was over. Thanks to Bern losing track of his place . . . and thanks to Mike as well. It was all thanks to him, in the end. He'd drawn them all together, created this whole new entity among the three of them, and now he'd stomped on the thing the second it slipped off its leash. The second that human nature hijacked the script, and—

He sat up straight at the sound of the lock flipping. "Sam?"

"It's me."

He stood, his legs feeling boneless, and met her in the hall.

"Let's sit down," she said. "I want to talk."

"Okay." Jesus, that didn't sound good. She had her business face on, and Mike had to wonder, how had his actions sounded, as retold by Bern? Psycho, no doubt. And had they been? He'd felt nothing but blind, searing righteousness in the moment.

Mike switched off the TV. Sam sat cross-legged on one end of the couch, and he did the same—close enough to take her hands in his and rub her knuckles. "What happened?"

"Very little. I told him I was sorry it had to end like this. He said the same. I thanked him for everything he'd been for us, and we said good-bye."

"Okay. That sounds civil."

She sighed, shaking her head, then met his eyes squarely. "Mike, it doesn't *have* to end like this."

"He has feelings for you. You . . . you have feelings for him. I know it's hypocritical—I know it's fucking ironic, given my fantasies, but this can't work. It could only ever have worked for as long as it stayed purely sexual."

"Do you think we're ever going to find someone as right as he was, ever again?"

"I don't know. I'm not sure we should ever even try, given how it's gone."

"You can't really mean that. Not after all the fun we've had these past couple of months."

"I know it sucks, but it's a catch-twenty-two. You need to feel something for a guy if you're going to feel secure enough to sleep with him. I won't feel secure if I'm worried you might have feelings for him, for real."

Another sigh, and she gazed down at their hands. "I just feel like . . ." She looked up. "I just kind of think that's bullshit, Mike."

He blinked, confused.

"It's bullshit, and it's unrealistic, and it's not fair. I drove around after I left his place, and I thought a lot about this. Before last night, all three of us were living our fantasies. You were getting cuckolded. Bern was getting watched and recorded."

Mike rankled at the man's mere name, whispered by Samira only last night, no doubt, too quiet for the computer to catch.

"I was getting to be with two men," she went on, "something I never realized would light me up the way it has. And he and I aren't teenagers, incapable of keeping our feelings in perspective. Now that it's all out on the table, I don't understand why it has to end. I told you already, I'm not going to leave you for him. If you can trust that, and he can accept it, why does this have to stop?"

"Be—"

"You've had *no* trouble dealing with me sharing my body with another man. Can't you see your way to sharing just a tiny piece of my heart? Just one little sliver?"

Mike didn't reply, way too muddled to make sense of his feelings. It all sounded so idealistic, so naive, after what had just happened.

She squeezed his hand. "I know I hurt you. We both hurt you, last night, but we never meant to. Maybe he does have feelings for me, but he didn't plan this. I believe that. I *know* it." She pressed a fist to her heart. "And the entire situation is so complex and intense, it feels like the only thing we can really control is our intentions."

"You have no idea how much that scares me."

"If he can accept that he and I can only be together within the bounds of the three-ways, why can't this go on?"

Mike didn't answer, paralyzed, too afraid to entertain logic.

"Why does the fact that I have feelings for him have to equal failure, Mike? Why does that have to be a bad thing? It's been so much hotter for me since those feelings developed, so much deeper. I went into this willing to do those things as a gift to you, but now I've found things in it that I want for myself, too. Because I value him, and what he's brought into our sex life, and because I feel valued in return."

Of course, when she put it like that, he felt like an ass.

"My body and my heart are a package deal," she said softly. "I don't want a man touching just one or the other. And I think if we'd tried those things with some guy I felt apathetic toward, we'd have found that out the hard way, and maybe turned me off the idea permanently. But instead we kind of hit the jackpot, Mike. Can you see that? Just a little?"

He kept his gaze on their hands, no words coming, just echoing uncertainty. Everything she said made perfect sense, but logic wasn't any comfort to his mangled ego.

"We could change the rules," Sam said at length. "There's no reason this needs to end, not for good. We can take a break, get some perspective, figure out what it might take so everyone's getting their needs met and everything feels balanced again, but then . . . Jesus, Mike. It seems wrong to throw this all away, after everything we've done, the three of us. I know how hot it's gotten you since it started. And it's done the same for me, and for him. What are the chances we'd meet someone out of the gate that we clicked with the way we did with him?"

"I know that, but—"

"All three of us have found a place in this arrangement—something about it that sets us on fire. And I've *never* known sex could do this to me."

The sting must have shown on his face; she hurried on. "Not just because of him—because of both of you, or just the taboo of it. I didn't know I could feel that way, like sex has gone from two dimensions to three. It's not something either of you could do on your own. It's not something he has that you don't. And I can only be honest and say I don't think I want to give that up forever."

Fucking Pandora's box, then, was it?

"Can I give it up for now to prove to you that you come first?" she asked. "Absolutely. Eagerly. But eventually, I think I'd want to get back there. I'll want to feel that fire again someday, when we're ready. Just like you should fight to keep what lights *you* on fire in your life. We can fix this, Mike. I'm sure of it."

He let her hands go to rub his face. "All I'm sure of is that I'm scared to fucking death."

"I'm just not willing to believe that we've wrecked this—not with one night of too-emotional sex, and not with one punch."

"He cares about you. More than I'm comfortable with."

"And he's also a thirty-six-year-old man. He can control his expectations and his emotions, if the payoff is worth it to him—if what the three of us can be for each other is worth it to him, and I believe it is. We need a little space and some time off, and some firm rules, if we all decide this is worth working on." She rubbed his forearm. "And, Mike, I really think it is."

He stared at her, long and hard, and took a deep breath. "I don't know yet. I just don't. Can you really promise that you won't . . . fall in love with this guy?"

She frowned, said nothing for a long breath, then broke his heart. "No, I can't promise that."

He buried his face in his hands, feeling he had his answer, right there. "I know it makes me a big fucking coward, and a hypocrite, yeah, but I can't deal with that. Pretending you want him more than me—even imagining maybe you do, for real . . . That, I can handle.

That gets me hot—I'll admit it. But love . . . ? I can't risk that much. I can't *share* that much, Samira."

She spoke calmly, plainly. "I can't promise I won't fall in love with him. But I *can* promise he'll never take your place. I'm never going to leave you for him. We've built a life together. We've been testing and strengthening what we've got for years. Whatever Bern and I are, it's new. In some alternate world, it might last a month or forever—we'll never know, though, because *this* is reality. You and me. We're the constant in all this. I think maybe I trust that more than you do."

"After watching that tape . . . Yeah, you probably do."

She winced, and he knew it had been a low blow.

"I can't ask this of you now," she said. "But in time . . . unless it'll tear you apart, in time I want to try it again. I want to crawl up inside your kink and take it as deep as it goes—with him. Let me be with a man I feel for. Not more than you. Different from how I feel for you. Trust that it'll always come back to you and me. Let's try, and I'll prove to you it'll always come back to you and me."

He turned that around in his mind, feeling blindsided by it all. Shocked by her insistence, when this morning she'd been so mired in remorse. *Remorse, or fear?* Fear that she'd hurt him—he knew that to be true—but perhaps also fear of losing what they'd found with Bern.

"You really care about this," he said.

She nodded. "I do. I think I want it as badly as you want the cuckolding."

Something she'd said earlier nagged at him . . .

"I never fought for my kink," he said. "Not like this." What he had fought for, though, was to keep Sam, back when his jealousy and dishonesty had nearly driven her away. He was struck now by the tone of her voice, its strains of both neediness and insistence. So like how he'd sounded himself, begging for a second chance, a chance to explain. A chance to prove he could control his emotions and articulate his wants.

We've been here before, haven't we?

"There's so much in this for you, for both of us," she said. "Where we are now, it grew out of your desires. I found my own along the way. Just tell me you'll *think* about it, and we can all maybe still have exactly what we want. Just with rules, so we don't end up back here again."

He breathed slowly, feeling lost and scared and exhausted and utterly uncertain. What if back when he'd fucked up, acted like an ass, and almost wrecked their relationship . . . What if she'd denied him a chance to fix things? To prove himself rational, just as she was pleading for a chance to prove herself trustworthy. What if she'd refused and simply ended it all, shot what they had between the eyes and walked away? He'd be years into missing her, years into wondering what might have happened, if he'd had a chance to fight to keep them together. Years into treading water, trying not to drown in all that regret.

A long breath hissed through her nose. "Say you'll think about it, Mike. Please."

He held her gaze and took her hands. "I'll think about it."

CHAPTER TWENTY-SIX

Six months later

Samira looked up at the sound of two men groaning in unison. It wasn't a sordid noise—not yet, anyhow—but enough to pause her hands in the midst of spooning guacamole into a wooden bowl.

"What?" she called over the breakfast bar.

Mike was on the couch, Bern kitty-corner on the easy chair, both their sets of eyes on the TV.

"They just scored," Mike said, reaching for his beer.

"Field goal," Bern added. "Not that it'll save them." He was wearing a yellow-and-black-striped beanie with a pom-pom on its peak, and Mike was in his supposedly lucky Steelers sweatshirt. It appeared to be working today.

"I'd sympathize, but I don't have a dog in this fight." Sam carried the snacks over and took her seat beside Mike, swinging her thighs over his.

"I'll convert you yet," he told her.

"No chance. I'll die a Giants girl."

Mike hooked a thumb toward Bern. "He switched, like a respectable citizen."

"I rooted for the Titans when I was a kid," Bern said, "but Kentucky doesn't have any real allegiances. It was nice to move to a city where people get rabid over this shit. Though on the flip side, around here it's like, convert or get lynched."

"Sam's not even from New York," Mike said. "I don't get where the loyalty comes from."

"Newark is, like, three feet from New York. Plus I lived there for twelve years."

"You marry me, you marry the Steelers."

"I took your name," Sam said, rooting through the chips for a folded-over one. "But I'll never take your colors. Everyone looks terrible in yellow, anyway."

"Blasphemy."

"Have we ever been in the Super Bowl against each other?" she asked Mike. She might own a Giants jersey, but she couldn't claim any sort of superfan status.

"Never. And we'll need marriage counseling if it ever happens."

Bern laughed and tipped his beer bottle to his lips.

Sam smiled, zoning out as the game came back from a commercial. She wanted to pinch herself, to be sure this was all real once more.

How had they gotten here, to this moment, on this lazy Sunday afternoon? Outside it was dark and snowy, with a bitter, biting wind, but here, by the glow of their little Christmas tree and the flashing television, all was so cozy, almost innocent.

It hadn't been easy, that much she knew.

Sam had pled her case with Mike, firmly, and repeatedly, and he'd listened, if not immediately agreed. She didn't speak to Bern for six weeks after the Incident—as she'd come to name that out-of-bounds night, and Mike's thuggish rebuttal—while she and Mike worked toward healing the scrapes she'd put on his trust. His anger and hurt had faded with time, thanks in no small part to Sam's willing abstinence from contact with Bern, and the fact that the man had respected their marriage and not reached out to her, either. Then in early September, Mike had come around. What had he said to her, late that night, after a long day of contemplative quiet and a near-silent, slow, intense bout of sex?

I think maybe I'm ready to try it again. If he's still interested, and if we can get the rules exactly *right.*

For all her optimism, Sam had been surprised.

Bern had been interested. Cautious but intrigued, and still single.

The cardinal rule was that all three of them needed to be present for any encounters that might happen, going forward. Sam had no issue with that, since the thing that excited her most was having both of their bodies there with her.

At first, the bulk of the control had been ceded to Mike—the tone of their encounters had been his to dictate, since he'd been the one violated by Sam and Bern's missteps. The reprised weekly meet-ups had felt much like their initial dates, to start—cuckolding was the driving dynamic once more, though Mike didn't pretend to catch them, the way he had at the start. He mostly watched, sometimes masturbated, always reclaimed Sam after Bern left, but didn't join in at first. He was stronger in his role than he had been before—less humiliated and helpless, and far more openly excited by watching them. Bossier, too—probably a touch eager to keep his alpha status clear this time around. Sam loved the change, loved this gruff new version of Mike more than the pathetic one he used to favor. He seemed like the conductor of his desires now, not merely a passive audience.

Sam and Bern kept their chemistry overtly physical these days, and their text and e-mail exchanges relegated to planning purposes only. For now. She imagined that might change, with time and trust, but the loss of those fun, dirty messages was a tiny price to pay to have him back in their lives, and their bed. Her crush was still there, but that summer's scare had been so painful, she felt no temptation to lose track of her heart that way again.

In time, as the cuckolding games went on and Mike's confidence grew, he'd proposed a change. They ought to switch who called the shots from week to week, he'd suggested, and Sam and Bern agreed.

Bern's nights to direct looked much like Mike's, though he favored the presence of the camera or a mirror, naturally. He liked sometimes for Sam and Mike to watch him masturbate while they had sex with each other. He liked to watch *them*, she thought. He seemed to find it fascinating in some way, if not as electric as being the show, himself. Ever eager to please, he often got caught up in Sam's fantasies by the end of his evenings and made sure she got to feel the both of them against her in the finale.

Of the three of them, it was Sam who pushed the most boundaries this time around.

Back in the spring, when this had all begun, she'd always imagined the arrangement was a gift she'd be giving her husband—orchestrated with enthusiasm, but ultimately for him. She'd never have guessed she'd find appetites of her own inside it. Never have imagined she'd *fight* to keep this in their lives, or guessed she'd feel the power she did, holding sway over them.

She eyed Mike, who was transfixed by the game. She eyed Bern, also distracted, though in time his gaze swiveled to catch hers. She smiled, and he returned it. A glance at the screen told her it was nearly the end of the fourth quarter, and that the Steelers were up by thirteen, their victory a foregone conclusion. It was time to shift this easy, platonic afternoon into a racier gear.

She curled her finger at Bern, and his eyebrows rose, smile turning mischievous. Sam patted the couch cushion beside her and he got up, skirting the coffee table to take a seat. She loved the way his weight dipped her cushion, and how she could already feel his heat. Feel the heat of both their strong bodies, and her own temperature rising.

Mike had lost interest in the game, studying her now.

"It's your night," Bern murmured, scooting closer. Sam's back was half to him, her legs still draped over Mike's lap, and he ran a slow palm down her arm, raising goose bumps even through her thick sweater. "What are you in the mood for?"

She craned her neck to regard his face and eased the hat from his hair. She knew every strand, it seemed, black and silver alike. "What a very good question." And one she had answers for. She wanted lots of things tonight. Wanted their two laboring bodies, first and foremost, but more. Since that punch had been thrown, since this affair had been destroyed and then resurrected, Mike and Bern had reeled back their physical contact. So much of it had been tied into Mike's desire for humiliation, and that had taken a backseat in their reimagined games, as his role had become more assertive, dominant, even.

"There's something I've been missing," Sam said, looking at each of them in turn. "And maybe its time has passed, or maybe it'd have to be worked up to gradually, but I miss when you two . . . touch each other. In any way, really," she added quickly. "It doesn't have to be hard-core, like it was, but just a little something." She'd not have come out and asked for this back in the spring and summer, even though she herself had been happy to exit her comfort zone for both their desires—her shyness about being filmed, for Bern, and the entire experiment to begin with, for her husband. But she had distinct wants of her own now, and the balls to name them.

"Like what?" Mike asked, his voice soft and receptive.

"Just about anything." She gave the scene some thought. She

wanted lots of things she didn't think they'd be ready for—to watch them kiss, and more—but less intense stuff as well. "If one of you is taking me, and the other's watching, or lying on my other side, it'd be hot to see your hands on the other guy's hip or back, sort of urging him, maybe. Just your hands on each other, in any way you're okay with. *If* you're okay with it," she added, glancing at each of them.

"It's your night," Bern said again with a smile. "Whatever gets you hot."

Mike was slower to reply, but she could tell from his tone that he knew his boundaries and was game to push them. "I'd be okay with it. With anything we've done in the past, but not much further."

Her heart leapt, and in the background the football fans roared their approval—surely of a game-clinching play, but to Sam it felt like she'd just triumphed, herself. How many times had she replayed those memories of Mike taking Bern in his mouth, these past months? Too many to count.

Sam looked to Mike, leaned in to kiss him. He accepted it hungrily and tugged her closer. She straddled his lap and got lost in this mouth she knew so well, excited and proud to feel her other lover's eyes on them—and then his hand. Bern's heavy palm stroked her back and neck, and she felt the elastic slide free from her ponytail. Soon she'd feel more—the bare, hot skin of both of these men against her, the flex of their needy bodies, the smell of their sweat as the sex turned the December chill into a figment of their imaginations.

As hot as Mike's mouth or Bern's hand was the tantalizing unknown of whatever might come after they went upstairs, when Sam let her desires direct these two men—everything in store for her tonight. They hadn't ruined it back in July. Not through Sam and Bern's fuckup, not by Mike's hand when he'd thrown that punch. They'd knocked it down, but in the end, all the bricks had remained, and a foundation of symbiotic need and desire, and they'd built something familiar, something similar but also entirely new, in its place.

Sam broke her lips from Mike's, breathing hard, feeling hot and tight and needy in the darkest shadows of her body. "Let's go upstairs," she told him, and let her hungry stare echo it at Bern.

Bern nodded and stood. "I'll be right up." And he disappeared to do as he always did now—to make a stop in the downstairs bathroom so that Mike and Sam could enter the bedroom together, first. Whether that little ritual symbolized his deference, or Mike's primacy, or some other subtle acknowledgment that he was still the guest in these matters, she wasn't entirely sure. But it felt right, and it spoke to that intuition he'd always possessed.

Sam and Mike headed upstairs hand in hand, and at the landing she asked, "You're sure about being ready to touch him?"

They paused inside the door. "It's your night," he said. "Whatever you want to see."

She smiled, and rubbed his shoulder. "You're a very indulgent husband."

"I learned from the best."

"Back in a minute."

He nodded.

Sam closed herself in the en suite bath, then grinned at her reflection as she dried her hands and smoothed her hair. Beyond the bedroom, she heard that telltale squeak, followed by the low rumble of male voices.

Through this door, two men waited, hungry to please her.

"Showtime," she murmured, and shut off the light.

Let the games begin.

Read on for a sizzling sneak preview
of the next book in Cara McKenna's Sins in the City series,

DOWNTOWN DEVIL

Available from New American Library in Summer 2016

Good as the movie was, it wasn't enough to hold Clare's attention. Not when she could feel Mica's body heat at her side, all but sense his pulse and every urge coursing through his body.

And I know exactly what that body is capable of. She knew exactly what it looked like, doing dark things to hers, knew how ably it could excite her, please her. She knew the feel of his skin under her palms, the smell of him.

Mica's attention was on her—not the film, not his roommate sitting mere feet away. She could sense it, real as touch. She glanced to the side and, sure enough, those eyes were waiting. Watching. His face was bathed in the restless glow of the TV, and he smiled.

Nothing about this man was more seductive than his smile. Her gaze dropped to the open V of his collar, to the soft, sparse hair and tempting skin. She inched her hand over, up his thigh to close over his. He clasped her fingers, thumb rubbing her knuckles fiercely, and the intention in those eyes went dark as pitch. Clare swallowed.

Take me to your room. It'd be so easy. Just stand, tug her to her feet, lead her down the hall. Vaughn wouldn't care. He was buzzed, same as them, and he had to know he'd walked in on the middle of a make-out session. And he'd been kind to Clare the morning she'd woken up alone in his best friend's bed, so he wasn't the type to judge. It wouldn't be rude if they just left. She held Mica's gaze, then flicked her own over his shoulder, to the hall. His grin deepened.

He leaned close and put that brazen mouth to her temple. "Something you need?"

"I bet you can guess."

"The movie not working for you?" he whispered, and she shivered as his lips brushed her cheek.

"It's fine, but I'm feeling a little distracted." A little distracted, a little drunk, monumentally horny. She freed her hand to rub his thigh, dipped her face so she could press her mouth to his jaw. Not quite a kiss, but she let him feel a hot, heavy exhalation, and hear the need in her very breath.

He turned his head, caught her lips with his. The kiss was deep and dirty, so good she wanted to drop her chin back and sigh aloud. Instead she held his head in both hands, let her fingers get lost in his dreads, let him feel her hunger, taste it on her tongue.

Something noisy happened on-screen, whisking her out of the moment just long enough to remember they weren't alone. She pulled back, flushed, and let Mica go. She felt silly and overcome, and surely he could see that in her dopey grin.

"We should go to your room," she mouthed.

"In a minute." And he was kissing her again, hungry and needy. No red-blooded woman could possibly say no to that.

His hand crept higher, warm palm cupping her breast, stealing her breath. A flash of worry chased the bloom of arousal. *We're not alone on this couch.*

It was dark, though, and Clare's buzz made it hard to feel scandalized. A glance in Vaughn's direction said he wasn't paying them any attention. The wine was making it very difficult to care . . . and to be perfectly honest, there was something a little wicked, a little hot, about going there with Vaughn sitting only feet away. With most any other guy, she doubted that would be the case, but Mica's sexuality was so bold, so provocative . . . It fit, somehow. And Vaughn seemed like the type of man who'd have no trouble excusing himself or calling out his friend if things got too weird for him.

As for Clare, the idea had her hot. Her cheeks were burning, her blood pulsing thick and fast from both nerves and excitement.

"Your room," she said again, rubbing Mica's arm.

He whispered, "Do you like him?"

Her hand stilled. "What?"

"My friend. Do you like him?"

Upended, unsure what precisely he meant, she said, "Sure."

"You want him?"

No reply came, not for long seconds. "I'm not . . . I don't know." She knew Vaughn was kind and respectful, and handsome. But what Mica was getting at . . . Shit, she wasn't thinking straight. The wine had left her warm and easy. If all Mica was after was a bit of kinky dirty talk, she wasn't opposed.

"Want him how?" she asked.

"You want to kiss him?"

"I . . . I don't know. Maybe a little. Does that make you jealous?" she teased. "Or . . . or did you want to see that?"

By the light of the TV, he smiled. "Maybe a little."

"It's all up to him, anyway," she said.

"Ask him, then."

She blushed, bit her lip. "I couldn't."

"You could. Just turn. Catch his eye. Ask him."

"Is that a dare?"

"If that excites you, sure."

Fuck, did it? She couldn't tell. All she knew was that the more they talked about it, the less scandalous—and the more thrilling—the idea felt. Mica had a way of making the filthiest, most *wrong* things sound irresistible.

His voice went low, all but growling against her throat. "It excites *me*."

She swallowed. "Yeah?"

"Yeah."

"I wouldn't even know how to ask."

"You just turn," he said again, "and you meet his eyes, and you tell him, 'I want to kiss you.'"

Her lips pursed, uncertain. If she did it—if she wasn't rebuffed and embarrassed and left never wanting to come by this apartment again—and if Vaughn was into it, where would this end, exactly? With Mica getting his kinky thrill and hustling her down the hall to his room? Or somewhere altogether unexpected?

"You want me to dare you?" he whispered.

"No."

"You want me to ask him for you?"

Another warm flush as she tried to imagine it. Imagine what Mica would even say to his friend. At length, she decided aloud. "I'll do it."

That smile deepened, carving lines beside his lips. "Good."

But not without another dose of courage, she thought, reaching for her wine.

Vaughn glanced to their end of the couch as she set the glass back on the table. His own tumbler was empty, and it had been his second. He was feeling the whiskey, no doubt. "I'll, um, I'll get out of your way, I think."

And faced with now or never, nerves muted by the alcohol, Clare was startled to hear the reply waiting on her lips.

"Could I kiss you?" Her eyes held his and the words seemed to float in the shadows between them. A bold question, spoken softly, warmly. Hopefully, even—she heard longing in her voice.

His brows rose. "Kiss me?" He looked past her to Mica, and Clare could only imagine what that man's expression must be saying. Something filthy. Something shameless.

She nodded. "Only if you want to."

His mouth closed, opened. He blinked, and she admired his eyes, those dark lashes she'd not really noticed before. If not for Mica's energy eclipsing everything around him, she might have met Vaughn at that party and gone home thinking he was the best-looking man she'd seen all night.

"So, do you want to?" She couldn't even say who this woman was, operating her lungs and lips and tongue. It was as though desire had turned corporeal, stolen her body and voice. No regard for what was appropriate, no cares beyond the wants of her mouth, hands, sex. "Would you kiss me?"

Another glance at Mica, a pause, a nod. "Yeah," he said softly, lids dropping low. "I would."

She stretched her arm along the back of the couch, angled her legs, welcomed him to come close. Their eyes met, and she saw her own wine-tinged uncertainty reflected back at her. But there was more. Curiosity behind the hesitance, and yeah, she felt that, too. Mica wasn't her boyfriend, after all—far from it. She wasn't worried about doing something that might complicate a relationship.

She could already feel Mica's heat and energy at her back, and now his fingertips joined the scene, alighting softly between her shoulder blades. He didn't urge, didn't push. Merely touched, letting her know, *I'm here. I'm watching. I'm excited.*

Vaughn edged closer and their knees touched. She stroked his collar, studied his mouth. Those stunning white teeth, framed by soft-looking lips. A flash of pink as his tongue wet them. He leaned in and she did the same.

For a moment, Clare barely registered the kiss. All she was aware of was Mica's watching, and for half a minute it was a performance, not a kiss. Then something changed. Something fell aside, and in a blink her attention shifted, captured by Vaughn's mouth.

His lips were full and lush, a touch hesitant. She let him know she wanted this, putting a hand to his face. His jaw was rough with the day's stubble, but other parts were soft—his cheek, his earlobe, his temple. As she touched him, his kisses deepened. Not dirty like Mica's, not that bold, but sensual and taunting in their own way. Mica's sexuality was a brushfire; Vaughn's was a smoldering hearth.

She tilted her face, invited more. A hand warmed her side, and it took her a moment to realize it was Mica's. She shivered, and heat rushed in as that pleasant chill subsided. *This is so wrong. So wrong and so fucking hot.*

Vaughn cupped her neck, his broad hand cool from his glass. With every stroke of their tongues, every exhalation that mingled between them, his hesitation faded, until she could feel the excitement humming deep in his chest. Mica's hand slid lower, kneading her hip. She felt its mate at her neck, pushing her hair aside. His breath caressed her nape; then came his lips. Two men's mouths on her. Two men's heat stoking hers. Two men's desires, at once intimidating and empowering.

She reached back to run her hand over Mica's hair, fisted it softly.

"You like how he kisses?" he murmured, loud enough for them both to hear.

"Yes." She spoke it right against Vaughn's mouth, and felt his body tense in reply.

Mica's palm on her hip rose and slid forward, closing her breast in its heat. The other was still in her hair, and she wondered if the two men's fingertips were touching. With every sweep of Vaughn's tongue, every soft squeeze of Mica's hand, she was sucked deeper into the lust, so deep that the wine was moot, its chemical intoxication *nothing* compared to this.

She was all but panting when Vaughn drew back, stealing that heavenly mouth. "Where's this going?" he whispered. His voice was thick, distracted. Sexy.

"I don't know." She suspected one person in this room *did* know, however. She suspected the man at her back knew exactly where he wanted this to end up. She craned her neck and met Mica's gaze.

"You like him?" he asked, dark eyes full of heat.

"Yeah."

"You want him?"

She swallowed and spoke the truth. "I think I do."

"You should have what you want," he said simply, and lowered his mouth to her throat once more. It snatched her breath for a moment; then she sought Vaughn's eyes and asked, "Do you want that?"

"If you do. If you're not too drunk, I mean." He looked flustered, but some clarity returned and brightened his eyes. "I mean, I don't know." His caution couldn't be faulted. The proposition implied that he'd shortly be getting naked with his best friend, and that didn't seem like a leap the average man would take lightly.

"I'm not drunk," she said, realizing it was true. She'd had two large glasses of wine—enough for a healthy buzz, enough to dull her inhibitions, but not enough to rob her of her judgment. "And I do want that. You, and him."

Vaughn didn't reply except to kiss her. Deep and dirty, with more passion and aggression than she'd yet felt from him—a taste of what Mica transmitted, when they did this. She imagined all that lust that radiated from his skin, doubled. Two mouths, four hands on her. Two excited male bodies. Two cocks.

This is really about to happen.

And as that fact sank in, she didn't think they could get there soon enough.

Photo by A. VanDerlip, 2013

Cara McKenna is the author of *Hard Time*, *Unbound*, and *After Hours*, as well as the Desert Dogs novels *Drive It Deep*, *Give It All*, and *Lay It Down*. She has published more than thirty romances and erotic novels with a variety of publishers, sometimes under the pen name Meg Maguire. Her stories have been acclaimed for their smart, modern voice and defiance of convention. She is a 2015 RITA Award finalist, a 2014 *Romantic Times* Reviewers' Choice Award winner, and a 2010 Golden Heart finalist. She lives with her husband in the Pacific Northwest, though she'll always be a Boston girl at heart. Cara loves hearing from readers!

CONNECT ONLINE

caramckenna.com

twitter.com/caramckenna